"Why do you want me, specifically?" McKenna asked.

His lips were at eye level, full and closed tight.

"Will you save me from the entire world, Blood Knight? Slay dragons on my behalf, along with more white-faced freaks? I wonder if you will save me from myself?"

She placed a light kiss on his mouth, absorbing the current that kiss produced. He didn't reach for her or devour her, though he could have. He didn't do anything at all, just stared down at her.

"Good night," McKenna said, turning from the man she almost wished would stop her, feeling his heated gaze on her backside as she limped toward the steps.

Turning her back to him was a mistake. If she had expected him to let that kiss go unchallenged, she was wrong. Seconds later, she was backed against the corner of the building with his body pressed to hers.

"You're making this hard," he said.

"Then do something about it."

IMMORTAL REDEEMED

LINDA THOMAS-SUNDSTROM

Waterford City and County
Libraries

First Published in Great Britain 2016
By Mills & Boon, an imprint of HarperCollins*Publishers*
1 London Bridge Street, London, SE1 9GF

© 2016 Linda Thomas-Sundstrom

ISBN: 978-0-263-92169-4

89-0416

Our policy is to use papers that are natural, renewable and recyclable products and made from wood grown in sustainable forests. The logging and manufacturing processes conform to the legal environmental regulations of the country of origin.

Printed and bound in Spain
by CPI, Barcelona

Linda Thomas-Sundstrom writes contemporary and paranormal romance novels for Mills & Boon Desire and Mills & Boon Nocturne. A teacher by day and a writer by night, Linda lives in the West, juggling teaching, writing, family and caring for a big stretch of land. She swears she has a resident Muse who sings so loudly, she often wears earplugs in order to get anything else done. But she has big plans to eventually get to all those ideas. Visit Linda at www.lindathomas-sundstrom.com or on Facebook.

To my family, those here and those gone,
who always believed I had a story to tell.

It wasn't hard being an immortal. And it certainly wasn't boring. But living out an extended life span could be lonely as hell, and that loneliness lasted forever.

Chapter 1

Kellan Ladd pushed the black custom Harley to eighty miles per hour on the open road, inhaling the wind, appreciating what might be his last moments on earth.

The purr of the bike's engine was the only sound in the dark fall night. His next stop was already a dim glow on the horizon. Out here he could breathe and see the stars. Disturbing thoughts were traded for the intricacies of pure sensation.

He liked the pungent scent of damp greenery and the faint odor of engine oil. Those things mixed well with the fragrance of his signature black leather pants and jacket.

In fact, the back of his neck tingled in honor of those things. But the pleasure didn't last. The dampness of the wind welcoming him to Seattle slipped beneath his collar to go head-to-head with the fiery burn of the intricate sigils carved into his shoulder blades...and the result wasn't pretty.

The sizzling sound of heat versus cold was imaginary. Discomfort wasn't. The marks on his back were as painful tonight as when he'd first received them. It was as if the scrolling tattoos were in on the secret part of his secret agenda. The temperature tug-of-war was a reminder he had never needed that after walking the surface of this planet for hundreds of years, he wasn't like the people he'd meet in an hour.

Not even remotely like them.

It wasn't as if he hadn't known that from day one. Sporting fangs and living forever made differences hard to forget. As did the oaths he'd taken that dictated his life's direction.

Tonight, he might have given half his considerable fortune to be completely free of the discomfort of the grooves on his back, if just for one day. He supposed the other six immortals in his Blood Knights brotherhood felt the same way by now.

Pain in the ass, though.

Chanting in a low-pitched murmur, Kellan willed the burn between his shoulder blades to ease, without much success. The magic woven into their creation continued to pulse with a steady beat the way it always did when he drew near the chaos of civilization. He considered cities to be a universal plague.

He didn't relish the thought of crowds. He never bothered with trying to fit in. Centuries ago he'd begun to agree with the freakish classification people would give him if they knew the truth of his origins. Luckily, very few mortals nowadays were in on the secrets surrounding his kind.

Most mortals were also ignorant of the part he played in protecting them—no easy task with humans occupying every corner of the planet. Add to those numbers the equally aggressive expansion of monsters that preyed on humans, and this modern world had developed its own recipe for disaster.

True, he just happened to be one of only seven immortals consistently going out of their way to do something about that. He was needed behind the scenes.

But he was tired.

Running a hand over his head made him miss the riot of shoulder-length auburn locks that had been his trademark for as long as he could remember. The new, shorter cut might make him appear more modern, but he couldn't actually outdistance reality. Short hair or long, he was the same immortal. Something he might not have to think about for much longer. Because...

She would help with that. She, her, it, or whatever the hell kind of spirit had ensnared his soul from afar with the promise of ending what had always been endless.

Kellan sensed her presence somewhere ahead. Not too far away. Well within reach. Someone unique awaited him in the rain-soaked West Coast city—a feminine soul with the ability to end his immortal servitude once and for all.

Maybe it wasn't actually a woman he'd find, yet he had a gut feeling it might be, and an uncanny sense of rightness about the perception. She had been invading his thoughts and his dreams for as long as Kellan could remember. From the beginning, actually, when he'd left his mortality behind.

So he was here in the States, heading toward one particular American city. Seattle, Washington, was ground zero for his private, personal agenda.

Finding *her* might be tough, though, since the whereabouts of his counterpart had always been a secret. The rare being he sought was a shadow, a dream. She was vagueness on the periphery of a memory he couldn't forget or completely recall. Yet she was there in his mind, buried deep.

Closing in on her true image might be like trying to catch hold of smoke. But he *felt* her.

He hungered for her and what she had to offer an immortal who had grown world-weary. She alone had the power to ease his restlessness. Only she would recognize his true identity and all that he had endured.

Hell, she might walk up to him on long, shapely legs and whisper her secrets in his ear.

Shots of white-hot anticipation streaked through him with that thought...before the chill returned.

"Damn sigils."

Kellan rolled his shoulders, cautious about lingering too long on treacherous thoughts. The brotherhood couldn't know about his mission or what he was after. All seven Blood Knights shared a special connection fostered by the type of blood in their veins. Tapping into the thoughts of the other six was possible, just as they were able to tap into his if he let them. Extra care was needed now to keep them out.

In truth, he was owed this trip, having stretched well beyond the concept of duty. Fulfilling his obligations had occupied the endless march of months, years, decades, that comprised his past. But having one of his brothers standing guard over the holy relic that lay at the heart of the Knights' creation meant that Kellan had plenty of time off.

An endless supply of time.

Ceaseless and unending.

The sound of the engine and the faint *ting* of the bike's spirit bell brought Kellan back from his thoughts. His speed was pushing ninety, and that just wasn't fast enough for an immortal with an important personal objective to ignore the disturbing feelings that lately had cropped up. Feelings of loss for parts of himself long ago left behind. Emotions dealing with an unforeseeable future and the mysterious *her* he could almost reach out and touch.

And there she was again, this mysterious soul at the heart of his search. Kellan imagined her scent floating in the wind. In the dark night he could almost see her eyes.

Those eyes would be blue.

His tattoos now stung with the force of a hundred scorpions. Each link of the inky scrollwork tied him to vows that made it a sacrilege for him to seek what he was after in Seattle. He had been created to exist forever, as long as he remained true to his pledge. It was too bad that *forever* had become too damn long.

Dangerous thoughts, bro.

Kellan reinforced his mental barriers against unwanted intrusion. He could shoulder the burden of all sorts of knowledge…if he could just deal with the damn tattoos.

"Might for right."

He spoke the old credo that he had once taken as his own, hoping the sentiment would offer comfort, even if false, to the blood-etched marks on his back. Those marks that now worked to keep him chained to an ideal that had long ago lost its shine.

Staring at the distant city lights, Kellan opened up the bike full throttle. Wearing the legend Blood Knights stitched on the back of his jacket as if he were merely part of an American motorcycle gang would either help his cause in finding the being he sought, or turn out to be the equivalent of painting a bull's-eye on his back.

Either way, this hunt had been a long time coming… and hunting just happened to be what he did best.

As the surgeon backed away from the operating table, McKenna Randall, RN, wiped her wet hands on a bloody white towel. They had saved this patient, and for that she felt immense relief, though saving only one out of three severely wounded people in a row wasn't great odds.

Nodding to the rest of the staff in the operating room, she headed for the door. Someone else would take over now. She'd been on her feet for twenty hours, and though at twenty-six years old she was the youngest nurse in the ER, a break was long overdue. She needed a shower, fresh clothes, food.

She was bone-tired. Her teeth hurt from grinding them together. Her shoulders quaked with spasms. She felt light-headed and a little dizzy from the kind of fatigue that brought back the long days of her past. Though she liked helping people, part of her still yearned for the excitement of her former profession. Nurse Randall tried to fix things that were broken, but Officer McKenna Randall had gone after the cause, hoping to keep things like slashed throats and stabbings from happening in the first place.

The injuries to the patients on the operating table tonight had been grisly. She'd had to keep a tight rein on her emotions in order to curb the desire to head out to the streets for a look at the crime scenes where her patients' wounds had been inflicted. Her old partner would be at those scenes, plus a lot of other guys she missed on a daily basis—guys who placed their lives on the line every damn day in the name of the law.

But that was then.

This was now.

The tickle at the base of her neck was a telling sign of her inability to remain upright for much longer. Also telling was the insistent ringing in her ears. Another ten minutes on duty and she wouldn't have been good for anything. Faintness had begun to hover like a big dark cloud. She was imagining things. Voices.

Hell of a thing.

In that operating room she'd been sure someone called to her. Lingering traces of that voice remained with her now, drifting like a breeze in her wake.

"Unacceptable," she muttered. She'd have to be careful when driving home to keep from becoming a liability.

The hospital was large and filled near to capacity. At 10:00 p.m. the corridor was busy, but no one seemed to notice when she stopped to take in a lungful of air and lean a shoulder against the wall. Not one person, staff or otherwise, paused to ask if she needed help, a stiff cocktail or a chair.

After all, she was the caregiver here.

But for the first time since she'd landed this job, McKenna wasn't sure she'd make it to the elevator. Weakness was overtaking her. Her nerves were dancing on thin ribbons of fire, as if her body were anticipating something she had no real knowledge of. As if the dizziness might be connected to some kind of premonition.

If she made it to that hot shower just one floor down, she'd get her core temperature back up and lose the shakes that came with too many hours spent in an icy operating room. She'd feel a whole hell of a lot better.

Just have to put one foot in front of the other.

Managing to push off the wall, McKenna headed for the elevator, forgoing her usual habit of taking the stairs. She avoided eye contact with the elevator's other occupants and fled when the door opened. In the locker room, she stripped quickly and stepped under the showerhead.

Head bowed, eyes closed, she let the stream of water bring new life to her overworked muscles. Turning her face to the rising steam, she tried not to think backward, but couldn't help it.

One bullet. One damn bullet with her name on it had ended her brief career as a cop. And that was just too frigging bad.

Fifteen minutes later she was dressed and out the hospital's front door, face scrubbed, wet hair combed. Walking was doable now that the quakes had ceased. Her car wasn't far away—just across the street in the new parking garage. The crisp fall air was bracing.

When the traffic light turned green, she almost stepped off the curb. Something stopped her.

McKenna spun around.

The sidewalk was fairly crowded with people heading in and out of the hospital. None of those people faced her, spoke to her or addressed her. Not one of them seemed to notice her at all.

Thinking that someone had called her name made McKenna reevaluate the current state of her health. Certainly her brain had been through a lot after being grazed by a bullet. Still, *voices*?

This time when the light changed, she made it halfway between the curbs before an odd sensation of being shadowed forced her to take a second look at her surroundings. Like most big cities, Seattle could be dangerous if people weren't careful. Single women out alone at night were wise to be on guard. No one knew that better than a cop.

Former cop.

Another look around showed no one suspicious and gave her no cause for alarm. Yet the sensitive skin at the base of her neck tingled. Strange fluttering sensations deep down inside her body forced her to briefly shut her eyes.

If this weird shit kept up, she'd be better off calling a cab or taking a bus the couple of blocks home. Hearing imaginary voices was scary stuff. The psychiatrist who had cleared her at Seattle PD after her incident wouldn't like this new turn of events any more than she did.

Not that clearing her had helped, since hopes of returning to the force had been lost with that damn bullet. The Seattle PD demanded retirement after an injury like that. Her next choice had been to finish the nursing degree she had started right out of school.

McKenna walked on. After hopping the next curb, she paused to search the street again. Nothing seemed out of the ordinary. She saw the usual long line of parked cars and the vague outline of a guy on a motorcycle pulling over.

Her smile was a symptom of feeling silly, because there was nothing unusual here. Plus, she had options. She could turn around, go back to the hospital, find a bed and sleep this off. A short nap might put things into perspective.

The stubborn tingle on her neck was a persistent sucker, though. She muttered a choice four-letter word she'd picked up on the force and tried to convince herself she was making things up.

"Where are you?"

McKenna whirled, nerves prickling, sure she heard that voice. If she was making it up, she had one hell of an imagination. That voice seemed real, even when logic told her the question couldn't have been addressed to her. No one waited for her or wondered where she was. She had no family left. The few people who mattered to her knew her schedule and were busy elsewhere at this time of night.

So why did the voice sound familiar?

Steadying herself with both hands on the nearest signpost, McKenna worked to calm herself down. This didn't have to be a premonition or a warning sign of disaster about to strike…though she distinctly remembered how the bullet entering her skull two years ago had spoken to her just before taking her down. As if that bullet had her name on it. As if that shot had been meant for nobody else.

She had experienced the same flutter of nerves back then, too, seconds before the bullet struck. She hadn't told anyone about those things. Cops weren't supposed to be crazy. She'd kept her mouth shut about premonitions and perceptions, though the nightmares persisted to this day.

She looked around, reliving a moment of uncanny connection to her surroundings, wanting to duck, but standing tall to await whatever was to come.

Nothing did.

No bullet arrived, though her weakening knees defied the notion of an all clear.

Holding on to the post, McKenna again scanned the sidewalk, fighting the impulse to cover her ears and block any further sound.

"Who are you?"

The question came again from out of nowhere, so real that she almost replied. Determined to ignore this, McKenna headed for the garage with a retort on her lips. "Not talking to you today, my invisible friend. I won't be admitting to the crazies anytime soon."

Under her breath, she added, "Definitely not today."

Before she finished the remark, her finely honed cop intuition set her teeth on edge. Someone was watching. Someone was there. She knew this.

Swaying slightly, shaking off the chills slipping under the collar of her thick wool coat, McKenna turned to stare at the guy on the motorcycle.

Chapter 2

Kellan got off the bike. His heart rate spiked as he eyed the woman on the corner. He waited out several more beats of time before breathing, each of those beats measured by the tick of the clock in the tower above him.

She was looking at him. Staring openly. Was she answering his call? If not, why the sudden interest?

The strange stirring sensations inside his chest didn't have to be meaningful since the odds of finding *her* just ten minutes after entering town were a million to one, or more like twice that.

Shaking off his disappointment, Kellan turned away.

Then he turned back.

The wind carried a trace of perfume—faintly floral, fresh, rich. He detected no hint of death in it, such as a Reaper might possess.

Tamping down the rise of anticipation, Kellan observed the woman closely. He had the advantage, of course. She would have no idea how effortlessly he could see every detail at this distance. She wouldn't know about the hunger behind his scan.

Her hair was fair, long, and hung past her shoulders. Although there was no rain tonight, the golden strands appeared to be wet. She had big eyes in a small face, high cheekbones and delicate features. She was tall and lean, her overall shape narrow. Faded blue jeans peeked out from beneath the knee-length tweed coat that didn't seem to warm her. Both of her arms were crossed over her stomach, as if that would help.

She was attractive, but not perfect. The eyes were a bit too large and her skin too pale. While she looked young, she possessed a worldly gaze. To anyone else, her bold stare might have been unnerving.

As their gazes connected across the distance, Kellan's nerves bristled. His muscles twitched. Strange as it was, after just seconds of scrutiny, he had an uncanny and urgent physical need for this woman.

Still, though she smelled delicious and stared back, she could be the wrong soul. Because he was immortal and a loner by necessity didn't mean he was immune to every temptation that came his way.

Under the scrutiny of his unwavering gaze, the woman turned from him with a small object clasped tightly in her hand. Cell phone for emergencies? Her steps stuttered on the sidewalk before she whirled again. Unbelievably, she wasn't running away. She didn't make any calls. After pausing to consider her next move, she walked straight toward him.

He hadn't used his power to influence her decision, so the move was all hers. Why, though? He was a stranger. Danger lurked on every street corner these days. Case in point, he caught a whiff of one lone werewolf to the south, potentially only half as deadly without a full moon overhead. And something dark-hearted with fangs perched on a rooftop halfway down the block.

Those things should have made him move. They should have been the center of this focus. He'd been blessed—or cursed, as he often thought—to feel the presence of these kinds of anomalies. He not only smelled them but saw into the shadows where they hid. He did his best to keep the monsters in check.

This time they weren't drawing his attention from the woman coming his way. They had nothing to do with his sudden sense of elation.

She was his focus.

His attention was riveted.

As she approached, Kellan's heart began to pound. Streaks of adrenaline created tension in muscles designed for fighting, as if she might pose a threat to those old vows. But the only fight here was for him to remain calm, because waiting for her wasn't easy. Meeting this woman could turn out to be a distraction he didn't need if she wasn't the woman he sought.

She stopped several feet away with a question.

"Do I know you?"

The huskiness of her voice made Kellan's nerves dance. Her tone was low and sexy. Her lips were full and slightly parted.

"I don't think so," he replied, economizing his comeback so that he could take in more details, like the dark crescents of sleeplessness under her eyes and the lovely lines of her long, graceful neck.

For the first time in a while, Kellan praised his special abilities for reasons other than ferreting out bad guys. He also amended his earlier conclusion. She actually was quite beautiful.

And if...

Well, if she was the one he sought...

All the better.

"Are you waiting for something?" she asked without backing away from the intensity of his keen observation.

Beyond Kellan's sigils, other parts of his body were

catching the fire of interest. Was this due to *her*, though, or did he just want it to be?

He had anticipated a more direct acknowledgment of being on the right track than an instantaneous craving for a woman. Then again, what did he really know about what his Makers had so carefully hidden?

Certainly he hadn't expected to meet a female who was the equivalent of a Grim Reaper, but also perfectly fit his personal preferences physically, when it could just as easily have been otherwise.

"I'm meeting someone," Kellan said.

"Oh. Sorry. I thought…"

"Yes? You thought?" he encouraged when she didn't finish the remark.

"I thought I might have known you from someplace. Guess I was mistaken."

She didn't leave. She stood her ground boldly, as if she wanted to add something, or else wanted him to.

Kellan purposefully kept his voice steady. "Do you work in the hospital?"

He stayed close to the bike so he wouldn't frighten her. Restraining himself from taking the few steps needed to reach her was hard. He wanted to press his mouth to hers in a kiss that might open Pandora's box. A kiss that might let him know if nearly overwhelming odds against him finding the one person he was after in Seattle meant nothing when it came to the magic of ancient souls and secrets connecting.

The pressure of his need to know about this woman was like a fist to his gut. Her presence was curious and captivating for a man who not only had searched for such a connection, but also had forgone serious female companionship in favor of more pressing pursuits.

She stood across from him as if he had conjured her.

Maybe he had.

Still, what was she seeing? She was telegraphing her interest in him by remaining close. His senses were loud and clear about that. Some sort of combustible chemical reaction was taking place between them. The air was heavy with it, and warmer than before.

Animal magnetism at work? Lust at first sight? An instantaneous attraction between strangers on a street corner was possible, Kellan supposed, though unlikely—which surely meant that the odds against this being a benign chance meeting were in his favor.

Are you her?

With his heart misbehaving, it was impossible for him to remain inert for much longer. In order to place her importance to his cause, he'd have to get a peek at this woman's soul. To do that, she'd have to be unwrapped. She'd have to meet him skin to skin for him to see what secrets, if any, lay hidden beneath those fragile feminine bones. And he was all for that skin-to-skin business.

"Do you recognize me?" he silently sent to her, hoping something deep inside her might rise to the surface and provide a clue.

"Yes," she said, giving him a start.

She waved at the hospital across the street, reminding him of the other question he'd posed. "I work there, at Seattle General. Possibly that's where I've seen you? Are you waiting for someone to be released?"

"Nope," he said, unable to lie about even the simplest things. None of the Blood Knights could.

Nor was he good at small talk, especially when trying to reason things out. He kept wondering how an ancient soul could survive by being passed along from body to body in a long line of new recipients, without those recipients knowing about it. Same soul, different housing, in a special type of reincarnation. Not a myth. Absolutely real.

If this woman didn't know what she carried inside her, though, how would she recognize him? In any case, why didn't she run?

Did she like his looks as much as he liked hers? His appearance had once been legendary, but he was much leaner and more chiseled now. Time had done that. Time and the efforts of his quest. He'd been frozen in the body of a twenty-eight-year-old, but Kellan knew he looked older, and that he had always projected a dangerous edge. The leather and the bike helped that image along.

"I stopped for a breath and to get my bearings," he told her.

As she continued to study him, his nerves burned. Seconds flew by in silence before she put a hand to her temple as if to ease an ache there. The brief flutter of her lashes gave Kellan the first hint that she wasn't all right. Not just tired. Possibly she was ill. Small quakes ran through her, suggesting that her strength had ebbed.

"You couldn't have called to me, I suppose," she finally said. "And I guess I'm way too tired to be making sense."

Her voice wasn't just sexy. It was flammable.

Was that also a sign?

"Do you need help?" he asked politely, carefully managing his excitement and his reaction to her. "An escort to your car, or a ride somewhere?"

The busy street wasn't the right place to hold an important meeting of any kind. The damn werewolf had got closer, as well as too many other people who hadn't received the memo about their lives being safer indoors after dark.

Kellan had to pay some attention to the monsters prowling the darkness because if he hit the road, this woman, in her weakened state, would be easy prey.

Her lashes fluttered again before she briefly closed her eyes, leaving Kellan certain that the ashen pallor of her face wasn't due entirely to Seattle's sunless climate. The bold blonde was no longer steady on her feet. She looked as if she could have been a patient at the hospital across from them.

"Do you need a ride somewhere?" he repeated in a soft, clear tone. "Help of any kind?"

"No." Her head shake displaced a few damp dark-golden strands that were starting to curl. "I don't need help. Thanks for the offer."

She inched backward without turning from him and ran into a post. After issuing a short bark of uncomfortable laughter, she muttered, "Hell, what a night," and looked up to apologize a second time. "Sorry."

It could have been the way she issued the apology—the rather forlorn enunciation of two drawn-out syllables—that caused Kellan to stir. He was beside her in an instant, utilizing the extraordinary speed and superior reflexes that had been built into him.

Chances were that not many others on the sidewalk had been paying attention to what might appear little more than a street-side tête-à-tête. Odds were also good that no one had noticed how frail this woman appeared to be, and how menacing he looked by comparison. He was two heads taller than she was and twice as broad. She tilted her head back to look up at him and met his eyes.

Her eyes were blue.

"I had a long shift, that's all. I need to get home and rest," she explained. "I used to be a cop, and that's my excuse for confronting you, as lame as it sounds."

Kellan's hand hovered less than an inch from hers. She

was in some kind of trouble and trying to make the best
of it. He zeroed in on the thin white scar that ran from her
right temple to beneath her ear, noting how the fingers of
her other hand kept returning to that spot.

She'd been damaged, and she seemed to him like a real
woman made of flesh and bone. Up close, he found nothing to suggest she might be a vessel housing an immortal
knight's off switch. She looked nothing at all like a Reaper
in disguise.

He eyed her thoughtfully. *Are you what my Makers tried
so hard to hide so that my life would go endlessly on? Or
are you merely a woman who appeals to my baser side?*

It was conceivable that she was just a woman, but how
could a mistake in identity happen between two souls in-
tricately tied to each other for centuries, or when the ter-
mination of his life might be in her hands?

Each Blood Knight had a counterpart soul, though no
one expected the two to find each other. They weren't supposed to meet. Weren't designed to meet. The Makers at
Castle Broceliande had seen to it that the seven Knights
could be taken down if they veered too far off track. This
had been accomplished by planting fail-safe switches in
seven other souls ultimately responsible for turning each
Knight off, dealing a final death blow if called into action.

The way they'd do this was top secret. None of the
Knights knew what their counterparts might have in store,
or where in the world they were. It had taken Kellan years
of research to pinpoint Seattle as the hometown of his,
plus a lot of underground bargaining with his considerable fortune. Then there was the call he had felt all the
way to his bones.

Was it this woman, then?

Is it you?

Will your touch end my existence? As simply as that?

I show up and awaken what's supposed to be off-limits, and you destroy me?

Her closeness produced feverish warmth in him. Yet he was minus the guidebook for unlocking secrets tucked inside someone composed by magical design, so he was on his own. And honestly, he now began to think that exploring this female's hidden assets, no matter what she turned out to be, would be extremely pleasurable. He might even die a final death with a smile on his lips.

As he stood there, the urge to touch her was becoming an outright necessity. He wanted to trace her facial scar with his fingers and feel firsthand the lushness of her lips. Burying his face in her damp hair would be a luxury. She smelled damn good, and it had been a while since he'd taken the time to enjoy anything of a personal nature.

"I'm willing to help," he said, gauging her reaction to his closeness. She shook so hard, his hand connected to hers automatically, sending shocking currents of electricity buzzing through him.

His excitement doubled. But was this a further sign?

Kellan smiled. While his sigils seared his skin and his heart beat wildly in his chest, raw physical need was trumping his internal warnings about having to use caution. Hell, he wanted this woman so badly, it was possible that sex held the answer to unlocking the Reaper, and all he had to do was insert a throbbing key into her lock.

"Let me help you..."

Had she heard that silent suggestion, too? She hadn't pulled her hand away. He watched her lips part.

"Are you a good guy?" she asked.

"Trick question," he replied. "Would I tell you if I wasn't?"

"Probably not."

"Everyone says I'm one of the good guys. Well, most people would, I guess, if they knew me."

She nodded warily, sighed softly, allowing these moments to linger because of his silent influence on her.

"Where are you headed?" Kellan asked.

"To my car. It's behind me, in that garage."

"Do you think you can drive?"

"I'm pretty sure I can't, but I'm going to try. My legs won't hold me up much longer, and I'd rather not be seen like this by anyone I work with. Besides, I doubt if I could make it back to the hospital's front door."

"If I carry you to your car, will I be responsible for the accident waiting to happen between here and your home?"

She stared at him mutely.

"How about if I take you home and we avoid all those other potential problems?" Kellan suggested.

"You can't take me anywhere, because I don't know you."

"Then I'm not sure what kind of help you need."

She shook her head, spreading more of her subtle perfume in the wind. That scent was like honey.

"This is seriously embarrassing," she said. "There's no need to worry about me. I'll call my partner for help. I'd be grateful if you'll just stay here until I do, so that no other…"

"Stranger?" he supplied when her sentence dangled. "So that no other Harley-riding yahoo might approach you on the street?"

"So that no other *person* dares to come to my aid, and I have to start over, behaving like an idiot," she clarified, looking up at him. "And so that no one looking out of a hospital window might assume I'm not up to the tasks assigned to me there."

Currents of electricity continued to slam Kellan through

his grip on her fingers. He had to monitor his reaction to each physical jolt.

The woman had palmed her cell phone but hadn't used it. Kellan wanted to know what she might be thinking. When would she realize that a stranger was holding her hand? This unplanned touch had to be unusual behavior for her. It certainly was unusual for him. He never made physical contact with mortals unless absolutely necessary, and he kept clear of them whenever possible. Too much contact, too much exposure to another beating heart's welcoming warmth, and a Knight's blood oath might be called into question.

This woman's fingers were cold, proving that she should have known better than to walk around with wet hair. Yet he sensed heat radiating off her, beneath her coat, and he wondered how long it would take before his desire to possess this mortal got the better of him, despite what she'd just said about having a partner to call. Another person in the picture could muddy things up quite a bit.

He detected something else. Silver. She carried a pocket-knife. The folded blade produced an additional buzz on the periphery of his senses.

"Are you ill?" he asked, releasing her hand.

Only then did she look at her fingers. "Tired," she replied. "Too damn tired."

"Okay. I'll wait for you to use that phone. Go ahead and dial."

She raised the cell phone, pushed several tiny buttons and held the phone to her right ear. "Officer Randall…" she started to say, then paused to clear her throat. "*Ex*-officer Randall on the line for Detective Miller."

As she listened to the response on the line, Kellan filed that information away. She had mentioned being a cop in the past, and had mistakenly used that old title now. Possibly her training was the reason she had spoken to him in the first place. The cop in her might assume at first glance that a guy on a tricked-out bike could potentially mean trouble, whether or not she was in any condition or position right now to address that kind of trouble.

Then again, maybe she had responded to his call.

Was she a doctor? Nurse?

"I see," she said to the phone. "No. Don't patch me through. I have Miller's cell number, and this isn't important. I'll get back to him later. Thanks."

Her arm dropped. Kellan caught the phone before it hit the ground, lamenting that there would be no lusty night ahead with warm sheets and warmer bodies, given this woman's current condition. If she wasn't sick, she was close to it.

She needed help. More than she knew. The damn werewolf was fifty feet away and closing in, drawn to weakness like a moth to a flame and unaware of what kind of fate awaited if it attempted anything monstrous here tonight. Blood Knights weren't known for mercy when it came to dealing with predators.

Since he couldn't tackle that problem at the moment, however, and in public, Kellan had to handle things another way. He'd see this woman safely off the street. Even if his hopes were dashed and she proved not to house a special spirit, the pretty blonde would be another in a long line of people he'd protected.

"No one else coming to the rescue?" he asked.

She didn't reply.

"All right. I guess that leaves me."

Kellan peeled her from the post and pulled her into his arms before any remark she might care to make was possible. The momentum of his action caused her head to rest against his chest. Her body molded to his from her shoulders to her hips.

Whips of fire licked at Kellan's bones, sending good-size shudders through him. These sensations were new. They were unique. But were they enough?

Her next words were muffled. Her hand closed on the knife in her pocket. "That was not an invitation, and if you don't back off, I'm going to scream."

"You asked for help," he reminded her with his mouth edging her damp hair.

"Not that kind of help."

"I'm not sure there's another kind at the moment. Can you walk?"

"Let me help you."

Her reply took some time. "Not far."

"Ten feet, to the curb? Should I actually carry you there, ignoring your protests?"

"Don't you dare," she said. "I'm not a child. I can…"

Kellan didn't wait for her to finish the argument. It was obvious to both of them that her legs wouldn't hold her up for much longer. It was far less obvious to anyone but him that if the werewolf came any closer with thoughts of pushing its luck, Kellan would be forced to deal with the beast for safety's sake, no matter who might be looking.

To avoid all that, there was only one thing to do—push his influence over her a little bit more.

"You must let me help you. Trust me to do that."

He waited until she blinked. Then he swung the blue-eyed enigma into his arms and headed for the bike instead of the garage. He set her gently on the Harley's seat and climbed on in front of her.

"Put your arms around me," he directed.

She did as she was told.

Although she shivered, her body heat penetrated his

leather jacket, reaching his skin as easily as if no barrier stood in the way. Kellan closed his eyes to absorb the impact.

Women didn't have a place in the oaths he'd taken. He'd known a few of them more than casually over the centuries, but had loved only once, long ago.

He was supposed to have turned out angelic. History painted him that way. Poets sang of his life. Some said he was a saint. He was one-seventh of a brotherhood designed to protect one of the world's most treasured holy relics. The Grail. Christ's chalice. But in truth, he had always been a rebel, and the gift of immortality hadn't changed that.

He might have desired this woman if they'd met in any century. He liked the mixture of strength and vulnerability she showed. He admired her looks, and had been mesmerized by those large blue eyes that somehow seemed so familiar.

Kellan ignored the soft click of his fangs extending in honor of his passenger. The razor-sharp canines rarely presented themselves and were a throwback to drinking the blood of his Maker in order to execute their plans. The outlandish teeth weren't for biting or hurting. He had never used them on anyone, for any reason, and never would, since he considered them an abomination.

Those fangs extending now were a complete surprise. They were also proof positive that though he was a monster hunter, by physical definition he was also one of those monsters.

Smiling sadly, Kellan kicked the bike to life. "Now," he called over his shoulder, ignoring the sparks of protest shooting from one of his shoulder blades to the other. "Where am I taking you?"

Chapter 3

Kellan maneuvered his way through the steady stream of traffic, drawing double takes from people in passing cars. He got more attention from pedestrians, who alternately viewed him as a threat or with envy while eyeing the shiny black bike.

He'd never been to Seattle. The streets had an uncomfortable look, as if the modern and older architectural styles were at war with each other. This, Kellan supposed, was another kind of metaphor for the dichotomy of the types of beings existing here. Humans versus their older, genetically modified nightmares. Werewolves. Vampires. And a whole host of other things.

Traffic, even at ten thirty, was thick. Horns sounded. Music reached him from the doorways of restaurants and clubs. Voices called to other voices, and a helmeted guy on a Suzuki gave him a thumbs-up.

Centered within all that chaos, Kellan's feelings morphed into something much more raw and anxious. If the woman behind him was the shut-off valve to his overextended existence, and he chose to activate that valve, his soul could be set free. At long last, he would be able to close his eyes and rest.

He had wanted this for more years than he could count.

"Turn here," his passenger directed.

Kellan did as she instructed, wanting to see where this beauty would take him. Having been a police officer, she'd know most streets by heart. She also would have recognized potential trouble when facing it, and when facing him, even before his understated commands had helped her to get on the bike. Maybe he didn't come off as scary as he thought. Yet tugging an old soul free from someone unknowingly housing such a thing might change her mind about that. It wouldn't be easy and could prove even tougher if he was up against someone trained to handle herself.

"Turn again," she said.

Simply wrenching secrets from this woman would cost him less anxiety and get him to the end point quicker. The problem was that he already considered her special, and these days he reserved muscle work for dusting monsters.

She had a death grip on him. If she truly was ignorant of the soul she housed, this woman couldn't possibly see the irony in that.

Fortunately, in this intricate game of hide-and-seek, he planned to come out the winner. That didn't mean he didn't like her arms around him and her heat. In fact, what he desired most right now was the time necessary for him to coax answers from her the old-fashioned way, by acting on an escalating physical attraction that would lead to sex. Nakedness and sex. Hard bodies on a soft bed that held lingering traces of this woman's wonderful perfume.

Hell, he amended. Sex on any surface would do. One last time. Would she allow him that? Could he get her to trust a stranger enough to invite him into her bed without using his influence?

After coming all this way, was he going to wait for her to decide, or help her along?

* * *

"Almost there," McKenna called out, and the handsome biker followed her directions without question.

It was all she could do to hold on to the stranger doing her a favor. He hadn't headed to the garage where her car was parked, so she opted for plan B. There was no way she'd let him know where she lived. In her present state she'd be an easy target for any pervert on the prowl, and he'd already had his hands on her.

Didn't matter that she'd liked it.

What did matter was why she had allowed such a thing.

"Fifth and G. Just a few more right turns and we'll be there," she said, not sure he'd hear that above the roar of the engine. But her gloriously muscled, incredibly handsome champion nodded his head.

He was a good-looking bastard for sure, from his cropped auburn mane to his boots. Everything in between seemed to have been molded to perfection by someone paying strict attention to detail. The fitted leather getup he wore enhanced his superior shape and smelled sinfully earthy.

She paid attention to the way he moved, and found him graceful and in complete control of the black custom Harley. With all his muscle and sinew, the guy was like a panther in motion. But he was too tall, too handsome and way too male. He might present himself as a white knight dipped in black leather, but in his presence she was experiencing a moment of moral and physical weakness.

It was a well-known fact that looks could be deceiving, so why the hell was she on this bike?

For the life of her, McKenna couldn't find a reason for that.

Her old partner at Seattle PD would have rolled his eyes mockingly when catching sight of this guy, suggesting that a package like this one was bound to be bad. The nurses on her shift at the hospital would have drooled.

So, okay, he appeared to be physically perfect. The odds of this biker being merely a Good Samaritan without an agenda of his own rang in at about fifty-fifty. Granted, she'd been near enough to fainting on the street corner to have seen the lights dimming, and there was no way she could have made it to her car. But did that justify accepting aid from a stranger?

Other then Derek Miller, her ex-partner both on the force and in her bed, she hadn't allowed herself this close to a bad boy without flashing her badge. Yet McKenna was pretty sure she had never wrapped her arms around anything so fine as this specimen.

"You can slow down now," she called out, wondering if she had a subconscious motive for accepting this lift. Could she possibly use this stud to punish Derek for not being the right man for her? By flaunting someone in front of Derek who was in no way right? The exact opposite of right?

No. That wasn't it. She'd never been the type to rub things into a partially closed wound. And Derek had, at one time, professed to love her.

"Fifth and G," she repeated. "Half a block down."

The guy glanced at her when they stopped for a red light. "All right," he said, rocking the windblown look with deep auburn hair only a few inches long that smelled like dangerous forbidden detours.

His worn leather jacket, soft against her cheek, had a logo on the back that she was too tired to lean back and examine. Anyway, it was probably best if she didn't know what he was up to when he wasn't volunteering to help ladies in distress.

Adding to the cliché of guys on bikes these days, her white knight had tattoos. Rounded edges of fine black scrolls were visible at the nape of his neck. Some sort of Celtic design, she guessed, and no big deal since she also had a tattoo.

In spite of not quite believing that she had accepted this guy's offer of assistance, she wasn't a complete idiot. McKenna felt relatively safe on the bike. The knife in her pocket was for protection. She also knew how to get an arm around this guy's throat if he misbehaved. For some reason, though, she had a feeling he was okay, and was sincere in his wish to help her out of a jam. In this case, McKenna preferred to trust her instincts.

When the bike swerved to the right, she hung on. But after they reached her destination, getting away from him would be the smart thing to do. And also the sensible move, since she was already imagining what a night with him might be like, and how he'd look without the leather—buck naked, bronze, intimidatingly perfect.

Would she stoop to that?

If times were different... If she was different and didn't know better, due to the things she'd witnessed both as a cop and in the ER, she might have taken this guy up on a night in the sack just for the hell of it. For reliving the thrill of her days on the force, when adrenaline surges were a coveted daily rush.

For a minute, she wanted to forget about taboos and melt into a guy's capable arms, free to express herself with a stranger in ways she never would have dared to address with Derek. She had been strong for so damn long. She wanted to experience what a man like this, with a body like this, could do to make her forget the nightmares. Only with a stranger could she indulge in that kind of vulnerability.

Pressing her face against his broad back, McKenna shut her eyes, loving the feel of the wind in her hair, hoping her instincts were right. This really had been quite a night. She was holding on to the sexiest man on the planet, who was also the kind of man all mothers warned their daughters to avoid.

Help was on hand, though. There would be plenty of cops to give reality a push when they reached the destination she'd chosen. She would wave goodbye to this guy, and he'd leave.

"Thank you," she shouted, leaning with him as the Harley swept around a curve. "I mean it."

He nodded.

Fifth and G was the location of the latest crime—the place where the last poor young man in the emergency room had got his throat slashed. Detective Derek Miller, in his recent career advancement, would have taken charge of the scene, and he would see to it she ended the night without making a bigger fool of herself.

With that in mind, McKenna almost regretted the thought that this handsome hunk of manhood, with his big serious eyes and body like leather-coated sin, might have given her a second wind on a mattress. And that he might have provided her with something to look forward to now that her more dangerous days had been left behind, along with her gun and her badge.

"You're sure this is the place?" he asked in a deep, silky tone as he pulled over to a curb marked off-limits by a length of yellow crime tape.

"I'm sure," McKenna replied. What she wasn't sure about was how she'd get off the bike now that she'd arrived, and if she even wanted to, good intentions and common sense aside.

Seriously, it wasn't like her to be torn on issues of safety. Strangely enough, she had begun to feel safe with her arms around this stranger's waist. Safer than she'd felt for a very long time. And that was a surprising revelation.

"I'm guessing you don't live here," he said, looking around.

"No. A friend of mine will take over from here. I appreciate your help in getting me this far."

"Your friend is Detective Miller?"

"How did you know that?"

He swiveled to hand her the cell phone she'd forgotten about. "You called him in front of me."

Losing the phone had been another unacceptable mental lapse and a slip in her safety net. Just how badly was she looking for trouble? She hadn't made any effort to get off the bike, a fact her biker would have noticed. She was sending mixed signals, damn it, and for no good reason.

"Maybe you could call the detective over," her companion suggested with his eyes trained on her. "Or maybe you'd like me to do the honors?"

"I'll find him on my own," McKenna said. "I'm not sure he'd like you."

"I'm quite certain he wouldn't," he agreed.

Easing back, McKenna checked out the logo on his back. Blood Knights didn't sound good. But it wasn't any local gang she was familiar with.

"What do you do, other than riding a Harley?" Her former cop tone came through on that question.

He shrugged. "I travel."

"That's all? You don't work?"

"Would that make you feel better about accepting my help?"

"Immensely."

The grin he flashed made her feel morally weaker, and quite prejudiced about the truth of beauty being everything. As if the smile were contagious, McKenna felt her own lips rebelliously upturn.

Those light blue eyes of his were a shocking contrast

to the sculpted features any male model would have given eyeteeth for. His eyes seemed to be lit from within.

She was starting to think she'd dreamed him up.

He was still staring at her.

"I didn't mean to pry," she said. "I have a tendency to speak too quickly and demand everything. It's both a habit and a fault."

"I get it," he said. "And it's okay."

And yet she still hadn't made that call to Derek. Minutes had gone by at the curb. An officer McKenna didn't immediately recognize had caught sight of them and was on his way over. She would ask that officer to get Derek.

"Maybe you should go," she suggested to the man beside her.

"With or without you?" he asked, as if he possessed the ability to read her mind and knew she didn't really want to be at this crime scene, now that she was. Maybe he sensed she was too tired to handle anything more, including another cop's biased queries about her condition and her ride.

McKenna also had an uncanny feeling that her rescuer might be reluctant to leave her, and the idea produced a thrill.

"Back to the hospital?" he asked. "Someplace where we can call a cab?"

McKenna bit her lip to keep from reciting her address out loud. In her mind's eye, she pictured the black jacket slipping off this guy's broad shoulders. She could almost feel the texture of his golden skin beneath her hands, and imagine the savage way she'd go for his pants.

Those brazen, totally unacceptable images scattered when another cop called out, "Randall, is that you?" He shone a flashlight in her direction.

She and her leather-clad knight turned their heads toward the young cop at the same time.

"Yeah," she called back. "Just checking things out for old times' sake."

Lowering her voice, McKenna whispered, "Hospital," willing her rescuer to take her away without further delay or remarking about her wishy-washy mental state. After all, he'd mentioned waiting for someone near the hospital. Quite possibly she'd been an unwelcome kink in his timeline, and he'd be glad to get back to whomever he'd been waiting for.

The streak of jealousy that came with the idea of this guy belonging to another woman was fierce and unexpected, arriving with the force of a sucker punch. Imagining some other woman's arms around his waist, inhaling the same musky maleness she'd inexplicably begun to desire, made her hot under the collar.

What if that other woman were to tug that zipper down slowly, inch by inch, to expose what waited to be discovered by a worthy mouth or hand? Trace the pattern of that rolling black tattoo on his neck with her tongue?

Damn it!

Several more choice words slipped out of her mouth before the guy said a gravelly "Hold tight," revved the bike's engine and lifted his feet.

"Don't have to tell me twice," McKenna muttered as the night wind again assailed her and the yellow crime tape disappeared behind them.

While he might never have imagined it, Kellan now found that he could be persuaded to wait a little longer to discover the extent of this woman's secrets. Not long. Just enough time to explore the hills and valleys of her beautiful body and indulge in some monumental lovemaking.

He sensed now that she might permit that kind of intimacy. As an experiment, he decided to let go of his own wishes and find out.

"Second left," his passenger directed in a hoarse, weary voice that also held a hint of invitation.

Kellan took another corner, knowing that turning where she indicated would eventually circle them back to the yellow tape and whomever she had decided not to see there just two minutes ago.

Change of heart?

Go with the gut?

To hell with instinct?

Was she back to considering him a threat?

"Stop," she directed after they had gone two more blocks, maybe as a test to see if he would do as she asked.

Kellan pulled over, planted his boots, waited to see what she'd do next and what she expected.

"Thanks," she muttered, loosening her hold on him slightly.

"My pleasure."

They were parked in front of an old commercial building that was six stories high and made of brick covered over with a dark coat of paint. Lights glowed in the third- and fifth-story windows. Weak overhead lanterns illuminated the entrance and its large metal door.

Kellan turned to look at his passenger. "You live here?"

"Yes. I won't be asking you in, though, for obvious reasons."

"Obvious reasons," Kellan repeated, nodding his head. "Completely understandable. Would you like me to walk you to your door?"

"I don't think so. You're too…"

She had a habit of not finishing her sentences. And they were about to return to the previous conversation dealing with what she might think of him.

"I'm too terrifying," he supplied, filling in the blanks. "I'm an unknown. As I said earlier, I get that. You don't know me, and vice versa. So, off you go. I can wait here until you get inside, and then I'll be on my way."

She didn't move. Either she wasn't physically able to hurry, or she was having second thoughts about leaving him.

"Okay, then." Kellan shut off the engine and climbed off the bike. He took hold of her elbow, absorbing the shocks of electricity accompanying the touch.

Christ, if she affected him so greatly, there definitely had to be more to this connection than merely a male-female vibe. And since he hadn't encouraged this latest round of compliance, the attraction seemed to be mutual.

"You're different," she said, studying him intently and in the way he'd want her to look at him once they were joined at the hips. A vision of entwining legs and limbs seared itself into his mind. Kellan shook his head to scatter the image.

"Different, when compared to what?" he asked.

"Everyone else."

If you only knew.

"Should I take that as a compliment?" he asked.

"Actually, I'm not sure it was one."

Smiling, Kellan let go of her arm and held both of his hands up in a gesture indicating he'd back off. "Then I will say good-night from here."

"Yes. From here," she agreed without moving or taking the fire in her gaze down a notch.

"I'm not sure what you want," he confessed after another minute of silence passed. Though he had a good enough idea. Chances were decent that she truly wanted him as badly as he wanted her and this fragile-looking woman had an edge he hadn't yet fully witnessed. She might even crave danger, when he was danger personified.

Slowly, carefully, he helped her off the bike and took hold of the collar of her coat. This time when she stumbled close, he tilted her head back with his finger, grinned wickedly when her eyes met his and dared to rest his mouth lightly on hers.

He waited for the slap that didn't come before applying more pressure. This wasn't a real kiss—more like a test of wills and a bargain between them that had finally been exposed.

Her participation in the kiss would be a green light and would shatter any remaining roadblocks leading to her apartment. If she didn't kiss him back, he'd have to regroup.

Ah, but her mouth was exactly as he had imagined it would be. Her soft, supple, wind-chilled lips tasted like mint toothpaste. They trembled slightly. Her eyes were closed.

"What are you thinking?" Kellan asked her silently. *"Who am I to you?"*

He waited, impatient, hopeful, until the lips beneath his finally parted and her warm breath seeped into his mouth.

Chapter 4

McKenna felt herself losing ground in a multitude of battles. Between her body and her mind. Between her principles of right and wrong. And between the possibility of falling into a dangerous situation that might lead to an experience of the sublime.

She was under this guy's spell. His mouth was an inferno, and she craved its warmth. He was an enigma, a face without a name, and though she was taking a chance, she'd been well trained in taking care of herself.

There was a nine-millimeter Glock in her nightstand and a revolver in a desk drawer by the front door. Her apartment was alarmed, armed with panic-button-type security. It was all there thanks to the bullet that seemed to have hit her in another lifetime, and the long recovery she'd endured.

Taking chances didn't seem so disturbing when, due to the severity of that injury, she felt as if she was already living on borrowed time.

She wanted to feel something. She wanted to explore the edges of the unknown and find a place ruled by pure sensation. If this stranger could give her that...well, all right, and God bless his perfect, leather-clad hide.

Surprisingly, his kiss was tender at first—not much more than a light pressure. He was judging her reaction, being honorable about waiting for her response. So she kissed him back.

Green light.

He got the hint and deepened the kiss. More pressure. More heat. The warmth of his mouth ignited fires deep down inside her that grew even hotter when he slipped the tip of his tongue between her teeth.

Yes, you beautiful bastard!

Her mind soared. Her body began to overheat. McKenna placed both of her hands on his shoulders and dug her fingers into the worn black leather, looking for a hold. In the back of her mind she conjured more unladylike four-letter words that described her wanton behavior.

But what the hell...

Her knight crushed her body to his, bending her spine, kissing her with a passion that was shockingly new. This kind of passion suggested a world far from her familiar one, a place of raw abandon where anything was possible. Having his mouth on hers created in her a hunger for something she'd never even sampled. That hunger began to take her over.

He was what she wanted right that minute. More of this. More of him. God yes, she might have gone temporarily insane, but she was going to have it all.

Damn you...

Each second in this man's embrace piled on more greed. Her skin buzzed with excitement. The deep V between her thighs tingled, anxious to be touched, entered, taken, filled, either gently or roughly, without caring about feelings, pain or hurt, and how she might hate herself afterward.

She longed to feel alive again, and this guy knew how to take care of that. He seemed to understand the things her life lacked and was willing to show them to her.

What have I become?

When he pulled back, she wanted to strike him in protest. She didn't want to go back to being bland, scarred McKenna. *Not now. Not yet.* When she looked up, it was to find a questioning glint in his unusually light, sky blue eyes.

"You need to know my name." The tone of his voice was like a second caress.

McKenna shook her head. "I'd rather not know that."

"Then at least tell me yours."

Without the heated pressure of his lips, she quickly chilled. "McKenna."

He said, "It suits you. I like it."

"Does liking my name make a difference?"

"It makes things more personal, don't you think?"

"I'm trying to avoid personal."

"Then we won't be going inside?"

McKenna was surprised to hear her reply. "Yes. We will."

After a kiss like that, she was wholeheartedly willing to put herself on the line.

"Yes," she repeated, holding back the urge to straddle the guy right here on the street.

He was infuriatingly calm. Taking her hand in his, her motorcycle-riding knight turned from the street and led her to her front door…straight toward the culmination of those wicked images she could barely keep to herself.

Before McKenna realized it, they were almost up the stairs to her fifth-floor loft. No further threat of fainting spells came. She didn't have to be carried since she was fueled by anticipation and adrenaline.

She handed him her key. Inside the high-ceilinged space, lights set on timers blazed in honor of her late return. Clothes from the day before lay strewn on the floor. The bed was unmade.

Her companion didn't seem to notice the disarray. Once the door closed behind them, his hands were on her again. He gathered her into his arms, his mouth moving greedily on hers.

Nothing was left of the gentleman now. These kisses were acts of ravenous, insatiable hunger that hurled McKenna toward a heightened emotional state. Breathing became a game between her mouth and his, her lungs and his. The tightness of his hold on her kept the world from tilting.

Her coat hit the wood floor with a clink of the metallic buttons. He undid her shirt far enough to slip one heated hand beneath. When he reached her breast, her heart exploded. Her breath hitched. She felt the beat of his pulse through the thin layer of lingerie she wore. That pulse was strong, erratic, and it lurched when her hands joined with his in the furious race for discovery.

The leather he wore was a unique kind of turn-on, smooth as velvet, with an old-world masculine scent. She ran both hands over his backside and the jacket emblazoned with the curious logo. Simultaneously, his fingers sailed lightly across her bare stomach before reaching around to her back.

Every inch of flesh he touched burned. It didn't take much for her to imagine what lay beneath his clothes and how much she would enjoy finding out.

"Off with the jacket," she whispered into his mouth.

Wanting to miss nothing, McKenna searched for a way under his black T-shirt as his leather jacket hit the floor.

The groan she heard was a sound she had made. The sheer beauty in front of her demanded it. Where Derek, her former lover, had been lean and wiry, this guy was composed of gracefully tuned muscle. Wide shoulders

stretched the cotton shirt tight. His chest was magnifi-
cently broad, perched above a narrow waist and hips.

He had the corded arms of someone used to performing hard work, without the calluses on his hands to prove
it. Since he was a knight, according to the legend on his
jacket, McKenna imagined him as a warrior of old, riding a horse instead of a Harley and swinging a sword. A
heavy silver broadsword was the type of weapon knights
with all that well-honed muscle would be trained to wield.

She imagined herself in his arms, back in those times
of castles and fierce men on battlefields...

And damn it, she was taking this whole rescuer thing
too far.

When his mouth recaptured hers, McKenna's mind fuzzed
over in favor of her body's new focus. Bed. This guy was
all hers for the next few hours, and she'd be counting them
not in minutes, but in orgasms like the one she was close to
having now.

Craving the feel of her skin against his, McKenna eased
back. He was in excellent shape, his skin tight, taut. His
abs were well-defined. He flinched when she touched his
bare skin as if he wasn't used to being touched.

Her fingers moved like lightning over him. When she
looked up, he was smiling. His expression held a hint of
sadness that made him look almost vulnerable. When their
gazes met, blue eyes to blue eyes, McKenna's internal fires
became volcanic, erupting, spreading, spilling over every
nerve she possessed.

She held her breath. He made a move.

First he tore off his shirt. Then he removed hers. He took
the time to glance down the length of her body before lifting her into his arms. Crossing the room in three big strides,
he laid her on the bed, pulled off her boots and leaned over

her with one of his hands on the pillow and his other hand resting on the zipper of her jeans.

McKenna struggled for each new breath. Anticipation caused her limbs to quake. The guy's damnably perfect face filled her vision, his features hurtfully handsome, almost supernaturally beguiling. "No one is this perfect," she managed to say, holding off the distant internal drumming.

He arched one auburn eyebrow.

"You're not going to have to work very hard," she added. "I'm afraid I might be too weak to last very long against all that…" She waved at his body.

"Then don't," he whispered. "Don't hold out."

"Damn you."

"I could stop," he said. "But we haven't even really started yet, have we?"

"One of us has." McKenna closed her eyes and dug deep for the willpower to ward off the storm threatening to overtake her.

She didn't want to feel any loss of control. She despised weakness. Weakness was a disadvantage for so many reasons. She'd been truly vulnerable once, two years ago, when a bullet was the cause. She'd been flat on the ground, on her back, nearly breathless and covered in blood. After that night, she'd had to kiss her job in law enforcement goodbye.

She had vowed never to allow anyone to take control of her life again, and so far no one had. She played tough, worked hard and avoided long-term relationships. She kept long hours so she'd be tired enough not to care overmuch about the past, and usually fell into bed exhausted and alone.

Tonight was special, but no big deal. She'd have sex, satisfy her cravings and usher this hunky nameless stranger out. She had condoms in her drawer from the few times she and Derek had shared a bed. She was hot, but not to- tally incompetent. There was no way she was going to shed the tough emotional shell she'd worked so hard to create for one night in the sack.

So what if her heart was pounding too hard and too fast as she waited for the sound of her zipper to slide on its metallic tracks? Sue her if she imagined what stroking her tongue over every delectable inch of this guy's incred- ible body would be like.

He moved his hand, taking hers with it as the zipper began its downward slide. "Are you having second thoughts, McKenna?"

He pronounced her name with a very slight accent she hadn't noticed before. British, maybe. Decidedly Euro- pean. Super sexy.

"Yes," McKenna answered truthfully, though that reply wasn't only about what was going to take place here. The second thoughts he'd mentioned had to do with her whole damn life, and how it had brought her to the point of lust- ing for a stranger.

Whispers of cooler air breezed across her stomach, a precursor to the next step in this brazen rendezvous. Grit- ting her teeth, McKenna whispered, "Kick it to hell," as the threat of an early climax rumbled upward.

There was just something about this guy.

Something to make her throw caution out the window.

And if the descent of her zipper wasn't enough, her tal- ented companion captured her mouth, letting her know that he planned to claim her tonight, in both body and soul.

As if he hadn't done so already.

The cry that escaped Kellan's lover's lips was one o imminent ecstasy. In that sound lay an unleashed emoti he found vaguely familiar, like a wisp of memory stolen from a long-lost dream.

The woman he was with felt things on a major scale. Her cry was just one example of that.

Slowly he worked his fingers farther inside the waistband of her jeans, pausing when he reached the thin barrier of lace beneath. McKenna's lingerie was delicate, ultrafeminine and way too fragile for a male with a mission. Delicacies like this were contrary to the kind of life he had endured, which made that scrap of fabric so very much more intriguing.

The woman beneath him snaked an arm around his waist. She raked his skin lightly with her fingernails and bit down on his lower lip with her tiny white teeth.

Christ. He was hard as steel. He was ready to take her and had to hold back, bide his time, sure a soul like hers needed to be confronted carefully in order for him to glean its secrets. If he went too far, too fast, crucial clues might be missed. He might fail altogether in his objective for coming here, and lose ground. Then again, maybe she was just a really attractive woman.

He didn't want to rush this in any case. But neither could he afford to get lost in the challenge. Focus had to be maintained when his willpower had already started to dissipate. McKenna's hands were like ribbons of molten lava, trapping him midway between lust and purpose. Those hands were heading toward his shoulder blades, a place no woman had visited since his only real love had pressed her lips there in goodbye.

McKenna was going to break that record if she had her way. He couldn't let her get that far. If she reached his blades, she'd feel the designs carved into him with the blackened blood of the seven Blood Knights.

If she were his Reaper, that one touch could awaken

her. Now that he was here, close, he wanted to prolong the pleasure.

When her fingertips found the lower edge of the tats, Kellan sucked in a breath. The sigils were scoring him raw when he already felt feverish. Part of his mind rebelled against the personal intrusion. His muscles spasmed with a dire kind of reminder that holy marks weren't meant to be seen or shared.

But he fought against the old rules. This woman's touch might be the only way for him to determine the sincerity of their connection.

These feelings he had for McKenna were a mystery, unless the two of them were connected. A woman's lips had been the last thing he'd felt before his new, resurrected life began. Now a woman's touch might cause the end of that second round of life.

He had to distract her from the tattoos, or he'd be undone.

Kellan rested his hand on McKenna's flat belly. He splayed his fingers so that his fingertips rested on her pubic bone, above the lovely spot his body now shuddered to enter.

He was used to observing every movement, gesture, tic, in not only an opponent but also everyone else around him. Danger in unexpected places was a constant for him. He found it funny now that enhanced senses used to working overtime couldn't quite get a handle on *her*.

While her sigh told him how much she liked this meeting of their skin, McKenna's tension hadn't eased. Though her face had flushed pink, her heart knocked out a swift-paced irregular beat. His heart matched hers pulse for pulse in much the same way that his body behaved whe taking on the aspects of his hunted prey.

Her long lashes fluttered. Her tongue darted to mois

her lips. Oh yes. He liked it all. Her. This. McKenna was doing a number on him. She had ensnared him on the street with the invitation in her eyes, and now he would return the favor.

Kellan pressed closer to her, waiting for her eyes to re-open, part of him hoping they wouldn't. Because he didn't want her to see the questions on his face. Or the fangs, sharp-tipped and throbbing with a need for something they'd never had.

Kellan hauled himself back, cursing silently with blasphemies from his past.

It was then that he saw the small tattoo on her upper arm. A tiny black rose with its petals unfurling. This could have been a coincidence. People today had tattoos. Women were partial to flowers.

But then why did he have one very similar to it, carved into him centuries ago?

Hello, Reaper, the voice inside his head said.

Chapter 5

McKenna's moan of pleasure stuck in her throat. Her arms dropped to the bed as if she'd been released from a trance. Opening her eyes, she found the auburn-haired stranger looking down at her.

His eyes were luminous. His shiny hair, lightened by streaks of gold, was just long enough to fall becomingly across his forehead. There was no upward curve to the lips she wanted to curse for being so inviting. He was serious now.

Her first instinct was to shy away from the intensity of his penetrating gaze. But there was more exploration to come. She and this man were only in the starting gate. Both of them were shirtless but still wearing their pants.

Wait. Could that be right?

In spite of finding herself half-dressed, McKenna believed that she'd been naked in his arms and fucked to within an inch of her life just minutes ago. The soreness of a long, drawn-out sexfest was there, deep inside her, aching, throbbing. Her thighs quaked with leftover need.

Of course, being almost fully clothed would have prevented any of that, so how could she have thought otherwise? She had to have been hallucinating. Wishing.

Her voice wasn't quite even when she spoke. "I though we just...that we..."

"Only the beginning," he promised in a tone as thick as hers.

Wary of losing track of events that couldn't have been more than a few moments long, McKenna made herself speak again. "I have a confession to make. I'm afraid that if you're good enough to make me imagine we've gotten to know each other a whole lot better without actually doing so, I truly might not be ready for the real thing."

He nodded. "We have a connection."

"You think?"

"My confession is that I find you irresistible, McKenna."

"You don't have to flatter me. I'm already right here, on this bed."

"What if I speak the truth?"

"Then I'd have to ask what's stopping you from taking what you want right now, and then see what answer you come up with."

"I'm savoring the moment," he said.

"Take your time. After all, I did just embarrass myself, didn't I, by jumping the gun? I suppose that says something about my love life, or the lack of it."

His brow furrowed. "I can't imagine why there isn't a man here, waiting for you."

"I guess it's because I have standards."

He nodded. "Then I'm honored to be here now. And I find your honesty refreshing."

"Yes, that's exactly what a girl wants to hear while lying in bed with a man. That she's refreshing."

The remark resulted in a smile that was as dazzling as the rest of him. Because of it, McKenna's mind began a new internal dialogue warning her about truly not being ready for this caliber of man.

His hand was very close to her private parts. One move of her hips and he'd find out just how much she wanted this.

He didn't make that move.

"You can leave whenever you want to," she said, testing his intentions. "There were no promises here."

"Did I say anything about leaving?"

"No, but I thought I'd get that out, up front."

"Actually, I'm fairly sure there *were* promises, and I rarely go back on mine."

"Promises? Such as?"

"Mouths meeting. Bodies merging. Two lost souls finding each other."

"That's deep," McKenna said. "And maybe too advanced for the possibility of an hour together in my bedroom."

"I'm a man of high hopes." He withdrew his hand and reached to the bedside table to turn off the light.

Darkness fell, but there was just enough light coming in from the streetlights for McKenna to make out her lover's sculpted silhouette. She mourned the loss of his baby blue gaze.

The mattress creaked beneath his weight as he shifted closer. Uncontrollably drawn to him, with a real need to explore what was so damn fine, McKenna's hands went to his chest. There she found the heat she knew would greet her, and she relished the burn.

The face she had thought angelic was close enough for her to feel his breath on her cheek. She turned her head toward him to offer easy access.

Sensation had tripled in the dark, awakened by anticipation. He swept her hair back from her face with his fingers, and she quivered. When he brushed her lips with his, without lingering, she wanted to break the standoff and tug him closer.

"Damn you," she whispered for what had to be the tenth time. Giving in to her body's demands, she reached for his shoulders.

"Soon," he whispered, his husky tone hurling more flames in her direction.

He felt solid, hard, as his body rolled onto hers, spread-eagle on the bed. There was only the briefest time to recognize how well they fit together and how good being beneath him felt.

He didn't have to move to let her know that he shared her excitement. His stiffness in all the right places made that perfectly clear. His hard length, and the friction of being pants to pants below the waist and skin to skin above, was a sensation like no other.

It would have been lying to say she hadn't known how good this would be.

McKenna stifled another moan when his lips feathered across her left cheek in a downward path that would lead to her throat. His next move was a soft bite to a super-sensitive spot below her ear. He did the same thing again a bit lower, and afterward placed a kiss in the valley between her breasts.

She was coming unglued. Her heart could not have beat harder. Catching her breath was a chore. She shook like a schoolgirl, fearing to move, not wanting to lose one gloriously sexy, unbelievably scary minute.

When his mouth grazed the lace covering her breasts, McKenna shoved her fingers into his hair. Her treacherous legs opened, urged into moving by the swift rise of another far-off internal beat that was pounding her insides to a pulp.

Hot breath on her nipples…

The sensation of her lacy bra being removed by the √'s strong hands…

Followed by a flick of his tongue over one raised pink bud.
She could not remain still. *Can't*.

This was too much. *And too little*.

"What are you waiting for?" she demanded breathlessly, the question loud in the darkened room.

"This," he replied, dragging his mouth to the other breast, where he closed his lips over that swollen tip of her raised flesh.

McKenna bucked beneath him. Her hands fisted in his hair.

God...

He stroked a hand over her jeans, over the sweet spot pulsing between her legs as he first licked, then lightly suckled her. Shudders of delight shot through her. His mouth was crazy hot.

Did he make a sound? Could the cry have been hers?

"Can't wait much longer," she whispered.

"We might have to," he warned as his hand stopped moving and the sound of knocking filled the room.

McKenna heard little over the sound of her own harsh breathing, but quickly realized that those knocking sounds weren't due to the pounding of her heart. They came from the door.

In the most untimely interruption imaginable, some-one wanted in.

Kellan swore beneath his breath and lifted his head. Drawing back, he sat up and looked to McKenna. "You were expecting company?"

"No."

He believed her. Using his extraordinary senses, he per-ceived that this visitor was a man. Presumably the elusive Detective Miller.

It was likely that the officers at the crime scene they

visited earlier had told Miller about them. It was also a good bet that the phone call McKenna made to the police department had been forwarded.

Maybe the idea of McKenna on a Harley was grounds enough for the detective to assume this was an emergency.

"Mac?" the newcomer called out softly between knocks. "McKenna? Are you there?"

"He'll go away," McKenna said, her body motionless on the lavender-scented sheets.

Kellan perched on the edge of the mattress, waiting for McKenna's next instructions and wondering what this detective meant to her. Friend? More than that? There was a new tension in the room that suggested *lover*. Was that title current, though, or a detail from McKenna's past?

When the knock came again, a jolt of anger hit Kellan. This was his time with McKenna. The importance of his agenda could not be overstated. He and the woman beside him had already opened a physical dialogue that might lead to the success of his mission. After all these years, he had also been enjoying himself.

"He won't like finding you here," McKenna said. She was looking to the door.

"Does he have a key?"

"Yes, but he won't use it. Not now, without my permission."

A liaison in the past tense, then?

"You don't think being seen with me tonight might be considered cause for concern?" Kellan suggested.

"There's always that," she conceded.

The knocks ceased for several seconds before the doorknob turned. Kellan stood as the sound of a key grated in the lock. Gracefully, quickly, with McKenna's welfare in mind, he moved toward his shirt.

Chapter 6

The man spanning the doorway looked like a cop, Kellan decided. It was all there—height, professionally short hair, wiry frame, condemning expression on a good-looking face. The scent of metal—his badge, and a gun hidden under an armpit—accompanied him. Underneath all of that, Kellan detected an almost feral nervousness.

The detective stopped dead in his tracks, trying to see into the darkened room. Once his eyes had adjusted, his focus landed on Kellan. Soon afterward, he flipped the light switch and transferred his gaze to the unmade bed, then to McKenna, who now stood at the window.

"Am I intruding?" he asked no one in particular. There was an explicit warning in his tone.

"Just leaving," Kellan replied calmly, sweeping his jacket off the floor.

"Good." The detective's eyes were still on McKenna. She had donned a sweatshirt in time to avoid being caught half-naked.

"I'll see you out," the detective added, facing Kellan.

"No need. I can find my way," Kellan said.

"Maybe so, but I'd feel better making sure you got to the street."

McKenna broke in. "Truly, Derek, does he look like he needs help?"

"Which is exactly why I'm offering it," the detective said.

"He brought me home," she explained.

"I see that."

Wanting to avoid more tension, Kellan shrugged into the jacket and zipped it up. After rolling his shoulders, he said to the detective, "See ya."

"I'll be back," the detective told McKenna as he followed Kellan into the hallway. "In the meantime, Mac, maybe you can turn on more lights?"

She offered no remark in return. Her eyes followed Kellan.

Ten steps toward the staircase, with the detective tagging along behind, Kellan stopped abruptly, alerted to a new problem. Looking up, he said to the detective, "You're going to keep an eye on her?"

"I usually do," the detective replied.

"That gun's loaded?"

"Are you wondering if I'll shoot you for taking liberties with McKenna?"

"I promise you there are far worse things than me around tonight," Kellan announced truthfully, able to smell the vampire on the roof and sense its bottomless hunger.

"Maybe so," the detective said. "Yet I think I'll deal with one thing at a time."

Kellan didn't want to leave McKenna and vowed the separation wouldn't be for long. He just had to take care of the little problem on the roof without this detective's prying eyes, and then get rid of the detective.

McKenna might wait for him. Then again, maybe she'd lock the door for good since she'd been afforded the chance to regret her actions and her invitation now that their night together had been interrupted.

Still, he'd find a second opportunity.

He had to.

Their footsteps were quiet on the steps. Once on the street, the detective waited with a shoulder against the building's brick entry for Kellan to reach the Harley. But Kellan couldn't leave. The fanged bloodsucker was clinging to the side of the building above them like an oversize spider. Really nasty vamps with bad intentions did that in order to peer into windows to locate their next unsuspecting victims. This one didn't seem to care about the two people below.

If Miller glanced upward, he'd see the danger lurking there. Possibly he'd even believe his eyes. At the moment, though, the detective's only concern was getting rid of the biker who had fraternized with his old flame. Like most mortals, Miller wouldn't catch a whiff of the supernatural threat that was almost in his face.

Leaving now was impossible. As soon as he exited the area, the dead fanger might drop, and Miller wouldn't know what hit him. It also might swing through the window and reach McKenna before Kellan could hit the stairs.

He saw McKenna at the window. The damn vampire was dangling a few feet above her, its white face gleaming with malice.

Kellan knew he could get past Detective Miller easily enough, but if he used his special speed, the cop would know there were things on this earth that lay beyond the realm of the possible. Miller's gun could slow the rogue vampire down if the detective got off a few rounds, yet those bullets wouldn't kill the monster, even if Kellan were to point the bloodsucker out.

This was his problem. Taking care of bad guys was what he did.

"Why were you with her? What's McKenna to you?" Miller asked as Kellan turned toward him.

"Is that your business?" Kellan asked.

"I've just made it my business."

Kellan figured he had a few seconds at most to play along with the detective's line of questioning.

"I gave her a ride," he said.

Miller's dark eyes were almost rudely assessing. "Yes. That's why the lights were off in her apartment, as well as your jacket. Mac's gratefulness for that ride being the reason?"

Kellan kept his eyes on the detective so as not to call attention to the monster closing in. He said, "I offered to get her home when she needed help."

"Mac seldom needs help. So if she did, you have my thanks for that."

Of course, Miller didn't mean that about the thanks. Most likely he'd been informed about the call McKenna had made, though, and would know she tried to reach him first.

This was checkmate when there was no need of it. Kellan supposed he would be pressed to honor his vows to the end, as he always did, so that humans wouldn't panic over seeing what hid in the shadows. He went so far as to think about showing his fangs to this detective, just to get Miller on board.

Turning to the Harley, Kellan peered over his shoulder. The vampire had reached McKenna's window, where she was standing very close to the glass. Another couple of breaths and the rogue would find its way in.

Kellan considered what might constitute the lesser of two evils. Reveal himself and his abilities to this detective and get to McKenna, or let Miller find out the hard way about one of the world's darkest secrets.

"I forgot something," Kellan said, rounding back to where the detective stood.

"I'll save it for you, whatever it is," Miller promised sarcastically, pushing off the wall to block the doorway.

"It's important that I go back up there, Detective."

Miller gave him a look that more or less translated to *over my dead body*. But by then the sound of breaking glass filled the night.

McKenna didn't know what happened. One minute she was looking at the two men on the sidewalk, and the next minute there were shards of shattered glass in her face.

She stumbled back, caught herself from falling on the bed and sprang sideways with an adrenaline surge as something barreled through the opening that moments ago had been a sturdy dual-paned window.

Intruder.

A shout lodged in her throat, but her police-trained reflexes rallied. She hit the floor and rolled toward where her gun was hidden in a drawer, figuring that timing would be her ally and provide the precious seconds necessary for her to protect herself from attack.

Unfortunately, she didn't get far. The guy was incredibly fast. Strong hands caught her by the hair and swung her around. Gasping, she was on her back before her next breath, smelling the rancid odor coming from her attacker's open mouth.

McKenna kicked out. Her bare right foot connected with the man's shin, but he didn't seem to feel it. He was a fighter, and superhumanly strong. Although she'd kicked with all her might, being shoeless wasn't in her favor. Her foot hurt like hell.

He was on top of her in seconds.

No way was she going to give up.

McKenna punched him with both hands and managed to rip the skin from his face with her nails. She struggled squirmed and fought with an energy born of both fear and anger.

She was against the wall without knowing how she'd got there. The attacker's face came close—a pasty angular death mask with dark holes for eyes.

"Freak!" she rasped as his hands encircled her throat and began to squeeze.

She got her arms under his and shoved hers upward to break his choke hold. Dropping her weight, she again hit the floor in time to slide out from under him.

He grunted once and again caught her by the hair. With a sickening heave he had her upright and shoved against the same damn wall. His hands returned to her throat.

She groaned as her breath left her and her lids fluttered toward stillness.

"What the hell?" The detective's startled shout preceded Kellan's race to the stairs.

Kellan was beyond caring about vows and secrets now. If anything happened to McKenna, he'd be one sorry immortal.

He was at her door in seconds and through it in less time than it took for Miller to gather himself enough to follow. One quick scan told him that the beast, in a blur of malice and motion, had McKenna by the throat.

Kellan pulled the vampire off her and held the abomination suspended in the air as he spoke McKenna's name, needing to know he was in time and she was all right. He had never faced the meaning of real fear until she didn't answer.

The vampire in his grip was young and unaware of beings with greater power. It spit and hissed and fought with the strength of two human men, but was no match for a Blood Knight.

Kellan threw the beast against the same wall McKenna had slid down. Hearing Detective Miller's approach, and regretful over not having the time to deal the bloodsucker some retribution, he clutched the vampire, moved to the window and tossed the beast out.

"Another time, fiend," he said, his voice low and threatening. "You'd better hope it's not anywhere near here."

"McKenna?" Miller was calling her name, kneeling by McKenna's side, turning her over. She was on the floor with her head against the legs of a chair. Her eyes were closed.

"McKenna, open your eyes," Miller directed. "Look at me. You're going to be okay. Tell me you're all right."

Kellan watched, wanting to help, desperate to go to her. Frustrated, he made himself wait, hearing the rapid patter of McKenna's heartbeat from where he stood and the staccato intake of her ragged breaths.

Miller turned his head. "Where did the bastard go?"

"It exited the same way it got in," Kellan said, withholding the part about throwing the bloodsucker out and onto its five-year-dead ass.

Miller didn't seem to notice the *it* part.

"Help her," Miller directed, pulling a phone from his pocket to call the incident in. "Jesus, there isn't a decent place left in this goddamn city to live."

Kellan relished the chance to get close to McKenna. As the detective barked orders into the phone, he took McKenna in his arms, brushed the hair back from her face and spoke in a soft tone. "You're not hurt, McKenna. I won't allow that, and neither will you. Do you hear me?"

He used his power of suggestion to convince her of this, adding, "Open your eyes. See me and believe that what I say is true."

She obeyed. Her sapphire-blue eyes blinked slowly.

"That's good," he said. "Now take a deep breath and push back the fear. It's over. You're all right."

Again she obeyed, taking one steady breath after another. Her face was ashen. So were her lips. "Window," she said. "He came through the window."

Kellan nodded. "He probably thought no one was home."

McKenna coughed as she shook her head. "No. I think he came for me."

"It's all right now," Kellan repeated. "Your cop friend will see to that. And so will I."

He ran a hand over her throat, noting the red marks where the monster had nearly squeezed the life from her. There were no punctures. No visible bite marks. She'd been reached in time to ward off that rueful fate.

Inwardly, Kellan chastised himself for allowing Detective Miller to keep him occupied on the street. That was what he got for being a good guy in a world gone bad. Any longer of a delay and he might have lost the one thing he needed most. McKenna.

Miller squatted down beside him. "Do we need an ambulance, Mac?"

She shook her head. "An ice pack would be nice. And a stiff drink."

Miller's relief was obvious and spoke volumes about the love he had for McKenna, no matter the status of their current relationship. His attention had been on her, and only her. Still, Miller couldn't protect McKenna if monsters had got wind of a developing relationship between McKenna and a Blood Knight, even if they didn't understand what a Blood Knight was.

He had to consider the possibility that his presence had played a part in drawing the vampire to McKenna's apartment, without the vampire realizing it.

Could this be a case of monsters recognizing on some level another monster's prey? Fang calling to fang, no matter how distant and seriously diluted the connection might be?

Miller offered McKenna a hand and she took it. She didn't look at Kellan again until she was sitting in a chair.

"Tall. White-skinned. Dark eyes. Black coat and boots. Black thinning hair," she said. "Maybe thirty years old." Wincing, she added, "With very bad breath."

"Good. What else?" Miller said after repeating that list to whoever was on the other end of the phone line he'd kept open.

"I think he might be sick."

"A junkie, possibly looking for drugs?" Miller asked.

"That's a good possibility," McKenna agreed, shifting her questioning gaze to Kellan. "Thanks for coming back in time to get him off me."

Kellan nodded.

Miller grunted an unintelligible remark, but Kellan searched McKenna's face for signs that she might know more about this intruder than she was willing to mention to the detective. The puzzled, frightened gleam in her eyes suggested she thought she'd seen a monster and was trying to come to terms with that.

"We're searching the area now," Miller said, pocketing the phone. "If the bastard is anywhere around here, we'll find him. In the meantime, it might be best if you stayed at my place. I'll drive you there myself. We'll want to go over this room for clues to this sucker's identity."

McKenna continued to study Kellan, as if deep down she was wondering if he had something to do with the attack. Did she believe he had been here to case the place so his accomplice could finish the job once he'd gone?

"No," he said to her, in case he was right about h

thoughts. "Don't entertain ideas that I could harm you like that."

Of course, his statement was a half-truth at best, since there was also a chance the vampire had come here for him and had got distracted after sensing McKenna's tired state. Vampires were too often hard to predict.

Also, since he was pretty certain McKenna was the special being he sought, he had no idea what might happen to her when he opened her up to the hidden soul inside her. Would she survive that opening? If she did, would she wake in a state vulnerable to every kind of predator on the planet?

He had to consider all the options, all the directions of his next moves.

"I can go back to the hospital," she said to Miller. "There's no need to put you out."

Kellan felt Miller's attention swerve back to McKenna. "I'll take you wherever you want to go," Miller said. "But you know you're always welcome at my place. In fact, I'd feel a lot better if you would take me up on that."

Kellan stood up. "I guess I'll take my leave."

"I'd like a word," Miller said to him pointedly.

"It might not be a good idea to leave McKenna alone."

"We can talk in the hallway with the door open. Mac, are you good with that? Just for a minute? Then I'll get you that ice pack."

After looking back and forth between Miller and Kellan, McKenna nodded.

Miller gestured for Kellan to precede him out. Kellan withheld a sigh, not liking the part he had to play in order to get along with these mortals. He was anxious to go after that vampire on his own. He needed to lose the biker's mortal semblance and get down to business with a fledgling vampire too willing to cross the line with someone else's treasure.

His anger was on the rise. That anger would soon become dangerous enough to burn away his calm exterior.

In the hallway, Miller lowered his voice. "I suppose thanks are in order for helping McKenna again. You ran up those steps like you were superhuman. But thanking you would mean I don't believe in the possibility of you having something to do with this incident. You do get that?"

"I'm not the bad guy here," Kellan said.

"I suppose that's a matter of opinion. So I have to ask some questions. The first one is, who are you?"

"I'm just a guy passing through."

"And you just happened to meet my...meet McKenna?"

"Yes. Near the hospital. She couldn't drive and asked me to take her to you."

That stumped Miller for a minute because he knew this was quite possibly true.

"Why didn't you leave her with me?" Miller asked.

"The lady changed her mind."

"So you brought her here."

"I followed her directions, yes."

"Maybe you can see how odd it is that this attack happened at the same time?"

"Our return could have interrupted the bastard's plans. McKenna probably would have been safe as long as I was there with her."

"It's entirely possible we have differing definitions of the word *safe*. You've known her for, what? Five minutes?"

"I've known her long enough to know I wouldn't want any harm to come to her."

"Maybe so, but I don't like this. I'm going to ask you to stay in the area until we figure things out."

Staying in the area went right along with Kellan's plans

though being part of a police investigation was never good. He didn't need the attention, or anyone scrutinizing his ID. He certainly didn't intend to play along with this detective for much longer. He had a vampire to catch and the timing was tricky.

He had to use more of his power of persuasion.

"I'll be going now," he said, sending the thought straight into the detective's mind, where it encircled everything else with the force of a command, urging Miller to let this biker go without a fuss.

"Okay." Miller raised his hands and stepped back. "I'll be in touch."

Fat chance of that, Kellan thought, since the cop didn't even know his name.

Catching a whiff of fetid air, Kellan turned his head for a quick look, able to detect the vamp's escape route from where he stood as easily as if the bloodsucker had left a trail of bread crumbs.

With one more glance over his shoulder to McKenna's open doorway, he headed for the street.

Chapter 7

McKenna stood in front of the bathroom sink, staring at her image in the mirror. She looked peaked, she thought, and gray. She was sporting an angry red ring of finger marks around her throat that would soon be a circle of bruises. Swallowing was difficult.

What she really didn't need was another miserable reminder of some asshole's evil intent.

Her gaze flicked to the scar on her temple. She touched the line of raised white flesh with her fingers before turning on the tap. Hot water felt good, soothing. She closed her eyes and let the water run as exhaustion again threatened to overtake her. Exhaustion aided by another close encounter with death.

She was finding it hard to breathe. The room was starting to spin, sending her stomach into free fall. Placing her hands on the sink, McKenna fought for enough breath to fill her lungs while attempting to get a handle on her wits. As a cop, she'd seen break-ins go bad on a daily basis. This one just happened to be hers.

"Mac? Are you ready?"

Her eyes found the image in the mirror of the man standing behind her. She wasn't sure why she'd expected someone else, but her heart lurched in anticipation of a face that didn't show up.

Derek had gathered ice cubes in a kitchen towel for her throat.

"I'll stay here," she said. "Unless you think I can't remember how to keep out of the way when everyone shows up."

Derek knew better than to argue. He said, "You won't get any rest if you stay, and you look like you could use a little first aid and a lot of sleep."

"I can take a day off tomorrow and sleep then."

He nodded solemnly. "How about the ice pack?"

She took it from him.

"Does it hurt, Mac?" His voice was a gentle reminder of old times, which made the idea of her attempted bedroom liaison with the stranger seem even stranger. She knew that Derek still loved her. Finding a guy in her apartment must have surprised him. He hadn't been able to hide the hurt in his eyes.

"It doesn't hurt much, thanks to you and…"

Wise to that telling hesitation, Derek's face became a mass of worry lines. "Seriously, McKenna? You don't know the guy's name?"

She didn't answer that question. How could she? Offering a weak shrug, McKenna turned off the water, hoping to avoid more personal scrutiny.

"You'll fill me in, Derek? You will let me know what the guys find?"

"I will," he replied after a beat.

She wanted desperately to get away from Derek's accusing expression.

"Maybe…maybe you can drive me back to the hospital? I've changed my mind about staying here. I'll find a bed somewhere. You can do your job here, and having you in charge will make me feel better."

Derek's face registered relief. "Great. Grab your coat. You can't touch anything else here. I'm sorry for that."

McKenna turned to face him. "Thanks. I know the drill."

What she didn't dare mention to an ex-lover was that she doubted if she'd ever be able to forget the gorgeous stranger who had rescued her twice in the span of an hour, and that she hoped to God she'd never see the biker again. Because owing someone your life was awkward. So was the fact that her body desired his heated touch, even now.

Kellan's arms were steamy beneath rivers of nerve-induced burn. His mind twisted with a new feeling of elation. He had found a contender for his search for the lost soul in Seattle. Her name was McKenna, and he knew where to find her.

He just had to make sure the vile creature that had attacked her would never bother McKenna again.

Where there was one vampire, there was usually another creature of the night. Monsters clung to others of their kind, believing in the power of numbers. This attack on McKenna might bring more danger to her doorstep.

There were many freaks amassing in the dark spaces that viewed humans as a kind of tasty dessert. And while ferreting them out wasn't the reason for this Seattle visit, he now had to take an unplanned detour. His current objective was to save McKenna Randall—he'd noticed her last name on her lobby mailbox. Save her for himself.

Her image wavered in Kellan's mind like a mirage. He could almost feel the softness of her smooth white skin. He rewound events for a replay of the look in her eyes when she appreciatively ran her hands over him, liking what she found.

He heard the lingering echo of the soft, sexy sounds

McKenna made when they kissed, and the way she pressed against him. He revisited the look of anticipation on her face when he'd tucked his fingers inside that little scrap of blue lace crossing her hips, and how those hips moved to help him find what she needed.

He contemplated that rose tattoo on her arm.

If given more time, he could have discovered if the thing he sought lay curled up inside her.

Police cars were arriving at the curb to assess the situation in McKenna's apartment. Since his presence was no longer wanted or necessary, Kellan climbed on the bike and took off, heading down the long block and around a corner, where he stopped to search the shadows with his highly defined senses.

The vampire that had hurt McKenna had landed and run, leaving in its wake a stomach-curdling mixture of odors: dried blood, dirt and the faint scent of lavender, picked up from its brush with McKenna's things.

Broken window glass couldn't have harmed this vampire. Vamps didn't bleed. Their ability to heal miraculously when injured was another one of death's creepy little bonuses.

This bloodsucker had been brazen, as most fledglings were. Hunger ruled them. Nothing else mattered but their need to feed. They weren't aware of the fact that one mistake on their end could create another bloodsucker, and so on. All it took to make a nest of them was a couple of drops of undead blood on a mortal tongue.

Or maybe they did know this.

As always, if the shadows were allowed to spread unchecked, mortals would soon become outnumbered and overpowered by the dark side. Not many people believed in the existence of monsters. They made excuses for the injuries and horrific deaths around their cities, failing to recognize the real danger until it was too late, if ever.

Fact was, it took a monster to find a monster.

"And it just so happens that I'm your guy."

Once he'd tuned in to the vamp's frequency, Kellan saw the atmosphere shift with a phosphorescent green glow. Anything moving with unnatural speed left a similar residual imprint in the air. Kellan supposed that he did, as well.

"Got you."

On foot, he followed the trail between buildings and into a narrow alley lit only by a small shaft of moonlight.

Carefully scanning the walls above him, Kellan called out a taunt, knowing he'd be heard. "Wouldn't you prefer to pick on somebody your own size for a change?"

There was a hissing sound, followed by the clatter of a can. Kellan perceived three vampires hiding out in this area. Obviously, none of them were willing to show themselves. Seemed that his reputation had preceded him and that these suckers were at least aware of the extraordinary strength he possessed.

"I can't leave," he said. "If you know what I am, you'll know why."

There was no response. Although silence settled over the alley, Kellan sensed the three creatures gathering into a group. Their plan to attack him was transmitted telepathically, in much the same way that furred-up werewolves communicated. To his sensitive ears, their minds were mostly a scrambled mess similar to radio static.

"You don't belong here," Kellan said. "Really, you shouldn't exist at all. You know this."

One of the goals of his brotherhood had always been to find that one immortal who had started the undead ball rolling by accidentally or perhaps purposely creating the first bloodsucker. Because that one original freak had bitten uncontrollably, the world today held more fanged abominations than anyone could count.

His blood brother, Mason LanVal, had finished that search for Bloodsucker Zero in France just one year ago, discovering the Maker that had wanted to create his own personal fanged army. However, that discovery had come centuries too late for anyone to turn back the red-tinted tide.

Kellan strode forward with his hands fisted. "Come out and deal."

The first fanger leaped into sight with the agility of a cat, landing on both feet not far from where Kellan stood. Unable to hold most metals due to Death's short list of rules governing the undead, this vampire wielded a brick in one grimy hand.

Kellan smiled. "Long ago in Venice, bricks were stuffed into vampire mouths once their heads had been cut off, ensuring those suckers couldn't bite one last victim as they were being buried."

Silence.

Maybe it didn't understand English.

Possibly it wasn't keen on metaphors.

"Bad plan, you being here," Kellan continued, taking the time to pull a short, sharp-ended wooden stake from his right boot.

Another vampire joined the first in the alley. Weaponless and seething with anger, it broke the silence, drawing its lips back to speak through the gap between long pointed teeth. "Traitor."

"I'm not like you," Kellan said. "You already know that. I don't harm the harmless. And you picked the wrong victim tonight."

"Heartbeat," that vamp hissed, spitting out dark blood that was evidence of a recent dinner engagement.

"Yes, my heart still beats."

"Alive."

"Very much so."

The third vampire arrived to stand with the others in a trio, which, in Kellan's opinion, made the alley too crowded.

The latest vamp to appear was the creature he'd chased back to this dark, grimy hole. The abomination moved disjointedly, as if the fall from the window hadn't yet been sorted out. Each step it took dispersed traces of McKenna's sultry scent into the air.

Kellan blinked slowly, tensed his muscles and waited for the three creatures to rush at him. He didn't have to wait long.

All three came at once, supernaturally quick, but no match for an example of the bigger gene pool. He had one fledgling down in under five seconds and reduced to a fluttering flurry of foul-smelling ash. The second vamp reached Kellan a second later, ramming him hard before Kellan swung the creature around by the back of its coat to look into its pale, pathetic face.

"Rest in peace." Kellan's stake found its mark.

As the vampire exploded, the third monster paused to note the swirling storm of ash filling the alley. A red-rimmed gaze slipped past Kellan. Despite the danger the creature faced, the thing greedily worked its jaw, exhibiting fangs that gleamed with a yellowish cast in the small puddle of moonlight.

Hell…

The hair at the nape of Kellan's neck stood up. He had a bad feeling about this.

Someone was behind him, and Kellan knew who.

* * *

McKenna stood at the entrance to the alley with her mouth open and her heart racing. Surely she was dreaming. She didn't dare blink, move or speak.

The scene was not only surreal but also fascinatingly macabre. Her beautiful stranger was here, fighting a creature that was human enough at first glance, yet when viewed more carefully looked anything but human.

Its white face was like death warmed over. Its body moved in an odd manner, as if it was composed of a combination of broken bones and murky liquid.

McKenna recognized the perp that had attacked her. The freak was now caught up in her stranger's steel-like grip. Had the man gone after the freak because of her?

McKenna took the Glock from her pocket. She wouldn't have left the apartment without it. The gun was loaded. She used to be a good shot.

"It's okay. I have him covered," she finally managed to call out through her aching, swollen throat, glad now that she had changed her mind about being dropped at the hospital and had searched for the Harley instead.

The man in the Blood Knights jacket showed no signs of the fear settling into her bones. He didn't even glance her way.

She tried again. "You can let that creep go."

The tall biker turned his head without doing what she asked. His face showed no sign of the rage she felt. It was impossible not to notice how lethally strong he looked in the alley's dim light as he stood there, motionless, with his hands on the jerk who had attacked her just two blocks from here.

Somehow he had found the asshole, and the perp looked sick and very small next to the impressive height and breadth of the auburn-haired vigilante.

"We can take him in," she said. "Case closed."

"What are you doing here, McKenna? Your detective was supposed to take care of you."

His voice was calm. Reasonable, even.

"Turns out that I didn't need a caretaker after all. Derek did his best, though."

"His best obviously wasn't good enough. Don't you listen to anyone?"

"I've been known to heed advice occasionally."

"Just not when it counts?"

"I'm okay." She was lying through her chattering teeth, because her bruised throat hurt like hell, and the creep the Blood Knight held on to looked like a creature from vampire movies.

"If I let this creature go, it will come for you."

"Why would this idiot want to finish what he started?" she asked, desperate to understand what was going on.

Reason suggested that she had to be hallucinating and that the creature in the biker's grip wasn't a monster.

Pure stubbornness had made her detour from her plan to stay out of trouble after seeing the black Harley parked at the head of this alley. She had gone to her car instead and rushed back to where the bike was parked. Adrenaline and anger had replaced her earlier fatigue. And now she'd found this. If a dream hadn't taken her over, what the hell did any of it mean?

She spoke again after swallowing the lump in her throat. "He won't get far with my gun pointed at his head."

"A gun can't hurt it for long, or for good."

"Don't be ridiculous. Believe me, no one wants to get shot. We can get him booked."

Her leather-clad knight shook his head as he raised the weapon he held in his free hand. McKenna couldn't clear see what that weapon was. It looked like some kind of branch.

Hell, it was a wooden stake.

"Is this a joke?" she asked. "That stick is supposed to scare him?"

"Go home, McKenna. Leave this to me."

"Not going to happen. If you hurt him you'll be held responsible for harming my criminal. You would then be considered a criminal in turn. That's not the way things are supposed to work in the justice system."

"This monster would have killed you. One more minute in your apartment and you'd have been dead, or worse."

"Worse? There's something worse than death?" She held the gun fairly steady in both of her hands despite the terror of the night's horrific events.

"Infinitely worse," her knight said.

What did he think could be worse than death at the hands of a freak? Was he thinking of rape? Sexual assault by someone as ill as this pasty bastard had to be? Was he worried she might have caught some horrible illness from this pale bag of bones? "Let him go," she repeated. "The cops combing the area will haul him in."

"I wouldn't advise having them try. You have no idea what we're dealing with, or how to handle things if this monster were to get loose."

"Let's try to do this by the book. For heaven's sake, please save yourself from prosecution."

Separated from him by several feet, McKenna watched his back stiffen. When he turned toward her, she was again struck by the sheer magnificence of the guy she'd been willing to offer her body to after hardly more than a brief hello.

Again, and quite wickedly, she experienced a moment of rampant lust for the guy, along with a healthy desire to have that climax he'd promised her. Those thoughts were absurdly misplaced and inappropriate at present, and didn't belong inside her head. Damn if she could shake them.

He was studying her in a way that made McKenna think he could see through her clothes and right down to her emotions in turmoil. In spite of the cold, her body flooded with heat.

"If you hurt him and get caught, we won't be able to..."

Damn it, had she just tossed that out there as if a rematch was open for discussion?

His gaze intensified. So clear. So blue. "All right," he said. "You win."

McKenna's mind circled wildly. If there was such a thing as a do-over, she'd forget everything else and have sex with this guy sooner. Even after all this strangeness, she wanted more than ever to discover what earthly delights this incredibly masculine package had to offer.

In a do-over, she'd suggest they go to his place instead of hers, where they wouldn't be disturbed and there was no chance she'd be assaulted. There would be no interruptions and zero time for guilt because the guy would be all over her.

Shame accompanied those thoughts. Her former decision had been to let this go. She'd vowed not to look for this guy. But their chemistry was incredible. She was drawn to him in a way she couldn't explain or ignore.

The leather-clad vigilante stepped back, freeing the perp as she'd asked him to do. The ill-looking bastard appeared to be stunned for a minute. Then he was on her before McKenna's next breath, going again for her neck. His needle-sharp teeth grazed the skin of her bruised throat.

Knocked back a step, McKenna cried out in stunned surprise. She hadn't seen the freak move. Had she blinked too long? Lost concentration? Struggling to fight him off, she heard her gun go off, but couldn't think fast enough to free herself from the freak's bony clutches.

Shit. She should have listened to Mr. Blood Knight. She should have gone to the hospital as she had originally planned and skipped all of this.

In a frightening replay of the former attack on her life, the simple act of breathing became impossible. Feelings of helplessness made a comeback. She was facing a being much stronger than she was, and the maniac had a grip like a vise. The maniac had fangs.

Light flickered like the flame of a candle in her darkening vision. She attempted to take one last breath…

And then she opened her eyes.

She blinked slowly without understanding what had happened.

She was alone, and standing. Miraculously, she was no longer under attack. The fanged monster was gone. No hint of him remained. There was no hint of her vigilante knight, either.

She stood on legs that threatened to buckle, beneath a rain of dark gray ash that chilled her face and smelled like sulfur. The alley was dark. A sudden absence of sound made the place seem sinister.

Widening her stance, McKenna looked around. Her skin was ice-cold. She felt sick to her stomach.

Voice hoarse and barely working, she called out, "Where the hell is everybody?"

Chapter 8

Kellan peered down from his crouched position on the rooftop above the alley, studying McKenna closely, ready to catch her if she fell.

She didn't.

She remained stubbornly upright, feet apart, eyes wild, with the gun dangling from one hand. It was some time before she moved or spoke.

"What the…?" As she surveyed the space in front of her, she muttered a stream of partially choked-off words, ending with "Where the hell is everybody?"

Helping McKenna wasn't an option at the moment unless it became absolutely necessary. She couldn't be allowed to ask about the monsters he'd put down or see the injury she'd caused him.

The bullet she'd fired off had missed the vampire and struck Kellan in the upper arm. While that bullet had passed clear through the flesh and the wound was already on the mend, McKenna would notice the hole in his jacket and the ring of black stain, when fresh blood should be red.

As he'd climbed to the roof to avoid her scrutiny, Kellan's second thought was that in an immortal's world, clothing should also be self-healing. That would have been fair.

Safely out of her sight, he considered what McKenna had nearly blurted out before stopping herself.

If you hurt him and get caught, we won't be able to...

In spite of everything that had happened, McKenna was up for a bedroom rematch. Nevertheless, he still wasn't sure how she had found him in the alley, after what she had been through.

Excitement over the thought of a rematch made the back of his neck tingle. Kellan glanced at his arm. Already, his wound was taking care of itself. His body hummed with an internal skin-splicing directive, repairing the damage from the inside out. The injured skin would be sealed and smooth again in no time. That was a good thing, because if every injury he'd ever incurred were to show up as a scar, he'd have been destined for a circus act.

In his favor was that twenty-first-century bullets were nothing compared to the muscle-ripping devastation of a sixth-century silver-tipped lance.

"Go to your detective, McKenna." Kellan directed those words to her in a whisper, with a slight push of power. "You'll be all right for a while in his care."

He grew quiet when McKenna glanced up. There would be no way for her to see him on the rooftop with the buildings looming over her and moonlight in her eyes...and yet he felt her eyes pass over him in a focused gaze that stoked the fires urging him to forget the bullet hole and jump down to her side.

Their connection was strong and growing steadily stronger. In placing a special soul inside McKenna's bloodline, his Makers had done their job well. Besides being a beauty in her own right, McKenna Randall was courageous, bold and possibly a bit too aggressive for her own good. No one could call her a wallflower. The cop she'd once been had come out tonight with full force. Nothing was going to keep her down.

He wondered what barred her from the profession she

seemed destined for. Also requiring an answer was the question of what really kept him from going down there to get what he wanted, and damn all else.

The answer, of course, was that timing was everything.

McKenna was human in all the ways that counted. As such, she'd need to be comforted, quieted. She'd need to be held and have sweet promises whispered in her ear. He wanted to do all of that for her, at least until the end. As Kellan watched her, he realized an honest closeness during the time he had left was what he desired most. That desire was so strong, he nearly shouted out loud.

He wished for his last few minutes on earth to be spent on scented sheets, with his body settled between McKenna's thighs. He was sure he'd die a final death in peace if he were to be granted those things.

Kellan also realized that he would have wished for all of those same things even if McKenna Randall didn't have a single secret to share.

"Go now, my beauty."

The urgent impulse to reach her made Kellan's muscles twitch. The involuntary reaction threatened to slow his healing process, so he was thankful he hadn't lost his wits altogether.

Now wasn't the time to reclaim McKenna. His healing took precedence, since he might need energy near the end. In the meantime, allowing McKenna some space was a good thing. Just enough space. Not so much that she'd reason away her attraction to him. Not so much space that she'd be in danger from forces beyond his control.

"I will watch over you, McKenna Randall."

As if she felt his presence, McKenna lifted the gun to point at the rooftop above her. She swept the weapon in a circle. Eventually she lowered the gun and spoke in a throaty voice. "I know you're there, but I don't understand how I know. Regardless of what I saw, monsters showing up here can't be real. This has to be a nightmare."

Her hand went to her throat. She winced, fingering the darkening bruises the fanged monster had left her with.

"Nightmare."

After repeating that word, her fingers found the scar on her temple as if that wound had also been part of a dream.

Although he couldn't speak to her out loud and fought to remain silent, Kellan sent his message directly to her mind.

"We'll find each other later. It won't be a long separation, I promise."

She swayed on her feet.

"Go, McKenna." His whisper was as tender as it was commanding.

Helpless to resist this directive, McKenna complied. Backing up one slow step at a time, she eased out of the alley. She paused when she reached the street. Her pale features drew tight, as if she'd fight the seeds of escape that he had planted in her mind.

"Go, McKenna. I keep my promises."

Except for one, he might have added. And that involved his intention to break the chains of his immortality.

His next question had to do with how long he'd stick around to protect McKenna if it turned out she wasn't tied up with his original objective. If someone else waited for him with a soulful come-hither, McKenna Randall would be nothing more than an untimely distraction. An incredibly beautiful, sexy, feisty distraction.

But again, there was a black rose imprinted on her beautiful body, and that had to mean something.

"Stay safe, my fair-haired lover."

Speaking those words eased the knot in Kellan's gut. Though the work wasn't over and nothing regarding his soul mate was set in stone, the word *lover* sounded right. The concept behind it produced an unexpected feeling of peace deep down inside him.

This wasn't over, though. McKenna wasn't completely free of other outside influences. Now that the bloodsucker on her tail had been dealt with, there was a chance she would be all right on her own, and an equal chance she wouldn't.

Her future safety depended on how many vampires made up this particular nest, and if her scent had been shared with more of them beyond the three he'd sent to their final deaths. Vamps were like supernatural blood-hounds. They were also like insects leaving decipherable trails to spread the word about a next meal. Interrupting that trail fueled vamp bloodlust to the point of no return.

He wasn't sure if that black-eyed vampire fledgling had latched on to McKenna by coincidence or for some other reason. But his next steps were now clear. As McKenna disappeared beyond the entrance to the alley, Kellan said aloud, "You have my oath of protection in return for a favor from you, McKenna."

He almost expected her to say something back.

Sadly, Kellan knew all too well that he'd hit a snag in his plans. Because he had begun to wonder how he'd leave this world behind if McKenna Randall were to remain in it. He wondered, for the first time, what would happen to her if the Reaper appeared. Would the human McKenna die?

The thought brought him to his feet.

Fingering the hole in his sleeve, Kellan examined the few drops of blood clinging on his fingertips. Dark blood kept him bound to the concept of Otherness. A very different kind of blood would also be the means of his escape.

Her blood. Red as a rose. The color a rose should be. Not the dark, colorless hue of the flower tattooed on his shoulder in honor of the woman he'd left behind centuries ago.

Heaven help him…

The life force flowing through McKenna Randall's veins would be his exit elixir. He had to be right about her part in this. His feelings for her told him he was.

Kellan stared after her. "Until death do us part," he whispered.

McKenna ran. Not particularly fast. Not fast enough.

Thoughts kept coming, speeding along, piling up. Maybe everything after that bullet hit struck her down two years ago had been a dream. She could be on a ventilator somewhere, her brain working overtime to create a fantastical existence.

Nursing school? Fixing the wounded in the ER? Was that just a trick her mind played to make her believe she was still doing her part in helping people?

No. This was real. *This* was happening. Her bruised throat told her so. The man she'd met tonight had gripped a creature right out of TV horror flicks. He'd held a wooden stake.

Unbelievable.

Insane.

Real.

She'd seen it with her own eyes.

The big problem facing her now was one of what to do next.

Tonight's events ensured that being able to rest anytime soon would be someone else's dream. She was hot under the collar and confused. This night had been weird beyond belief. Cops did love a good mystery, but this was lunacy.

She drove to her apartment house, parked and sat down on the low wall beside the building's front door. Cops were parading in and out of the building. Derek's car was double-parked at the curb.

She considered marching to the street to search for evidence substantiating her belief that the Harley had been parked there not long ago. Though she couldn't ask Derek directly, he surely had taken down the Knight's name and address…an address she would not use to find him because something wasn't right about that Blood Knight and the immediacy of their attraction. She now knew firsthand that lust made idiots of perfectly sane people.

Was that guy going to fight the creature in the alley? Could it really have been a vampire?

Hell, were there more things going undetected in the shadows like the freak that had attacked her? If any of that was true, she felt sorry for the cops trying to piece together this scene. She felt sorry for the world in general, because it would mean that nothing was like it seemed.

Vampires?

She swayed, caught herself, faced the fact that she was terrified. Being a cop had taught her not to show that kind of fear, but her stomach was in upheaval and her nerves were fried. She wasn't sure what to do next. How insane would she sound if she were to tell anyone about what she thought had taken place in that alley?

"Mac?"

Derek was standing beside her and she hadn't even noticed his approach. McKenna glanced sideways, constructing a perfectly good excuse for returning to the crime scene. "I had to know what's going on."

Once a cop, always a cop.

What she did not mention was how badly she needed to know if tonight's events had been real or make-believe. If the CSIs on this scene dusted her, would they find a monster's prints on her neck and evidence of the biker's hands everywhere else on her body?

As an ex-cop, she had to consider the possibility that

the Harley-riding knight showing up and a freak breaking into her apartment on the same night were connected
events. Derek was going to think so, and how could she
argue? Derek was a good detective who followed all paths
that might lead to solving a case.

But the Knight had called the thing in the alley a monster. He said her gun couldn't keep the monster down,
which led her to believe the biker knew about...vampires.

Derek's disappointment in her behavior registered now
as a series of worry lines on his not-too-cleanly-shaven face.

"The deal was for you to rest, Mac."

"Could you rest, in my place?"

"Probably not."

Derek sat down beside her. Neither of them spoke again
for some time before McKenna decided to take a chance
and probe, giving herself permission to sound like an idiot.

"What if I told you the asshole that attacked me wasn't
going to be found tonight, and that your guys are wasting their time?"

"Have you turned psychic on me?" Derek asked.

"Did you find prints?"

"Not yet. And you made the question sound like you
think we won't."

"Merely a wild guess."

"Is my face transparent, Mac? You knew this wasn't
going well?"

McKenna shook her head. "It's a good cop face, Detective, if a bit too pretty."

He didn't smile at her attempt to lighten the mood, like
he would have in the past when they briefly were partners.
He said, "You didn't mention that the attacker might have
worn gloves—if that's what you meant about not finding
fingerprints."

"Sorry. He could have worn gloves."

This was the best response she could come up with in a line of questioning she had ridiculously started. She couldn't come right out and say that she doubted if the walking dead had viable prints, or suggest that city cops should start carrying wooden stakes along with everything else in their arsenals.

Derek went by the book, as most cops did. He wouldn't accept anything having to do with the supernatural. She didn't believe in hocus-pocus, either, other than imagining she'd heard that bullet call her name two years back, and swearing that someone called her name tonight before she met the hunk on the Harley.

Right now, she wasn't sure that some outside force wasn't having one over on the people occupying this planet.

As she stood up, her skin chilled. She'd never been so freaking cold. Her mind kept framing images of the Blood Knight wielding a wooden stake as an instrument of death. Nothing about those images suggested to her that the leather-clad vigilante was in cahoots with the dark-eyed bastard in her place and in the alley, unless his plan was to eliminate a weak link and get rid of any salvageable evidence against him.

"You okay, Mac?" Derek got to his feet.

"Yeah. Okay."

Maybe not so okay, though. She held back a bad case of shakes by tensing every muscle in her body.

"I'd like to stay with you tonight after all, Derek. Is that all right? Am I still welcome?"

His relief was immediate. "You know you're always welcome. Can you wait for me, or should I have an officer take you there?"

"I'll wait."

There was no way she was going to be left alone near her apartment when she not only was scared but also couldn't be trusted. On her own, she might cave to the urges piling up, get into her car and go in search of that damn Harley. Chances were that she wouldn't rest until she found the guy in the Blood Knights jacket and demanded answers about what the hell had happened tonight and who he really was.

"I didn't need this." Her whisper was low. Barely audible. Her throat, so extremely raw and bruised, ached like crazy. The night sucked so badly that she was in need of *normal*. Derek epitomized normal. At his place, she'd find some peace. Derek would protect her without waving a wooden stake, and without knowing what hid in the shadows of her mind and in that dark alley.

There was something to be said for normal. At the moment, McKenna loved Derek for perfectly embodying that term.

"Why don't you wait for me inside the lobby where it's warmer? You're shaking. I'll grab you a better coat and dig up something hot for you to drink. One of those guys must have a thermos," he said.

"That would be great. Thanks."

As her words echoed, McKenna fought off a pang of guilt. Though Derek was being helpful, she pitied him for not actually knowing her at all, or the full extent of what she was capable of.

Derek had no clue that a dangerous, dark place nestled inside her that she had only recently begun to notice. And that nightmares sometimes took over that place, making her emotions go haywire.

How could anyone who knew about that dark place love her or want to be around her? After following her to the lobby, Derek took hold of her arm and turned her around to face him.

"I won't ask you to explain, if that's what you want. Is it what you want, Mac? A free pass on this one?"

He wasn't talking about the attack. Derek's thoughts had looped back to the handsome stranger in her apartment.

"Yes. For now" was the only thing McKenna could say.

Just how long a time *for now* might cover was beyond her at the moment, because swear to God, she believed she could feel her Harley-riding bad boy watching her. She sensed his presence, and shuddered to think what that kind of perception might mean if the word *supernatural* wasn't just a concept coined for TV.

Who are you?

How have you gotten to me so quickly?

The truth was that she wanted to see him in spite of the possible danger he represented. He ruled her thoughts in the same way he'd rule the road on his badass bike.

Nothing normal about that.

"Mac?"

She couldn't look at Derek.

"Mac?" Derek's grip tightened on her elbow.

McKenna continued to avoid his familiar brown eyes. Her mind was churning up the word *computer*. The internet would help her regain her footing. She would look up a few things, like where the Blood Knights motorcycle gang hailed from and who among them were bad guys with records.

Search engines would dig up theories on the existence of creatures like vampires. She'd investigate how that thing called animal magnetism worked, and if there was a pill to avoid it.

She wasn't going to lie back and let a steamroller of mythical proportions run her over. Could she rest? *No.* Could she sip a hot beverage from some cop's thermos, close her eyes and forget about *him* for a while—the bad boy who had quite possibly saved her life tonight?

"I'm worried," Derek said. "Talk to me. Are you really okay?"

"No." That was her first honest reply. "Sorry, Derek. I'm not okay. Not even close."

Apparently her answer satisfied Derek more than anything else she might have said. He'd have noted the earnest tone, the unusual confession and the shakes that escaped from her net of willpower. Her answer was something Derek could deal with. It was an example of vulnerability that allowed Derek to believe he could take charge of both her and the crime scene.

McKenna's last thoughts before being hugged briefly and then ushered to a chair were about men being hardwired to enjoy their place as the stronger sex.

Equally as universally accepted was the fact that sometimes, like now, for the sake of everyone's ego and sanity, women just had to play along.

Chapter 9

McKenna was in the detective's care, under Miller's protective gaze, but Kellan didn't like it. His hunger for her hadn't lessened. He craved her more with each passing second.

He had followed her from the alley to her building, now bustling with police presence, keeping a watchful eye out for signs of a further threat. Another wave of vampires hadn't materialized, and yet Kellan perceived unnatural ripples in the fabric of the night. Trouble was brewing without showing itself. More darkness was gathering, and that was too damn bad for a plan that had been so promising.

His mysterious *she* had a name. McKenna sat in a chair with her eyes closed. Surrounded by the frenetic activity of people coming and going, she looked as if she'd been turned to stone. Shock had done that. Scared her. Changed her.

He wasn't proud of the part he'd played in that. There was, however, a larger picture to consider, and a goal in further engaging her.

I'm not finished with you yet, McKenna.

He couldn't afford to show her the mercy his heart begged him to render, though he badly wanted to go to her and ask for her forgiveness. The ache he felt inside was the very thing he had longed to avoid. His preference in the past, as well as his reason for wanting to forsake his future, was to feel nothing at all.

And now there's you.

McKenna's eyes had been opened to a whole new realm of thinking in that alley. Where would she go from here? If she saw him again, would she scream and run? Shoot first and forget the questions?

"McKenna." Her name slid pleasurably over his tongue. The sound of a lover's whisper.

McKenna's head came up. She turned toward the open doorway, her knuckles white from her grip on the chair.

Kellan found himself in that doorway, looking at her without realizing he had moved. For the briefest second, no more than a blur of time, he stared. She wouldn't see him. She was safe. For now, that was all that mattered.

Spinning away in a flash of speed, he was afraid he hadn't been fast enough, and that her soul might have tuned in to his desperate frequency, because she managed to get to her feet. Her bloodshot eyes were wide-open. Her thin face was wan.

McKenna had sensed him there.

"Connected." Kellan spoke from the other side of the street. "We're held together by the links of a silver chain forged without our permission or knowledge. What do you make of that, my soul-survivor?"

She took a step toward the door as if he had asked her to. Kellan held up a hand to stop her, though she wouldn't be able to see the gesture.

"Tomorrow," he said. "Rest now. There's so much more to learn. You'll have to be ready for what we're going to do."

Leaving her wasn't an acceptable option. Neither was remaining close enough for anyone else to see him. Detective Miller might be good at his job, but against otherworldy forces the man would be out of his league.

If McKenna went home with Miller, Kellan couldn't visit her tonight. He would have to watch over her from a distance. In her defection to Miller's care, McKenna was being smarter than she knew. Vampires were one thing, but a Blood Knight on a mission posed the larger threat.

Miller joined her now. Kellan's exceptional hearing allowed him to listen in.

Miller handed McKenna a blanket. "Put this around your shoulders."

In the detective's place, Kellan thought, he would have enfolded her in his arms. But McKenna took the blanket.

"We can stop for coffee on the way to my place, if that won't keep you up," Miller said. "I don't have anything to brew."

"Nothing could keep me up. I'd like that."

Miller's smile unsettled Kellan, though jealousy wasn't often part of a Blood Knight's agenda, or even part of his plan.

"I have paperwork at the department, so I'll take you home after we stop for a bite, then join you later. I won't leave you for long, I promise. You'll be able to get back in here tomorrow afternoon. I'll post a car in front of your apartment tonight, and we can call about a new window in the morning."

Wrapping herself in the blanket, still shaking, McKenna nodded numbly.

"Give me one more minute." Miller turned to head up the stairs.

Seconds after he'd gone, McKenna's big blue eyes returned to the doorway. Her lips moved with a remark she didn't say out loud. *"I know you're there."*

Kellan felt as if he were standing inches from her. The

air seemed to move with her presence. Her scent wafted between them. He felt every beat of her pulse. Those beats continued to echo in his own arteries as if they were his own.

McKenna Randall was his final quest. His last challenge. And she was so much more than he could ever have anticipated.

Still, after all the years he'd spent longing for this moment, and for release, Kellan now wanted something else first. McKenna's body beneath his. Her blue eyes meeting his in a moment of passion.

The intensity of his desire for her as a woman, and not only as an instrument for his demise, was a genuine surprise. So were his feelings of sadness.

McKenna had finally given in to exhaustion when she reached Derek's apartment, and curled up on his bed.

His tiny two-room apartment was neat and organized. His bed, unlike hers, had been made. No clothes had been left on chairs. The sink was free of dirty dishes. Derek had always been neat, while she was a mess. But with all their differences, she wished he was there with her instead of at work. She didn't relish the thought of being alone.

Midnight had come and gone. Though Derek had promised to return after finishing up, that could be anytime between now and daylight, since it was as usual for cops to work all night through as it was for ER nurses.

She hadn't come here for company, though, but to hide. Derek's place was far enough from her loft to provide a safe barrier between her and the leather-jacket-wearing Blood Knight with his mesmerizing eyes. In theory. That barrier of distance did nothing to ease her mind.

She put a hand to her mouth, able to feel his kiss. Her

hand moved to her throat, seeing again his calmness in the face of trouble, and how he had rushed to her side. This biker was special, no doubt about it. The fact that his dangerous edge had been so well contained made him seem all the more threatening.

Had she been used as bait for the break-in? Would this guy have saved her if he'd been part of that kind of scheme?

McKenna sat up, thoughts scattering. "Derek?"

Someone was there. She dragged herself out of bed. Heart hammering, she moved toward the dresser.

"Who's there?"

Her coat was slung across the back of a chair. McKenna found her gun in the pocket. Ready to use it, she aimed at the door leading to the living room, advancing one step at a time and cursing under her breath. What the hell was wrong with tonight? Why was so much shit piling up?

The front room was dark, and she had left it that way. She didn't rule out an ambush, but what were the odds of that when this was a detective's home base?

"Get out or lose a limb," she said clearly.

Nothing happened. No one jumped out or replied.

She fumbled for the light switch and dropped to a crouch with the gun in both of her hands, hoping she was pointing in the right direction to scare the hell out of whoever this was. Light flooded every corner of the small space. None of that space was occupied by burglars, hoodlums or black-eyed vampires. McKenna nearly collapsed with relief.

Recovery took time. Eventually, she straightened and lowered the Glock. She moved to the window on legs like rubber and, without exposing herself, peered out. Her breath caught. From a patch of cloud-diluted moonlight came the silvery gleam of polished chrome.

* * *

Kellan was aware of the bloodsucker on the outskirts of the light. While he had feared that more of them would come, the turnout was disappointing.

As he waited for the vampire to show itself, his skin prickled with anticipation. Any confrontation would be easier at this time of night. The city was quiet. McKenna's detective lived on a short street, and it was a weeknight. Most people were in bed, Kellan guessed, by the number of darkened windows.

Deserted streets like this one would have favored a vampire if a Blood Knight hadn't been standing guard over the person this oncoming bloodsucker wanted to locate.

"Sorry," he muttered. "It's just not going to be your lucky day."

Senses on full alert and tuned in to McKenna, he knew that she was awake, on her feet and aware of him on a level she didn't dare acknowledge. Her uneasiness ruffled through him like a stiff winter breeze. One glance at the detective's window seconds later told him that McKenna stood behind it. "I've got this," he said to her.

"Go to hell," he heard her say as if she'd heard him and was fighting the extraordinary bonds tying them together.

He had to tear his attention from her. He was needed elsewhere. Down the block, and like a dab of coagulating ink, the new fanged intruder flowed toward the streetlight as though it had no real form. Near the bike, the dark countenance solidified.

Kellan stepped forward. "I thought you would have taken the hint."

He had known from experience that this visitor would be larger, older and stronger than the minions Kellan had hunted earlier that night. Vampire circles worked that way. Concentric layers of fledglings surrounded an older set of vampires. Just as hives supported a single queen bee, one ancient vampire usually ruled from the center of every bloodsucker nest.

This vampire wasn't ancient, or a vamp Prime, though it was old enough to be used to a mouthful of fangs. It spoke clearly, cocking its head to one side as if to capture more of Kellan's potent otherworldly vibe.

"Who are you?" the newcomer asked.

"No one you'd care to meet in good times or bad," Kellan said calmly.

"You're a brother."

"Looks can be deceiving."

"Yes," the vampire agreed in a voice as smooth as butter. "So what is your purpose for being here?"

Kellan shrugged. "What's yours?"

The vampire's thick mane of tangled gray hair matched the concrete sidewalk, and also its gaunt, wrinkled face. This one had to have been turned near the ripe old mortal age of seventy, though age was irrelevant for the undead. The creature did, however, radiate a high level of power.

"You have secrets." The vamp's comment was direct.

"My business isn't any of yours."

"Killing some of us was my business."

"Your fledglings got in my way."

"They sensed you, perhaps without knowing how or why."

"As you do?"

"I do not know fully what you are, other than perceiving the dark blood that runs in your veins, in the same way it runs in mine."

Kellan shook his head. "Not the same. Blood doesn't rule me."

Flat black eyes searched Kellan's face. "They said your heart beats."

Kellan nodded.

"Yet Death has visited you."

"I know him well," Kellan conceded.

"You will hunt here?"

"I hunt only what hunts them." Kellan gestured to the buildings in front of him with a wave of his hand. "I'll hunt whatever hurts these people."

"People are the source of our survival." The vampire also waved a hand. "You'll turn on us though you're not like them and not one of them?"

"It's what I must do. Call it a quest."

"Then you'll hunt me?"

"If you take innocent life, and if you've made more creatures in your image, then yes."

The vampire fell silent while it thought that over. Kellan waited for what might happen next.

Finally the vamp spoke again. "You are strong and confident, golden one, but I think you do not know everything."

"Golden one?"

"I see in your eyes the flash of gold that separates us. I see the blue color that Death has left intact for a purpose of his own design."

"I do not serve Death," Kellan said.

"Don't you?"

"Some of us chose to serve the light."

The vampire turned its head toward the window McKenna was standing behind. "Many of us did not have such a choice. We do what we were meant to do in order to thrive. And we have waited here, as we have vowed to do."

Kellan felt McKenna stirring. She was restless, agitated, but he was sure she couldn't see this meeting from her vantage point.

"Waited for what?" he asked the vampire, latching on to that part of its remark.

His visitor, Kellan soon found, wasn't going to answer that question. Nor was it planning to try its luck in attacking a holy crusader tonight. The bloodsucker had come to see who the interloper was and to gauge a best line of defense against the possible destruction of its nest.

This vampire hadn't come after McKenna. Kellan now knew, with a feeling of having been knifed in the gut, that he might very well have been the cause of the attack on McKenna tonight, as well as the reason she was in jeopardy now.

Not having to fend off an attack wasn't Kellan's only surprise. In his mind's eye he saw McKenna heading down the stairs, en route to the street. *Stubborn woman!* He couldn't direct her or stop her with his focus on the vampire across from him. He had to remain vigilant, gear up, in case that vampire also sensed McKenna.

Kellan stepped forward, fists clenched, when he heard the door to the apartment building start to open. His attention remained fixed on the old vampire.

In a gesture straight out of olden times, the articulate bloodsucker inclined its head in acknowledgment of Kellan's superior strength. Instead of moving forward, or toward McKenna, who was ready to burst through the doorway, it backed away from the pool of moonlight, smiling wryly without showing fang.

Kellan continued to stare at the spot where the vamp had been standing. His sigils ached with a warning he didn't have time to address because of McKenna. But that bloodsucker's knowing smile haunted Kellan more than anything else had in a very long time.

That fanger knew something Kellan didn't, and relished whatever that was.

Chapter 10

"I saw your bike from the window."

Out of breath, McKenna spoke quickly, in short spurts, sensing the man nearby as if she had the ability to see him clearly without enough light.

"Why are you here?" she asked.

"Why is it you insist on placing yourself in danger?" the velvet-soft voice countered.

"Why are you here?" she repeated.

"Merely to make sure you're safe."

"That's not your job. I've taken up enough of your time and energy. I'm grateful for what you did tonight. I've thanked you."

"Watching over you is what I need to do."

"Are you mocking me?"

"On the contrary, I'm trying my best to save your pretty little ass."

"From what, exactly? According to my ongoing nightmares that might never end, you've taken care of the freak that broke into my apartment. Or was I imagining what happened in that alley?"

"It might be easier if you believe you imagined it."

"A whole lot easier," McKenna agreed. "And preferable. But unless you're prepared to explain what actually took place, you have no further obligation here, where I'm concerned."

"I didn't intend for you to see me. I'm sorry you did."

His sincerity made her pause. She rallied. "That's the strange thing. I can sense when you're around. It's as if you're sending signals to me on a subconscious level. It's as if I have radar that picks up your presence."

"Maybe you just like me."

There was a lightness in his tone that indicated he might be smiling inside.

Clearing her throat hurt like hell, but McKenna refused to let him see that. She said, "Your possible involvement in tonight's attack can't be ruled out."

"In which case helping you wouldn't have been to my benefit, and wouldn't benefit me now."

"Maybe you only want it to look like you're a good guy, and have other plans."

"Like what?"

"Gain my trust. Do something awful to me."

"You're right to be skeptical, of course," he agreed. "You don't know me."

"I know nothing about you. For instance, I don't know why you're hiding from me right now."

"I didn't want to scare you."

"Too late."

"All right." He stepped closer to her, bringing with him a round of chills. How could she have forgotten the impact he had? His face was that of an angel, she had thought.

One step is all he took to reach her. He had been very close to begin with. She didn't know jack about this guy, and yet she hadn't raised the gun in her hand.

It took several breaths to calm herself. In that time, the man beside her didn't make any sudden moves or do anything to frighten or scare. Instead, he faced her quietly, though there actually was nothing quiet about him. The guy gave off enough electricity to light up the block. Those same currents were what had attracted her to him in the first place.

Little hairs at the nape of McKenna's neck moved. The scar at her temple pulsed. This man was larger than life. He had an honest face and a smoking-hot bad-boy aura. If he had a part in tonight's break-in, meeting her on the street here would be premeditated. If his goal was merely to see her again, he'd won.

"Why do you think I might not be safe here?" she asked.

"The freak might have friends."

"That would mean the creep in my apartment had a motive for attacking me other than theft. For the life of me, I can't imagine what the motive might be. I'm not a cop anymore. I'm a nurse. I don't possess jewelry or valuables. I no longer put people away, but help to save them. Besides, no one could possibly know about Derek's place, and that I'm here."

"I did," he said.

"You must have followed me."

"So can they."

"Whoever this mysterious *they* are."

McKenna looked for a furrowed brow or other sign that the man facing her was as confused as she was. His beautifully chiseled features showed nothing like that. His expression registered concern.

"I'm sorry you were bothered. I didn't mean for you to see me here," he said. "My plan wasn't to disturb you."

"Please tell me you're not a stalker."

"I suppose I am. But only in a good way."

"Are you a cop? Is that why you care about what happens to people and know how to handle yourself?"

"Something like that."

"Ex-military?"

"I was in the war, yes. More than one of them."

Though she had a soft spot for the men and women fighting for their country, that didn't necessarily mean all soldiers returned home as good guys. There was good and bad blood everywhere, and in every circumstance. War did strange things to people.

"You mentioned a plan. What might that be?" she asked.

"Right now it's to make sure you're safe and out of harm's way. Nothing more."

"Why should I believe you? Why do you care about me? We only met a few hours ago."

Her voice sounded strained, and McKenna knew why. She was already starting to cave on the tough-girl routine. Her instinct was to believe this guy was again being sincere, and she usually went with her gut on decisions like that.

After a beat of time had lapsed, he said, "I can only tell you that after our brief time together, you've become important to me."

Anything she might have said after that would have been like going around in circles and frustratingly repetitive, so McKenna simply asked, "Why would you think so?"

His devastating smile lit his face, highlighting his angles and recreating the angel analogy. Fallen angel, she thought. Not too repentant. Sex was in the smile, as was confidence and enough testosterone to junk up half the women of Seattle.

So, sue her. McKenna wanted him now more than she had wanted him earlier. As she faced him like this, the wooden stake she thought she'd seen him wield seemed a preposterous mistake on her part. A trick of the eye. This guy was a virtual chick magnet, and she wasn't immune.

But while he might possess leftover energy from a night of intrigue, her energy had waned. Her throat hurt like hell and she was barefoot, standing in front of Derek's apartment house with a gun in her hand. Yet damn if her womb didn't thrum for this guy, a clear warning of how far over the edge of reason she'd gone.

"Derek will be home anytime now."

He nodded. "I'll wait until your detective arrives, and then you won't see me."

That was nice sentiment, and well-spoken, but his eyes hinted at something else altogether. The liquid blue gaze ate her up, clothes and all. Bright as jewels, those eyes were caressing her. His silver-tongued voice made matters worse.

This guy wanted his mouth on her, his hands on her, and he was barely holding himself back. The really bad thing was that she wanted those things, too. Whatever desires he had were rubbing off. Highly contagious.

The situation was dangerous. He was dangerous, and possibly tied to the night's perversions.

Damn it. Her excuses were fading.

"Derek knows where to find you?" Her voice reflected her frustration.

"Drifters don't have addresses," he said.

"Well, that's damned inconvenient, because I have a need to get to the bottom of who you might be and what you want with me."

"You don't believe a word I've said?"

"The problem here is that I'm not your concern, and you're ignoring that."

"Maybe I'm just selfish and have a stake in what happens to you."

Unable to defend her next move, McKenna stepped

closer to him. Rising on tiptoe, she ignored the throb of pain in her injured throat. "Why do you want me, specifically?"

His lips were at eye level, full and closed tight.

"Will you save me from the entire world, Blood Knight? Slay dragons on my behalf, along with more white-faced freaks? I wonder if you will save me from myself?"

She placed a light kiss on his mouth, absorbing the current that kiss produced. He didn't reach for her or devour her, though he could have. He didn't do anything at all, just stared down at her.

"Good night," McKenna said, turning from the man she almost wished would stop her, feeling his heated gaze on her backside as she limped toward the steps.

Turning her back to him was a mistake. If she had expected him to let that kiss go unchallenged, she was wrong. Seconds later, she was backed against the corner of the building with his body pressed to hers.

"You're making this hard," he said.

"Then do something about it."

She watched him blink. She could see his eyes very clearly in the night, despite the lack of light. His bronzed face smoothed to a perfect rendition of managed calmness that McKenna easily saw through. He was fighting to keep from taking what he wanted. In another minute, he'd give in.

She held the gun in her right hand and was ready to use it.

"This can't be rushed, McKenna." He searched her face with a focus like a laser beam—looking for what? Cracks in her reasoning?

"Meet me." His breathing was as inefficient as hers was. His heart raced.

"When?" she asked.

"Tomorrow night."

"I might change my mind by then. Anything could happen." After a pause, she added, "Where?"

"Your house."

"Derek will have someone watching it."

"Does he have a say in what you do?"

His lips were so close, McKenna felt them moving. His hands pinned her to the brick.

"I owe him honesty," she said. "At the very least, I owe him that."

He nodded, then feathered his lips over hers, igniting a new round of sparks deep inside her body. She'd never felt this hot and needy. She wanted to ask somebody, anybody, if the night could possibly get any odder.

"This is my fault." She spoke through quivering lips. "I've encouraged this, and you."

Admittedly, she deserved the kind of trouble she found herself in at the moment. She had allowed this illicit liaison to continue. There was no denying that or how badly she wanted this connection. Though she had always been a rebel, she had never got off on trouble. This wasn't like her. She could put a stop to the nonsense once and for good. All she had to do was leave. Leave him.

"Tomorrow." His hands dropped to her hips before slowly rising to her waistline with a provocative pressure.

Without the coat, she was only half-dressed and should have been cold. But the man radiated heat. When his fingertips slipped under her sweatshirt to meet with bare skin, McKenna stifled a groan. He didn't stop there. His warm palms slid to her breasts.

This was going to happen. Who could stop it now?

McKenna wrapped her arms around his shoulders with the gun still clasped in one of her hands. As she breathed in the richness of his masculine scent, feelings of wildness began to flower inside her.

Too late...

He was rubbing her, stroking her softly, and each move brought a new discovery. His fingers were hot. His breath was hot. She couldn't resist the extreme pleasure he gave her.

His hands moved to her backside, then lower, with tender touches. Lifting her by the hips, he wrapped her legs around his waist so that her sex, tucked inside her jeans, slid over his swollen, leather-clad erection.

He swore in a fiery breath that McKenna breathed in. His mouth covered hers, tasting like...

There was no time to complete the thought. He was unzipping her jeans. His fingers delved beneath, in search of the spot he had headed for earlier. The one she so badly needed him to find. He sighed when he found it, and paused. This was where they had left off.

Unwrapping her legs from around his waist, standing her on her bare feet, he tugged her jeans down. That became an exotic adventure by itself. Without bothering to remove her pants completely, his hands found their way back to her, locating and separating the folds of her sex.

One of his fingers dipped tentatively inside her. The intimacy made her sigh. McKenna threw her head back, hit the brick and didn't care. She squeezed her eyes shut, picturing what Derek would see if he were to return home that minute. But she didn't really care about that, either. Danger had become her middle name, and for the moment it suited her. After all her wavering, she was now determined to have this outlandish deviation from the norm.

Growling his pleasure, her lover unleashed himself from the formfitting leather pants. The creak of leather sent shocks of anticipation through McKenna as he pressed closer, ready, rock-hard. The tip of his cock replaced his fingers. Slowly he eased inside her.

Forgotten, the gun in her hand dropped to the grass. Muffled cries tore through her sore throat, one after the other. She couldn't have stopped this if she tried. The reality was that she was going to demand for this man to take her hard and fast, and give her a thrill she hoped would cancel her absurd addiction to him.

The flashes came suddenly to McKenna with the brilliance of lightning. Vivid color swirled in a vortex of moving landscape.

She caught a glimpse of white stone walls. A fur-draped bed. There was a strong scent of melting candles.

Voices joined the vortex, all of them urging her to run away as a tall man walked toward her—powerful, beautiful beyond belief, notorious for his past.

Vertigo struck hard, bringing with it serious stomach upheaval. More images swam in the visual current, in an almost subliminal string—distorted fantasy images that made no sense and didn't stick around long enough for McKenna to focus on.

The scent of candles filled her nose, leaving a bitter aftertaste in her mouth. She was frozen to stillness and suddenly chilled, but as the smell dissipated, so did the whirling pictures. They stopped altogether and McKenna was back in the moment as her new lover penetrated her body.

With his hips against hers, he drove his hardness toward her core, where she longed for that kind of touch. The intensity of their merging forced her eyes open. His blue eyes, so very compelling, waited. He was asking her if she wanted to go on.

She nodded.

And she didn't regret it. As she took her lover in, she became one with the rhythm of his beautiful assault. Adding movement of her own, she encouraged and urged until the distant rumble of vibrating internal drums began.

He was talented, this Blood Knight. Repeatedly, and with precision, he reached the spot that had never been fully awakened. McKenna was tethered to sensation. Mesmerized by it. Enslaved. Every nerve in her body came alive, sparking mercilessly, bonfire hot, triggering a level of ecstasy that was as ruthless as it was divine.

His mouth was a wicked delight—sinfully damp and extravagantly malleable. It was difficult for McKenna to discern which sensation overrode the others—the stroke of his tongue over hers or the simultaneous stroke of his cock against her overheated insides.

She wanted more. Wanted it all. Her lover was taking things too slowly. He was biding his time, teasing her with a promise of the explosive climax soon to arrive. His mouth was sealed to hers. His hands held her steady so that each slow thrust he made hit straight and true.

The experience was exceptional, new and unlike anything in her past. The pleasure of having him inside her was ceaseless. He played her perfectly, hitting hard, relenting, hitting hard again, until the strange flash of fantastical, dreamlike images returned to her mind as though they were tied to this intimacy.

Chapter 11

Kellan was aware of the exact moment McKenna's mind began to travel. He shouldn't have been surprised. He had anticipated this discovery, sure now that McKenna housed the soul he'd combed the world to find.

But the moment also marked the beginning of the end.

He would soon lose what he had worked so hard to find. And McKenna was so very delicious, so supple and warm and silky, he had nearly forgotten his purpose in testing her. He'd been waylaid by the burn of the build-up of friction between their perfectly matched bodies, enjoying everything about this clandestine meeting on a Seattle side street.

The revelation of finding *her* was therefore a victory that also felt like defeat.

As his body took over, speeding up, gaining momentum to move in and out of McKenna with a madman's drive, a thought came to him that with McKenna by his side, he could have gone on in his endless campaign. Nestling inside her and against her on a regular basis might have made *forever* worthwhile.

There was a flaw in that reasoning, though—a big, insurmountable flaw.

He wasn't mortal.

Nothing they could do would change that.

And while her soul was as immortal as his, the rest of McKenna belonged to another world that he had merely been layered on top of. He was a guardian, a holy champion, an overseer. McKenna Randall was his secret salvation, his exemption from more years of the same kind of existence. And yet she was human.

Had this level of challenge also been foreseen by his Makers? Was that why it felt so necessary to be with McKenna? Had the beings at Castle Broceliande seen to it that the Knights' Reapers were so seductive, if ever found, that they could change a Blood Knight's mind about relinquishing his vows? Had they used the lure of attraction as a last resort?

Damn them all.

He still knew nothing. As the first Knight to find his Reaper, how was he to know what his Makers had been capable of? Certainly, he had never come across anything like McKenna Randall. The woman in his arms had a huge capacity for passion. She was taking on a stranger, letting him in, when she had to know this was a bad idea.

She moaned each time he plunged into her fiery depths, appreciating each thrust, inviting him back for more. The muffled earnestness of the sounds she made touched his heart. When she moved her hips, lifting them to accept and guide him, he wanted to howl like the damn werewolves downtown.

For him, things could end now, this minute, on a dark street in a damp city. McKenna was within his grasp and under his power. She was the one. She was seeing things behind her closed eyes that turned her skin ashen and made him take stock, even as she accepted the physicality of his ardor.

Her mind was traveling to foreign places, and he had

sent her there. If left in that other place for too long, she might find the past—her soul's past, as well as his own.

What are you seeing, my lover?

He had to make those images stop. He couldn't allow McKenna to discover the thing she housed too soon, before he was ready to open her soul. She might resist what had to be done. She'd fight that. She'd fight him.

She might die.

Although he was experienced in so many things, this situation was precarious. He had no real idea of how to go about unzipping what lay hidden inside McKenna, and would have to wing it, torn by the knowledge that she had utterly and completely bewitched him. McKenna had turned the tables, mastering him, throwing him into an unexpected contemplation of his objective in coming here.

The situation had changed. If he was to die, and McKenna survived her soul's opening, the vampires might get her. And if she were to die with him... Hell, he didn't want that.

Stay with me, McKenna. For now.

He dragged her back to the present with a thrust that pushed her against the wall and made her lashes flutter. He felt the shudders of her climax barrel through her, chasing the dreams away in favor of her body's need for release.

He was a fool, a damn fool, for letting his goals slip.

Bless him, he couldn't help it.

Take it. Take me, sweet soul.

Kellan's hips picked up more speed—faster, harder, as he listened to her soft cries and the sound of her back hitting the wall—until he drove himself home and she wrapped herself around him. He pinned her to the rising climax as he pinned her to the old brick, aware of the rolling rise of his own ecstasy.

McKenna screamed, and he let her. Within that cry lay

something more substantial than release. Her mind was breaking away from its moorings.

As the tension left her body, McKenna's mind again soared with flashes of color and sound, abstract images coming together to form patterns of pictures that Kellan recognized.

God...he recognized them all.

As his heat merged with McKenna's, his mind joined hers in that distant place. He again saw castle walls that had been guarded by the three beings no one would ever dare to cross. White stone turrets rose high above the ground, windowless, gleaming in the moonlight. Gardens filled with bloodred rosebushes, each the height of a man, displayed night-blooming blossoms. Above all of that came the tinkling noise of water dripping from a golden fountain that had once hidden one of the world's most precious and coveted holy treasures. The Grail.

With his body pressed tightly to McKenna's, Kellan relived those things and grieved. He had wanted to forget about that castle. It was at Broceliande that he had forfeited his life and his first real lover. Due to what went on in that place, he was now in another country, in a city foreign to him, caught up in the arms of a woman named McKenna.

This wasn't quite right, wasn't the way things were supposed to be.

Strangely, now that the way to erase all those memories for good was within his grasp, Kellan found himself backpedaling, loath to let go of the woman who could give him his wish.

Saints be damned. He liked McKenna. He liked being inside her. If McKenna's lineage had been chosen to house something special, she deserved better than to confront what lay hidden inside her by fornicating with an immortal in front of her former partner's house. She deserved a gentler send-off to the great unknown, and maybe even an explanation as the end came near.

Will you die when I steal your soul?

If you knew what lay hidden inside you, McKenna, would you willingly give up your life to save another— you who have believed in and fought for justice?

Now that I'm here, can I ask that kind of sacrifice from you?

Lost in her incendiary heat, Kellan's heart pounded painfully. Then his world exploded. As their orgasms danced in perfect unison, Kellan locked his mouth to McKenna's.

Kellan Ladd, an immortal who had once gone by the name of Galahad, the knight who had been positioned at the right hand of Britain's Arthur, at a round table, before accepting a holy quest that changed his life forever...whispered her name as ecstasy shuddered through him.

But in that moment, in his soul, he knew that this sparkling union was merely the postponement of an ending that remained ahead. And that because the world had become such a painful place, he could not postpone a final confrontation forever.

His eyes opened to find McKenna's blue eyes looking back. She was breathless and therefore could hardly speak. Her face was paler than usual as she voiced a question.

"Who the hell is Damaris?"

Aftereffects of the exotic pleasure she'd experienced continued long after they both had stopped moving. McKenna's heartbeat refused to slow down. Her question hung in the air between them, when there wasn't much space.

She had wanted this man to want her. If she had been mistaken about the depth of his interest, the position she found herself in seemed almost obscene.

Another woman's name had been on his lips.

Rage gathered within McKenna as she looked into the face of the man still inside her and found another surprise. He was more than a little familiar—those angles and shadows. Sparks of leftover dream images nagged at her consciousness, suggesting to her that his was the face she had seen in the vortex of odd images. This man had been there, in a landscape as fantastical and unearthly as anything her mind could have dreamed up.

Of course, that was absurd. Her mind had to be playing tricks, mistaking an orgasm for fantasy. Either that or the old head injury was catching up with her in ways she had not expected.

But to utter another woman's name?

She managed to repeat the question. "Who is Damaris? "Wait," she quickly amended. "That's none of my business. A man like you could probably have any woman you want and not suffer any consequences."

He didn't address the question of whose name he had called out in the throes of passion. Maybe he didn't remember, having taken so many women to bed, he was unable to keep all those names straight.

A hint of sadness added more shadows to his features.

When McKenna's heart rate finally began to slow, the sound of her labored breathing was the loudest thing in that otherwise silent world. She hadn't moved. Neither had he.

The sexy stranger who had just sent her to the gates of either heaven or hell spoke at last, with question of his own. "What did you say?"

"Just so you know, mentioning someone else while having sex can be a turnoff to most people."

The remark had offended him. His face sobered. He said, "I'll escort you inside now."

A wicked kind of angry laughter rose within her over

the simplicity of his avoidance technique. Then again, what had she expected, an *out of all of them, I love you most*?

That laughter didn't emerge, though.

Damn it, you beautiful bastard. I saw stars and don't even know your name. Was I even here for you, or was Damaris here with us, whoever she might be?

That thought was tinged with an emotion too reminiscent of jealousy.

This man's hands lingered on her body possessively. McKenna felt the rise and fall of each breath he took. If he was planning on walking her to the damn door, he made no move to do so.

She changed tack. "What was this?"

"Pleasure," he replied after a beat.

His eyes met hers again. His expression remained serious.

Careful...

Her next move would be important. It was a fact that she was way too interested in this guy for her own good, no matter what kind of rogue he'd turned out to be. He alone had led her toward an ecstasy unlike any other. In his embrace, she had left the known world behind. Still, she felt uneasy, awkward, embarrassed and used.

"Well, we got that out of the way." McKenna dropped her arms. "We had to. I had to."

"Yes," he agreed. "We had to."

Placing both hands on his wide, solid chest, McKenna pushed. Though he didn't have to step back, he did.

She stood on a tiny square of green lawn edging the wall, sure she made a pretty picture with her pants and underwear down around her ankles and her hands on her hips. To an onlooker, she'd appear as silly and as slutty as she felt. With the main event over, she was feeling too vulnerable to come up with a witty remark that would put what they'd done into any kind of acceptable perspective and allow her some dignity.

She pulled up her pants. The grass was wet. Her bare feet were cold. The gun she'd waved around was now a dark spot on the ground beside her.

McKenna leaned over to retrieve the weapon. Her biker lover watched her without comment. Holding the Glock, she said, "That was good," and started toward the door to Derek's building, hoping this guy would let her go. Hoping to hide the shame coloring her cheeks.

He called after her. "Kellan."

McKenna hesitated on the steps.

"My name is Kellan. And that was better than good."

She peered at him over her shoulder. "Yes. But it's over. You can go now. It's obvious that no one else is coming to bother me."

"All the same, I'll stay awhile."

"I won't be able to sleep knowing you're out here."

"I won't be able to rest if I go."

McKenna turned around. "You're not my keeper. I'm really grateful for your help tonight and for…" She let that thread trail off before starting over. "What we just did wasn't payment for saving me from the freak, you know. It wasn't a reward."

He nodded. "I didn't assume that it was."

"Then why would you stay?"

"For my own peace of mind."

"What about mine?"

The remark couldn't be retracted, and McKenna was sorry for that. What she'd said let him know exactly how much his presence messed with her equilibrium.

She covered that mistake with another question. "Will you answer something truthfully before you go?"

"I'll try."

She put hand to her swollen throat. "You didn't answer me the last time I asked this question, so here it is again. Did I see what I think I saw in that alley tonight?"

"What do you think you saw?"

"That freak looked like a vampire."

"Might have been a junkie, out of its mind, like your detective friend suggested."

"What happened to him?"

"He went away."

"Tell me the truth."

"The truth is that I killed that creature with a wooden stake." He said this soberly, without smiling to suggest he'd made a joke.

McKenna thought she heard him add "*You don't believe that*," though his mouth hadn't moved. And he was right. She didn't really believe it.

As a cop, she'd been trained to read gestures and body language. This guy's quiet demeanor suggested he might be telling the truth, but maybe her people-reading skills were rusty. After all, she'd thought he wanted her, and not just as a surrogate for another woman.

"I was hoping you'd confirm what happened in that alley for real, because it could mean I'm not nuts," she said.

"You thought you were nuts?"

"Well, who would believe such a story? Vampires in Seattle?" She fingered her neck.

"Very few, which is why you don't believe it, either."

Weary, sluggish, sexually sated and angry, yet wanting a rematch with the bastard despite the awkwardness of not being the woman he really wanted to be with, McKenna frowned. "I'm not sure what's going on here. Maybe you can also tell me what this is between us, and what kind of world this one has become if it houses freaks like the ones in that alley and men like you who aren't afraid to deal with them?"

She didn't wait for his answer. In another minute she'd fall over. Then what? Would he come to her rescue again, like her personal guardian angel? He'd take her into Derek's apartment, where they'd start the arguments over if Derek returned too soon and caught them together? Would this guy continue to have her fill in for someone else?

Instinct told her that Kellan would make good on his promise to stay here, whether or not she was with him, and in spite of his refusal to come up with answers she could use. As for her own behavior, that had spilled into uncharted territory, where she was fast losing ground. If Kellan wasn't going to tell her the truth about that alley, or about whom he'd used her in place of, she couldn't make him.

She wasn't a cop anymore. Derek's front lawn wasn't an interrogation room.

"I don't suppose you actually know anything about a castle with white stone walls and golden fountains?" McKenna said.

Maddeningly, he didn't address that question, either. His bright eyes reflected the same kind of lust she was afraid showed in her own.

The word *idiot* didn't even begin to describe her.

"I don't want to believe in vampires, wooden stakes and men who aren't afraid of either of those things," she said. "Equally as disgusting is the scenario where a nasty creep reappears for a second chance at getting his hands around my throat. I don't believe anyone will find me here. They won't come after me. I'm not your responsibility, Kellan. Your work here is done."

His face remained serious. "Given all those things you don't believe in, what do you believe?"

"That we'd be better off not seeing each other again."

He didn't respond to that. Didn't verbally agree.

"Why don't you get some sleep?" he suggested.

"Sleep is a nonissue. And you're not helping."

For all McKenna knew, she really could be hallucinating and in need of the kind of medical help that lay beyond her area of expertise. Chances were also good that this whole night would end up a bad dream obliterated by the rising sun. Dreams and hallucinations were the only viable ways to explain what was going on. Right?

"Good night," she said with finality, wondering if the talented Kellan might disappear in a puff of ash like the rest of her nightmares if she took a closer look at him.

"Wait." Kellan called to her again, his damn voice sexy as hell and all the more disturbing because of it.

She had to turn. She didn't want to, but did.

"I'll be here if you need anything," the handsome bastard told her.

"Suit yourself."

With a stiff back, McKenna entered Derek's building. Inside, she passed a trembling hand over her lips, able to feel the impression of Kellan's ravenous mouth as if it still rested there.

Her hand came away wet and flecked with red.

Warning lights blazed in her mind. Stopping abruptly, McKenna stared at her fingers, then the door, quickly completing the description she'd left dangling earlier.

Kellan's lips had tasted like…blood.

Chapter 12

They were coming.

Kellan leaned over the railing of the porch he was using as a vantage point to watch Detective Miller's front stoop. Sunrise was an hour away, at most, and the vampires were making a comeback.

So had Detective Miller. The man had arrived a while ago without turning lights on in the apartment. He probably hadn't wanted to wake McKenna, though Kellan knew she wouldn't have been sleeping. McKenna was thinking about him, unable to get him out of her mind. He felt her awareness breeze over him now that they had connected body to body. Taking his mind off her wasn't easy, but he had to attend to pressing business.

Carefully observing the shadows, he sensed the darker spot within them. The oncoming unearthly presence brought a chill that made his sigils burn.

Two vamps were on their way—youngsters whose minds were hazy from being out of their nests so near daylight. Because a raging thirst was upon them, they'd be mean, frantic, desperate. Because there was no sign of the older vampire he'd met earlier, it was conceivable that the old vamp hadn't missed these two fledglings yet. Then again, maybe the old monster had sent them.

The bloodsucker's words continued to taunt him. *You*

*are strong and confident, golden one, but I think you do
not know everything.*

Over the years, Kellan had heard so many threats. Nevertheless, these words, and what they implied, resonated dangerously.

Most vampires were too impulsive and ruled by their hunger to have long-term plans. The two coming toward him, hugging the dark spaces, weren't up to long-range thinking or dealing with much of anything at all other than sniffing out breakfast. Their appearance here, however, so near to McKenna and far from her own apartment, was highly suspect.

Seething with anger, Kellan leaped from the balcony to land directly in their path, stake in hand.

"Well, that was ghastly." Leena Day, McKenna's co-worker, exited from one of the utility-beige bathroom stalls in the nurses' lounge with the swiftness of a comet, heading for the next available sink. "I've never seen anything like it. Or this." Leena alluded to her own image in the mirror. "I look like I could use a stint on that operating table. Do we have any plastic surgeons on call? I've got bags under the bags under my eyes."

From her position at the next sink, McKenna said, "If you find a good one, give me a call."

Leena leaned sideways with a hip against the porcelain, her green scrubs mottled with the evidence of the seriousness of their last patient's wounds. "Honey, if I had your face, I'd be dating that plastic surgeon, not begging for his services."

McKenna waved her comment away with a spray of tap water. "Have you been inhaling the good stuff when we weren't looking?"

Case in point for eye bags and dark circles, she hadn't

slept for the past two nights, waiting for Kellan to show up again unannounced. She'd stayed with Derek, which was okay since Derek had been at work most of the time.

Her throat still hurt and looked even worse. From a distance, the ring of black and purple beneath her chin was like a gothic collar. She'd covered the bruises with a blue turtleneck shirt worn beneath her scrubs.

Certain other body parts had ached for several hours after her close encounter with Kellan—the effects of a crazy, over-the-top sexual indulgence of the *we'd best forget it afterward and move on* kind. Rogues without roots weren't relationship material, despite how mesmerizing they could be. Rogues with wooden stakes and stories about vampires didn't deserve a second look.

Maybe that was why she couldn't stop thinking about him.

Leena smiled wryly, making a beeline for the towel dispenser. "I'm changing clothes before we're called back to the operating room. If patients woke up and saw me like this, they'd get the life scared out of them."

"Right behind you," McKenna said as Leena exited the room with perkiness no fiftysomething-year-old woman should have possessed after the long hours they'd just put in.

McKenna had requested the long hours this time, needing to concentrate on her job and nothing else, thinking that being at the hospital would rule out unwanted visitations of any kind. The forgetting part wasn't working. Hands on the sink, she drew deep breaths while attempting to get a handle on letting thoughts of Kellan go. That didn't work now, either. Nothing had worked.

"I know you're there," she said, convinced the statement wasn't merely wishful thinking, concerned that she actually wanted Kellan to be nearby or on the street waiting for her. It would have taken a lot of money for her to admit that out loud.

She splashed warm water on her face and wiped it off with her hands, staring at her fingers as if the blood she'd seen on them after her night with Kellan still remained. Since then, she'd taken several showers to scrub off his scent, and hardly smelled him now. As she checked herself out in the mirror, the lights in the room flickered. Winking lights were a bad sign. Power outages in a hospital filled with sick people weren't a complete anomaly in Seattle this time of year, but were never good. Clouds had rolled in overnight, gathering for a bigger storm that was brewing.

The lights went out, throwing the dingy beige space into near-total darkness.

"Damn storm." Sighing, McKenna waited patiently for the backup generators to kick on until her gaze was drawn to the mirror again, guided there by a faint, wavering light. Although the light was barely bright enough to see her reflection in the glass, there was a hazy outline. Was it hers? Had to be, right?

Maybe not.

Something wasn't quite right.

A glance over her shoulder proved that no one stood behind her and the rest of the room was black. McKenna took a step backward, wary of what she was seeing, rubbing her eyes.

The figure in the mirror didn't rub hers.

A woman stood there, motionless. Soon other details began to fill in.

A fringe of blond hair, the same color as McKenna's, curled over the woman's forehead. The rest of her hair was pulled back, also like McKenna's. Her face was thin, wan, with prominent cheekbones and a wide brow. She had a full mouth and unpainted lips. Her eyes were dark-rimmed, with bluish crescents beneath, as if this woman shared McKenna's fatigue.

All those details were vaguely familiar and reminded McKenna of herself. There was an uncanny resemblance between them, and yet this image wasn't hers. She was in scrubs. The woman in the mirror wore black.

"What the hell?"

Chills washed over her. Nerve endings fired in stunned surprise. Leaning forward with her hands braced on the sink, McKenna stared at the image in the mirror in an attempt to make sense of what she was seeing.

"I just need a minute. This isn't happening. My mind is playing a trick. It's been full of things like that lately. If I wait this out, you'll be gone."

The generators hadn't kicked in. If the room was dark, why was the woman's image in the mirror getting clearer?

Panic made McKenna unsteady. Her head hit the mirror with an impact that stung. The glass was cold. Her breath caused a fog. "Who are you?" she asked the strange image, feeling foolish for doing so.

Another ripple of panic struck. Jesus, who was *she*? Why couldn't she remember her own name all of a sudden?

Mother's name? Father's? Type of car I drive? The location of my apartment?

Her inability to answer even one of those questions made McKenna's stomach tighten and her pulse skyrocket. Fists raised, she pounded on the mirror. "What the hell is going on?"

Wait.

Buzzing sounds accompanied by a slight vibration made her run both hands down the length of her body, where she discovered a small object attached to her waistband.

"Pager."

The room around her flashed bright, then dark again, as if there was a short in the electrical system. When the lights finally came on, McKenna found herself sitting on the floor with her head in her shaking hands.

The door across from her banged open. "Mac, we're up," Leena announced, stopping just past the threshold. "Damn generator took long enough. Shit. What happened? Are you okay?"

Leena. Yes. I know her.

"McKenna? Talk to me." Concerned, Leena came closer.

McKenna. Of course. McKenna Randall, RN. That's me.

"I'm fine." That didn't sound convincing. "Had to tie my shoelaces and was too tired to bend over."

"Oh, right. It's okay to sit on a filthy floor when we have one minute to get our butts back in there," Leena said. "Another one just came in."

"Another..." McKenna's pulse began to settle. Her heartbeat slid toward slow.

"Throat-slash victim, I hear. Serious wound. You might want to hurry up. They're paging us."

When the door closed after Leena, the ensuing silence seemed deafening. But the room, thankfully, stayed bright.

McKenna got to her feet. She adjusted her turtleneck to make sure the bruises were concealed, then stuck her hands under the faucet, where the water still ran hot. After splashing more water on her face and taking several deep, settling breaths, she turned for the door...easily answering each of the questions she'd been unable to answer just minutes ago.

She did not give the treacherous mirror a second glance. Whoever was on the operating table deserved a nurse with all her wits intact, and by God, by the time she got to the ER, she planned to have recovered all of hers.

* * *

The surgery had been long and arduous. McKenna paused in the corridor after it was over, sensing trouble. Her heart stuttered.

Kellan.

The back of her neck tingled as excitement rolled in. Ignoring those things didn't make the anticipation of seeing him go away. Running away wouldn't, either, because Kellan, who was ground zero for these palpitations, would probably be faster.

He was here. No doubt about it. Kellan was here, waiting to show himself to her. To find him, all she had to do was twitch the thread binding them together. Part of her wanted to. Part of her wanted a lobotomy so these feelings could no longer take precedence over everything else.

Widening her stance to keep from tipping over, McKenna scanned the hallway. Four nurses were making rounds. Handfuls of other hospital workers were busy with various tasks. There were only two ways out of this hallway, and suddenly *he* was blocking one of them.

There were ten feet of polished floor between them. To her, that distance felt like centimeters. She didn't try to close it, debating whether to address him at all, afraid that if she managed to, her voice and flushed cheeks would be a dead giveaway of her true feelings.

What about all those promises she'd made to herself about what she would do if she saw him again?

What about that?

Her willpower was weakening. She felt it go. Kellan moved first, walking languidly toward her as if he owned the space. When he spoke, it was as if his voice had a direct line to the place tucked between her thighs.

"Is everything all right here?"

He seemed to fill the hallway. Kellan's dark attire, so

sexy and perfectly suited to him, looked out of place alongside the peaceful gray and white walls. He carried nothing in his hands. No box of chocolates. No flowers. No
pointed wood stake.

Beneath the lights, the streaks in his auburn hair shone
like burnished copper. His artfully handsome features
looked to have been carved from stone. McKenna's heart
stalled. The urge to jump into his arms was counterbalanced
only by Derek's warning to keep away from the mysterious biker if he returned. And her own remaining common sense.

"Yes. Everything is fine," she said. "Except that the police haven't been able to find you. They've been looking."

"That's strange, since I haven't gone anywhere."

One of the nurses interrupted their locked gazes, smiling as she passed Kellan and offering McKenna a con-
spiratorial grin behind his back. The fact that this nurse
saw him made McKenna feel better. The knowledge that
Derek had seen and spoken to Kellan on the night of the
attack in her apartment confirmed that he was real and not
a figment of her imagination, as she had begun to believe.

Too bad you're a drifter was her next treacherous thought.
She might have come up with an excuse for seeing him again
if he stayed in Seattle. Her feelings for him might have been
acceptable. There might have been more one-night stands.

"Why are you here, Kellan?"

"The lights went out. I was worried."

"You're again assuming that I might be in danger?"

"Anything is possible these days. Dark forces are gathering in this city at the moment."

"Are we back to the vampire scenario?"

"Didn't you treat their latest victim just minutes ago?"

McKenna hesitated, considering his remark, applying
it to the young man on the operating table who'd nearly

had his throat torn out tonight. That would have been bad enough, but he was the second patient with similar wounds this week. Still, believing those injuries had a supernatural cause was insane.

She flashed back to the freak that had attacked her, and put a hand to her throat. There had been too many unwelcome flashes lately. She was sick of them.

"This one survived," she said. "Barely. He can't help put an end to this supernatural nonsense, though. He was so damaged, it's likely he will never wake up again."

Kellan's eyes were steady, his focus unwavering. "He will leave here soon, and nothing remotely human will exit from this hospital when he goes."

The shakes McKenna had tried so hard to be rid of returned like an incoming tide. Her voice reflected that. "Meaning what? That patient won't recover? He'll die and go out in a body bag?"

"That patient will rise and walk out on his own if he isn't stopped."

This beautiful bastard could be maddeningly stuck on one theme while being so incredibly charismatic that he almost had her believing he could be right.

Fully dressed as she was, McKenna wanted to cover herself up, save herself from his scrutiny. She never would have pegged herself as someone shallow enough to allow a man's looks to affect her, but Kellan was a healthy reminder of the ease with which he brought her to her knees.

"Next you'll tell me zombies are real," she said.

He shook his head. "No zombies."

"Good. For a minute I was worried."

She pressed her hair back—a nervous gesture since it was already tied behind her neck. "You do realize that people are looking for you?"

"Not hard enough, I guess."

"I'm okay. Really." The lie slipped out.

"You're also off work," he noted.

"How did you know that?"

He gestured toward the nurses' station behind him with the same hand that had pleasured her three nights ago.

"Must have been your charming smile," McKenna remarked before noticing the hole in the sleeve of his fine leather jacket. "You're hurt?"

"Merely in need of new clothes."

Relief came swiftly. "I don't think anything else would suit you as well as that leather."

Her cheeks burned hotter. She was a fool to offer any kind of compliment.

He smiled briefly, devastatingly. The kind of smile that made her heart race. His laser-like gaze swept over her face, more than likely missing nothing.

"Come with me, McKenna."

She stood her ground. "I don't think so."

"Wouldn't you like to talk?"

"What good would it do? You'd evade my questions like you've evaded Derek's search. Besides, talking isn't really the point between us, is it?"

"It's one of them," Kellan said. "I see that now. You need to know what part you play. Maybe then you'll understand."

The tension between them could have been cut with a knife. Not all of that tension was bad, McKenna supposed, unless unresolved sexual issues with a stranger who'd wrapped her around his little finger once already meant more trouble in the future. However, she was having difficulty making sense of every other word he said.

The part she played? In what?

The real problem here was that this guy was so damn fine, common sense didn't stand a chance. Reason went south. Kellan was a vision of masculine perfection. Sex on legs. Trouble with a bite. Her body was ready to give in to the emotional rush of being with him, near him. That very moment, she was reliving sensations having to do with being pinned to a brick wall with her pants down.

But her body wasn't in charge this time. And Kellan was still a short distance away. The erotic dream of having him beside her, inside her, would have to be saved for bedtime. She'd put things in their proper place. She had to redeem herself from her former slipups. Get a grip. Move on, just like this guy would when he decided to leave town.

When she looked up, it was to find Kellan's hand raised. It was clear to McKenna that he wanted her to take his hand, touch him, trust him.

"I can't do that."

"*Can't* and *won't* are two different things," Kellan said.

He was right. She wanted badly to take him up on his offer. When confronted with his powerful presence, her determination to avoid him at all costs seemed ludicrous.

"Just to talk," he added. "Someplace safe."

"What place could be safer than this one?"

"Not tonight. Not for you, McKenna."

Hands on her hips, she said, "Maybe you should go now."

"You want proof that I speak the truth?"

Her eyes met his in challenge. "Proof would be nice."

Backing up, Kellan gestured for her to follow. When she took a step, he turned and walked off. She couldn't wait to see what he'd come up with next. Along the way, she figured that they'd stop off at the psychiatrist's office, where this guy would get thunderous applause for his unique worldview.

Without pausing to consider how he knew his way around

the hospital, McKenna followed him to the intensive-care recovery unit, where he stopped beside the door.

"Can you get me in?"

"Why?"

"I'd like to show you something that might change your mind about me."

Waving to the nurse rushing past, McKenna ushered Kellan through. What would it hurt? All the patients were behind glass, so he couldn't reach any of them.

She found it odd, though, that he walked right to the victim she'd just worked on in the ER. Attached to tubes and other devices, the young man in the bed looked as if a miracle would be necessary for him to eventually open his eyes, despite their best efforts on his behalf. The guy had been very near death before reaching the ER. On the table, his heart had stopped twice.

"Go inside," Kellan said. "Take a closer look at him. See what you might have missed."

"I can assure you that we miss very little."

"Humor me, McKenna. Please. What harm will it do?"

"All right. If this is what it takes." She moved to the door. "What am I supposed to look for?"

"What lies behind his lips."

"It's a tube."

"There will be something else."

She would humor him, McKenna decided, and then she'd be on her way to accepting him as a nutcase. Things would be easier after that. She would have to forget him.

Going to the young man's bedside, McKenna rested a finger on his lower lip, checking the tube. She glanced at the window where Kellan stood. He nodded his encouragement. Carefully, she lifted the young man's upper lip. After a pause, she raised it higher.

Both of her hands hit the bed and were necessary to

keep her from sitting down. McKenna couldn't look at Kellan, breathe or stop the whirl of outlandish thoughts about the alley, the freaks with white faces, her broken window, Kellan's wooden stake. They had all been real. Very, very real.

The guy in the bed had unusual teeth. Inhuman teeth. Nothing that should have been in a mouth. Either no one in the operating room had noticed this anomaly, or the guy in the bed had just grown a pair of fangs.

"Not safe here tonight. Not for you."

When she glanced up, Kellan wasn't behind the glass partition. *Damn him.*

Damn this.

Damn it all...

Dazed, scared, moving quickly, McKenna headed for the door to the corridor and pushed through. Kellan wasn't there.

Someone else was.

Chapter 13

"Derek." Reeling from the shock she'd just had, Mc-Kenna knew she was pale. Her legs felt like putty as she stood before him in the hallway.

"Are you finished for the night, Mac? I'll drive you home," Derek said. "It's not safe out there tonight. We've had five calls in the last two hours."

Not safe. Everybody thought so.

"Calls from around here?" McKenna made herself sound as normal as possible. But why did she bother to act as if nothing unusual had happened? All she had to do was take Derek to the young man's bedside and show him those fangs. If she didn't, would the entire hospital be in danger? Would that young man wake up at all, after what he had suffered through?

Hell, did those teeth have to mean that he was a vampire?

"Not close to the hospital," Derek said. "But we can't be too careful. There's a really bad guy on the loose, Mac. Possibly a whole gang of them. They're scaring the shit out of everyone."

McKenna blinked slowly to get a handle on her emotions. Too many strange things had happened lately. First that dreadful alley. Then the image in the mirror, Kellan here in the hospital and what she'd seen in the ICU.

Derek didn't know half of what she had been through.

He had no idea what was going on. He was just worried about a danger he knew about outside these hospital walls.

She tugged at her scrubs. "I'll change clothes and get my things."

"I'll be right outside your door," Derek promised.

One of the two men who had come to see her tonight knew something she didn't, though she had been somewhat enlightened twice now about the possibility of humans sharing the streets with creatures that could no longer be considered human.

There was another explanation that she grabbed on to greedily. Young people today did odd things to emulate their heroes. Since the surgery had been more or less routine after jump-starting the patient's heart, there was a possibility that patient simply liked vampires and had modified his teeth to look like them. Stuff like that happened.

Yet if that was the case, how would Kellan, in town for just a few days, have known about the guy they had worked on tonight? Unless Kellan had something to do with it.

Her head hurt. Shooting pain needled the backs of her eyes. Even if Kellan was right…even if it was a vampire she had seen in the alley…she wasn't in a position to do anything about it.

McKenna walked with Derek in silence for a few minutes before he asked, "Have you seen that guy on the Harley since the other night?"

She nodded and leaned against the doorjamb. "He stopped by here tonight."

How could she lie to Derek again, when he'd been so kind and considerate and was doing his job? Obstructing an investigation was serious business. Besides, why should she lie about Kellan's visit anyway, when tonight had nothing to do with panties around her ankles?

Concerned, Derek perked up. "He was here? At the hospital?"

Nervous, McKenna again tugged at her scrubs. "He showed up minutes before you arrived."

"What did he want?"

"He wanted to talk."

"Where is he now, Mac?"

"I have no idea. I went into a room, and when I turned around, he'd gone."

Perplexed, Derek came closer. "I'm starting to think that guy is a shadow. We found nothing about that logo on his jacket in the system. Blood Knights has to be some secret gang, if it actually exists."

Derek ignored the buzz of the phone attached to his belt. "I couldn't find where I'd written down his name, so he could be anybody, with any agenda. You have to be careful, McKenna. Call me right away if he shows up again."

Having done her own research regarding the name on his jacket by calling in a few favors to old friends on the force, McKenna knew most of this already. The trick was going to be figuring out what kind of secret tribe the Blood Knights were.

The first thing that came to her mind was that they might be self-appointed vampire hunters. That would explain the *blood* part of their logo. It would also be a reason for Kellan looking at the guy in ICU.

"His name is Kellan," she said.

Derek looked up. "He told you that?"

"Yes."

"Did you get a last name?"

"I didn't ask."

She could see that Derek wanted to press her about the name thing and held himself back. However cordial he was acting, Derek truly hadn't forgiven her for finding

Kellan in her apartment, just as she hadn't forgiven Kellan for whispering another woman's name when his hands were all over her.

"He didn't mention where he's been staying, by any chance?" Derek asked.

McKenna pointed to his buzzing cell phone. "Are you going to get that?"

"Not yet."

She nodded. "Reason tells me you would have searched all the local hangouts already, and that without a name, a description didn't get you very far."

"Not so much as a whisper," Derek admitted. "I find that suspicious. Don't you?"

"It's hard to hide a bike like his." *And a body like his.*

"And yet he obviously has."

McKenna mulled that over. "You think he might be connected to the mayhem going on?"

"The guy comes into town and chaos starts. Wouldn't you be concerned?"

"Actually, the trouble started long before then, and you know it."

"Okay. You're right," Derek conceded. "But then things got worse a whole lot quicker. We don't know if the guy—"

"Kellan," McKenna said.

Derek started over. "We don't know if *Kellan* could be involved, and if he might have been in town a while before you met him. Hell, Mac, we don't know anything about him at all, and that isn't acceptable."

She wanted to agree with Derek, but there was another side of the story to consider. "We know that he didn't hurt me, and that he in fact helped me in a time of need."

"It's just too convenient. You have to see that. You meet him. You're attacked. He's Johnny-on-the-spot and reaches you, but the attacker gets away."

Tell him, McKenna's inner voice directed. *Tell Derek everything. See how he takes it, and if he thinks I've lost my mind.*

Tell him about the alley and the wooden stake.

Tell him about what we did on his front lawn, and how much I liked it.

She put a hand to the door, sensing that Derek was waiting for her to agree with him. In the old days, as partners, they had often run various scenarios past each other. That was what cops did.

"There could be a possible connection," she said. "I don't believe it, but it's a path we have to go down in order to find the truth."

Derek tilted his head. "Has he mesmerized you or something? I can hear the hesitancy behind what you said. You do understand how serious this is, and that this stranger can't be ruled out?"

"I haven't lost my mind, Derek. No one understands how this could have gone down more than I do. But the guy walked right in here to check on me tonight, which makes it look like he's not hiding from anyone."

"Where is he now, then? You don't think he could have seen me coming and hit the road?"

Actually, that was worth considering, McKenna realized. Kellan had been there one minute and had vanished the next. Was he hiding from the law?

Sick of the presumptions, she closed her eyes to ease the migraine getting worse with each passing thought. That was a mistake. With the rest of the world shut out, she sensed Kellan again as though he was some sort of distant, wavering mirage.

Kellan stood in a corner of the corridor, observing the man who was trying his hardest to keep McKenna from him. Miller.

He and this detective weren't enemies. They weren't even rivals, really. McKenna's body language told him this as she had walked side by side with Miller to the staircase, allowing the detective to hold on to her elbow without leaning into him.

Miller would protect McKenna with his life, and at the same time make getting close to her from this point on more difficult. However, not much lay beyond the control of a Blood Knight, and McKenna Randall remained an integral part of his plan. Time, since he always had plenty of it, was on his side. He would let this game play out while he took care of that damn nest.

The vamps' return near the detective's apartment was more than a case of lingering scent and a bloodsucker's job left unfinished. The fight in the alley and on the street, and going after McKenna, had meant something to them—which had suggested to Kellan that a hospital thrown into darkness, with McKenna inside, was a bad omen.

Why McKenna Randall was of interest to a bunch of brooding vampires was a puzzle he hadn't yet worked out. Filmy threads bound them all together somehow, and those threads had to be severed.

Placing a vampire inside the hospital had been a stroke of genius on that nest's part. It also spoke to being part of an organized plan, which again made this a highly unusual, highly charged situation. Sending in a victim who would die on the operating table and then awaken as a bloodsucker without suspicion meant havoc would reign in Seattle General once that creature opened its eyes.

He wondered again who the ancient vampire at the center of this Seattle nest was, and how that master had conceived of such an idea. Right now, and more than ever, he looked forward to meeting that monster face-to-face.

Anxious about how soon he would get that privilege,

Kellan glanced at the clock on the wall. After five minutes, McKenna and Miller had not returned to the ICU floor. She hadn't shown the detective what she'd found in that intensive-care unit. Not yet, anyway. Surely the omission meant that she believed what he had told her.

If she changed her mind later and decided to point things out, it would be too late. No proof of the vamp's existence would remain. Kellan would see to that personally, because if he didn't, the little fanged bugger would wake half-starved and go after the first body within reach. After that, the fledgling would bite its way through the rest of the incapacitated people, draining them all dry. Sick people unable to defend themselves would be the ideal beginner vampire buffet.

And then what? Would its task be to go after McKenna? This was a problem requiring a quick solution.

Leaving McKenna in the detective's care, Kellan headed down the corridor. He slipped into the ICU with one hand in his pocket.

"Do you have something further to say?" Derek asked when McKenna emerged from the lounge. "I can almost hear the questions rolling around inside your head."

"I just want to go home and sleep. I want a hot shower and a soothing drink."

"Anything else?" There was a hopeful hint in Derek's voice.

She nodded. "Pizza. I'd kill for some pizza."

Derek's familiar grin was automatic. For the moment, he had forgotten about Kellan. "I'm pretty sure we can manage that pizza. Let me make one call first. Then I'll take you out. Will you wait here where I can keep an eye on you? The lobby's pretty crowded. I'll step aside and get out of the way."

"Fine."

Standing in the center of the main-floor lobby, McKenna searched the faces of the people coming and going. None of them was the one she wanted to see. *And what will you do if you find him, Nurse Randall? Turn him over to Derek?*

Barely a second later, she sensed his presence behind her in the form of a sudden, warm, pleasurable breath on the back of her neck. Her quakes returned, just as they always did when Kellan was near. McKenna willed herself not to turn her head.

He whispered, "It's done, my beautiful lover. You needn't worry about that one."

Right after that, the sense of Kellan's presence scattered as if blown away by a strong wind.

"The car is at the curb," Derek said.

Hell, how had he missed Kellan?

McKenna took a long moment to rid herself of the warm sensations Kellan had left her with. It took a lot of internal chatter to do so.

Derek's hand on hers brought her around. As she walked beside him, McKenna began to worry about what Kellan had meant when he said something was done.

What had he done?

She almost missed a step, because maybe she knew.

"I'm sorry, Derek. I forgot something."

Her throat was dry. More pain stabbed at nerve endings behind her eyes.

"Okay," Derek said. "Let's go and get it."

"I'll go. Cell service is better here, so you can stay and finish those calls you need to make. I'll be quick."

Although Derek didn't look too pleased with this, he inclined his head to her and palmed his phone.

Anxiously, McKenna raced up the stairs and along the corridor toward the ICU. There was no sign of Kellan in the hallway. Everything looked normal until she reached the unit where a crash cart had been discarded and nurses were speaking to each other in hushed tones.

They quieted when McKenna approached.

"Just checking on the surgery patient," she said amiably. "I thought I'd see how he's doing."

That sounded reasonable enough, she thought.

"Yes, well, good luck with that," one of the nurses said with obvious frustration. "He's gone."

McKenna stared at the other nurse, blank-faced.

"There's no way he could have gotten up, or past us if he did manage," another nurse elaborated. "He hadn't even opened his eyes and should have been under for several more hours. You can call it a miracle if you want to, but I call it weird."

McKenna moved past them with her heart in her throat. "That's ridiculous. His wounds were life-threatening. We weren't sure he'd make it past tomorrow."

The other nurses followed her to the bed the patient had occupied the last time she checked, which hadn't been more than fifteen minutes ago. Two doctors arrived behind her, looking as shocked as she felt.

It's done. You needn't worry about that one.

Had Kellan taken that patient away?

McKenna's chills multiplied as she eyed the empty bed.

"What's that?" a young doctor asked, running his hand over the sheets.

McKenna's stomach turned over. Her gaze dropped to the bed, now bodiless but covered in a dusting of fine, dark gray ash.

Chapter 14

McKenna would soon find him, Kellan was certain. She'd find him and demand the answers she had every right to. She would do so without the good detective by her side.

Kellan waited outside her apartment house, sitting quietly on the Harley, deep in thought. Although the rain had stopped, more clouds were gathering. Wet pavement glistened under the streetlights. Water pooled near the curb.

Detective Miller was now occupied at the hospital, checking into the missing patient. Since Kellan had taken care of that problem, the hospital was safe again, and he and McKenna would have the alone time they needed. She'd come to him armed with a new sense of purpose, and maybe the Glock.

Anticipating her arrival, he glanced up to see her coming toward him. She was running, and out of breath, as if she had sprinted all the way from Seattle General. She must have parked her car down the street. There were keys in one of her hands. She ran up to him. Her right fist connected with his torso in a decent punch that at any other time would have made him smile.

"What did you do?" She went on without waiting for a reply. "Why couldn't he have been saved? What about transfusions? Specialists? Dear God, what was that guy?"

Her voice dropped to a whisper as she reached for her throat. "Why was he there in the first place?"

"I believe he was put there to gain access to you," Kellan said, getting off the bike.

She shook her head. "That's…"

"Only the beginning, McKenna. You and I seem to be caught up in something. This is the third time they've gotten too close."

They were inches apart. McKenna removed her hand from her throat and placed it on his chest, planting her palm over his heart. That simple motion sent ripples of heat through him that felt like a bad sunburn. The heat grew stronger when her eyes met his.

"Tell me what's going on, Kellan. Fill me in."

"I wonder if you'd believe me now."

"I've seen enough to make me want to try."

Needing to capture the last remnants of innocent warmth that would soon turn cold, Kellan placed his hand over hers and forced himself to relax.

"There are vampires in Seattle," he said. "I think you know that now. The young man in the hospital was going to be one of them, and the transition would have been just as unacceptable inside a hospital as it would have been anywhere else in this city."

McKenna's lashes lowered, as if she might be struggling to comprehend what he was saying. "How do you know about that? About vampires?"

"I travel the world to make sure the really bad ones don't harm anyone beyond those they've hurt already. I can't take care of them all. No one could. I do what I can, wherever I can, to protect the public from finding out about the parasites in the shadows."

Her hand on his chest slid toward the bottom of his rib cage, sending shock waves of pleasure through Kellan. This was the kind of intimacy he had always wanted, and what he had searched the world to find. *And of all the beings in the world, it would have to be you, McKenna Randall. At the end.*

The acknowledgment of that kind of bad timing brought him great sorrow and a terrible sense of loss.

"You chased the vampires here?" Her voice pitched higher due to the stress building up inside her. "You wanted to hunt them in Seattle?"

She was no longer questioning the existence of bloodsuckers. That was a first step. Kellan carefully considered what else to say and how much to tell this woman who had been a cop, and therefore had already experienced her share of violence in the past. He had to figure the odds were good that McKenna would now accept at least some of what he had to say. She might hear him out.

"I came to Seattle to find you," he told her, getting right to the point. "Not to find them."

His sigils fired up a warning. He was treading on dangerous ground, but as usual, he went on anyway. "These vampires are merely a sideshow to deflect me from my purpose in seeking you out."

Her gaze lifted to the level of his chin and stopped there. Kellan kept himself from willing her to look at him. He wanted honesty tonight, not mind control. He was tired of having to urge people into action.

"There are other things in this world that people aren't aware of until it's too late," he continued. "Beings that hug the darkness and feed on humans. Beings that shouldn't exist, but do."

"You say *humans* as if you're not one of us," McKenna noted.

While he had planned on telling her nearly everything, Kellan found that he couldn't. Not all of it, when so much

was at stake. He captured her hand in his, felt how fragile and cool her fingers were when the heat between them
was rising.

His tattoos were on fire with a warning he could not
heed.

"I'm not like you. Not completely," he said.

After his remark had settled, McKenna shook her head
to negate it. "No. You either are like me, or you aren't.
There's nothing between those two things. The freaks in
the alley weren't like me. The guy in the hospital might
not have been like me if he was what you say he was. But
you…"

Finally her eyes again met his. In them he saw hurt,
and also a flicker of defiance. "You are not like them at
all. Not the least little bit."

Smiling sadly, wanting desperately to agree with her,
ease her mind, take it all back, Kellan knew it was too late
to do any of those things. He had told her the truth. Now
she had to deal.

"I'm the transition, McKenna. The bridge that spans
the gray space between the two. That's where I live, and
where I've existed for more time than you can possibly
conceive of."

He stopped her from pulling back. "I'm no innocent
bystander. My kind is responsible for the creation of the
bloodsuckers, and for that we do what we can to eradicate
the worst of them."

She tugged again. He held firm. "Somewhere in the
past there was a slip of a fang and the creatures known
today as vampires came into being. We weren't aware of
this mistake for some time. By then, like a plague, their
species had spread to all corners of the earth."

"Who is *we*?"

He should have predicted that she'd pick up on the nuances. McKenna's skills were focused on the holes in his confession. The things he left out.

"There are six others whom I call my brothers. We're in this together and have been from the start."

"Blood Knights."

"Yes."

"Not a motorcycle gang. I'm not stupid, you know. I did look that up."

"No gang," he said.

She stopped trying to break away. "Only seven of you? If all of what you say is true, how could that possibly be enough to keep the nasty breeds in check?"

"It was enough for our original purpose, before things got out of hand."

"And that original purpose was?"

"Protecting a holy relic from those who would abuse its power. Hiding that relic. Keeping it safe."

As she thought that over, Kellan could almost hear the wheels of her mind turning.

"It's a good story, but no help in connecting the dots," she said. "Is it safe? That relic?"

"Yes."

She took more time before speaking again. "What do you want with me? Why did you come here to find me?"

They had arrived at the crux of the matter—the reason why he was standing here now.

"I came here hoping you'd kill me," he said.

McKenna dropped her chin to her chest. The ringing sounds in her ears were getting louder. She had been in no condition to run into Kellan. She wasn't in any condition to hear all this nonsense, either. She'd been sick since she saw those ash-covered sheets. She was going to throw up if she didn't sit down.

What Kellan said made no sense. She couldn't wrap her mind around his explanations. *Kill him?*

With uncanny perception, the man, or whatever the hell he really was—madman, escaped lunatic, vampire hunter—scooped her up in his arms. She kicked out, struggled to break free with such vigor that he put her down. But he led her to the building by holding her hand.

He was ten times stronger and faster than any man she had known. They were at her door in seconds. He managed to get them inside without a key or kicking down the door.

Registering those things made McKenna feel worse.

The apartment was dark. She hadn't expected to come back here tonight. The window had been repaired, though McKenna expected a shower of glass at any moment. Left-over tension seemed to hover in the air.

Kellan led her to the bed, where light from outside chased some of the shadows away. He sat her down and sat down beside her. Being with him here was like a reboot of the last time they'd been together on this bed. Her expectations on that other night had been high. Currently she wasn't feeling much of anything.

"Miller sent a car to watch over you," Kellan said, turning his head as if listening to sounds on a frequency she couldn't share. "Your guard dog just arrived."

Her voice wasn't as steady as she would have liked. "How could you possibly know that?"

He smiled sadly.

"What if it isn't a police car?"

He didn't answer that.

"Let's say I do believe you about some things. Explain how you figured out that the guy in the hospital was trouble."

"I've been watching his friends. I've met a few of them.

When the lights went out tonight and I found out about this latest victim in surgery, I became suspicious."

"Those suspicions might have proved false."

"Rarely am I wrong about this one thing," he said. "About them."

"Why are you so sure of yourself and your perceptions?"

"My blood recognizes theirs because a distant part of me resides within that blood."

McKenna fell back to the pillows with both hands covering her face. "Blood. Vampires. You do realize how crazy that sounds?"

"Are you crazy for believing me?" he countered. "For believing what you saw?"

"Yes. I'm nuts. I'll admit it. I think I've been heading in that direction for some time. But you..."

Kellan traced the scar on her temple with his fingertip, and the meeting of their flesh was exhilarating.

"Why would I kill you?" she demanded. "How could you possibly believe I could do a thing like that?"

After all the pleasure they had shared, was his plan to hurt her somehow? She was alone with him in a dark apartment. According to Kellan, there was a cop on the street, but what good would that do with Kellan so close?

Should she shout? Run? Could the man her body hungered for so desperately, the man making such absurd statements, mean her harm?

"You would kill me because I asked you to," he said.

"Then I hope to God you don't."

His fingers rested on her scar. "Was it bad? Whatever caused this wound?"

"*Bad* is an understatement."

"Tell me."

"A bad guy shot me. The bullet entered my skull because I ducked to avoid the shot. And that was the end of my job as a cop."

"The incident cost you the things you most desired."

"All of them." She looked at him. "I thought my life was over. For a while, I wanted it to be over."

"Then you might understand what it is to want to die," he said. By the dim light from the window, his expression registered as serious.

Thinking was difficult when he was near. With his hand on her face, her concentration was divided between remembering the pain of her past and wanting this man so very badly. For a potentially crazy bastard, Kellan knew a lot about the fine art of manipulation. She might have vowed to keep her mind in check where he was concerned, but the rest of her was already surrendering to his touch, his addictive masculine vibe and the look in his eyes.

She waited for his lips to find hers, sensing how much he wanted that, but hoping they'd get a few more things straightened out first. Instead of finding her mouth, though, he replaced his fingers on her scar with a light kiss and said, "Pain makes us all feel fragile."

And for the first time in two long years the dull, continuous ache behind her eyes just melted away...as if this man had simply erased it.

Kellan's lips followed the raised ridge of her old wound. As he willed her to forget about that wound and the physical pain it caused her, McKenna began to release the tension she might not have realized she carried.

Her eyes blinked open. She stared at him for some time. Then, no longer a prisoner of that stockpiled pain, she reached for him, grabbed hold of his jacket.

"I do understand about death, Kellan, though I no longer dwell in that dark place. You're right. I have experienced the desire to end it all. But that feeling passed. Maybe I can help you, if eluding pain is truly what you came here for. I can find someone for you to see. There are plenty of good people in my business."

McKenna Randall was so very beautiful and completely sincere that Kellan couldn't even shake his head. He had temporarily freed her body of its leftover aches, and yet her mind would always retain remnants of that dark time.

McKenna was struggling to pigeonhole their relationship, such as it was. She was hurting on a level as deep as his, but unlike him, she didn't know why. Possibly the soul she harbored influenced this.

His Makers had to have been out of their minds to play with life and death, going so far as to manipulate the gray zone in between. Obviously they hadn't foreseen what such a state could do to the innocent mortals who'd been forced to be a part of their schemes.

McKenna was an unsuspecting victim of their foresight, such as it was, as well as their plotting and plans. He was attracted to that air of innocence her human side possessed. McKenna's spirit made her want to accept him even if she wasn't completely on board.

Maybe it was the same for him, and soul to soul was how this attraction thing worked. Resisting her was futile. Completely out of the question. They were chained together by forces that lay beyond their control, forces set in motion long before McKenna was born. He wondered if McKenna would believe him if he told her that part.

She was looking up at him with those big blue eyes. Her lips were slightly parted. She was unbelievably alluring, feminine and brave. What man could resist such a combination? What kind of immortal could resist her?

He knew that she was going to argue, and he couldn't let her. Explanations and secret plans of secret sects didn't begin to cover what he wanted to do with her. The moment was almost too rich to bear.

Kellan covered McKenna's mouth with his in a kiss that was savagely demanding and the culmination of thoughts, feelings and emotions running rampant. The sheer force of his hunger for McKenna drove her deep into the pillows. Contrary to what he might have expected, she didn't fight him. On some level McKenna understood their mutual attraction existed on a scale that no one else could possibly comprehend.

The kiss loosed something wild inside her. She tore at his jacket, seeking to get closer to the bare skin beneath. She breathed him in as if oxygen-starved. She nipped at his tongue, made small sounds as she moved her slim hips provocatively.

Talk went by the wayside, making room for baser things. He knew McKenna wanted answers to her questions, but at that moment wanted him inside her even more.

He thought this might be a trial by fire. A test to see how far he could go, enjoying her, loving her, before he did what he had come to Seattle to do. He wondered if he'd ultimately fail, because the closer he got to that objective, the more regret he felt.

Would loving her so fiercely in this bed make her soul, passed down through centuries, take flight? When it did, would a lifeless McKenna remain, or would she wake refreshed, free of her hidden burden?

Why don't I know these things?

McKenna. Stay with me. Stay as long as you can.

The night darkened when his mouth lifted from hers. His tattoos all but screamed for him to stop the madness. Mating with his Reaper had to be against the rules that had governed him all this time. Then again, maybe this was the way his objective was to be achieved.

McKenna's soft, husky moan sent him over the edge of reason. Thoughts scattered. He joined her in the act of tearing at his jacket. In a voice as hoarse as hers, he warned, "I will have you. I'll selfishly have it all, though you might damn me later."

"Then you'd better hurry," she said.

It didn't matter what they had been through or what she really thought about him and his stories about vampires and dying. They were on fire and going down in flames. The room was as sultry as their mingled breath.

McKenna helped him remove his shirt, not bothering to hide the extent of her greediness to reach what lay beneath. Kellan stripped off her coat, her sweater, her pants, one item at a time.

Her quakes had stopped, replaced by desire. Fully naked, she was a masterpiece. Her creamy skin gleamed. The sharpness of her hip bones and the edges of her shoulders cast shadows over long stretches of perfectly smooth, unblemished ivory flesh. Small round breasts sat high and firm on her chest, beckoning him with raised rosy tips. Below her flat belly, the space between her thighs vied mercilessly, again, for his attention.

Damn the Makers for this.

He had loved her once already and had got away with it.

Kellan allowed McKenna's eyes to drink him in. She smiled briefly before that smile fled.

He pulled her legs out from underneath her, and she fell onto her back with her arms open wide. That singular moment made time stop. The position seemed familiar to him, as did the ivory gleam of McKenna's beautifully naked body.

He felt as though he had been here before, seen this same pose in the past. Hell, was he reliving a lost memory with really poor timing? Hadn't he seen this same look in a different pair of blue eyes?

Was that a further warning for him to be careful?

"It's okay." McKenna's whisper broke the spell temporarily holding him back. "I want this."

Finish, Kellan's mind insisted. *Stop playing around. Open her now. Find out how to expose the secrets you have given up everything to find. Take from her what you need. Get the kind of peace you covet. You will know how to do this when the moment arrives.*

"It's okay," she repeated, her expression deadly serious.

This really was a trial by fire, and his sigils were in on the deal, firing up with a scorching heat. McKenna was giving him permission to do what he wanted, and he was losing control. He wanted the peace he had come here to find, and he also wanted her. The woman, not just the soul McKenna Randall housed.

Suddenly he wasn't sure which of those two things he wanted most.

More thoughts nagged at him, delaying his next move. Possibly McKenna's permission for closeness was the first step toward attaining his original goal. Maybe his Reaper had to offer herself to him willingly.

She certainly was doing that.

Her legs parted on the sheets in an open invitation. He stared at her, wanting very badly to accept that invitation.

His fangs dropped with a soft clicking sound.

He had to clench and unclench his fists, tighten and loosen his jaw in an effort to keep those fangs to himself. If he had never used them, what were they for? Hadn't he often wondered?

He and his brothers had become immortal by drinking blood from a golden chalice. It was for the protection of that chalice that the Knights had been created. Their mission was to keep the Grail safe at all costs in order to prevent that holy cup from bestowing the gift of immortality on others less willing to adhere to the rules of the civilized.

Oh yes. He knew Death well. He had felt Death's black breath on his face, felt Death's hand reach inside his chest to rip the life from him. He had mourned every last second. He had seen darkness fall. But he had been resurrected. He and his brothers had risen again as beings no longer in fear of Death's kiss. Seven Knights with a golden purpose.

One sip of blood had done that to him. The blood of his Makers, added to the ring of caked, dried blood that the chalice had once collected, had stolen his mortal life, and then remade him with unfathomable strength and a purpose to match.

Blood Knight.

His fangs now ached, pulsed, as if they, too, had a purpose.

God...

Was he supposed to sink them into McKenna's beautiful neck as if he were one of the vampires he fought on a regular basis?

Were the fangs meant to open a vein, so that the soul McKenna hid could poison him? So that he'd die a final death with her blood on his lips?

The thought was so repulsive, he groaned out loud.

But what if it was true, and he had to taste the Reaper to suck that soul free?

He felt sick, and no more enlightened than when he had started this personal quest. The how-to part of attaining his goal was too damned elusive, so who knew how this might end?

Will you die, my beautiful McKenna?

If that were true, what then?

What had become clear to him since day one in Seattle

was just how reluctant he was to hurt McKenna. Taking her life to ease his pain would be a terribly selfish act.

He had become emotionally involved with his Reaper.

Her neck, like the rest of her, gleamed in the light from the window. Veins Kellan was now all too aware of throbbed beneath her ears, raising the skin near her black-and-blue throat. Those things weren't acceptable for him to notice if he cared for her. In harming this mortal being who cared so much for others, he would have no peace at all. After he'd served the light for so long, Hell would surely come calling if he took that bite.

In essence, he'd be damned if he did what he came here for, and he'd be damned if he didn't.

So Kellan waited, his skin damp with the effort of holding himself back.

McKenna...

Don't let me do this. You must not allow it.

Send me away. Please.

The problem was that she didn't seem to hear him.

Chapter 15

McKenna sensed how badly Kellan wanted to make love to her. His intentions were obvious. But he made no move, and that was unacceptable.

He was perfect. Even better when viewed half in the buff. Everything was molded, honed, toned. The fine dusting of chest hair led her focus to the narrow hips that balanced his broad shoulders. Beneath that were lean, strong thighs.

He was erect. Real effort was necessary to bring her attention back to his face, which was sober and so very fine. In the dim light, the scrolling tats she had noticed earlier cast black tentacles over both of Kellan's shoulders in perfect symmetry. Those tats seemed to move each time his muscles tensed, as if they were alive. Though she had seen a lot of tattoos in the ER, none were quite like these.

She passed her legs over cool sheets in an effort to ease the incredible buildup of heat accompanying his stare. She smoothed one hand down her body, gliding her fingers provocatively over her stomach and between her hip bones, hoping to lure him there.

She was hot for him, aching for him. Any further delay just would not do. This was a moment she had tried not to think about but had been waiting for. The Blood Knight was going to be naked in her bedroom.

Uttering a growl low in his throat as he watched her hand's progress, he finally took the bait. He sank down between her legs, placed a kiss on the inside of her right thigh and ran his hot mouth over her flesh. Again, and in spite of how desperate she was to get on with things and have it all, Kellan was going to make her wait.

The man was going to make her squirm.

When she felt the lap of his tongue on the folds of her sex, McKenna cried out. It was too much. And it was too little.

She reached for Kellan's hair, sighed as the pleasure of his actions washed over her in wave after wave of sexual bliss. She rolled her head on the pillows and thrashed on the bed. As the pressure of his mouth increased, her limbs flexed and curled. The inner drumbeat began.

Unable to fight the sensations, too weak to ward off a pleasure that was so damned extreme, she came, hard, with a feral cry.

The sound of her cry echoed thunderously inside Mc-Kenna's head. She flicked her eyes open.

She was lying on a bed, and the bed was moving. Or maybe it was the room that moved. A man was lying with her, his weight heavy but comforting, dangerously lovely and familiar. He was inside her, his hips tight to hers.

But it wasn't real.

White walls drifted past her vision, beneath a ceiling too distant to see. Her lover moved in and out of her, thrusting hard, waiting for her to whisper his name before retreating enough to goad her into lifting her hips to meet him.

The joining of their naked bodies was the only other sound in a room filled with the lush scent of melting candle wax. Lavender wax. Her favorite.

Her lover's hair, long, dark copper interspersed with flecks of gold, tickled her throat. His skin was damp from the fierce athleticism of their coupling, yet also smooth to the touch. He was hers. This act proved it. She loved him more than words could say. More than anything else, anyone else. More than life itself.

She closed her eyes as she came with a climax that went on and on as if it were the only kind of feeling left to her. And maybe it was.

Her talented lover spoke her name when the lights went out, and that name hummed inside her skull like an echo. His sigils, newly carved and still a raw, swollen, bloody red, curled beneath her hands as if they were separate entities and alive.

McKenna's cry of surprise woke her. When her wits came spiraling back to the present, large blue eyes were searching her from a face filled with concern.

The man those eyes belonged to was shaking. His hands gripped the edge of the mattress. He was not inside her, hadn't been inside her, she now knew. Not this man. Not this time.

They hadn't got that far.

With her eyes and her heart, McKenna recognized each curve of muscle that tensed his wide shoulders. Both his body and his face were intimately familiar in a way that denied knowing him for such a short time.

The room she had awakened to also was familiar. These were her things. This was her apartment. The window beside the bed overlooked the street. The lamp, now dark, was an item she had purchased in a downtown store.

There were no white walls or candles.

Cool sheets reminded her that she was naked, and how

she had got that way. The man beside her was half-naked and breathing hard.

She focused on his bare shoulders, on the tattoo tentacles that were obviously no inker's free-for-all. She had seen those marks before, in her dream, and had thought them to be alive.

Kellan. That was his name, and yet the moniker didn't ring true. Was this name an alias? Did he have another? Another name for him was on her lips, so close she could taste it.

She had been dreaming again, when she should have been attentive to what was going on in this bed. Had she been the woman in that dream, or did the dreams belong to someone else?

She had a feeling those images were trying to tell her something that she was finding hard to grasp. Possibly that message was nothing more than that Kellan might be her soul mate.

His concern was a surprise.

The man with her in her current reality didn't smile or offer small talk. He was watching her as if waiting for something. Was she supposed to speak? Apologize for losing control of her faculties when she should have been paying attention?

You are tied to my dreams, she wanted to tell him. She knew that for sure because of the tattoos that were like no others.

What are you? she wanted to ask.

What does being a Blood Knight really mean?

With the holy relic they guarded safe, had he and his brothers become vigilantes bent on dishing out their own form of justice? What had happened that made Kellan want to come here to die? He had told her that he had come here hoping she would kill him. She. *Me.*

Looking directly into his eyes, McKenna said, "Having only met me a few nights ago, how could you possibly imagine I'd have anything to do with your wishes?"

Did he follow that? His gaze tracked hers.

"Who are you, really?" she added, because hell, his inky tattoos had sparked a brand-new level of fear. She wanted him to turn around. She wanted to see the tats, touch them in order to understand what they meant.

At the same time, she knew that though she had bared her body and her soul to Kellan, her reticent lover wasn't ready to respond in kind.

Kellan closed his lips over his fangs. The abominable teeth had urged him to cross a line, and that urge was strong enough to make getting close to McKenna's neck impossible for him.

He couldn't trust himself to kiss her again. He feared to touch her until ready to decide which way this was to end. Leaving McKenna for good, the way he had left another lover so long ago, seemed an impossible task.

But time was short for decision-making. McKenna had seen the castle twice. In her soul's memory, she had visited Broceliande for a taste of what went on in that forbidden place. Out of all the memories she could have chosen, she had picked the last one, the moments preceding a long farewell, on the night before his new, endless life began.

He had not dared to think back on that night until McKenna showed it to him. He couldn't have gone on with the golden quest if he had dwelled on his past. This jolting backward look showed him how two important things had been stitched together in that past purposefully to confuse him.

This woman, McKenna, not only hid the soul he was never supposed to find but also carried particles of another woman inside her. Not just any woman, either, but the one who had once known him better than anyone.

The woman he had once loved with all his being.

Why else would McKenna have been to the castle in a daydream to see, to feel, to be inside his former lover's body? The lover he'd left behind in order to fulfill his vows. The lover who had cried mercilessly over her loss.

Those same cries had moments ago escaped from McKenna's lips, this time in pleasure. But in them he heard an echo of the pain and suffering of another woman's darkest time.

God help him...

More than one imprint of the past resided within McKenna Randall's DNA. The fair hair, blue eyes and delicate angles were similar to those of the lover he'd left at Broceliande. That woman hadn't been part of his crusade. In the years after he'd left the castle, he hadn't tracked her. He hadn't dared to try, fearing what his Makers might have done to her if he had. The seriousness of the golden quest demanded his undivided attention. God himself, it was said, demanded his fealty on this matter.

Tonight, here, Kellan relived the pain of that separation. Being with McKenna brought it all back. The irony was that while she alone stirred those ancient memories, McKenna also possessed the power to free him of them. In McKenna Randall he'd found not only a woman worthy of his attention but also memories of his lost lover.

Who are you? McKenna had asked him. Perhaps she sensed that submerged past.

"I planned to tell you everything," he said to her now. "Tonight was going to be the night to come clean. Plans to tell you more about myself before this were derailed because of my hesitancy to involve you further. I believe it's only now that I might have figured out why."

McKenna's eyes were wide.

"You and I have met before. Not as we are now, but in another lifetime," he explained.

She blinked but didn't reopen her eyes for some time.

"Hear me out, if you will," he said. "The story is fantastic, and yet I swear to you that every word is true."

He didn't wait to go on. "I was born with another name that I'll soon tell you about. I was born in a time when things like honor not only counted but reigned supreme above all other things."

"That must have been a very long time ago," she said in a raspy voice. "Not many people today recognize what honor means."

"Of course you'd need to take that tack when cops often see the worst in people, and morals, as well as attitudes, have slipped into noticeable decline."

Clearing her throat reminded him of what she had been through a few nights ago in this apartment, and how close he had come tonight to tapping into the same kind of evil.

"I'm supposed to believe you think I'm going to kill you for some reason," she said. "Do you actually believe that, or is the word *kill* a metaphor for something else?"

Kellan's fangs had not retracted and continued to pulse dangerously in time with the visible beat in McKenna's neck. If he were to show the teeth to her, she would have to believe him. There would be no mistaking his intrinsic differences. She might run away and save herself from whatever fate had in store.

He might let her go.

But he couldn't do that. Not yet. Not with her sweet scent in his lungs and on his lips.

He spoke around the fangs.

"As far-fetched as it sounds, I believe you were created to terminate my life, and that was your only purpose from the start."

As much as he hated that statement and how absurd it sounded, Kellan began to see more and more truth in it. Maybe, he now thought, Damaris, the woman who had captured his heart so long ago, had loved him for reasons other than he'd assumed. Possibly putting the two of them together had been his Makers' plan all along, so that the particles inside the soul he sought would have this surprising effect on him.

McKenna's right cheek twitched. He knew how unbelievable this must sound to her.

"You need help," she said. "And you're not the only one. I need help for allowing what's between us to get this far."

Kellan shook his head. "Let me explain. Hear me out, and then believe what you want to."

"Because you think I owe you?"

"Because I'd very much appreciate you giving me that time."

She nodded. Waited.

"This is between you and me, McKenna. It has always been between us. It's a dance of love and death."

"That," she said, pointing between her legs, "was between you and me. Mind games are a whole other matter. And if you mention the word *death* again, I might find my gun and take you up on those wishes."

"You will help me," Kellan asserted gently. "You'll have to. It's what you were meant to do if I showed up here or, conversely, if someone brought you to me."

"Hand me my gun."

She didn't mean it. Whatever she thought about his feeble attempt to tell her the truth, she wanted to believe him. He only had to make her see the light before stealing that light back from her.

As the wickedly fickle hand of fate proved once again, though, something outside of their conversation intervened. That untimely interruption came in the form of gunshots on the street.

At the window in a flash, Kellan looked outside. McKenna rushed to his side. When he pressed her back, away from the glass, she swore.

"Too close," he warned. "Keep clear of the glass."

"Sounds like it might be the cop parked downstairs."

"Possibly. How fast can you get dressed?"

"Don't worry about me."

"Will you stay here if I ask you to?"

When she didn't answer the question, Kellan repeated the cussword she had muttered.

"Don't tell me it's vampires," she said. "Unless shooting is a new part of their routine."

Kellan gave her another cautionary glance. "I doubt if your cop friends would know what to do about it if it were vampires."

"Maybe you planned for this to happen," she challenged, "so that you wouldn't have to finish your story. In two sentences or less, can you explain why vampires or anyone else would be after me, if in fact that's what's been going on?"

"I don't know why," Kellan admitted.

McKenna didn't touch him, though he felt as if she had. The air seemed to compress, closing the slight distance. He couldn't shake the sudden sense of impending doom.

He scrambled for an idea on how to keep McKenna safe in case this turned out to be a repeat of her attack. If anything were to happen to her because of those bloodsuckers, his hopes for salvation would go with her.

"It might have something to do with me," he finally

confessed, leaving the window to pick up his shirt. "If so, I honestly don't know what that reason is."

As McKenna quickly dressed, her arm bumped his, unsettling him further, taking his mind off the street. Her face was earnest, set and very pale. She couldn't have been more beautiful.

She tossed her hair. "They might be interested in me because you hunt them and have been visiting here. Could they want to get back at you for something you've done?"

Again, the cop in McKenna was evaluating all options, going over multiple scenarios in order to find answers that were never going to make sense in the long run.

"That's entirely possible," he agreed, tugging on his boots.

She watched him. "Will they keep coming? Do you know how many are out there?"

"Vampires, you mean?"

She stopped dressing. "Yes, given that they actually exist, and that's what's going on."

"You've seen the proof, McKenna. What more do you need?"

She didn't answer that because she couldn't, considering all she had been through.

"A city this size could support one nest or a whole slew of them," he said.

"Nest?"

"I don't have time to go into that. If the cop on the street was shooting at a vampire, that cop doesn't stand a chance of being around much longer. I have to go down there, and I have to do that alone."

"That officer is guarding my place. I'm responsible for what happens to him, so I'm coming along."

"You're mortal. Like the cop, you're an easy target."

Her hand was on his shoulder, inches from the sigils that felt as if they'd be the end of him if she wasn't.

"Wait," she said. "Now you're admitting to me you aren't mortal?"

He turned to her.

"You're immortal and you want me to fix that? Take that away? That's what you want from me?"

He choked on the word "Yes."

"Well." She took a big breath and let it out slowly. "As far as excuses for strange behavior go, that's rich."

Before he could reply, more shots sounded from the street below.

Chapter 16

There were advantages to being his kind of immortal. One of those perks was that he could move faster than a human's sight could perceive. Another one was his ability to direct the way things could go by talking directly to mortal minds.

Kellan used those gifts now.

Reaching the street before the building's door had closed behind him, he found the cop Miller had sent to watch over McKenna squatting down behind his cruiser, gun in one hand. There was no sign of what he'd been shooting at, only the usual lingering stink of vampires having been too close to the building.

Those suckers were not going to let up.

Mentally directing the cop to lower the gun, Kellan raced for the sidewalk, wondering if that officer had any idea what he'd been aiming at. There was no one else on the street. Not one car. As far as Kellan could see, nobody hung out of their windows to find out about the shots. In the aftermath of the gunfire, the area had gone quiet.

Kellan had no doubt that the bloodsuckers were present. More than one of them. He wondered why they bothered to hide.

What did you see? he silently asked the cop.

"Not sure," the man replied without seeming to notice he had more company. "It's too damn dark."

How many were there?

"Two or three. Maybe four. I warned them away."

Good job, Officer. You can relax now and wait for whomever you called to show up.

"Thanks." The cop stood and rested his gun on top of the car. "Backup will arrive any minute."

Kellan heard the sirens. Glancing to McKenna's window and not finding her there, he swore, dredging up a curse from Arthur's time. McKenna, rebel that she was, wasn't on the stairs, either, or in the doorway. Maybe she had listened to him for once.

Without reaching out to her with his mind, in case the vamps caught wind of that message, Kellan took off down the street at a run, tracing the scent of the suckers doing their damnedest to ruin his plans.

Instead of heading down the stairs, toward the street, McKenna ran up. Heart racing, she burst through the door to the roof. Familiar with the low-walled expanse, she rushed to the edge and peered over.

The street was clear. She identified the cop and the cruiser. Oncoming sirens were hard to miss. She didn't see Kellan.

No chromed Harley glistened in the streetlight. There was a marked absence of sound down there, when this part of Seattle was usually busy, whatever the hour.

"Where are all the people?"

Her fear escalated suddenly. She forgot to breathe. Chills on the back of her neck warned that she wasn't alone on the rooftop…and that wasn't good.

She spun around, both hands on the Glock, to face a whole lot of nothing.

"Come out. Let me see you," she called.

The shadows moved, stretched, seemed to flow toward her. Kellan's voice looped inside her head. What he'd said.

It might have something to do with me.

"FYI, he's not here." McKenna stood firm against the impulse to run away. The last time she'd faced off with a monster, two years ago, that monster had been a drug dealer with a gun.

"I'm getting tired of the likes of you, and find it hard to believe you might be what Kellan says you are."

She heard chattering, the kind of sound big groups of birds made when they perched en masse on a telephone wire. The strangeness of the sound brought more chills and a sensation of having ice water poured down her back.

She shook that off. "So what's it going to be? I start shooting and claim self-defense, or you step forward and tell me what the hell it is you want?"

The chattering ceased, leaving a noticeable hole in the quiet. After bracing herself by widening her stance, McKenna filled it. "Explain, or come and get me."

When the creature stepped forward, her first instinct was to scream.

Perceiving a silent cry of alarm, Kellan halted. The vamp trail had brought him to the entrance of the same alley he had visited before. He found this odd after what had happened there. Once the site of a nest or a pathway to a nest had been discovered, that site was usually, almost universally, abandoned. In a hurry.

An image of the calm, lined face of the gray-haired vampire returned to needle Kellan's mind. That vamp should have known better than to mess with him. Obviously the bloodsucker and its master didn't care to consider the ramifications of a Blood Knight's misplaced affections.

He didn't like anything about this new turn of events.

"All right. You got me here." He didn't bother to raise his voice. "Now what?"

Suddenly, with the force of a hammer coming down, he realized what was going on. His angry bellow shook the trash cans lining the alley. More bricks tumbled down from above him. These bloodsuckers had succeeded in separating him from McKenna. He hadn't often been a fool. Not like this. As he backtracked using all the speed he possessed, Kellan could almost hear the gurgle of bloodsucker laughter behind him.

He streaked through the rain that had started to fall, damning himself for playing into the bloodsuckers' hands. What he still couldn't figure out was why they were going for McKenna.

Two police cruisers were at the curb when he arrived at McKenna's apartment. Miller wasn't among the cops massing at her door. Looking up, feeling McKenna's presence high above the street, Kellan moved to the side of her building. Without showing himself to the others, he placed a hand on the brick, then a boot, and proceeded to climb.

He reached the roof in seconds.

Seconds too late.

The door to the stairs swung open. Miller stood there, gun in hand, finger on the trigger. "Where is she?" Miller demanded.

On the floor, near Kellan's feet, lay McKenna's gun. Nothing else. No sign of her.

As the detective advanced, Kellan closed his eyes and sent his senses skyward.

Darkness filled McKenna's vision. Her body ached from the rough grip of too many hands holding her down—bony hands that forced her to believe what Kellan had been telling her about vampires was true.

She hadn't got one shot off. Before she could pull the trigger, a gang of them had jumped her from behind. More of them had come from both sides of the roof. Too many of them to count. Gaunt figures with ashen faces and dark, inhuman eyes exhibited features she supposed bore some resemblance to the people they had once been. No one would have mistaken these freaks for people now. Not living people.

Stunned by the sight of them, she should have fired. If nothing else, the sound would have alerted the officer down below. These monsters had been so damn fast, they were like a blur of moving darkness. They were on her in seconds. She didn't have a chance to do anything to save herself before they carried her away.

It was too late.

Too damn late.

She opened her eyes slowly, disoriented. Her lips wouldn't move. Neither would her limbs. Her abductors had done something to keep her quiet. They'd made sure she couldn't struggle. Drugs, maybe. She had lost the feeling in both arms. Her legs weren't faring any better. The only movement she managed was blinking her eyelids.

Her face was wet, which meant that she was outside in the rain. How these creatures had got her off the roof was a mystery, with an officer on the street. Someone in this building should have noticed a pack of vampires carting a body down the stairwell if they had chosen that route.

She was at their mercy. A prisoner of the dark side. Kellan had warned her about this. He had tried to warn her, anyway. She was screwed for being born with a stubborn streak and for being independent. All she had left were her reasoning skills, but what good was a mind that worked well when only one thought kept repeating?

I survived death once, only to fall right back into Death's grimy hands.

If offered a choice, McKenna would have preferred a bullet to the brain rather than death by vampire fangs. Or, God forbid, the thought of becoming like them.

Worse than death, Kellan had once said to her, before she began to comprehend the truth.

Given that that much of his story was real, how about the rest of it? How about him?

Immortal?

There was no such thing. Immortality was a concept reserved for fantasy. No one lived forever. Not even close to that. Although half the things Kellan said might have been true, the other half remained suspect because her brain just couldn't wrap around the facts being presented to her.

Thoughts halted when the monsters carting her stopped. Either the rain had ceased, or she had been taken inside a building.

Why can't I move?

Why can't I speak?

Fear crept up her spine, forewarning that the nightmares were starting over. She had been paralyzed once before and had woken in a pool of her own blood. What would happen to her tonight if she survived?

Fight, Mac.

All she needed was the use of one hand. She'd throttle one of these freaks before the lights went out for good, and feel better for having done it. With a working voice, she'd shout "Kiss my ass!" and maintain her dignity to the end.

After she'd been shuffled a few more steps, the hands holding her let go. She didn't fall. McKenna found herself placed on a soft surface that gave slightly beneath her weight. A voice whispered to her from somewhere close by, and that voice was more frightening than anything else.

"Welcome to our humble abode, Mistress," said the freak she assumed must be the vampire grand pooh-bah.

"What did you do to her?"

The question rang in Kellan's mind like the chiming of a bell. Inhaling deeply, filling his lungs with the scent of what had gone on here and who had got to McKenna first, he finally looked at the detective.

"I can't talk," he said, turning to face south, peering over the side of the roof. "McKenna's life depends on timing."

"Where is she?" Miller repeated, stepping closer.

"Would you have me explain things you won't like hearing, or have me go after her?"

"You're not going anywhere until you explain this."

"Vampires have taken her," Kellan said.

Miller took another menacing step. "Don't toy with me, whatever your name is. I have a personal stake in this one."

Kellan turned back. "So do I."

"How could you? You don't even know her."

"I know enough."

"Like where she is?" the detective pressed.

"I'll have that location in a minute."

"Using a special skill set of your own, I suppose?"

"Yes."

"And what might that be?"

"Knowledge of the creeps that took her."

Through the light sheet of rain, Kellan sensed the trail the vamps had taken. That trail didn't lead him toward the alley he had visited earlier, but in the opposite direction. The idea of that alley luring him in a well-planned bait and switch created by vampires was a mind-numbing reminder of these vamps being guided by an intelligent hand. Either the monsters in this nest were masters at manipulation and the art of the dodge, or they had outside help.

Who would help a nest of bloodsuckers for any reason, and to such a great degree? Why would anyone want to sacrifice a human life to these creatures? What could be gained if someone did?

Questions stirred Kellan's insides until he seethed with anger. A previous remark replaced the ringing in his ears.

We do what we were meant to do in order to thrive. And we have waited here, as we have vowed to do.

Damn their pasty dead vampire hides, this had been their plan all along. Test him. Thwart him. The old vamp he'd met had hinted as much in a foreshadowing of McKenna's abduction. But why? Taking McKenna made no sense. They couldn't possibly know what McKenna housed inside her. So this vampire nest had waited for what?

What type of vow could they have made for them to await the opportunity to face him? To whom had such a vow been made?

Kellan's power, usually well hidden beneath a calm humanlike exterior, began to simmer. In another minute, if that anger were to be unleashed, he would become something else. Something more.

He preferred to make that transition alone.

"You can't help her," he said to the detective. "Not this time. I'm the only one who can."

Too much time had already elapsed. Looking the detective in the eye, pushing the weight of his will toward that man, Kellan said, "Stand down, Miller. Let me go. Trust that I will do everything in my power to find her."

Without waiting to see how the detective took his command, Kellan whirled, gathered himself and vaulted over the edge of the rooftop.

Chapter 17

"What the…?"

Kellan heard the detective's final words as he fell. Catching a ledge on the building's brick exterior with one boot, he pushed off, managing to grab hold of a pole supporting an awning three floors down. From there, he swung and dropped to the ground, landing silently in a crouch near the corner of the building, twenty feet away from the cops on the street.

This show of agility was a trick all of his brothers had performed on occasion. The ability to jump from high places without sustaining permanent injury served him well. Immortal bones weren't like those of human composition. His were flexible, fluidly pliable and incredibly strong. If broken, they healed quickly, just as his muscles and other body parts did.

Supernatural strength had got him through centuries of war and skirmishes, though he'd hoped, by coming to Seattle, not to have to call upon his powers again.

So much for that.

Speed was necessary once he hit the sidewalk. Too much time had been wasted on Miller. Each minute McKenna remained in vampire hands was a minute too long.

His sigils, despite the convoluted situation, flared with

the heat of an exploding star, sending shudder after shudder of electricity through him. With this power surge, his body shifted, morphing to a more fine-tuned appearance— harder, larger, each angle defined by the shadows he'd gathered to him for hundreds of years.

As he stood, his body thrummed with a power he felt to the roots of his hair. His eyes burned with a new kind of vision. Turning from the street, he heard a cop say "What was that?" But by the time the question reached him, Kellan had already left the scene.

He moved quickly, following the line of the curb, thinking, worrying about what this abduction meant without reaching a conclusion. The questions on a perpetual loop in his mind wouldn't stop. What possible connection did this nest have to McKenna? If they were trying to get to him, why take her when he was right here?

Fighting corruption and holy wars and monsters, as he had in the past, left him little tolerance for ambiguousness, and yet Seattle's vamp behavior eluded him. Annoyed him. Without McKenna in the world he would have no choice but to go on like this, as he was, forever. Only one off switch existed for him, and she housed it. If he didn't find that switch and McKenna were to die, living even longer seemed an inconceivably vast and empty idea to him.

One more corner.

The scent here was foul. Between the two large buildings closest to the road, the streetlights were out. Shards of their broken glass covered the ground. Kellan cursed in disgust. To hell with *trying* to find them. The filthy parasites were now leaving a path to their door.

And he was nothing if not ready to oblige their invitation.

* * *

McKenna's tongue felt heavy. Both eyes watered, and she almost managed to move a finger. Her ears worked just fine, and so did her brain.

Feeling heat in one toe, McKenna got excited. After numbness, anything was welcome except the sensation of heaviness on her chest. It was as if someone sat there. Breathing was difficult.

The scratchy sound of static, like the irritating noise from an untuned radio, began to fill the darkness. Clicking noises joined in. Damn it, were her abductors going to speak to her again, offering an explanation for attacking her twice?

Was this about holding a grudge?

She moved her left foot and withheld a shout of triumph. Then she moved her right leg. Working hard, exerting herself, McKenna curled her fingers into a fist, panting with the effort.

"It won't do any good."

The remark came as a grating tone that sifted through the static. McKenna worked even harder to gain control of her lips so that she could respond.

"He will come for you, of course," the voice continued. "Though we promised long ago not to harm him, old vows weaken considerably with time."

The freak was talking in words and sentences. Worse than that, McKenna had a good idea who this monster might be talking about. Kellan had faced off with members of what he called an unholy nest in a back alley. It looked as though he might have dusted a young vampire in the ICU that very night. Her abduction could be retribution for Kellan's actions if these creeps assumed Kellan cared for her enough to find her.

Did he care?

Did she give a damn if he did?

Yes. She did give a damn. Even numbed up in some dank, stinking room, thoughts of Kellan were what she clung to.

"You are another matter," her abductor pointed out in a voice composed of darkness.

His closeness demanded her full attention. McKenna wondered if he was going to hurt her, touch her. She wondered where Kellan was, and silently called out to him.

"We didn't know about you until the knight arrived," the freak said.

She whispered, "Knight?" as if she didn't comprehend what this monster was talking about. Obviously, whoever this was had seen Kellan's jacket.

"What were the odds of him finding you when no one else could? And so quickly?" he asked.

Kellan's words came echoing back to her. *I came here hoping you'd kill me.*

She had worried about that statement. After Kellan had made it, she'd concluded that he meant her specifically, as in…she'd be the only one who could do that awful deed. Taken to the extreme, the remark could also mean he had come to Seattle to find her. Only her.

The idea was as ludicrous as the existence of vampires. Yet vampires were real. And here she was, captured by them. She went over the list of strange events that had occurred since meeting Kellan.

The castle in her dreams. The woman in the mirror. A Blood Knight waiting on the street corner, and the immediacy of their attraction. Kellan's hungry mouth on hers, against a wall and on her bed. The emergence of monsters out of myth, in the shadows of this city. Wooden stakes. Rooftop abductions. Piles of gray ash on white hospital sheets. Kellan, looking fine in black leather.

She wanted to run her fingers down her scar the way Kellan had, to remove the pulsing pain. Each time she blinked, a searing bolt of fire struck a soft spot behind her eyes.

"There's no one to ask about you, and what's to be done," her host continued, still not showing himself to her. "After finding you once, the knight would easily do so again. There is no going back."

The pain behind her eyes made McKenna want to shout. She was afraid to shut her eyes, dreading what might happen if she did. This monster's voice seemed to be the catalyst of that pain. His remarks required too much concentration. His accusations were outrageous.

"Promises are tricky," he said. "In hindsight, this one wasn't smart on our part. If the knight had remained true to his causes, with a desire to continue his work in other places, things would have worked out. Neither you nor I would be in this predicament. But he changed. And he has come here."

"What are you talking about?" McKenna demanded.

The voice came closer, whispered in her ear. "Can we believe he hasn't told you, and that you don't know what he is?"

She managed the briefest shake of her head, desperate to understand, determined to get away at her first chance.

"You did not care who shared your bed?" her captor persisted. "Perhaps you couldn't help yourself, since you are connected?"

"Hunter. He said he's a hunter." Her voice was faint.

"Not just any hunter. *The* hunter. One of seven of them who are our very distant relatives."

She shook her head again.

"Yes. It's quite true. The Seven were fashioned as a superior breed, and born by drinking the blood of a special

Maker. The first Maker. As such, this knight looks down upon others of less fortunate origin."

"You're lying. I don't believe any of this."

"You must believe. This knight has come a long way to find you. He has crossed continents and seas, drawn by your soul. It's highly likely that he is both addicted and repelled by what he has come all this way to do, given the vows he and his brothers have taken to protect the innocent."

"Not true." McKenna fought with herself and her rising fears. The freak speaking to her was Kellan's enemy. She was in enemy territory. If this wasn't a monster with fangs, why didn't he show himself? Nothing he said explained anything. Not one shred of these events made sense.

Kellan, a vampire? A beast that drank blood? *Absurd.* Kellan was warm, sexy, kind and solid. His dangerous edge came from being a vigilante that fought the kind of freaks that preyed upon others.

These dark criminal thorns in Seattle's backside might be using her to get to Kellan, as Kellan had suggested. They were using her to lure him here, to them. She was the bait.

Shouting for Kellan to stay away would accomplish nothing. She had no clue where she was, and Kellan wouldn't, either.

If they planned on killing her, why didn't they get on with it?

"Trust is a unique thing," her creepy host said. "It's supposed to be sacred, even among thieves. That doesn't seem to be the case here."

He was so close, McKenna could smell him. The odor was a shocking combination of dust and decay.

He said, "Someone must have told him about you, girl."

McKenna squirmed and managed to lift her head.

"Here is the dilemma we face," he went on. "If the knight's life ends, my kind might flourish unchecked."

He made a growling sound that was scary as hell.

"On the other hand, if the knight were to cease to exist while in this area, it will be because we have broken our word to those who wield great power. Because we swore never to try to harm him, those powers would see any act of violence as a transgression on our part worthy of the severest type of punishment."

McKenna's reasoning skills were working well enough for her to see that both scenarios he presented were based on Kellan dying. *Why?*

The creep rattled on. "Who can conceive of what might happen then, or even guess if those powers still hold sway today? It's a big chance we'd be taking by harming a knight."

"This isn't about me," McKenna said.

"On the contrary, you are at the heart of it all."

"How?"

"No one else can deal him a final death, once and for all. Only you can do that. You, and you alone."

"That makes no sense. I won't. I wouldn't."

"If you don't kill him, this knight will stay and hunt. Some might think that would be better than having the rest of them come here to do the same. But who is to gauge what kind of destruction might occur if a knight doesn't get his way? Or if his brothers come running?"

"What brothers?"

"The six just like him."

Six. Like Kellan. The thought nearly robbed McKenna of breath. She pictured a line of tall, unbelievably sexy men, each of them sharing Kellan's aura of danger.

Or maybe these creeps had merely bought into Kellan's story.

She struggled to lift a hand, found that she could. "I told you I'd never harm him."

"You will pull the plug on his life if he wants you to. If he wills it, then it will be so."

"You believe he has that much control over what I do?"

"With the mastery of managing a puppet on a string."

The freak was speaking nonsense. Kellan's *will* had nothing to do with her. Hopping on his bike that first night had been her idea, as was her wish to take him to her apartment after that.

Kellan wasn't mesmerizing her into being attracted to him. Any woman in the city would have wanted to see all that muscled perfection up close. To believe he had control over her feelings and emotions was a ridiculous notion.

She had to speak to release the rising tension, and to quell her fear. "So, you're keeping me from him in case Kellan does or doesn't make me kill him? Either way?"

"If only it were that simple. Given our dilemma, when he comes for you, we're hoping that perhaps a bargain can be struck."

"If you think he would bargain with monsters, you don't know him at all." McKenna pushed herself to a sitting position. She wasn't tied down. Her limbs were free and warming up. The pressure in her chest was easing.

"Perhaps a pledge," her captor said. "Your life spared in return for this knight going away. Going home."

Would Kellan accept those terms? Would he want to save her, and in turn save himself?

"Why would he want to die in the first place?" she couldn't help asking. Kellan hadn't answered that question, either. They hadn't got far enough in their last conversation to clarify much.

"I cannot answer your query. No one can," her host replied. "Rumor has it that the key to ending his life was intended for another purpose."

"What key?"

Her heart thundered in her chest as pieces of an elusive puzzle snapped into place. Since everyone assumed she was to take Kellan's life, including Kellan himself, were they saying she was that key this monster mentioned, or that she knew where to find it?

"If no one has a say in what Kellan does, then why tell me any of this?" A quiver in her tone underscored those words.

"Merely passing the time," he replied. "Time is something I have a lot of."

"Until he takes it from you."

A moment of silence followed her remark.

"You understand that he is closer to us than to you, in terms of species," her captor finally said. "Such knowledge might have influenced your future."

"Didn't you say that he would find me, no matter what?"

The freaks were toying with her, unsettling her, and she didn't appreciate it. Anger began to simmer, battling for dominance with her fear.

"Well, it's too late to continue our little chat," the monster she hadn't yet laid eyes on announced. "He is here. Your Blood Knight has come."

Chapter 18

She was there. Here. In the basement of an old abandoned building that looked as if it might have been slated for demolition. Four stories' worth of windows were either boarded up or missing. From those empty brick sockets, Kellan sensed more than one set of eyes trained on him.

This was the perfect place for a supernatural showdown, and for hiding McKenna. With no lights in the area to offer even the dimmest glow, no one would see vampires coming and going, or dare to trespass on this block.

Without bothering to slow his pace, Kellan strode to the front of the building, then paused to glance up. Though vampires usually preferred dark, windowless basements, any dark space would do in the dead of night, and this one was as good as any.

He waited, feeling uncommonly edgy. Anger soothed the tattoos on his back. Fighting vampires was the task he had taken on for more years than he cared to count. Ridding the world of parasites was his purpose these days, and his body was in accord on this objective.

For someone who had lived through so many lifetimes, the wait this time for someone to acknowledge him was agonizing. Because of her. Because McKenna was in there somewhere, and she was afraid. She was calling to him with her mind. Warning him. Her fear was like a wave of terror.

Kellan widened his stance to keep from jumping the gun and going through that damn building floor by floor to find McKenna, ignoring possible consequences. He had to be patient a few more minutes, until the vampires came to him. Then he would tear apart every bloodsucker in his way—the whole damn nest of them—to get to her. If they had harmed one hair on her pretty head, he'd go ballistic and let his power shine. Tonight would come to be known as Seattle's own World War.

The aged, gray-haired vampire finally emerged from behind the cavernous front door with the same calmness the monster had exhibited during their last meeting.

"You didn't mention about being the spokesman for this nest when we last met," Kellan said, controlling his tone.

"A lapse on my part," the vamp replied, having taken less than ten steps past the entrance.

"You have her," Kellan charged.

The vampire nodded.

"Bring her to me."

"And no one gets hurt?" This was said with irony.

"Or everyone gets what they deserve."

Again, the vamp nodded. "We know you can back up that claim."

"Then why make me show you?"

"This is important. You need her. You will need to deal with us in order to save her."

"Are you so sure I'll wait that long?" Kellan snapped.

"Quite sure. You see, we know what she is and why you're here, so far from your home."

"If that's true, why wouldn't you have left her alone? Left her to do her part?"

"There are far too many scenarios to consider. In the meantime, she is our guest."

"She's mortal and in the dark."

"If that mortal body were to be done away with, what it hides will go with it. Isn't that right?"

Kellan fisted his hands. "You're threatening me?"

"You weren't meant to find her."

"And you mentioned something about promises the last time we met. Were those promises made to keep me from her if I did show up?"

The vampire smiled without showing fang, which made the answer quite clear.

"Someone," Kellan said slowly, "had the foresight to place a nest of vampires in my way, in case I wanted a change of scenery?"

"We did not know the full extent of things until recently. You do understand why the Reapers were created," the vampire said. "And now so do we. Perhaps no one could have foreseen what you might be planning, though."

"You dare to think you know my mind?"

"Enough of it to offer a bargain that might benefit us all."

"It will take an army to keep me from her for much longer," Kellan warned.

"An army of the dead," the vampire agreed.

Kellan unzipped his jacket, freeing his arms, needing the extra space to allow even more power to rise to the surface. In much the same way that werewolves transitioned from their humanlike forms to their more animalistic sides, his muscles rippled and stretched as if searching for some mystical connection to the moon hidden behind the clouds.

But this wasn't about the moon. It was about honor, retribution, the concept of *forever* and a Blood Knight's curse. It was about saving a woman he already cared for too much to lose in such a manner. He would risk anything to get her back.

McKenna...

The gray-haired bloodsucker took a reactionary step back. "You only have to go. Leave here. Leave us alone."

"And you will just let her go, when she knows about you and what hides in the shadows? When she was a law enforcer bent on keeping the peace, and your kind laughs in the face of that? I'm to trust that you will hold to that bargain?"

"Do you have a choice? *She* has her."

Without an inkling of who the mysterious *she* might be, Kellan recognized the significance of the threat. He sensed fear in this old vampire. As formidable as this bloodsucker was, and along with thoughts of an army of the undead as this sucker's backup, the building in front of Kellan hid something worse.

Kellan let his jacket fall to the pavement. Senses blazing, he searched the night, looking for answers, seeking the truth.

With a spasm of disgust, he found it.

They had left her to attend to other business.

Big mistake.

With feeling flooding back into her body, McKenna pushed herself off the mildewed thing she had been lying on and got to her feet.

So far, so good.

She swayed, not steady enough to take a step. Being surrounded by darkness didn't help her equilibrium. She had no sense of direction in the pitch-black space and no pinpoint of light to follow. In order to maneuver here, the monster that had spoken to her must have had the eyes of an owl.

Daring a step forward, McKenna held her hands raised in front of her. Inching slowly ahead, afraid the floor might cave in or contain a large black hole to nowhere, she breathed heavily, sucking in mold spores that had probably been here for years.

She found a wall. Something solid. She ran her hands over it, feeling for, praying for a doorway. Crossing one foot over the other, she continued sideways with a few brief pauses. In darkness this complete, up seemed like down, and vice versa.

Staring straight ahead of her, McKenna frantically searched for a way out of this icy-cold version of Hell. Thoughts of Kellan were the only warmth she was allowed. If anyone could save her sorry ass tonight, he'd be the one to try.

She stumbled, too scared to curse. Each move she made strengthened the odor of decay pervading this awful place. There could have been other bodies here. Hers might have been scheduled to join them.

She wanted her gun. She wanted fresh air and a flashlight. Most of all, she wanted to live long enough to see Kellan again.

"I'm here!" Her muffled cry was a whisper. Anything louder would have been suicidal.

But then… McKenna was sure she heard an answering voice. Not the monster's voice. *His.* Kellan's.

She hoped she wasn't imagining that.

Kellan heard McKenna's distant cry and fought to ignore it. The game these vampires were playing required that he stay focused. These monsters had called in a beast.

"You have outdone yourself this time." He spoke to the gray-haired vampire with his gaze trained on the bloodsucker. "And you've gone too far."

The vampire nodded, refusing to cough up an explanation willingly for why he'd called an extraordinary monster to this nest. Their ace in the hole was a Nosferatu, a fanged invader rumored to be one of Hell's minions. An executioner, and now a hired gun for the undead.

These bloodsuckers had raised a monster's monster from the deep earth. A defender of the dark and an enemy of the light, Nosferatu were unparalleled hunters in their own right, two-legged bloodhounds created for one purpose—the annihilation of the seven Blood Knights.

He had faced Nosferatu before, as some of his brothers had. In Kellan's favor was the fact that none of these hellhounds had ever been successful in a standoff with the Seven. He wasn't even sure why they tried.

"If you know anything, you'll realize that one of them can't take me down," Kellan said.

"Perhaps not in a fight," the old vampire agreed. "But they can destroy the things you work so hard to protect."

"It would take a very strong master vampire to handle them. You are fools for calling this beast here, and for believing any of you could manage such a creature."

"We didn't call it," the vampire said.

That confession came as a surprise. Kellan quickly adjusted his thoughts. If the master of this nest hadn't dialed up a Nosferatu, who had? To get here, the beast had traveled thousands of miles from wherever it had been hiding, without showing itself. The only way to accomplish that would have been for it to stow away deep in the bowels of a transatlantic ship bound for the States.

God help the crew of that ship.

"The bargain we proposed is your only option for ending this soon," the vampire across from Kellan suggested.

"We both know your word is worth nothing," Kellan returned.

"Yet some of us have adhered to our word about watching for you."

"So it would seem to one of us just learning about it. I wonder if you'd care to elaborate."

He had to think over what he had learned so far. The vampires wanted him to leave the city, forget his goal in coming here, and believe that if he did those things, they would let McKenna go.

The whole thing was preposterous. He could count the number of honorable vampires he'd met on the fingers of one hand. None of them would have called on a Nosferatu to do their bidding. The fact that these vampires had taken it upon themselves to do so, without admitting it, was unacceptable and unbelievably shortsighted. A monster like that in Seattle would mean the obliteration of dozens of innocent people a day in the name of sport.

"We did not call it," the vampire repeated, as if it had read Kellan's mind.

"Who did?"

"An ancient curse set into place before my time summoned this creature."

"You are uncommonly frank, vampire."

"Perhaps that is a fault."

And perhaps that's the source of the fear I smell on you. You don't like having such a beast here any more than I do.

"I will make a new bargain with you," Kellan said. "Bring McKenna to me and I will take her away from here. We will leave Seattle together. Old oaths will then mean nothing."

The vampire inclined its head. "I will take that suggestion to my Prime, though I fear it's too late to turn back the..."

"Beast?"

The vampire hesitated a beat too long for Kellan's liking. Then it said, "Perhaps you are the only one who can face such a creature now that it's here."

"And possibly Seattle's bloodsuckers will be taking bets on which one of us will alert the public to the presence of Others first."

"No one wants the beast here," the vampire said.

"Nor do they want me."

He thought the vampire shrugged.

"So you need my help in dealing with the monster when you've taken McKenna from me? That's rich. You have two minutes to bring her to me. Tick. Tick."

"Even a Blood Knight can't take us all on at once," the old vampire warned.

"Yet I'm willing to try."

"So be it." The vampire returned to the doorway, trusting Kellan enough to turn its back.

With that little chat out of the way, and with power rising within Kellan like an incoming tide of hot white light, Kellan bared his fangs and followed.

McKenna fell to her knees and scrambled to get back on her feet. Kellan was here. She felt him. She would have sensed him without the vampire's announcement of his arrival.

She had to find him, show him she was all right, help him take these suckers down. There would be no peace within her if he were to be hurt because of her. There would be no way to live with that, even though everyone around here believed she was going to be instrumental in doing him harm.

No time to worry about that.

Have to find a way out of here.

Groping again along the wall, pausing to shudder when

she heard shuffling noises nearby, McKenna moved on with her heart thundering.

Yes, Kellan. I believe you now. I've seen them.

Empty space beneath her hands meant the end of a long stretch of wall. At last. Relief swelled within her. Hope seemed to shine in the dark. McKenna closed her eyes, thanked her lucky stars. Finding a doorway was a start—one positive step in a night that had gone terribly wrong.

Heart in her throat, she walked forward, hugging her body, holding her breath for long periods of time. She was in a narrow corridor with few twists and turns. Daringly, she picked up speed, before stumbling again as she tripped over an object on the ground. She went down hard.

Pain shot through both knees. Something sharp had penetrated her jeans and the skin beneath. Her hand came away wet when she blindly searched for damage. Withholding a scream took all of her willpower.

The night seemed to hold its breath. Air around her began to pulse, pushing against her, pressing her back. A curtain of heaviness hung in the dark, as if the atmosphere had thickened. McKenna waited for what felt to her like hours. Her knees hurt. Breathing took real effort.

"Damn you," she finally whispered, crawling on all fours until she again found a wall and pulled herself to her feet. "Damn you all, and the fangs that made you."

Her bravery in continuing was rewarded with one small detail of consequence. A stream of air, either from an open window or door, reached her. Pulse skyrocketing, McKenna turned her face to that air, choking back a sob of triumph.

Chapter 19

Kellan's sigils were alive, and the pain was about as tolerable as having a ball of fire glued to his shoulders. Pain so hot it felt icy on the back of his neck. He wasn't supposed to save McKenna. Anger made his breathing harsh as he entered the dark hellhole with the force of a battering ram, his sense of McKenna growing stronger with each step.

Two black-eyed vampires met him inside the doorway with a pathetic display of stupidity and were reduced to ash before they uttered a sound. Two more vamps attempted to stop him in the hallway, with the same result.

Three more came at him, followed by another four, all of them of no consequence. He took them down with vengeful swipes of his sharp-ended stake, as if he were swatting at flies.

This kind of pathetic fledgling barrier couldn't last, he knew. Vampires didn't welcome invaders. Eventually older, stronger suckers would arrive to save the day. The building was large enough to house hundreds of them. An army of them, the old vampire had said.

Protecting their master was paramount to the survival of the nest. In essence, that master was their pimp, sending minions out to do its bidding. Several times more powerful than the others, and many times more resourceful, that master, often also called a Prime, kept tainted blood flowing while waiting to be served dessert.

Would this master be strong enough, intelligent enough, canny enough to deal with this situation wisely?

Another pair of unprepared fledglings approached, hissing through their fangs—mindless idiots with no inkling of imminent peril. He'd lost his sense of the presence of the Nosferatu. All he could bear to think about was McKenna.

As he turned a corner, he heard her shout. Whirling in the dark, Kellan saw her.

His heart soared. For the first time in years, he felt real joy.

"McKenna."

She rushed forward, toward his voice. Her face was bloody. Her knees were bloody. She was limping, and dragging one leg.

"I didn't... I hoped..."

"It's okay. I'm here," he said. "I have you."

McKenna's legs gave out the moment he reached for her. They were almost out of time, so comforting her wasn't possible. The master of this nest was here somewhere, and so was the Nosferatu. Kellan had seconds to get McKenna well beyond their reach.

He fought the desire to pull her close, to feel her body against his and to hold her, and withheld the impulse to tell her that things would truly be all right. He couldn't lie. Not even after everything she had been through. Comfort wasn't to be found in a place this dark, this evil.

The world had a hidden side, and McKenna would never be the same after witnessing it. Having already been wounded in her past, she'd have to rise high above this and accept that humans shared their precious earth with Others, some of whom were far less than desirable.

No one deserved such a rude awakening.

Retracing his path to the doorway with McKenna in tow, Kellan felt whatever strength she had remaining leave her. She weakened with each step and couldn't go much farther on her own. He'd have to carry her out of here, but with McKenna in his arms, they would be vulnerable. Nonetheless, saving her was all that mattered. Making sure she survived this night became his only goal.

As he swung her into his arms, she groaned. Her fierce independence had been compromised tonight.

Calling up his power for speed, Kellan rushed from the building. He reached the center of the cul-de-sac swearing beneath his breath, and tossed McKenna into the arms of the stern-faced man standing there.

Blinking back tears of gratitude for being able to see again, McKenna looked from the face above hers to the other. Derek and Kellan. Their expressions were grim. But there was another surprise in a night full of them. Kellan's face had changed. Kellan no longer looked entirely human.

Light beaded on his skin, the way water would if it had still been raining. Although the features were recognizable as his, they were somehow also *more*.

Kellan had become someone else. Something else. The logo on his jacket wasn't a joke. The vampire who had spoken to her in the dark hadn't been lying. *Blood Knight* wasn't just a label. It was a calling that separated Kellan from the human world. He was a creature who'd been created for a quest.

Was it wrong for her to crave someone like that?

He had seemed so human at first. Almost too good to be true. With her cheek pressed to Kellan's chest, she had felt the familiar beat of his heart and wanted to drown in that beat. She felt a longing for him now that was so deep it was bottomless, endless. Were those cravings real, or had he created them?

This was a being who walked like a man and talked like a man, but wasn't one. Nevertheless, Kellan was an opponent of the undead, and that was terribly important.

What kind of a being made vampires anxious?

One of the seven knights created to hunt them down.

He was talking to her silently, telling her that he was going to do his best to make this turn out all right. When she looked at Kellan, it was to discover that new shadows contoured his features. His eyes reflected an emotion she couldn't quite comprehend.

Derek was holding her tightly. His grip was firm and possessive, and yet the closest thing to safety she had ever experienced had been in Kellan's arms. Without Kellan holding her, feelings of hopelessness added to the fear icing her bones. The terror of the night's events threatened to overwhelm her.

Have to hold on.

Must hold on.

She glanced up to see that Derek's face was ashen, proving how shocked he was about confronting someone not entirely human. Derek didn't know about Blood Knights. He had no idea that if the monster had been right, Kellan and his brothers were designed as a kind of master race. Derek wouldn't know that vampires recognized and feared him.

So why had Kellan, whose past was supernatural, come to Seattle to end his life? And why had he chosen her as his executioner?

She wanted to be in his arms again. In bed with him again. She wanted his breath in her lungs, his mouth savagely taking control of hers. After having all that once, how could he imagine she could harm him?

She loved him.

God yes. She loved him.

"Take her to safety," Kellan said to Derek. He didn't look at her. She would have cried if he had.

Right then, she would also have given her life for his, traded her soul for his survival.

"Backup is on the way." Derek's voice sounded steady enough now that his initial shock had worn off. He'd obviously found a way to track them both to this house.

Kellan shook his head. "Not a good call. Look at what we face, Miller. Turn them back. Keep others away. They don't need to know about monsters until they have to. Maybe, if we're lucky, they never will."

Derek said stubbornly, "It's not what you think. Not the kind of backup you might be anticipating."

Kellan zeroed in on Derek's face. He tilted his head in a questioning posture and took in a lungful of air. Then, in a place as dark as anything the mind might conceive of, and while facing an attack by undead monsters with fangs… Kellan threw back his head and laughed.

"I should have known," Kellan said, as if Derek would understand and appreciate the comment.

"We've adapted," Derek soberly returned.

Kellan's smile quickly faded. "You're not at all what I would have expected."

"I'll take that as a compliment, even while knowing it wasn't one."

"Pure-blooded?" Kellan asked.

Derek inclined his head.

"And the backup?"

"A few of Seattle's finest. I hear them coming now."

"Finest what?" Kellan asked.

McKenna's focus darted from Kellan to Derek. Tension electrified the air, not all of it due to the threat housed in the building in front of them. Part of that tension was her fault. She hadn't stayed put when Kellan had asked her to.

In the silence following Kellan's last question, McKenna heard the buzz of a helicopter in the distance. On the boulevard, two streets away, a fire truck hit the horn. For a brief moment it seemed to McKenna like any normal night. But of course it was light-years from normal.

Vampires chose that moment to attack. Hell opened its gates. Ten, twenty, thirty of them poured from the building's windows and doors in a mad, oddly disjoined dash toward where she, Derek and Kellan stood.

At the same time, the moon broke completely free of cloud cover, bringing with it a symphony of angry shouts and guttural animal howls that echoed behind her.

Before she knew it, Derek turned. Taking Kellan up on the suggestion of getting her to safety, he headed for a side street as fast as he could, carrying her, ignoring every plea McKenna made to put her down.

She wasn't helpless now, just hurt and scared half out of her wits. In the past, on more than one occasion, she had been hurt far worse.

Finding a quiet place away from traffic, Derek finally set her down. After waiting to make sure she could stand, he placed a hand under her chin so that she had to look at him, and spoke to her softly. "I've always loved you, Mac, though I've also worried that things could never really work out between us. I have secrets, things I've kept from you. Sometimes remaining emotionally distant was the only way to deal with those secrets."

"What secrets, Derek?"

"You're about to see one of them now. Since you've already had more than one shock tonight, this one shouldn't make things too much worse."

He kissed her—a light touch of lips that lasted only for

seconds. Looking into her eyes, he said, "Get away from here. As far as possible. I'm begging you."

Moonlight flooded the street beyond the overhang where they stood. Derek touched her mouth with his fingers, then backed up into that light.

Already missing a jacket, his belt and a badge, he tugged at his shirt. Buttons pinged as he peeled the shirt off and his bare torso began to twitch and realign.

The terrible sound of bones breaking heralded a new emerging outline. Muscle contorted and danced as Derek shifted rapidly, smoothly, from one shape to another with an effort that left him panting.

His hair began to grow, as if months of time were rushing by. More hair dusted his chest and arms. As his face elongated, the question she had posed seemed to hang in the air. *What secrets?*

"Werewolf" was the last word Derek got out.

When he straightened, his brown eyes pleaded with her for understanding. Those eyes were the only recognizable detail in his new silhouette. Opening his mouth, he let out a growl that joined similar sounds in the distance.

"Derek!" Afraid she might be hallucinating, McKenna blinked slowly and rubbed her eyes. The world had come unglued. Derek was a goddamn werewolf.

The wall behind McKenna kept her upright as she grappled with this new revelation. Damn it, why hadn't she known any of this?

Derek held up a hand to keep her from approaching. Each of his fingers ended in a lethal-looking claw. He took the time to examine those claws before glancing again at her. With one more harrowing growl, the werewolf turned from her and sprinted away.

Any normal person would have fainted, whimpered, checked into the closest loony bin, McKenna supposed as she watched him go. The problem was that she had never been normal. Neither, she now knew for certain, was a good portion of the rest of the world. And that included Detective Derek Miller.

There weren't just good guys and bad guys to deal with. Suddenly there was an actual place between the two, a hazy area that covered more ground than anyone, except those dwelling within it, knew of.

Was she the only human left? Were the other citizens of Seattle what they seemed? Without powers or claws, did she stand a chance of helping in a fight that pitted vampires against werewolves and a Blood Knight?

"Shit."

Ignoring the sting of pain in her legs, McKenna pushed off the wall. She might be tired and injured, but there were weapons in her apartment, and she had to get them.

Like it or not, she was involved. She had made a promise once to protect and serve the people of Seattle, and stopping vampires from preying on those people was paramount to that cause.

The bloodsuckers moved like a black wind, infinitely quicker than the furred-up, teeth-baring werewolves that now lined the street. Their eyes were wild, dull and red-rimmed. All of their faces were skeletal. Collectively, these vampires put out signals of palpable wariness at the arrival of so many new opponents.

Fifteen werewolves had joined the fray. Detective Werewolf's friends. Miller would soon return to bump up that number. With McKenna safe, at least for the time being, it was with some relief that Kellan faced the vampires flooding into the street.

Werewolves coming to the aid of a Blood Knight wasn't a new experience. Weres and vampires were two opposite ends of the species spectrum, and ancient enemies. The dead versus the preternaturally alive. One had a Prime. The other had an Alpha. Both species had fangs. In the old days, they fought over prey.

The sound of bodies slamming together split the night. The Weres were large. Their muscles rippled. The vampires snapped yellow fangs and lunged in a blur of incredible speed.

The time for bargaining had officially ended.

Gathering his power, Kellan palmed the wooden stake in one hand and pulled a sharp silver dagger from his boot with the other. He faced the fanged horde with the silver weapon in his grip.

Come on, you bastards.

He missed a broadsword's balanced weight. But what good were swords these days against automatic weapons?

Honed by centuries of fighting, his arms tensed as he swung them, arcing with fluid, almost poetic motions. To the right and up, then left and down. Vampires dropped without realizing what hit them. So many he didn't bother to count. More emerged from the building in a vast, seemingly endless supply.

No Nosferatu presented itself.

Not yet.

Why the postponement?

The beastly Nosferatu possessed the strength of ten aged vamps with one-track minds. Some of these Weres would have gone down before such a creature, no contest, if they tried to deal with the abomination.

Right now, the Weres were holding up. Whether or not they had ever seen a vampire, they exhibited no signs of shock. Werewolves were a ferocious breed. In these, the fearless combination of cop and wolf served them well.

Fortune had been on his side tonight with a full moon overhead.

Kellan tore the air apart with his weapons, slashing with the silver dagger, dealing death blows to creatures unable to stand against the only metal with power over them. A weapon of reflected moonlight, wielded by a knight who had, like them, at one time been a man, before being chosen to fulfill a dangerous destiny.

"Rest in peace," Kellan whispered as each vampire exploded in a final death and the street became a funnel of ash. The werewolves weren't quite so polite. They went for the throat of their fanged opponents like wolves in the wild. Getting a firm hold, they shook their prey until vamp heads were severed from their emaciated bodies. Several of the Weres roared ferociously as they fought, as if this was what they had been bred for.

The vampire hordes had been decimated by the time the rain again started to fall. Able now to stop his choreographed dance of death, Kellan lowered his arms. His weapons were black. The asphalt was a dark dappled gray.

He tilted his head to listen. In the aftermath of the fighting, the silence rang in his ears. No vampire had been left standing, and no evidence of the carnage remained. It was as if the battle had never taken place.

The Were pack, still numbering fifteen, stood beside him. In front was a rangy, brown-pelted Were that finally uttered a soft growl of victory. Miller. Pack Alpha. As a full-blooded Lycan, with the purest wolf blood running through his veins, the detective was werewolf royalty, and knew how to mask his scent from an immortal.

Minutes passed without any hint of movement, though none of them let down their guard. Then, from the yawning, darkened doorway of the hellish abode, the gray-haired vampire reappeared, its black eyes on Kellan.

"You have friends," Gray-hair observed. "With more in the distance, circling closer. Round one has to end here, knight. I'm sure your furry friends would agree, given their present state."

"You'd like to keep your hiding place secret," Miller said after slipping gracefully back to his human form.

"We all have something to hide, do we not?" the vamp returned.

Kellan stepped forward, his gaze steady on the old bloodsucker. "You will leave her alone."

"That is not my call."

"Make it your goal or I will burn this place to the ground."

"Hell, I'll do that for you," Miller interjected. "Get rid of the rest of them all at once."

The vamp's eyes searched the half-naked detective. "The consequences of that would not suit you or this city, I promise. Do not mistakenly assume that we are alone in this place."

Kellan stopped Miller's heated comeback by raising a hand. The old vampire's warning was a pointed reminder of the existence of more nests like this one tucked into Seattle's shadows. Already he'd seen more vampires here than in any other city he had lately visited. If there were more, heaven help them all.

"Leave her alone," Kellan repeated firmly.

Sensing Miller's agitation, Kellan kept his hand in the air, a gesture that Miller thankfully heeded as half of the Weres behind him turned their heads.

Wailing sirens were closing in and almost on top of them. Police sirens. The approach of more law enforcers wasn't what had Kellan worried, though, and Miller's wary change of expression told him the Lycan sensed the same thing.

As he and Miller turned around in unison, Miller said, "Holy mother of…" without finishing the remark.

Glock in hand, shirt torn down the front, jeans bloody at the knees…and showing off her throat bruises in the same way some people might display a fancy diamond necklace, McKenna Randall advanced like an avenging angel.

Before anyone reacted, she fired five shots.

Chapter 20

All five bullets hit the vampire in the doorway, knocking him back. The bloodsucker glanced down. Covering the chest wounds with both hands, the creature looked up again with a withering expression.

"That's for the less-than-stellar hospitality," McKenna shouted, hating the creature with every fiber of her being. "And for ruining my night."

Kellan was beside her before the others at this party had time to blink. Though his expression was grim, McKenna was glad the rest of him looked fairly normal again. He had tucked the Blood Knight persona back inside where it was less obvious and more user-friendly to the crowd gathered around him.

Kellan wanted her to lower the gun, but she wasn't finished here. She wouldn't be finished until every last one of the black-eyed bastards inside that bricked-up hovel were gone for good, as in wiped from the face of the earth.

Despite Kellan's closeness, she kept the gun aimed at the monster across from them, refusing to back off, ready to fire again if the vampire made the slightest move in any direction. If five bullets hadn't done the trick, she'd go for six.

Kellan had other ideas. Taking her by the shoulders, he

spun her around and stepped in front of her, acting like her own personal suit of armor.

She was unable to see around Kellan's broad shoulders. Whatever the vampire did now was out of view. Her goals shifted quickly, adapting to Kellan's closeness. She fought the impulse to jump him from behind and hurl herself into his capable arms.

Power continued to radiate from him with the warmth of a space heater. That power crackled like wayward electricity with nowhere to go and raised the hairs at the nape of her neck. Just looking at Kellan from behind had the impact of sticking her finger into a wall socket.

"I'm not used to surrendering," she said breathlessly, hurting from head to toe and everywhere in between. "I won't allow it."

"Bending keeps us from breaking," Kellan returned. "Your bullets are wasted on the vampires."

Leaning sideways to look, McKenna saw that he was right. The monster was still standing, uninjured after five good shots to the chest because the creep was already dead. An animated corpse. If weapons like hers wouldn't seriously damage vampires, the world would have to learn to whittle parts of trees into weapons that would.

With the shooting over, she felt light-headed and useless. No one was moving. The sirens right on top of them signaled the arrival of more cops. Doors slammed. Men were shouting, and all she could think about was how unprepared the good men and women of the Seattle PD were for finding out some of their brothers were werewolves, and that the city had buildings filled with the fanged undead.

"Time to go," Derek said.

Before he finished that clipped directive, McKenna was moving, following behind Kellan, holding his hand. The strange part was the direction they were taking. Instead of making himself scarce like the scattering werewolves, Kellan walked toward the vampire in the doorway. Dragging her feet did nothing to deter him. Begging him to get away would have been equally as useless when Kellan had something on his mind.

The gray-haired vampire in the doorway stared at them silently with a bland, colorless face. Five perfectly placed bullet holes were ringing the spot where its heart should have been. Seeing those holes made McKenna feel sicker.

Remaining calm was not an option. Doing nothing wasn't the plan. She raised the gun but didn't fire. Kellan laid his hand over the barrel to stop her. Without looking at her, he spoke to the vampire. "You didn't let all of them loose. Not by half."

"They were meant as a warning, not to kill you," the vampire said. "We both understand what the only thing is that can do you great harm."

The implication of that made McKenna's stomach turn over.

"There are so many of you that fifty were expendable?" Kellan asked.

The vampire's pale mouth contorted. "Replacements are being created as we speak."

Those words and the terrible threat behind them made McKenna take a step back.

"Hey!" a cop shouted behind them. "Turn around slowly, hands where we can see them."

Showing the briefest flash of its fangs, the vampire in the doorway backed away, blending into the darkness behind it. She and Kellan were the only ones left in the street. These new cops would shoot if threatened. They'd be anxious and anticipating trouble. In the past, she had often been on the other end of this kind of call. She knew exactly what to do.

Highlighted in the beam of several headlights, she raised her hands slowly with the gun pointed at the sky, wondering how she and Kellan were going to explain their presence here.

Turned out she didn't try. Couldn't have managed one word. Chills dripped down her back. Her mouth went dry. A trickle of blood from a scrape on her forehead stung her right eye, but there was more to digest. So much more.

The vampire was gone. And so was Kellan. She was alone on the street with a dozen cops, their service weapons drawn and aimed at her.

Kellan looked down from the rooftop above the dark street with reluctant satisfaction. *It's only for the time being*, he silently sent to the white-faced woman he would have done anything to protect. *In police custody you'll be safe, my beautiful lover.*

He had thrown her to the cops to keep her off the streets, figuring she'd eventually invent a way to extricate herself from this mess. Miller would help her. The good detective who, it turned out, was no ordinary human being, either, could come up with a satisfactory explanation for the inexplicable. Hell, Miller was probably used to doing that, given what he and his pack became every time a full moon rolled around.

McKenna's current state—her wounds and bruises, plus the ongoing investigation of an attack on her life a few nights ago—would also work in her favor. The sorting would take time, though, and time was what he needed to settle a few scores.

As he watched McKenna being seated in a cruiser, Kellan's heart ached. His mouth formed the shape of two speechless words. *I'm sorry.*

Studying the disappearing lights, he added, "I could

have kept you from all of this if I'd done what I came here for the first night we met. Now…well, now, I'm afraid that I can't."

If he'd done what he came here for, he would also have saved himself from the agony of putting himself to this particular test. With all his wounds, in his long past as a Blood Knight, he'd encountered few things equal to the pain of this moment. Being separated from McKenna Randall was like losing a piece of himself. And though his body possessed the ability to mend rapidly, his heart, he found, was destructible.

"You," a familiar voice growled from the street once the cops had cleared out. "Up there."

Kellan peered over the edge of the drainpipe.

"What kind of a son of a bitch would leave a woman to take the fall?" Miller spoke from the shadows below. The Were's exceptional eyes had found him.

"Can you think of a safer place for her than under lock and key?" Kellan replied. "If the fates were kinder, she'd remain behind bars for at least a night or two."

Miller huffed thoughtfully. "For Mac's protection, I'll concede to that making sense. After what she's been through and when left to her own devices, McKenna can be her own worst enemy."

Kellan waited, sensing this detective had more to say.

"After fighting God-knows-what by your side, can you tell me who and what you are?"

"Name's Kellan Ladd. Lately."

"An alias, I presume?"

"I liked it."

"And the *what* part?"

"Knight of the Round Table. Defender of the faith."

"This isn't the time for jokes," Miller said.

"I never believed it was."

Silence ensued before Miller spoke again. "What are you doing here, in my city?"

"Searching for something."

"Would you care to be more specific?"

"Afraid not."

"Why McKenna? Why involve her?"

"McKenna is tied to my search."

"Are you saying she can help you find the thing you're looking for?"

"I believe so. It was worth a shot, anyway."

"Or five of them," Miller quipped. "Dead-center in some fang-bearing schmuck's chest."

"I didn't mean to involve her." Kellan glanced at the roof tiles beneath him, thinking of McKenna with the gun in her hand, remembering her face in that moment and the look in her eyes.

He said, "Did you know about the vampires, Miller?"

"Not in numbers like this. But the calls coming in lately have been getting harder to explain."

"They'll get worse," Kellan warned, offering the detective a hint of Seattle's future with a Nosferatu hellhound on the loose.

"Is that a promise, or some Round Table shit?" Miller asked.

It was obvious to Kellan that the detective didn't believe his credentials.

"Their actions make it clear that they have plans," Kellan said.

"Then I'd like to suggest we do something about it."

"I applaud your willingness to face them again, Detective. Your pack did good work tonight, but this is my fight."

"You think so because...why?"

"This nest of vampires wants to keep me from finding

what I've come here to find. To that end, they're likely to do anything. As I said, it's my fight."

"And this is my city."

"Yes," Kellan conceded. "I don't belong here."

Again, the detective took some time before speaking, as though weighing all of his options concerning a being unlike any other he'd come across to date. There was agitation in his voice. "You're not like them, yet you don't fear them."

"Fear has no place in my line of work."

"Which is?"

"Keeping the peace. Like you. Trying to, anyway, in places where aid is needed."

Miller stepped clear of the shadows, looking up, still shirtless. "You're a vigilante, then? I have to worry about what you might do in the future?"

"I wouldn't want to give the wrong impression by answering that question in any other way than to promise that you won't have the pleasure of my company for much longer."

"Good. You make me nervous," Miller confessed.

"Really? A Lycan of your lineage?"

"Even werewolves have common sense, Kellan. Especially Lycans. You didn't seem concerned when we showed up tonight. Maybe you've met a few of us before?"

"Many times."

"No love lost between you and my kind?"

"No lasting animosity, either."

Miller nodded. "You won't tell me more about your agenda?"

"Speaking about it is forbidden."

"By whom?"

"The rest of my kind."

"Christ. There are more of you?"

Miller's remark echoed between the walls of the buildings, unanswered. The detective sighed as moonlight once again shone through a hole in the clouds. He rolled his neck as if his muscles ached.

"You're not telling me half of what's going on," Miller said with a long look at his hands.

"Not your fight," Kellan reiterated. "But I thank you for helping here tonight, and am in your debt."

The Lycan raised a hand, then closed and opened it several times, testing the sharpness of the claws that had appeared.

"Does that hurt?" Kellan asked.

"Like hell," Miller replied.

"Then it's good you have so many good days in a month."

Miller smiled sadly. "I wish that were true."

Lifting his face to the moon that lured him to join the world of the beast, Miller's body began its transformation with the sound of wet meat being slapped on a counter. Once his shift was completed and the man in him had been shoved to the background, he growled fiercely and turned away.

Kellan rocked back on his heels, deep in thought and attentive to a new sound. Through the connection binding him to McKenna, he heard her call his name.

Crouching on one knee, he ran both hands over his face, then through his sheared hair. For him, McKenna's voice was like Miller's moon. Her lure was overwhelming. Her call was a temptation that pierced his heart. His anxious body urged him to give in and go to her, but the sigils on his back hadn't lost their burn.

"Can't," he said aloud, answering McKenna in a way she couldn't hear.

He had placed her in police protection for her safety.

Vampires couldn't touch her there, true. Yet that was only part of his reasoning for allowing cops to take her away.

He had also done so to ensure that he couldn't reach her. He had allowed her to be locked up in order to keep McKenna Randall from a Blood Knight selfish enough to have endangered her in the first place.

Chapter 21

McKenna knew the two cops sitting across from her at the precinct. Thankfully, her cuffs had been removed.

Her gun lay on the table. In the two-way window behind the table, her image reflected the ravages of a horror tale.

"Randall," Ben Thompson said, addressing her in the way all the cops addressed each other, by last names. The tall, brown-haired cop had been a rookie at the same time she was. Now she looked at him for signs that he might also be something else besides a cop. Something furry on the inside.

"Miller just called in. He asked us to hold you until he can get here," he said.

"You didn't read me my rights."

"What rights would those be? The right to look like something the cat dragged in?" Gene Wilson, another cop, asked. Though Wilson was in fighting shape, the man's hair was now peppered with gray. His practiced cop face almost completely hid the hint of a smile.

"You're not under arrest, and you know it," Wilson continued. "As far as we're concerned, the permit you have for that weapon allows you to engage in a little target practice near abandoned buildings, though your choice of this location left something to be desired. There wasn't one damn light out there, Randall. What were you thinking?"

He eyed her sheepishly. "You didn't have anything to do with those shattered streetlights, I suppose?"

"If I'm not under arrest, why am I here?" she countered.

"We had to answer the call and follow procedure."

McKenna rubbed her wrists. "The cuffs were tight."

"The cuffs were on you in case anyone was looking," Thompson said.

"Given that it was so damn dark, how could anyone have seen what you did or didn't do?" McKenna tossed back.

Wilson shrugged. "I guess you've got us there. Seriously, we honestly didn't recognize you at first. I doubt if anyone here could have. So the question we have now is… what the hell happened to you?"

"I fell down a few stairs that were in dire need of repair and hit the ground hard."

"Why did you fall?" Wilson asked.

"It was pretty dark, and I thought someone was chasing me. After the attack in my apartment, I got scared."

Both cops nodded. Wilson said, "We will get to the bottom of the other night. Have no doubt about that. Right now, though, you need some towels. And maybe some coffee."

"I'm a nurse these days," McKenna said. "I'm fine. And I'd rather go home."

"Not happening until Miller arrives," Thompson told her. "I'll see to those damp towels myself, and rustle up some Band-Aids. Will you be okay here for a few more minutes?"

McKenna sat back in her chair, too damn tired to do anything but nod. As soon as the cops left her, she put her head on the table and closed her eyes, wondering where Kellan was and if he would return. Wondering if she would see him again, and why he had left her to fend for herself after rescuing her from vampires. Wanting to see him. Hopeful she might.

"Kellan…can you hear me? Why did you leave me here?"

For now, she was a prisoner whether she liked it or not, and trapped in a loop of her own making. The wrong person would eventually come. Which Detective Miller would show up to spring her? The man who had confessed to loving her, or a goddamn werewolf?

There was no use in pretending he'd stay away, because that wasn't going to happen. Even if it were only to catch sight of McKenna from a distance, Kellan had to make sure she would get through this night with her soul, if not her body, unscathed.

Was he being selfish again by waiting around? *Absolutely.* He was just too far gone to care. McKenna Randall had taken hold of his heart and squeezed. She alone, out of everyone he'd met since taking his vows, moved him.

After parking the bike at the curb, he leaned against the corner of the precinct building with one shoulder to the wall. Cops came and went, though the hour was late. Actually, he wasn't sure what time it was. Other than when extremely necessary, he never bothered to keep up with hours and minutes because those were things he'd always had an abundance of.

Tonight, he had to face facts. His plan to stop time altogether had backfired, along with his reason for coming to Seattle. When the vamps had taken McKenna, and after finding her in their nasty lair on her feet and fighting, he realized that he loved her, and that he didn't want anyone to hurt her, ever again.

I mean it, McKenna. For what it's worth.

She was in this building, surrounded by officers, many

of whom probably still cared for her. Her character was strong. She was continually fighting to preserve her place among these people.

He wasn't sure what he would do next. Wait? See if Miller's common sense would fail him and he'd allow McKenna to go home when she insisted? Surely she would insist. And as to what might be waiting for her there, without a Blood Knight on guard…well, no Lycan he knew of was strong enough to fight the Nosferatu on his own.

Kellan turned his head.

Miller had arrived and was parking his black car beneath a large portico connected to the precinct. The detective was alone and fully dressed in jeans and a blue shirt. Miller didn't have to worry about the big silver disk in the sky causing an untimely shift when the werewolf wasn't concentrating. The fact that Miller seemed able to shift shape at will had to be some kind of a specialized purebred Lycan trait.

Sensing Kellan there, Miller paused. Looking a bit ragged around the edges, the detective gave Kellan a warning glare before entering his work domain by the front door.

Let him have her, Kellan told himself. Miller was a man most of the time. McKenna could handle the rest.

A last warning came for him to heed his own advice and get the hell out of there before anyone else saw him.

There was a Nosferatu to catch. He alone had the power to face such a creature. He knew what to expect because he'd done this before. McKenna would then be safe from the worst thing on a long list.

On Miller's heels as an invisible blur, Kellan headed into the heart of police central.

McKenna sensed Kellan getting closer. Her heart thundered. She got to her feet in anticipation of his arrival with a knot of hope stuck in her throat. But it wasn't Kellan who came through the door. It was Derek.

"I thought…" she began, realizing she was about to say something she might regret.

Derek closed the door behind him and leaned heavily against it. "Were you expecting someone else, Mac?"

The night had also taken its toll on Derek. His face was lined. Strands of dark hair, once again its normal length, curled over his forehead. Derek was tired and out of sorts. God only knew what being a werewolf was like.

She would have given a lot to have been able to make Derek feel better about what happened on that dark street with Kellan, yet saw no way to begin.

"He's outside," Derek said.

Her heart beat faster, harder, with that news. McKenna wasn't sure if werewolves could pick up on things like that, though he had obviously read her mind.

"It's him, then, Mac?"

She understood what he was asking and answered honestly. "Doesn't really matter. He won't stay."

"Until he goes, though, he's the one?"

"I'm not sure what I feel. That's the truth."

Derek shook his head. "Hell, your pulse is accelerating with the mere mention of him."

Yes. McKenna felt the drumming in her neck without having to reach for it.

"You realize he's not anything remotely human," Derek said.

She stared him down, driving home a point about people not always being what they seemed, including Derek.

Derek sighed. "Like I said, there were secrets. Maybe I should have trusted you with them. We have to be so careful these days."

"Will you take me home?" McKenna purposefully

avoided adding more emotional turmoil to the list they were already dealing with. The knot in her throat had slipped to her stomach.

"It would be better if you stay here until morning. I'm not the only one who thinks so," Derek said.

McKenna glanced down at herself. "I need a shower and the bandages the guys were going to get for me."

"We'll get those bandages and some clean clothes. You can shower in the locker room."

"With you guarding the door?"

A rush of cool air preceded any reply Derek might have made. The door to the interrogation room had opened, shoving Derek aside. A voice much deeper than Derek's and twice as welcome to her said, "I don't see why he'd need to stand guard, since I'm already inside."

"Damn it. How did you get in here?" Derek's voice was close to a growl.

Facing McKenna calmly, Kellan said, "Miller is right. You need to stay here. Nowhere is safer for you tonight."

Her body was already being sucked into that impossibly strong voodoo Kellan had going on. There was no way she could have stayed away from the man who had heard her silent calls and returned for her. He was here, and because of that McKenna understood he might have left her to the cops with only her safety in mind. Having her end up in police custody had been part of his plan.

"Hell, McKenna. Shout if you need me." Derek left the room, and that was a good thing.

She wasn't in control of her reaction to Kellan, hadn't resisted him from the start. They were connected by an unbreakable thread that made it impossible for her to avoid his almost mystical allure.

Limping over to him, then standing close enough for

their chests and hips to touch, she looked up, spoke softly. "What do you want from me?"

"Nothing less than your soul," he replied.

And McKenna believed him. Deep in her heart, she knew he had spoken the truth.

Derek's warnings seemed distant, hazy and irrelevant. Kellan's blue eyes were searching hers for a reaction to his confession. His unwavering gaze brought familiar heat.

He touched her face, gently dusted away blood caked on her forehead. His fingers slid to her temple, to the scar she had forgotten about until right then.

"I can make you forget," he said, each word like a caress, like the brush of silk over sensitive skin.

"Forget what?" she asked.

"Everything. All of this."

"Will the making-me-forget part happen before or after you're finished messing with my soul?"

Kellan's face reflected his seriousness.

"Why me?" she asked Kellan, thrilled over the tender way such a large man touched her, remembering what had come after that same kind of touch in her apartment and on the street. Remembering also the sheer ecstasy of having him enter her body during that street-side encounter. Reliving each blissful thrust.

With her eyes shut and Kellan's fingers so very near to her mouth, the world began to turn. White walls again appeared in her mind, rising to impossible heights. The sound of water tinkled over the image of a shadow-filled garden. Moonlight pierced the clouds, cold, silver-bright. In that moonlight, beside a fountain, stood the figure of a man who was looking at her, raising a hand, whispering her name.

When her eyes opened, her heart was accelerating. Shudders accompanied each beat because more pieces of that strange, elusive puzzle were falling into place. The picture grew each time she viewed it, and yet she had no warning about when the images would come. She had no fast-forward button.

Kellan's exhaled breath made the edges of that picture fade. His fingers rested on her mouth invitingly, seductively, causing a longing for him that electrified nerve endings and woke muscles too exhausted to move. McKenna couldn't hold on or keep her eyes open, and she needed to keep Kellan in focus. In another minute he might be gone.

"Why me?" she repeated with more force.

"There is no other," Kellan said. "No one else for me."

She was mesmerized by the special being beside her. She ached for him, craved him, loved him way down deep. In his arms she felt whole. On his face she saw light, and something else...

Truth.

With her eyes shut, McKenna let herself go, seeking and welcoming the rush of images bombarding her overworked mind. The only way to understand what was happening was to solve the mystery of these dreams. See where they led.

Steep castle walls rose in sheets of white stone that were ethereal in the moonlight. Beside them were the garden and the fountain. He was there, too...the faceless man, waiting as if he expected her.

She was walking toward him, careful not to trip over the hem of a long black gown that McKenna remembered seeing before.

What wasn't clear was whether she was in this dream or merely seeing with someone else's eyes. Was she tapping into a moment carved from somebody else's life?

The air in the fantastical garden was cold. Her breath preceded her like a fog. Although she walked briskly, she got no closer to the man. Her hand, someone's hand, shook, clutching the skirt of the dress. This was to be an anxious meeting.

The images began to waver in the manner of a desert mirage. White walls started to tumble. The moon disappeared.

"Wait!" McKenna shouted. "Wait!"

Strong hands shook her. Confused, McKenna found the precinct in chaos when she opened her eyes. Alarms were going off around her.

Kellan's elegantly chiseled face was so close to hers, McKenna saw little other than his eyes. They were shining with emotion. Nestled in that blue gleam lay hints of a great sadness.

"I promised that you'd never be hurt again," he said. "That promise didn't include the kind of damage I could do."

"Do what you have to. If these are to be our last moments together, I will at least have that."

Their mouths met with an impact indicative of hunger and rage. McKenna kissed him back, straining to be closer, reaching for him with both hands and fearing that their time was short. She was afraid of the look she'd seen in his eyes.

His breath warmed her on a night that had grown cold. The strength of his ardor bent her backward. Every bit of his hard body molded to hers as if two bodies could actually become one.

His tongue tortured her senses with the promise of more to come, but she didn't dare contemplate what lay ahead. This wasn't just a kiss. Was it their last? A final goodbye?

Kellan drew back abruptly, severing the connection. His whispered oath was the last breath to meet with hers.

"Please stay here, McKenna." Leftover passion made

his request seem harsh. "Believe that it's best. If not for yourself, do it for me."

Derek chose that moment to return from wherever he'd gone. He stepped forward when Kellan stepped back. Derek's firm grip on her arm kept her from following Kellan, who was heading for the door.

"Calls are coming in from all over the city," Derek announced, facing Kellan's retreating form. "Do you know what this is about, and why it's happening now?"

Kellan paused, answered. "It's because of me. They are shaking things up in order to shake me loose."

"Who the hell are you to be so important to these monsters?" Derek demanded.

"I'm one of the first."

"First what?"

"Monsters."

Derek balked, blinked. "You're some kind of goddamn vampire?"

As he exited, Kellan glanced over his shoulder. "No matter what you care to call me, I'm about to become their worst nightmare."

"That shouldn't be hard," Derek called after him with audible animosity. "Since you're already mine."

Chapter 22

Kellan stopped when he reached the street. Light rain was falling. The wind had picked up. He stood at the curb listening, gathering himself for what lay ahead, and wondering about what the vampires were trying to prove with this open display of aggression. The old one said they weren't out to kill him, but alerting humans to their presence wasn't to any vamp's benefit when secrets and shadows were what kept bloodsuckers fed. In light of that, what could they hope to gain by openly causing chaos?

The night was alive with the shrill sounds of sirens. Police. Fire. Ambulances. His proposal to the vampires had been to take McKenna away from all this and out of their reach. No vamp he'd ever heard of cared about adhering to ancient promises, especially those leading to exposure.

He couldn't wait to meet the unusually sharp mastermind of this nest. That meeting would be item number two on his list. First, he had a beast to hunt down—a particular nasty two-legged beast.

He opened a rift in the night with a flash of lightning-like power that allowed him to see beyond his extensive list of senses. "Come to me," he said. "It's time for that chat."

The response was immediate. Not in words. Nosferatu had long ago lost the ability to speak. This answer came in the form of an abnormally icy wind.

Kellan turned into that wind. Discerning the location of the beast was easy. Tuning McKenna out was another story. Her voice sang in his mind. Her calls tugged on his soul. His name, spoken from her lips, brought both excitement and pain. The images haunting her had spiraled her closer to the truth. His truth. And hers. Still, even he could not see it all.

The Harley roared like a lion when he fired it up. Bits of polished chrome glistened under the lights as he raised his boots. He shook McKenna from his mind. If he thought about her again, he might turn around and go back. How many people might die tonight if he did?

Anger bubbled up inside him. Perhaps, he thought, his Makers would be pleased to know McKenna's allure was a successful trap that forced him to reconsider his goal. If his Makers had the foresight to look so far ahead, and he survived his initial impulse to end what was endless, maybe his next step would be to track those Makers down. Make sure they were gone for good.

He rode with purpose toward the scent of death in the distance. *Not long now.*

Turned out the battleground was going to be an old, no-longer-used bus station on the west side of the city. At least that was in his favor. No one would be around.

For the first time in ages, instead of trying to ignore the power etched into him, Kellan called on the full strength of that power. He'd have to deal with this crazy sucker quickly and hope his sigils would aid him when aid was needed.

Driving the bike into the building through a gap in the walls, he braked on the concrete in a squeal of tires. He was off the Harley and standing tall beside it when the Nosferatu stepped from the shadows.

Remembering this thing didn't make facing one any easier. Hell no. Nosferatu were grotesque terrors designed to represent the worst part of the dark human psyche. Made of mounds of undead flesh stitched together with spikes of sharpened horn, it was huge. Where a mouth should have been, the gaping hole had been filled in with some sort of rusty connectors. There were no eyes, merely two deep, empty sockets. Those sockets were trained on Kellan.

Kellan braced himself. This one was worse than others he'd come across in the past. Leather cuffs wrapped its wrists. A black helmet caressed its ugly head. Its clothing consisted of little more than a draping of mottled animal hide.

In this sucker's right hand was a long, narrow sword. Not silver—nothing that shone in the brief flash of moonlight passing through clouds and the holes in the roof. The weapon carried the dull scent of whittled animal horn.

Nosferatu, like other forms of the walking dead, detested metal. For most preternatural species, silver in any form was deadly. This Nosferatu, with its long sword, seemed to be stuck in olden times. But these weren't mindless creatures. They were animated by the hatred of whoever had sent them. These beasts were supernatural minions doing the bidding of a master puppeteer.

Time and time again, these beasts had been called out of their dark dungeons with a specific quest, when killing a Blood Knight just wasn't possible. Whoever had sent the beast either didn't realize how this would go down, or wanted to enjoy the show.

But if the local vampires hadn't sent it, who had? What did the old vampire mean about an ancient curse rising on its own?

"Here I am," Kellan said. "I believe you've come for me?"

The wind whistling through the walls accompanied the rise of Kellan's power. Electricity streaked across the surface of his skin as he began, measure by measure, to shed his earthy disguise.

His skin whitened. Ripples of extraordinary muscle expanded his outline. Kellan's sigils, as if seeking freedom, began to burn through his clothing, free to do what they were designed to do.

Kellan ripped off his jacket and smiled. "You wanted something?"

The monster rushed forward. With a skilled knight's dexterity, Kellan sidestepped the sword's first dangerous thrust. Faster than anything that large had a right to be, the beast whirled to strike again. The point of its sword missed Kellan's midsection by inches.

Kellan's power refocused. He nodded his head as if giving the thing he had become over the centuries permission to appear. It was that knight, the Blood Knight, who bested the ever-expanding lineup of villains. That knight now rallied to his call.

His spine crackled with live energy and light. His body lengthened until he stood four inches taller. Then his face began to morph, taking on what Kellan knew were the aspects of the angel the knights were created to emulate—Michael, God's champion.

As the beast returned in a smear of determined speed, Kellan raised his arms. Old battle scars, long hidden, reappeared to crisscross his skin. His sigils, carved in blood, burned with the ferocity of the hellfires from which this Nosferatu had sprung.

Though terribly fast in reality, the beast seemed to lumber in slow motion as Kellan's transformation was completed. The perception of time slowing down was another Blood Knight trick that allowed them to see more clearly. Because of it, Kellan was the more frightening thing now. He had become the nightmare he had told Miller he was.

With relative ease, Kellan reached out a hand and caught hold of the monster's sword. The edge of that weapon sliced through his skin, sending up a spray of blood as black as night. As that spray hit the Nosferatu, the beast stopped in its tracks with a soulless groan of surprise. Then it began to wail.

"You see," Kellan said without anger or malice, "I fight for the righteous. And that is what sets us apart."

He stole the sword from the beast as it clawed at the blood on its face. That face began to sizzle. Drops of Kellan's blood burned their way through the monster's unearthly flesh and bone as if they carried the properties of holy water.

Turning the sword, gripping the hilt, Kellan plunged the tip into the monster's throat. He waited as the beast writhed, then slowly hefted his silver knife.

"Gold, covered in silver," he said. "I am not immune, but long ago learned to bear the pain."

With a single well-placed thrust to the monster's chest, in a direct hit to the place where the beast's heart should have been, if in fact it had ever been alive, the Nosferatu shattered and fell apart as if it hadn't been solid in the first place.

Quiet returned. Moonlight fled. Rain pattered on the roof, some drops finding their way inside. The Nosferatu's remains smoked, caught fire, then disappeared, leaving black scorch marks on the concrete. Kellan waited until no other evidence of the monster's presence remained, then whispered, "Go in peace," as his wounded hand began to mend.

They had left her alone in the precinct interrogation room. Mistake number two.

McKenna strode through the hallway of the police station as calmly as she could, hoping to avoid unwanted interest in her flight from custody. Outside, she paused only seconds to listen to the sirens and formulate her own ideas about what was going on in Seattle. Then she hit the road.

She had no money for a cab. She was dragging one leg that hurt worse now than it had an hour ago. Running was out of the question. So was hailing a passing police cruiser. She was blocks from the hospital and farther from the apartment she never wanted to go near again.

In their biggest mistake of the night, after cuffing her in the first place and then leaving her in that room unsupervised, Officers Thompson and Wilson had left her gun on the table. The arrest had been a ruse arranged by Kellan and Derek. She had been part of this force, and they had treated her as such.

That gun was now in her hand.

McKenna had no idea what time it was. Night was night, and this one seemed endless. The rainfall was steady, quickly soaking both her and the ground. She was underdressed and chilled to the bone before managing to make it one long city block.

Gritting her teeth, she tucked the Glock into her waistband to keep it dry, leaving her hands on it just in case. Seattle had become a foreign place where monsters roamed and people with exemplary fighting skills killed vampires. Oh yeah, and some of the Seattle police force were werewolves.

So, what was her next move? She didn't have any idea where anyone was. Her cell phone was long gone. The only place she could think of to use as a temporary regrouping spot where Kellan might more easily reach her was Seattle General. Even looking the way she did, she'd find shelter there. Everyone who mattered would know where to find her if they decided to come looking.

She limped on.

In spite of the late hour, there were cars on the streets and people on sidewalks. Hidden under their umbrellas, the few pedestrians she passed paid her no mind. That suited McKenna just fine. Out here in the open, she could think. Breathing was easier. The rain seemed to wash away a portion of the fear coating her like thick, supernatural syrup.

By the time she had limped halfway to the hospital, McKenna realized she was truly spent. The rainfall had got heavier, and the downpour hampered her vision. She had to look at the ground, at her feet and a few inches ahead. Her hand, clamped to the gun, started to cramp.

"I could use a little help here," she muttered, fighting on, taking one labored step at a time. "Also it would be nice if everyone was exactly as they seemed."

What about her, then—the ex-cop ER nurse with a penchant for bad boys on motorcycles, and for finding trouble wherever it lurked?

Those thoughts bolstered her determination to make it to the hospital's revolving front doors. She just had to get her body on board.

Blinded by the rain, so cold she had become a block of ice, McKenna plowed on, muttering to herself so she wouldn't break spirit. Head down, and leaning into the wind-driven raindrops, she didn't see the object in front of her until she had rammed into it.

He had found her.

McKenna was again in his arms—if not willingly, then out of necessity.

Though he had again tucked his own power inside, Kellan sensed the pain radiating through her limbs. Her knees were bloody. One of her ankles was injured. The cut on her forehead was sore but had stopped bleeding.

McKenna was bruised, battered and speechless. She had begun to doubt everything and everyone. And rightly so. Kellan knew he was pushing things by finding her like this and surprising her in this way. Yet she had called out to him with her mind. She was silently repeating his name now, over and over in the manner of a chant. She was fighting to accept him in the way she wanted to, unable to reach a decision as to how to react after everything that had gone down.

"It's all right," he said to her. "I'm here, and I'm sorry. My intention was never to let things get this far off base."

"I'm no weakling," she said. "No freaking damsel. This isn't like me. I hate this." She pointed to her leg.

"No one believes you're anything like that," he said. "How did you get out of the station?"

"I walked."

"Right out from under their noses?"

"There was too much going on for them to pay attention."

"What good is Miller if he can't do two things at once?" Kellan added a silent *Damn it, Miller. Do you pick and choose your battles?*

McKenna raised her face to look at him while blinking back the rain. "I think Derek handles two things quite well. Does a full moon hidden by clouds dilute what resides inside him, keeping the werewolf part at bay? In the years I've known him, I'd never seen a clue."

"Secrets define those of us touched by the supernatural," he said. "Care of those secrets is highly personal and completely necessary. Only Detective Miller knows the answer to your question."

She lowered her head and leaned into him. Her voice

made a rough comeback. "Am I the only person in this mess who's human through and through? No genetic tweaks? Nothing hiding internally? Please tell me I'm in the majority, and there are more people like me than like…"

When he didn't answer or offer further comment about her unfinished question, McKenna backed up. Again, she looked at him. "Hell. I'm wrong?"

"Let's get you out of the rain," Kellan said.

"Stop avoiding me. Stop distracting me. Don't I have a right to know what you meant by that sudden silence?"

"You do. I told you I was going to explain."

"And we always seem to be interrupted when you try."

"By nothing I had a hand in," Kellan said.

McKenna's hair was soaked and hung down her back. She was shivering in her thin shirt and jeans. "My part. That's what you said. You were going to tell me what part I played in all of this. Meaning that I have one."

A good-size shudder rocked her back a step. Kellan's hands on her shoulders kept her close. She said, "If I do have a part, there was obviously a plan. Did it have to do with what you already told me? That you were hoping I'd help you die? Are you sick beneath that gorgeous exterior? Is that it? I'm a nurse and you need my help?"

She shook her head and went on without waiting for a reply. "Why did you want to die, Kellan? And why are vampires after me? Possibly that's only the surface of what's happening. Am I right to think so? Tell me everything. Please tell me before I go insane."

"All right," he said. "Once we're out of the rain."

She grabbed hold of his jacket. "No more excuses. Tell me now."

She was distressed, white-faced, fielding tremors that would soon drop her to the ground. Kellan pressed the hair back from her forehead with both of his hands, then kept her pale face centered between them. He spoke slowly, carefully. "You are human, McKenna. Just not one hundred percent, and through no fault of your own."

Chapter 23

The woman in Kellan's care stopped shaking suddenly, as if someone had simply thrown a switch. She was so still, so motionless, he wasn't sure she knew where she was and who he was.

Her lips were bloodless. Her eyes were closed. Only the thump of her erratic heartbeat told him she was conscious.

Kellan spoke to her in a gentle tone. "You might never have known about this, or about the others, if I hadn't come here. Yet it was a quest I had to take up, a final task to complete."

She repeated one word. "Quest."

"All of my life has been directed by that term," he explained. "I took it up willingly because I believed in the job. Having experienced the power at the heart of this quest, I knew it to be worthy of my allegiance."

Kellan dropped his hands. McKenna kept standing as if she'd been frozen in place.

"Quest," she said again, as if trying to analyze the word.

"Nowadays, you might label this a *calling*. A call to action for a specific purpose."

She opened her eyes without looking at him. "Like a monk, or a priest."

"Yes. Like that."

Her gaze began to travel upward. "What am I, then?

Something or someone important enough to bring you here?"

"Important to me," he said. "Seemingly also important to a lot of others, though I hadn't expected to find either that or the unwelcome reception."

Her eyes met his—blue eyes shot through with the red lines of sleeplessness and fatigue. "They want you, not me? Those vampires?"

Kellan nodded. "Their goal is to keep us apart."

"Why?"

"Because you are the only person on this earth who can take me down. Only you, my sweet, sweet McKenna, can help me find the exit I have yearned for."

Her gaze intensified. McKenna had gone past the point of registering minor aches and pains. Information was what she craved. But the rain had grown fierce. He needed to get McKenna out of it and off the street.

Kellan took a step back, and as if truly physically connected, she followed. He took another step. So did she. When he finally took her hand, she snatched it back. She wasn't going to touch him in any intimate way. Things between them had changed.

Kellan thought about the Nosferatu and its intent to do him real damage. He thought about the gray-haired vampire that had told him the nest wished him no harm. He searched McKenna's face for further signs of her willingness to hear him out, and found her staring back.

"They want to separate us," he reiterated. "As long as I'm in Seattle, the vampires will continue to push that agenda, at your expense."

McKenna seemed to realize right then that they were in the open, and not only exposed to the elements but also vulnerable to the shadows surrounding them. She had emerged from her near-dazed state with a series of labored breaths. Her bloodshot eyes blinked slowly, twice.

Kellan couldn't help noticing how her wet shirt was pasted to her slim body, showing off every delicious detail beneath. The lace covering her breasts formed a pattern on the wet, white cotton. Under everything, her skin was only slightly darker than the colorlessness of her insignificant attire.

"I promise," Kellan said to her. "I promise to tell you as much as I know if you will follow me out of the rain."

She turned her head to scan the street. "Is anyplace safe?"

"Will you trust me to find a place that is?"

"Okay," McKenna said with her hand glued to the butt of her gun.

It wasn't much leeway, Kellan supposed. But it was a start. McKenna would have a hundred questions, and a Blood Knight couldn't lie. A promise was a promise. He would tell her everything concerning her, and why he was here. She would either accept his explanations or run away. He hoped the odds of her acceptance were better than the odds he had considered when trying to find her in the first place.

He would tell McKenna how unsure he was about the decision that had brought him to Seattle, and how meeting her had altered that.

Gesturing for her to move, Kellan headed toward the hospital. Her knees and her ankle needed care. Due to those injuries, the going was slow. He had to accept that and stop himself from lifting her in his arms. Any attempt to touch her now might push her over the edge of her hardwon battle with self-control.

Some part of her mind continued to call to him, though.

Part of her wanted to be in his arms. As McKenna walked, she stared straight ahead.

All of a sudden, Kellan wondered if maybe it wasn't McKenna's wishes that he perceived. Maybe the soul curled up inside her was reaching out now that he'd got so close. If that was true, they were making headway. But in what direction?

They didn't reach the hospital before the worst of the storm blew in. The rain became a torrent. Water ran like rivers at the curb. Speaking now would likely end all negotiations before they had begun, so Kellan eased McKenna's agitation with a soothing chant, using only a little slip of power.

He wished those particular powers of persuasion worked on himself, because McKenna wasn't the only one affected here. His heart felt heavy. His insides churned. A Nosferatu was nothing. This small woman and what he was going to tell her had become the things he most feared.

McKenna walked on long after remaining upright became a struggle. She didn't care where Kellan took her as long as he kept his word.

They were moving in the direction of the hospital. She knew this city by heart. Kellan was going to take care of her first, before getting to those tough answers he owed her. Funny how little her legs hurt now when all she could think about was getting to the root of the past few days, and Kellan's place in the nightmare that had become her life.

He was wrong, of course. She didn't carry anything strange inside. With all the blood tests she'd had in her lifetime, most of which had been in the past two years, any abnormality would have shown up, raised red flags. Kellan was messing with her for a reason only he knew about.

At the hospital where she was well-known, she would

be safe. Other than a random newly-turned vampire or two in the ICU, nothing dead got out of the building or rose from the beds. Not that she knew of, anyway.

She was putting her faith in Kellan when being around him had proved dangerous from night one. However, she did believe he would take care of her to the best of his ability, and that he was intrinsically good. In spite of all that had happened, Kellan had her back. Even if he hadn't earned it, this Blood Knight had her respect.

When the hospital came into view, McKenna let him take her arm. Being in her company when they entered the building would take suspicion off a stranger roaming the hallways.

Two ambulances were pulling around the side, making for the emergency entrance. One police cruiser accompanied them, which usually meant there was a bad guy inside an ambulance in need of watching. Kellan was probably better equipped to know what kind of bad guy that was.

She and Kellan entered by the front door, drenched. With all of her injuries and minus a coat, she probably looked like a homeless person seeking shelter. And that was pretty much the case at the moment since her apartment seemed to be a magnet for attracting monsters.

Rain and all, Kellan looked like the angel she had first compared him to. Hell, maybe he was an angel and that was what this was all about.

With that assessment, more chills piled on top of those already icing her skin. McKenna waved to the attendant manning the registration desk behind a glass partition as they passed through the first door. She waved to another woman in the hallway beyond, drawing stares from everyone they passed.

If anyone noticed her torn jeans and her limp, no one addressed it. Mostly their gazes fell on Kellan, dark in his black leather and looking as though he didn't belong in the halls of healing.

Rounding a corner, they found the door to the staircase and climbed slowly, McKenna leading with her uninjured leg. Kellan was patient. He did not again offer assistance, understanding that she wouldn't take it.

No damsel, damn it.

Near the third-floor landing, Kellan stopped. He leaned against the wall. Glancing around, McKenna asked, "Here?"

He nodded. "Can you think of a better place? Who takes the stairs these days if they don't have to?"

McKenna sat down on a step, weary and anxious. "All right. Talk, please. From the top. From your arrival here, and what brought you."

"You brought me," he said. "I mentioned that earlier."

"From where? Where were you last?"

"England. In the north."

"Explain how I could bring you here."

"Your soul called to me. That's the truth you asked for. I followed that call to Seattle."

"You do realize how crazy that sounds?"

"My life reads like that," he agreed. "You have no idea."

"Especially when there's no proof there is such a thing as a soul," she pointed out.

Kellan's arms were loose at his sides. He didn't appear to share her nervousness about what this interrogation might entail. Then again, he held all the cards, while she was in the dark about so many things.

"Oh, there is a soul, I promise you," he said. "Those who lack souls are notably different."

"Like the vampires?"

"Vampires are what's left after the death of their mortality is resurrected in a different form by an infusion of blood from another vampire. Their souls take flight when the humanity in them passes on. What's left isn't pretty, as you have seen."

"They're all evil bastards because they have no souls?"

"A few of them retain their souls. I believe that has to do with the timing of the soul's flight. Maybe the behavior of the person who dies is also considered. The souls of good people might linger longer, influencing their behavior when the new blood takes over. That's one theory."

McKenna stood up to face him, afraid to ask the next question sitting down. "Are you a vampire?"

His eyes softened. There was, McKenna noted, a glint of gold mixed in with the blue. Kellan looked like a rebel, but those eyes were special.

"Not a vampire," he replied. "I don't bite. My soul was retained in its original form as a special gift. I carry it with me now."

"Retained?" McKenna sucked in a breath. "Are you saying you died?"

His smile was one of infinite sadness and lasted for a few seconds before the lines around his eyes smoothed out. "I died centuries ago. Long before vampires as we know them today existed."

Standing up hadn't been such a good idea. McKenna sagged back to the step. The pain in her ankle flared as if Kellan's confession called that pain back to life. Maybe the weight of his remark was just too much to bear. He had taken away her pain on another occasion. What kind of creature had that kind of power?

Believing Kellan's stories took a giant leap of faith when McKenna wasn't sure she had quite that much trust left in her. Who could have understood any of this and called it reality? She chastised herself for being fascinated and wanted to cover her ears.

He had died. And the beautiful creature opposite her

was the result. This was mind-blowing stuff. Still, there had been blood on her lips after kissing him, and the taste of blood in her mouth. She was too caught up in what any of that might mean to come right out and ask Kellan if he had fangs. She was afraid to see them.

McKenna squinted to dim the harsh stairwell lights and tried not to look at his lush, talented mouth. "Tell me about what brought you to me. What part of that *not one hundred percent human* were you seeking?"

She saw that Kellan was dreading this conversation as much as she was. He couldn't have dreaded it more, though. No one could have.

She had gone off the deep end.

She wondered if anything Kellan said could dissuade her from what she was feeling. Her craving for him was a desire so deep-rooted, she couldn't see where that desire ended. What she felt was like love, though she was a rookie when it came to that kind of emotion. Being apart from him hurt. Worrying about the truth of his stories hurt. If he was a goddamn enigma, what did that make her for caring for him with her heart and soul both? Certifiable?

"We're not really strangers," Kellan said. "I realize how difficult this might be to understand, but I honestly believe I've been in the presence of your soul before, and that I once loved the woman it belonged to."

"My soul belonged to someone else?" she asked.

He nodded. "That, I believe, is the reason you see things from her past, like the castle and what went on there. Possibly that's the only reason I could find her soul again. I didn't realize this until tonight, and it's the only explanation I have for locating what my Makers tried so hard to hide."

"Makers?" McKenna put a nervous hand to her temple. "Hell. What are those?"

"That's what we call the beings involved in bringing us back to life."

"Meaning they raised you from the dead? Then they made you into something else?" she asked, sick over the thought of Kellan dying, what that must have felt like, the agony that would have caused.

She stood up again by holding on to the railing, anxious to get on with this interrogation.

In rising too fast, she became light-headed. Despite the wet clothes, she had started to sweat. Shock often did that. She was on the edge.

"You're suggesting that someone else's soul is inside me. Inside my body," she said. "And that's how you found me."

There had to be a way to make sense of something so nonsensical. McKenna was desperate to find it.

She flashed back to the name Kellan had whispered in place of her own the night they had made love on the lawn in front of Derek's apartment.

"Damaris." She spoke the name slowly, watching for Kellan's reaction. That reaction came swiftly, altering his expression, causing him to tense.

"That's the name you spoke," she said, thinking back to the images of the white castle and the man in the garden. The man near the bed. The bloodred roses and the golden fountain. Tying all those images together with what Kellan had just said made her want to find a place to retch.

"Those were her memories? Not dreams? They had nothing to do with me?" She looked to Kellan for confirmation, hardly daring to breathe, and spoke again, needing to get this out. "The white castle. You know what it is. You've been there. Been there with her."

He nodded.

McKenna flashed to the woman in the mirror. "She dressed in black."

Kellan nodded again. His forehead furrowed in surprise.

McKenna lowered her voice. "Then it isn't me you're attracted to. It's her. Her soul called to you. The soul you say is inside me is hers."

"Possibly that soul lured me here. I didn't stop to question why the call was so easy to follow after spending so much time looking for it."

"Love," McKenna said numbly. "Maybe your love for her never died."

"That's not it," Kellan returned adamantly. "What she and I had was intense, but it ended centuries ago. What happened to change things in Seattle is that I met you, liked you."

When his eyes searched her face, McKenna felt the familiar heat. Wanting to go to him, wrap her arms around him, she instead stood her ground.

"In you I found something that made me question my reasons for coming here," he explained. "You did that. Getting to know you did that."

Her heart rate escalated dramatically when her eyes found his. Yes, she was certifiable. Because she loved him when she had no right to, when he wasn't human, and he would surely go away, leaving her eventually. She felt so very small in comparison to what he had been through; so human, against the concept of immortality.

Kellan stepped forward, seeming to fill the small space. "I don't see that soul when I look at you. I don't see a past lover. I've wanted only you since our first meeting, though others in this city mean to keep me from you. The visions we shared made me realize whose soul this had to be."

"Why would others want to keep me from you?"

"One of them implied that he and others have waited

for me, watching for my arrival. I've come to believe that a monster in this nest has made a promise to my Makers to keep me alive, and therefore away from you."

He paused before going on as if searching for answers as he spoke. "That line of thinking would mean that the beings at Castle Broceliande had a reach far beyond the scope of its walls. They would have had to set things in motion really far back by creating a species that wasn't around when the seven of us took up the quest. That alternate species, known now as vampires, would have been given a task of their own, if what the old vamp said carried weight. Abducting you should have backed up that purpose."

"And yet if their plan was to kill me, that didn't happen," McKenna said. "So why didn't they?"

Feeling a dire need for solidarity in a rapidly deteriorating world, McKenna rested her hand on Kellan's arm. The familiar buzz of electricity tingled through her, spreading like wildfire. But was it her own response to Kellan, she wondered now, or a reaction from the mysterious soul she was supposed to carry inside her?

"Perhaps they face the kind of dilemma I now face," Kellan replied.

"You said that you came here to die and told me I'm the only person who can help with that. Did you mean me, Kellan—that I was the one to do the deed—or was that objective tied to the soul you say shares space with my own? Is that the dilemma you're talking about? Is that the question here?"

When Kellan didn't answer, she knew it might be because he didn't want to hurt her any more than he already had. However, she was still in the dark about the details of this supposed special liaison. In spite of that, she believed what he had told her so far. She'd seen the castle.

She'd seen the woman in the mirror. Making love to Kellan was unlike anything she had experienced, and well beyond the norm. Was that because another woman's soul shared in her pleasure? Doubled that pleasure and pushed it to extremes?

Were any of her thoughts or feelings her own?

Kellan brought her to him with a snap of his arm. If more bad news was coming, his plan might have been to catch her when she collapsed beneath the weight of that information.

Chapter 24

"They can't kill me." Kellan searched McKenna's face as he spoke. He couldn't tell her what he didn't know. All he had were the ideas he had been formulating.

"Only you can kill me. Given such a strange scenario, I asked myself why the vamps would take you. I'm their enemy. Why not allow me to end my life by your hand? In that way, the vigilante they and others like them fear would be gone." He took a minute to think that over before speaking again.

"It's the promise that bothers me. The oath the old vampire mentioned. This told me I am not supposed to die, either by their hands or yours. I am to continue on as I have, further extending my long existence. Removing you from my future assures everyone of this, even though it also means ongoing trouble for the undead."

"Then they should have killed me when they had the chance," McKenna said. "So I couldn't harm you."

"There's where the real problem lies. If you don't take my life, no one else can. You hold the key to ending my existence. If I were to go mad, go rogue, change sides or simply give up helping others, there would be no way to stop my rampage without you. Keeping you around would be an asset to the world in general, McKenna. You do see the problems in all of this?"

McKenna nodded. She had grown paler, though he would have thought that impossible. Kellan slid a hand down her arm, closed his fingers over hers. She let him do this. Both her pulse and her heartbeat were racing.

Her voice was hushed. "How was I supposed to kill you? Who could possibly have conceived of something like that, foreseeing all situations from the time you were reborn to well in your future?"

"Those who called that castle their home."

"Can't you go to them for answers?"

"They were to take their own lives after sending us forth on our quest. That was the deal they made with those who trusted them. The Blood Knights were to replace the original three Makers, and the castle was to be destroyed."

"Blood Knights," McKenna whispered, as if the words had taken on more meaning for her. "If only I could take you down, turn you off, does that mean your six brothers can be destroyed by souls embedded in humans, and that there are more like me? One secret adversarial soul per Knight?"

He nodded solemnly. "Our Makers hid you and the others to ensure that we would continue forever. They had no contingency plan for allowing us to decide the life or death question for ourselves."

"Why couldn't these Makers do all the things they created you for? Why did they need Knights?"

"They weren't fighters."

"How did those creatures get this soul to me, coming all this way, through all this time?"

"I have no answer for that, and can't even imagine one," Kellan admitted, feeling terribly ill-equipped for this discussion. McKenna wasn't supposed to know any of this. A hefty flaw in this whole scheme was that he had fallen for the person hiding the soul he had wanted to destroy him.

"So if these vampires can't kill you," McKenna said, "and I won't, the vampires have no real stand. They have no stake in what happens, really. It's checkmate. Things could conceivably go on as they had before you arrived in Seattle if you simply left the city."

Her delicate brow creased. "Besides, if your Makers are gone, what binds these vampires to an old oath anyway? What would be the point? You do see how absurd this sounds? Supposing that I am the vessel housing the soul you sought, how would anyone access it with those Makers gone? That soul would have had to migrate from body to body, one lifetime after another, without being traceable."

She glanced up at him. "What do you call a soul that's able to do all that?"

"Reaper."

She winced at the term. "That's an ugly word."

"It is," he agreed. "Though it best describes the reason behind its creation."

Kellan watched McKenna's jaw tense before she spoke again.

"What happens to that special soul after serving its purpose?"

He had to be truthful. "I don't know. I wish I did."

Her eyes met his. "So I'm the test case."

He nodded, barely able to control the guilt already pummeling his insides for placing her in this situation.

She held his gaze. "When you met me on the street, you knew I was the… Reaper?"

His eyes traveled over her wan face. "I thought you might be."

"Why did you think that?"

"The instantaneous attraction. Your boldness in approaching a stranger. The feeling I had when I looked at you."

Her eyes were very bright in the artificial light of the stairwell. "Those things could have been nothing more than a man's normal interest in a woman," she said, and then immediately added, "even though there's nothing normal about you."

She broke eye contact. "How long did it take you to figure things out, for real?"

"Our first kiss."

She eyed him warily.

"The vampires confirmed my suspicions by going after you," he said.

"What if they were merely following your lead in thinking I'm the one you needed to find? What if I'm not the one, Kellan? Are you so sure now that I am? Can you really be sure?"

"I'm sure. And so, I believe, are you."

McKenna's gaze came back to his. "Yes," she whispered. "I saw the castle. I suppose nothing else would explain that. But I was hoping these feelings for you were my own."

Kellan wanted to take her to a place where they could be happy together, at least for a while. Where the alternate soul she housed no longer mattered. Where it could be just the two of them. But his Makers had ruined the promise of a rosy future for any of the Seven, who were unable to find and keep love without immortal women.

Creating an immortal partner was forbidden and the greatest sin. Without passing along the black blood in his veins, there was no way to create a mate with an equally long life span. The mortal-immortal differences made any future he might have considered with the woman beside him daunting. This was a pain he had to endure when he had already endured so many.

McKenna deserved more. He could make her forget all

of this with a few whispered words, just as he had told her. But she was in danger now, and he had put her there. Making her forget about vampires and fangs would only compound that danger. Without what she knew already, she'd be helpless. She would probably die a gruesome death by their hand. And he couldn't accept or fathom that.

One bite...

One slip of his fangs into her beautiful veins, and she'd be his. *Maybe.*

And... God...maybe not.

There was a possibility that the extra soul inside her wouldn't allow him to have her that way. The human might die once that extra soul was activated. Who knew how any of this worked, when the details were so damn important?

Frustrated, Kellan slammed his fist against the railing. The building shuddered as if an earthquake had passed through. McKenna rocked on her feet.

"It's too late for what-ifs, my lovely McKenna," he managed to say before the door behind them blew open.

The body rushing through the doorway belonged to a nurse McKenna knew well. Leena.

"All hands on deck," Leena said, passing them, paying little attention as she raced up the stairs. "Five just came in. We could use any and all help."

"Five what?" McKenna asked before stopping to consider how that might sound. But Leena was running and thankfully hadn't heard the remark.

Kellan had taken on the motionlessness of a statue. He hardly seemed to breathe before he tightened his grip on her hand and turned so quickly, McKenna wasn't sure what was happening until she found herself running. They didn't head up the stairs after Leena, but back through the stairwell door and into the hallway, where hospital personnel were massing for the arrival of victims of a major incident.

"Wait," she called out, but Kellan didn't stop. He led them through hallway after hallway, past trauma units readying for an influx of patients, and down another set of stairs leading to the underground labs.

McKenna had no idea how Kellan knew where he was going, but he didn't falter. They ended up at the back of the hospital, near the emergency doors, and were on the street before anyone noticed them.

The rain had stopped. Her bad ankle was numb. With sparks shooting through the damaged nerves in her knees, McKenna limped along as fast as she could, helped by Kellan's possessive hold on her and his strength of purpose.

That unstated purpose scared her half to death and nearly as much as the transformation she began to see as she stared at Kellan's broad back.

He was rigid, his unflappable calm visibly dissipating. McKenna had a feeling she had glimpsed only the outer edges of this angelic being, and that possibly she wasn't going to be able to handle the real deal.

On the back of his neck, the scrolling black tattoos stood out like midnight-hued stains. Those tattoos appeared to be moving. Kellan's shoulders shuddered as if something foreign had slipped inside his jacket to burrow beneath his skin.

Under the streetlights they charged past, his auburn hair had taken on a shine like a halo. His marvelously chiseled face seemed harder, more angular, barely recognizable. Kellan had again become something more than Kellan, his transformation tripped by the danger surrounding them.

This is real.

This new Kellan is real.

Her lover was from the past, born centuries ago. He wasn't a time traveler, but had lived through each year of time's passage. How many decades had he seen so far? She wondered who had bestowed these Makers Kellan spoke of with power over life and death.

Vigilante.

The word struck a chord as they hopped a curb and hustled along the boulevard. Rumors about the existence of such a vigilante came back to her now. Reports on TV from the Carolinas. News feed from Texas about a mysterious man turning up on the sidelines to lead cops toward a hefty bust and clean up the streets. Never more than one mention of the mysterious guy, in one place at a time. In and out. There and gone. That was how the vigilante operated, remaining faceless, nameless. A phantom.

Because that man was a shadow himself.

That mysterious man was Kellan.

Given the chance, she might have been able to track Kellan's route across the States until his arrival in the West. In Seattle.

I've come for you, he had told her.

Instead of shock, the puzzle pieces snapping together brought friction. Fright was there, too, spreading like a plague inside her. Nothing was as it seemed on the surface. *Nothing at all.*

Kellan turned a corner onto another street that would eventually lead them out of the heart of the city, if they made it that far. He had not looked at her again. His grip on her hand was tight.

Kellan. A man who wasn't actually a *man* at all, in the typical sense of the word.

Kiss. Bed. Naked...

He'd had her heart and maybe even her soul with that first opened button.

Sex. Mystery. Danger.

All that in spades, and ongoing.

Smile. Eyes.

He used those unearthly blue eyes to see into her soul, even if that soul wasn't completely hers to begin with.

Protection from...vampires.

That was the kicker. The sticking point. Reason enough for the current evasive techniques.

So, what's next, my sexy immortal?

Hell, if they'd just stop, she would show him what she thought of him. Tell him this adrenaline rush brought back the best days of her life, and he didn't have to be sorry. She would tell Kellan that at the very least, she would have loved him for this.

They were moving away from the direction of her apartment and were nowhere near the alley where he'd fought the vampires. They weren't remotely close to the building where the beasts had taken her, hoping to draw Kellan into the open.

McKenna didn't bother to inquire about where they were going. She didn't really care. Being with Kellan was what mattered. Finding out about his true nature was important. Chasing monsters was a worthy cause and made him a good guy, no matter what else he might be. Helping him was the only thing she could do now. She had to rally to his cause and remain strong.

She would try.

She sucked in great gasps of air as he helped her along with his strong grip. She hoped that mysterious soul she was supposed to carry around would eventually jump-start back to life, be useful for something other than starring in strange fractured pictures. Maybe it would heal her damn foot.

Two more blocks filled with people and their cars were

behind them. Most of those folks were oblivious to the supernatural rift in their midst. They paid no heed to two soaked, underdressed people moving along the boulevard hours after midnight, on what had turned out to be the longest night of McKenna's life.

When Kellan halted, she stumbled to a stop with him. Without a warning glance in her direction, he whirled to face shadows that began to undulate like the marks on the back of his neck.

Not again…she silently prayed.

Chapter 25

"Come out," Kellan commanded, staring at the darker bit of night sandwiched between two buildings. "This has gone on long enough."

Although no one appeared, a voice familiar to him spoke.

"There is nowhere to run in this city that will take you far from us if we wish to find you, Blood Knight."

"That's the thing," Kellan said to the gray-haired spokes-monster for this powerful, enigmatic nest. "We weren't running away. On the contrary, we were coming straight to you."

"As if you knew the way?"

"Oh, you can be sure I'm well aware of you now. The stink here is particularly strong."

The vampire glided free of the shadows. "Why would you come to us?"

"Wasn't it just a matter of time? I'm sure your Prime is expecting my visit."

"We don't want you here, knight. I thought we made that clear."

"That's just it. I'm not at all clear about your purpose. Perhaps you can enlighten me. Better yet, maybe your Prime can. In person."

The gray-haired vampire's gaze darted to McKenna.

"Wasn't taking the woman warning enough of the danger we represent?"

"Checkmate, bud," McKenna said boldly, in what Kellan supposed might be the only reply she could get out when facing the monster she had shot.

"You must go," the vampire warned, changing tack.

Kellan shook his head. "You know better than to suggest such a thing."

"There is nothing more to be accomplished here."

"You can't have it both ways, vampire. Either you want me gone and actually let me go, or you wish me dead. Which is it?"

"Your fate is not up to me."

"Neither," Kellan said with a tug on McKenna's hand, "is hers. Why, then, did you involve her?"

"Take her away," the vampire said. "Now. Tonight."

"Is that your final offer of enlightenment? A free pass to leave Seattle?"

"No," another voice answered in Gray-hair's place.

Kellan experienced a moment of pure sensory suspension before drawing back as if he'd been struck. His heart thrashed. His sigils stung.

He knew this voice.

Can't be.

Some mistake?

"I assure you it's no mistake," the female in the shadows confirmed, as if reading his mind.

But then…she always had been able to read minds and hearts and his innermost desires. The female this voice belonged to hadn't almost been burned at the stake as a witch for nothing.

"How is this possible?" Kellan peered into the gloom, catching sight of movement too fluid to belong to anything other than ancient vampire royalty.

Her scent was of aged wine, tinged with fresh hemoglobin. She was the brains behind the plan he had doubted, and intelligent enough to be the master of a big city like Seattle.

In all of his years, he'd never felt sicker than he felt right then. The ravages of time came down hard to press in on him, threatening with the force of a lash to send him back to the last time he had heard that voice. Her voice.

His lost lover.

A surge of power slipped from him to lighten the darkness. Shadows shrank. In Kellan's peripheral vision, he saw the gray-haired vampire shield its eyes.

And there she was. *It* was. Standing before him, as beautiful as anything on earth. Dark as a winter storm and twice as deadly. Dressed in black. Hair the color of spun gold. Wielding power the likes of which Kellan had never sensed in a vampire.

Eyes he had once likened to cornflowers now had the red cast of the blood she had ingested. Her face was thin, almost skeletal, and so pale, fine tracings of black webbing were visible beneath the surface of translucent skin.

Through lips he had once devoured, lips that had intimately roved over every inch of him, this vampire showed off the tips of two ivory, lethal, razor-sharp fangs when she smiled.

"Hello, Damaris," Kellan said hollowly.

McKenna backpedaled a good three feet. She had to shift weight onto both legs in order to remain upright. The rest of whatever color and expectations she might have had escaped her as if poured down a drain.

She looked first to the Kellan who had grown, filled out, stretched. His face shone with the colorless luster of a South Sea pearl.

When her focus moved to the abomination across from Kellan, McKenna teetered. Pain, hard-hitting and unendurable, struck her, nearly sending her to her knees. She staggered sideways with both hands on her stomach, staring into the shadows with the understanding that this female vampire was inflicting the pain on purpose, without even looking her way.

"You shouldn't have come," the blonde abomination said to Kellan in a voice like steel.

"I couldn't resist," Kellan remarked. "And now I begin to understand why."

"No hug? No I'm-happy-to-see-you kiss?" the thing in black quipped, red eyes flashing in the light Kellan had created from nothing more than a look and a raised hand.

"How can this be?" Kellan asked.

"Wasn't it a perfect choice, Ladd? Who better to watch and wait? Who better to predict what you'd eventually do—you, out of all of them, because you were different from the start?"

"How?" he repeated.

"You must see what an easy choice this was. I knew you best. I loved you with all my heart. Who better to guard your life, should you decide to lose it?"

The terribly fearsome vampire appeared solid one moment and diaphanous the next. Looking straight at this apparition caused a burning sensation in McKenna's eyes. Maybe this was some sort of defense mechanism to deflect attention. Supernatural voodoo this extreme was quite possibly the reason vampires were still around.

She couldn't help but think of the unsuspecting victims this wickedly beautiful vampire had come across. The vamp master must have been conceived under intentions as black as the night to have existed for centuries.

Another stab of pain threatened McKenna's balance.

Gritting her teeth, fisting her hands, she withstood each fresh round of agony sent to her from Kellan's former lover.

This was the woman whose name Kellan had whispered. The woman a Blood Knight had left behind at the white-walled castle in order to pursue a quest.

"Damaris," McKenna said.

Red eyes turned her way before Kellan stepped in to provide a barrier between the two females. Anxiousness radiated from him. The air around them carried the scent of metal. Despite the danger, McKenna wanted to know if Kellan, having loved this thing once before, felt anything for her now.

This monster was killing people and making more bloodsuckers…and yet McKenna felt jarring pangs of jealousy for Kellan's past affections.

"If you're as undecided as your minion on what to do next, I'll make that decision for you," Kellan said to the scary, fair-haired vampire.

"Meaning that I can back off and let you be?" the vampire returned.

"Isn't that the only option?"

"One might assume so, since I've become the kind of creature you chase and stake on a regular basis. Perhaps the plan, conceived so long ago, was to have us face each other again. Putting your vows to the fire would be the ultimate test of time and honor, would it not, my love? Do you not see the beauty of such foresight?"

Kellan bowed his head as if this new turn of events had become too much to bear. "Did you volunteer for this task, Damaris?"

This was the second time he'd said her name, beyond his initial whisper. Hearing him say it made McKenna want to strike out.

Tensions were mounting. The night pressed in.

"No," the female vampire at last replied. "I did not ask to become the thing you see before you. I'm not sure anyone would ask for that."

"You're a long way from home," Kellan said.

"As are you."

"But you knew I would come here someday."

She nodded. "To find her."

"The woman you were to keep me from."

"No," she corrected. "The *soul* you were to be kept from. There is a difference."

"That soul called to me."

"Wrong again," the vampire remarked.

Kellan appeared to think that over. Letting the comment go unchallenged, he said, "You run this city's nest."

McKenna sidestepped Kellan, needing to view this confrontation, tired of being in the dark.

"Oh yes," the vampire confirmed, casting an eye to her gray-haired minion, who moved back as if struck by an invisible blow.

"What do you want, Damaris?" Kellan asked calmly. "Is there something you'd require of me after waiting all this time to do me the honor of your presence?"

"I want to kill her," Damaris replied, sliding her gaze to McKenna. "Kill her so that I don't have to, and so that I have something good in my memory to hang on to."

"I can't do that," Kellan said. "You know why."

"Yes. I know why. I wonder if you do?"

McKenna felt Kellan's fiery attention on her, his glance there and away in a blue-eyed flash. The vampire was insinuating there might be more to this story than Kellan had previously thought. Was Kellan as confused as she was?

Just at that moment, however, in a move that made McKenna want to kiss whatever cop sat behind the wheel, a cruiser pulled to the curb. Over the speaker, the cop said, "Everything all right here, folks?"

And that, McKenna wanted to shout, had to be the question of the century.

Kellan reached out a hand too fast for even a Prime vampire to escape. When he touched what was left of Damaris, his sigils burned so badly, his skin began to whine.

Behind him, McKenna spun around to face the cruiser. Kellan supposed she had figured out by now that these vampires could open that car as easily as ripping open a can of sardines. She would be afraid to involve anyone else in this unbelievable situation because McKenna was selfless, but she was also aware that they were in danger, and that this creature confronting them had once been his lover.

He heard McKenna stumble toward the cop. He had made her run on a bum leg.

His plan could turn out to be a bust now that he saw just what kind of entity ruled Seattle's shadows. Witch, warrior, lover, Damaris's predictions were what guided the Makers' actions, once upon a time. She had always been ruthless in love and war. Damaris was no mere vampire Prime. She was like death itself.

"Go," he said to McKenna over his shoulder.

Go.

Stubbornly, she balked. He used more power.

Go now!

"Name's Randall," he heard her say to the cop in the car. "Officer Randall. I need a lift."

Damaris hissed through her fangs but made no move to retain McKenna. Kellan knew the reason for that, too, and what this vampire was waiting for.

As soon as the cruiser left the curb with McKenna inside, the rest of Damaris's welcoming party swarmed the sidewalk, dropping like spiders from the building above.

Chapter 26

McKenna was on the radio and calling for Derek without alerting dispatch to the cause of the emergency. He responded in seconds as if he'd been waiting for this particular call.

"Second and B," she said without going into more detail. To the cop beside her she added, "I'm undercover. Drop me here."

She was out of the car one block down the road, and running as if her injured ankle was nothing more than a minor inconvenience. A lot was going on in the city tonight, some of which could be part of that vampire's plan to divert attention elsewhere while waiting for Kellan. Derek might not get that, but he sure as hell would understand the risks of ignoring her plea for backup on a night that already defined the word *bad*.

She had to head back to where she'd left Kellan, but it didn't take a cop's intuition to realize that rushing in empty-handed, by herself, would be suicidal. She had to think. She needed time, when time was scarce.

She had nothing to offer. No special weapon. No knowledge of how to fight the supernatural, whose numbers had swelled to alarming proportions. Her next thought was that this poor city stood no chance against the encroaching shadows.

McKenna prayed for an epiphany to help her make a smart move. When she got back to where she'd left Kellan, it was to find him standing inside a ring of fang-snapping monsters. And that thing at the center—their Prime—was the bloodsucking headmistress.

How the hell had this many vampires cropped up in Seattle without being noticed? Didn't anybody other than a few good guys pay attention to what was going on?

Hugging the building on the corner, McKenna stared with her heart in her throat. If beasts like these were drawn to a beating heart, she was a veritable beacon.

Think, damn it.

The saving grace was something Kellan had told her tonight in the stairwell about these vampires not really wanting to hurt him. They couldn't kill him, he said. Only she could end his life. McKenna Randall, unsuspecting Reaper and keeper of lost souls. So what were they hoping to accomplish by surrounding him?

She counted each second that passed, because each one was a second too long in the wait for help to arrive.

Kellan, stunned and sorry things had turned out this way, dropped Damaris's wrist and watched as she inched back to gain a better vantage point for seeing his face. He almost recognized the woman in the gaunt vampire she had become, though very few original details remained.

"Is your plan to coerce me into killing McKenna by presenting me with an army?" he asked. "By lighting up this city to get my attention?"

He heard McKenna's thundering heartbeat close by and offered up a silent curse. Why hadn't she gone somewhere safe?

"She will bring help," Damaris said. "You know this."

He nodded. "Your secrets will be compromised if she does."

"By then, my job will be done."

"Meaning that you'll kill her for me and save the day?" Damaris's eyes flashed red fire.

"You'd give this up, after all this time, when you rule with an iron fist?" Kellan asked.

"I once thought you knew me well, Galahad," she countered. "Was I mistaken?"

Kellan's heart thumped with her use of his true name. But he was missing something crucial. He was surrounded by vampires that would eat themselves with their own fangs if their Prime commanded them to, and yet this display of vamps was all for show if she adhered to the promise the gray-haired bloodsucker had mentioned.

What was he not getting? Forgetting? The lapse in understanding wasn't like him.

"Come," Damaris said. "We can talk elsewhere."

"What's the point? We're now at opposite ends of the golden quest. My instinct is to rid the world of your kind. If you can't kill me, what's stopping me from hurting you by killing her?"

Damaris moved closer to him, gliding as if she wore skates, her feet not seeming to touch the ground. "Call an extended visit my reward for the long wait."

She was close enough for Kellan to sense Death's hold on her. Damaris had been overcome by the dark, and it was far too late for her to fight the consequences of that transformation.

"Feeling sorry," she whispered, "is a useless emotion. For instance, were you sorry when you left me at that castle? Would you have been sorry if you'd known what I soon would become? I wonder if you would have tried to rescue me, the way you have taken to rescuing the mortals you've grown to love?"

"If I had known what awaited you, I would have tried," he said.

Damaris's eyes closed briefly. She spoke through her fangs. "I know that, my fine Galahad. I think I have always known that, which is why I never asked."

She raised her head, sniffed the air. "Company comes without an invitation, my lord. I suppose it won't be difficult to see which side you choose, so I don't think I'll hold my breath." She laughed maliciously at her own joke, then added, "In the end, however, certain choices will be made for you."

In the time it took for a mortal to blink, every one of the vampires had gone from the street, leaving a whiff of Death's evil tidings behind them. Only the rustle of Damaris's black garment remained as a subtle final torment.

McKenna was unable to make her feet move in Kellan's direction after dry-heaving near the base of the building beside her with a stomach already empty.

She felt heavy, dizzy, way too ill to shout. Her legs kept buckling. Her injured throat felt tight.

The vampires had gone. *Why?*

When she glanced up again, Kellan was standing beside her. Worry lines etched his brow. The tails of his tattoos were writhing.

Two more cars pulled up, unmarked, no sirens blaring. Derek jumped out of one of them and rushed over. "McKenna?"

"Fine," she said. "There are a lot of those fanged bastards, Derek. Too many to go unnoticed for much longer. Too many to count."

Derek looked to Kellan. "Do you have anything in your

bag of tricks to help this situation? Pockets of trouble have broken out in five more places near the city center. None of the rioters have been detained or caught. We both understand why they weren't caught, don't we?"

Kellan nodded. "I know where they are. They have moved since the last time we showed up in force."

"You mean since two hours ago? Show me," Derek said.

"Too many of them," McKenna repeated. "Derek, you have no idea."

"I'm pretty sure I do," Derek argued. "This whole street smells like rot." He turned to Kellan. "Am I right about that? They're here somewhere, near where we're standing?"

"Underneath where we're standing," Kellan said.

McKenna looked at the ground with disgust. Derek did the same. "That's just plain nasty," Derek muttered. "Can we drop something down there that will kill them all at once? Those of them still down there, anyway? Hell, we should have burned that other place to the ground when we had the chance."

"And brought innocent firefighters to the scene for slaughter?" Kellan asked.

"Jesus."

"Anything strong enough to affect them that you could put under us would also risk taking down buildings and infrastructure."

Derek ran an agitated hand through his hair. "What do you suggest?"

"Let me go to them," Kellan said.

McKenna pushed off the wall, her adrenaline rush making a comeback. "You can't do that."

Kellan's blue eyes were soothing when they shouldn't have been. Calm, when the night had been anything but. "It's the only way, McKenna. She is my problem."

"She?" Derek looked back and forth between them. "Who are we talking about?"

McKenna was adamant. "That's what she wants. Why else would she confront you now, when all she had to do was let us go?"

"Who are we talking about?" Derek repeated several decibels louder.

"The vampire queen is, or was, someone Kellan once knew," she told Derek.

Derek got up in Kellan's face. "Someone you once knew? No joke?"

"Not much of a person anymore," McKenna said. "Powerful. Scary as hell. Too smart to leave her nest open to attack."

Derek came back to Kellan. "What do you think you could do on your own? Reason with them? Don't forget I've seen those things in action. Going in alone would be crazy."

Kellan said, "I won't be alone."

McKenna's gut tightened. Her insides knotted. She knew what was coming without comprehending why. She raised her face to the sky, waiting for the words that would announce her doom.

Kellan spoke those words slowly, deliberately, as if they pained him more than anyone could ever guess. "McKenna is going with me."

"No way." Derek's protest landed on deaf ears because McKenna had already made up her mind to accompany Kellan.

She was the soul he sought. She was the reason he was here. But none of those old truths addressed what might actually happen if she were to perish before Kellan got his wish for a final death.

He'd been right when he figured out there was a problem with the reasoning behind all of this. Having met Damaris, she could easily guess what that problem was. *Love.*

Maybe Damaris couldn't kill Kellan, but there was a chance she wouldn't have anyway. Kellan, her long-lost lover.

The concept of love had been conquered by the merciless confines of duty and honor, plus a whole slew of pledges so old they had lost their shine. Kellan wasn't alone in his adherence to ancient vows. Six others like him had also given up their mortal lives. Damaris must have suffered, too—even as an evil fanged queen with vampires at her beck and call.

Love.

Love was a concept that ruled McKenna Randall, as well. If wishes came true, she'd want Kellan to hold her one more time, make love to her again, even with Death nipping at the mattress. Kellan was everything she had hoped for in a man, despite his immortality. Any way this ended, she'd lose him. There was to be no happy ending here.

"All right," she said to Kellan over Derek's vehement protests and curses. "I'll go. But I have one more question for you."

Kellan's piercing gaze connected with hers.

"Why do you suppose Damaris became what she is, taking up the task of watching over me and waiting for you?" she asked.

Kellan didn't answer that, though McKenna knew he must have formulated his own ideas.

She needed more air to continue. "Did she do this in order to see you again, whatever the circumstance and no matter which side you were on?"

When Kellan smiled sadly, the emotion in his eyes set fire to her insides.

In that instant, she saw the man Kellan had once been. The honorable knight fighting for justice. The champion driven to complete an unending task worthy of changing the futures of seven good men. Her last thought on the subject was to ponder the scope of his original task, a task that had elicited such extremes in loyalty and sacrifice. The kind of sacrifice that made being a cop and facing peril on a daily basis pale in comparison.

God yes. She loved Kellan. She had to see this through by his side.

"All right. Let's do this," McKenna whispered as the lights on the block went out, throwing them into total darkness.

Chapter 27

The vampires had returned, their approach preceded by the smell of a moving wall of filth and rotting debris.

In near-total darkness, McKenna lunged to the side, toward the building next to her, in an automatic reaction of self-defense. She hit the brick hard, stunned by the severity of the blow.

Hands reached for her that weren't Kellan's or Derek's. Bony fingers tore at her clothes. Pointed talons raked deep grooves into her overly-sensitive skin. The scent of her blood whipped these bloodsuckers into a frenzy.

She heard Derek swear, and the sound of fighting—fists connecting with bone, muttered jeers and hisses through fanged mouths. She swung both arms at the vamps clawing at her, using her body to deflect several jabs. She punched back and kicked out with her good leg.

The realization that forceful contact didn't deter these monsters eventually came to her, and still she refused to give in when she was pushed to the ground.

Dragged away from the rest of the fighting, McKenna let out one final muffled cry.

Kellan fought like the machine he was trained to be, cutting a path through the bloodsuckers that resembled the parting of the Red Sea.

Vampires fell before him each time he moved. Ashes swirled. He shouted, "McKenna!"

There was no reply.

Derek was fighting beside him and holding his own. Some Lycans possessed the ability to shift shape during a full moon without that moon instigating the transformation. Miller was obviously one of those. His growls were as deadly as the tremendous power behind the claws he wielded like blades.

Both of them could see in the dark. When the way had been cleared and the last vamp dispatched to wherever what was left of them went, the big Were roared in satisfaction. But that sense of accomplishment didn't last. The Were faced Kellan with another threatening growl deep in his throat.

"She's gone," Kellan said.

And they both started running.

McKenna didn't close her eyes to block out the horror. She had to note the details of where these vampires were taking her. Why they hadn't yet killed her remained a mystery. She could only assume that Kellan's ex-lover wanted to take care of that business herself.

In a twisted way, McKenna understood how this whole thing was going to play out. It took a woman to comprehend fully that love sometimes obliterated not only reason but also the highest stakes...and that jealousy posed a terrible threat to everything.

She hated that Kellan had loved the woman this vampire Prime had once been. She would have envied anyone he'd been intimate with. Hell yes, she was jealous. She couldn't dismiss the fact that Damaris was also exhibiting signs of jealousy, and blaming McKenna Randall for that.

McKenna despised this vampire and her nest of monsters for hurting people and for existing on the same planet humans occupied. She cursed the fanged hordes for what they were about to do to her now.

Her shirt was in shreds. Gritty, uneven pavement sliced into her back as they dragged her over glass shards and pebbles. Each new horror made her more resolved to face down Damaris.

Humans were too damn fragile, she decided. If she were to be so easily destroyed, the soul she was supposed to harbor would have been better off placed elsewhere. Inside a werewolf, for instance, where it would have stood a better chance against ruffians and rogues that had lived for hundreds of years.

When they finally came to a stop, McKenna could have cried with relief. Darkness ruled this place. The bad smell had intensified, as if too many vampires were centered in one small spot.

She felt Damaris's presence without the use of her eyes.

"What have we here?"

The voice she dreaded posed that question. Hissing sounds followed that were reminiscent of steam escaping from a hole.

"He isn't yours to keep, you know," Damaris said. "You, my dear girl, are merely a vessel, and the infamous Galahad is used to protecting vessels. In no way could you aspire to keep the affections of a Blood Knight. No woman in the world can."

Galahad? McKenna suddenly felt colder. The dark world around her seemed to collapse in on itself as tales from the past came rushing back to her. Galahad and the Knights of the Round Table. Galahad and the quest for the Holy Grail.

"But you tried to keep him?" she worked hard to say,

finding it difficult to tear herself away from the idea of who Kellan actually might be.

The slap came before she could blink—a sharp, open-handed blow with a practiced delivery. McKenna swallowed blood, as well as a groan, but she'd had worse in her short career as a cop. She could stand this, at least for a while longer.

"You do not fathom how this goes," Kellan's ancient paramour said.

"Then why don't you enlighten me?"

"Why would I bother?"

"I'm not sure, when we both know that you won't kill me."

"Won't I?" Damaris challenged.

"Not until he comes."

When the vampire fell silent, the only sound in the area was McKenna's harsh breathing.

"Why do you suppose he came here to find me?" McKenna asked. "He has never spoken of that to me."

"Why would he speak of something so personal?" Damaris snapped.

"Well, then, how could I not be aware of an extra soul inside me?"

"Am I to provide you with those answers, as the last things you will hear?"

"No. I'd rather hear the story of how much you loved him, and why you've endured all this time just to see Kellan again when that outcome wasn't guaranteed."

Damaris laughed wickedly. "Kellan, is it? That's what he calls himself these days?"

"Yes." She was pushing things, wasting time, hoping to delay the inevitable. However, McKenna really did want the information this vampire possessed.

"He was a lord. A knight like no other. Famous. Handsome. Headstrong. Mythical from a young age for his prowess in combat and his goodness of heart."

"And he was yours?"

"Oh yes. He was mine, body, heart and soul. I saw to that."

"Until he answered a higher calling."

"Yes. Until then, when the inhabitants of that castle took him from me."

McKenna hardly dared to breathe now that secrets were being revealed. Damaris's revelations were going to snap that elusive puzzle into a comprehendible form.

Galahad. The knight who roamed the country espousing the use of might for what was right. Just like Kellan did.

Galahad.

If that was his true identity, he was here, centuries later, even though the holy relic he'd been designed to protect was safe. He'd come to Seattle to look for the soul that would end his long existence. Hell, he had finally grown tired of immortality and the ceaseless quest for right.

McKenna heard pieces of that puzzle snap together. All of those pieces seemed to fit.

"So you see, dear girl," Damaris began, her voice very close to McKenna's ear, "I had to do something. Some part of me had to remain in this world, hoping someday to lure Ladd back for one more look, one final kiss from a man torn from my arms to do what they said was God's bidding. After all, who could turn down God in favor of something as meaningless as love?"

McKenna choked out more words, riding out crests of unconquerable agony and a new fire building behind her eyes. "You…you became a vampire for that reason?"

"He was immortal. I gave up my soul, sacrificed my very being so that I would be immortal, too. Don't you see, little human…that the soul I gave up now resides within you? It's my soul you carry."

Yes. Kellan had explained his beliefs in the hospital stairwell without seeing the horror of the truth he would soon face.

"The Makers were happy to choose me for the task. I let them take my life and my soul because I had to. I stayed close to that soul, patiently waiting," Damaris said. "I knew he would come for it because I always understood him and anticipated his loneliness."

The soft swish of the fabric of Damaris's dress made McKenna shudder.

"It was my soul that Ladd came to find. It's me he needs in the end. The part of me that was left. He did not come for you, little human. Nothing else but that soul could have lured him once his decision had been made. None knew him better than I did. And now that he's here, I cannot allow the last part of me to be the end of him. After all of this time, I find that I can't watch the only thing that has ever been beautiful to me die."

Damaris still loved Kellan. McKenna found that concept as oddly touching as it was terrifying. Carnage and blood and the sacrifice of so many lives…in the name of love.

"So, you'll kill me and take away his ending," McKenna said.

"That's the plan."

"You will part from the soul you once possessed, the soul you've stood by, for him."

Images of those damn white walls returned to McKenna's frazzled, exhausted mind. The garden, the roses, the golden fountain. She again saw the man standing in the moonlight. This time, she knew whom Kellan had been waiting for. She understood the heartache Damaris had felt because she, McKenna Randall, a mere mortal who had stumbled unknowingly into the world of immortals, loved Kellan—Galahad, Blood Knight—with her own heart and soul.

And the world still needed him.

"All right," she said. "Do it. Kill me, and get this over with."

Strong arms encircled her. McKenna was one breath away from losing consciousness, and she figured that was probably a good thing. The scent of blood was cloying. The damn vampire's eyes glowed.

Her hostess wasted no more time. She pulled McKenna to the floor, almost completely cutting off her air supply. Her head was drawn back. She was held in position by Damaris's hold on several strands of her hair as something very sharp grazed her neck.

Fangs.

It was over. Nearly so. Death was sliding closer in the form of a dark, dank mist. She had no real family left to mourn her. She was the last in her line to carry the Randall name, so that, too, would die with her. Maybe Derek would never find her remains.

Please don't let her make me a vampire.

The first nip of those fangs didn't break her skin. McKenna prayed for the searing pain in her temple to claim her first, before those unnatural teeth punctured a vein.

Cold vampire fingers brought waves of chills across her skin. The hold on her hair tightened, threatening to tear those strands out by the roots.

And then...

Then...

There was light.

Chapter 28

"Damaris."

Kellan stood inside the blaze of light he had created with a wish and a call to a higher power cultivated by years of righteousness.

"Harming her will solve nothing," he said. "McKenna is innocent of our past transgressions."

He saw McKenna on the ground, injured, dirty and bleeding. The vampires he had vanquished to get to her in this underground cavern had been salivating at the door where their Prime toyed with McKenna and was precariously close to taking a bite.

"I knew you would come," Damaris said, looking up.

"I would have come sooner, had I realized what you needed. I told you that."

"What I needed, Ladd?"

"To be free of these chains. To be released from the obligations that brought you to this point, this minute. And to lose the pain you're carrying inside."

"You cannot die," she said. "This is the only way to ensure it."

"Do my wishes mean so little, Damaris? Have I not served out my time? Done the right things? The time for pledges is over. Mine and yours. In lieu of my Makers' presence, I release you from the promises you made and, in return, ask that you release me."

The red eyes narrowed. "It's that simple, when nothing else is?"

"We'll make it so."

Damaris glanced at McKenna. "She can end your life."

Kellan shook his head. "In fact, it's just the opposite. McKenna has saved my life."

After a beat, Damaris spoke again. "She carries my soul inside her. Part of me."

"Then I will love her even more because of that."

Damaris's eyes trained on him. "Love her? This?" She tugged at McKenna's hair. He wanted more than anything to go to her but couldn't do that quite yet.

Hang on, McKenna. Bear it a bit longer, my love.

"You do love her," Damaris snarled.

"Yes. How's that for a strange twist to an even stranger tale? I wonder if anyone could have predicted an outcome like that. I wonder if you did."

Big red eyes blinked slowly. "Her family carried my soul, passing it on. I followed them here, far from where you roamed. I kept watch over it and waited. But I feel what she feels, Ladd. Inside me, my lost soul's imprint lingers like a quarrelsome vibration. It hurts. Every damn day of this wicked existence hurts me."

Kellan took a step. "There is good in you. That goodness has not been abandoned or lost. Your sacrifices have saved you instead of destroying you. You are nothing like the others and never were. Prove that once again, Damaris. End this. Let McKenna go."

"Will you kill me instead, my love?"

"Never."

For a brief moment, in a flash, he again saw the woman behind the pale mask. All that beauty had been traded for a quest of her own. For love. For him. Now memory was Damaris's greatest torment. Pain had become her ally in a world where she was unable to walk freely. Was that why she inflicted pain on others? Did she hope by doing so she could rid herself of some of her own?

Damaris had spent centuries without sunlight, existing in the dark, following the soul she had lost due to a sacrifice much darker than his. His Makers had asked her to do this, and Damaris had complied.

"You will have to kill me, Ladd. Once I sink my venom into the woman in my grasp, you will change your mind. Maybe my soul will be returned to me if I take this bite."

"Would you wish your curse on anyone else?" he countered. "After the hundreds of vampires you've already created?"

"I didn't create them. I despise them all. I send them out to be eliminated, and more turn up. If I don't see to the culling of this nest, another master will double its size."

Kellan's heart banged inside his chest. This was news he hadn't anticipated. Damaris purposefully sent vampires to their final deaths in order to keep their number down? Hell, if that was true, it set his ideas about vampires into a tailspin.

She was soulless, and yet she wasn't a monster. Could it be that staying close to her soul all this time had saved her from the depth of darkness most vampires existed in? Could it be that love had saved her from a fate worse than death?

A master like this was unique, and useful to the world. Damaris's intelligence and resourcefulness were sorely needed in the shadows.

He stood silently for a few more seconds, absorbing that, then repeated, "Let McKenna go. Let me have this last chance at happiness, at least for a while. Please."

He saw how the request disturbed her. In her agitation, Damaris loosened her hold on McKenna. She said, "You will be reminded of what her soul can do, and will never be far from that temptation. How long, I wonder, can you avoid its call once you tire of the human housing it?"

More news. All of it bad. Most of it true. He had sampled the pull of this soul's curse already and had avoided McKenna's neck. He was no vampire, and yet McKenna's blood remained a heady allure that frightened him when nothing else did. Was that kind of lure due to the fact that the soul's original owner was now a vampire?

Damaris spoke again, as though she had read his mind. "Yes. Maybe. That isn't all, Ladd. I cannot be parted from her if she lives. I can't leave my soul. You will have to find a way to release it from her body in order to be free of me. That soul will never allow you true closeness to her when it belongs to me."

"I will take that chance," Kellan said.

Damaris eyed him again. "Then why haven't you taken her from me, when you're so much stronger?"

"It is as much your decision as mine to let her go."

"You suppose I won't kill her, even if it's to end my own agony?"

"The woman I once knew could not do such a thing."

As unbelievable as it was, Damaris let McKenna fall to the ground and stood. "If you take that chance and cannot resist the temptation later on, you will die. But she will also die. A life for a life, Ladd. That's the way this works, and the best fate can do."

There it was…the worst thing he could have thought of. If he had opened McKenna to get at that extra soul, she would not have survived the process.

He closed his eyes.

Before he reopened them, McKenna was in his arms.

Stifling a soft sound that was only the merest indication of her pain, and shuddering, she had managed to stand on her own two feet.

Kellan's arms went around the woman who felt so small and light. Somehow, McKenna had survived this night, so far.

"I will not harm her. Neither will you," he said firmly, glancing up to find Damaris no longer there.

He strode through the fighting that had taken to the street, with McKenna in his arms.

Werewolves were there again, and ruthless beneath a moon that had broken through the storm. Hell, Kellan thought as he maneuvered McKenna to safety, maybe Weres knew how to control the weather.

The night carried a taste of the imminent arrival of morning. There were few cars at this hour, and those had been detoured away from this location by perfectly placed police cruisers.

Kellan's heart demanded that he join the fight behind him, since he had started it, but he had one more thing to do first. Something important.

He had to stop this seemingly unavoidable pattern of manipulating fate, once and for all.

It was to the hospital he went first. His bike was there. "Can you ride?" he asked the very weak mortal in his arms.

She nodded and climbed onto the seat.

He took her to her apartment, far from the fray. Inside, he led her to the bathroom and turned on water in the shower. He tore away what was left of her shredded shirt and jeans, careful not to harm her more.

She stood naked in front of him, strong and glorious in her wobbling stance. He helped her under the water and held her there, searching her face, loving her for her bravery, and for so many other things.

You didn't ask for any of this, my love. I'm so very sorry.

He rinsed her face, her chest, her back, willing her pain to ease, taking some of that pain into himself. All the while, she watched him in silence.

When the blood of her wounds had been washed away and the whiteness of her skin showed again, he kissed her. Just a kiss, without other contact. Her trembling lips responded to him, parted for him. By the time he pulled away, she no longer shook quite so hard.

As his fangs had dropped, he thought again about what Damaris had said. Take that bite, find that soul, and McKenna would die. McKenna had been freed from the grip of one kind of danger only to head toward another.

Though he didn't want to take his eyes from her, something drew his focus downward, past where McKenna's pulse beat steadily in her neck, to the inky black spot on her upper arm that was the size of a quarter.

It was her tattoo. The black rose with its petals only beginning to unfurl. He stroked the mark with his finger. McKenna's hand covered his.

Kellan experienced a strange sensation of falling through space. His own tattoos had set fire to the muscles beneath them. His fangs ached. But those things were now the pain of enlightenment. That rose had bloomed at Castle Broceliande in the magnificent midnight garden. Tattooed on McKenna, the rose had always been the key to what she carried inside her.

"How did you get this?" he asked, fingering the tattoo.

"There was a birthmark in that spot. I had it defined."

The rapid buildup of a new pressure inside Kellan was obscene. He was the one shaking now. Hers was the steadying hand.

"I know you have to do this," she said. "You have to do

something with me or to me, though I don't know what that is. I'm not deaf. I heard everything said in that horrible place. There's no choice, is there, if I'm always to be the highest form of temptation?"

She reached up to press on his lips. Finding the fangs, she shut her eyes.

Kellan tore his gaze from the rose.

"I might be a pawn, but I don't want that vampire's soul inside me," she said. "Get it out. Take it away, whatever the cost."

Kellan found his voice. "That would be the end of us both."

"What's the alternative? You leave me, and I'll have that thing, that vampire, shadowing me forever? I'd rather end things here than be a vampire's plaything. I don't want your love if it's mixed with the feelings you once had for her."

"You are not her, McKenna."

"Then why do I feel her teeth on my neck? Her beatless heart in my chest? Why do I see those same questions reflected in your eyes? I'll never be whole if I can't stand on my own. I'll never be able to have you if you know these things are true."

He understood perfectly, and yet he couldn't move. He didn't dare address what McKenna was asking of him. Another sacrifice was one too many in a long line of them. He loved McKenna. How could he let her die in his arms?

"Do it now." McKenna's whisper was desperate and tugged at his heartstrings. Desperation was another emotion he understood all too well.

"Please," she said. "Don't leave me a victim. I can't live that way. I don't want to live that way."

His fingertip went to the scar on her temple. Kellan wondered if Damaris had anything to do with that bullet McKenna had taken, and probably would never be sure.

What he was sure of were his feelings for this woman.
He knew that Damaris would be waiting for her around
every corner if he didn't do what McKenna asked, and that
he would be torn from her no matter what.

Perhaps they would die together.

It was McKenna, his brave cop, the competent nurse,
who moved first. With his hand in hers, she stepped from
the shower wet, naked, somber and willing. To die.

She led him to the bedroom, to the bed, and sat down on
it, encouraging him to do the same. His heart was beating
loud and fast. In his long existence, he couldn't remember
the last time he'd wanted to run.

He could have her taken away to somewhere safe, far
from Seattle. Even then, though, Damaris could easily find
them. He would have gone away and left her in Miller's
care if Damaris wouldn't have been hovering.

None of those things gave either of them what they
wanted.

Was there only one way out?

Despite her wounds and abrasions, McKenna lay back
on the soft bed. Her eyes never left his. The fire in those
eyes matched the fire in the grooves on his back.

If he caved to McKenna's wishes, he would commit
that ultimate sin.

McKenna was beautiful, exceptional, one of a kind. For
a few more minutes, counted in heartbeats and suspended
breaths, she was his.

He tore off his wet clothes and stepped out of his boots.
He crawled up beside her and eased his weight on top of
the woman he loved with all his being.

He was inside her in seconds.

Their tears mingled on her cheek.

Chapter 29

Walls of white stone towered around her, over her. Candlelight glowed from windowless recesses. The scent of lavender wafted in the air, along with another, more nose-twinging fragrance.

Her pale hands gripped a pair of male shoulders reddened by freshly carved sigils. There was blood on the sheets, on those hands and on her mouth. His blood. Her blood. Mingling.

No sound penetrated the walls. Darkness surrounded their small pool of light. She was naked, and so was her lover. He was inside her, where he belonged, and where she would keep him always if she could. But fate had other plans for him, and this was to be their last night.

She writhed as she took him in, massaging his hard length, striving for a feeling that might last long after he'd gone. He gave her everything he had, with a series of powerful thrusts that might easily have either split weaker women in two or sent them running.

She wasn't a weakling and wanted to hurt. Needed to hurt. To that end, she urged her lover to a faster pace by raising her hips, wrapping her legs around his waist, allowing him free rein to do as he pleased with her, to her.

He went deep, hitting her core again and again, sinking into her, stroking her depths with an effort that made his arms shake and caused her thighs to weaken. She did not cry out. This was what she lived for. The pain would be all that was left after he had gone.

She cried. Tears of overwhelming sadness slipped down her cheek, pattering to her throat. Concerned, her lover drew back. His blue eyes found hers.

"I love you," she said.

"And I, you," he whispered back.

The cry McKenna heard was her own. The whispered affection had come from her mouth. The reply her lover gave hadn't been part of the dream.

Kellan loved her.

As in the dream, her legs were wrapped around the man who was loving her. Kellan moved in and out of her with strong strokes, hard strokes, burying himself inside her with his eyes closed as if he were eradicating demons. There was a good possibility he was.

McKenna took him in, matched the force of his ardor. Like the woman in the white castle, she encouraged him, closed herself around him, greedy for more, wanting it all, desperate to see this through to the end.

Inner rumblings came and went with the fury of a roller-coaster ride. She found ecstasy in every thrust and each withdrawal. The movement of his hips and the flexing of Kellan's back were torturous turn-ons.

She rode the waves of pleasure that built and receded, breathing only when she had to, shouting silently each time her wounds hit the sheets. Pain was part of this. His pain, and hers. The finale was up for grabs. When it would come was anyone's guess. She wasn't sure how Kellan would do it, yet knew that he would.

Where did a soul reside? What would happen to it when

she was dead? There would be no further use for it without its Knight. Maybe Damaris would end, as well.

When Kellan slowed, she complained with one more lift of her hips. When he became still, she looked deeply into his eyes.

"Do it," she said. "Do it at the peak of my love for you."

"Are you sure, my love?"

"Aren't you?"

His last thrust sent her over the edge of a vast precipice. She let loose the cry that had threatened since the start. The rumble reappeared from where it had been banished, careening toward Kellan like a flash fire.

Her lover went rigid, his muscles as hard as quarried marble, his cock buried deep. Then, with a single blasphemous cry, and as his own orgasm hit, he opened his mouth, exposed his fangs…and slid his teeth not into her neck, but into the heart of the rose on her upper arm.

The world became a wonderland of color before spinning off into black and white. Kellan drew back with the taste of blood in his mouth and looked with horror upon the puncture marks on McKenna's arm.

He had made those.

Her eyes were closed.

But he was still here.

Had he been wrong about everything?

"McKenna. God, McKenna."

She screamed. Her body seized. The bed shook, and the floor. Kellan held her down, pressed himself against her, whispered to her, scared now that the deed had been mangled, afraid he had done the wrong thing.

Her mouth opened as if she would speak. No words came out, but something else did. A swirl of gray fog emerged like exhaled cigarette smoke.

That fog came directly to him, breezed over his shoulders, caressed his neck, easing the fires on his back, calming his flaming sigils to a more manageable degree. He welcomed the coolness of that vapor. He waited for it to do what it had been intended to do.

There was a flash of a face at the window before the glass shattered. A vampire clung to the sill, hunched over with her red eyes wide and staring. Her long hair blew in the wind. Her black dress shone in the moonlight.

Damaris.

She held out both hands and whispered through her fangs as if casting a spell.

The fog left him, wafting toward Damaris as if it were a part of her, though it was no longer hers to claim. As she squatted there, the swirl of mist passed her by—this wisp of gray vapor that held the power, the secret, to ending what was otherwise endless, yet had not done so.

And then…the fog was gone.

Kellan had to look down at himself to prove that life had not been terminated. A thought came that perhaps he had been spared because he wanted so badly to remain with McKenna.

Panic struck. McKenna was motionless on the pillows.

Kellan slid his arms around her and pulled her close before turning again to the window. Damaris gave him one long look that told him she had done this. She had not allowed her soul to end his life. She could not condone any part of her harming the man she had loved so deeply.

And then she vanished in a flurry of black silk.

"McKenna. My love."

He had used his fangs, broken the rose, and he was alive.

He pressed back McKenna's fair, tangled hair, kissed her forehead, her cheek, her mouth. She didn't wake up.

She had to wake up.

She wasn't breathing.

"No!"

This could not happen. Not like this. He knew of only one way to wake her. This way was forbidden. Sacrilege. A sin. It wasn't how he had envisioned things, but what the hell? What good were rules now, when he did not want to exist without her.

Kellan parted McKenna's lips with a trembling finger. Biting down on his own lower lip, tasting the blood, he gathered drops of that blood on his hand and let it drip into her mouth. He replaced his hand with his lips.

He kissed McKenna, willing her to open her eyes, demanding that she obey. He kissed her as if there would be a tomorrow, and more days after that.

Come back to me, my love.

Breathe. Now. Accept this gift.

His lips left hers. She uttered no sound. He kissed her again, pushing his silent power into her over and over. He sent commands of waking, of breathing and of the vastness of his love for her. He felt that power spark.

Light appeared at the window. Dawn had arrived. Kellan went on kissing her, breathing for her, refusing to give up.

And he was rewarded. As the rounded edge of the sun began to rise somewhere beyond the city's buildings, McKenna took a breath.

"Yes, my love. I'm here. It's all right."

Kellan's power raged as her lashes fluttered. Her chest rose once, twice, and then she opened her eyes.

"One more choice," he said to her. "It's yours to make, my dear, dear McKenna. My love. But you must decide now, and the decision must stand."

Chapter 30

The Harley purred on the open road, taking the bumps like a Thoroughbred, without missing a stride. McKenna, in black leather, spoke in Kellan's ear.

"I'm not sorry about leaving Seattle to Derek. Where are we heading?"

"To LA."

"Plenty of shadows there, I suppose?"

"I hear it's a dropping-off point for every bloodsucker west of Texas," Kellan said. "Though that isn't the reason I want to go. I have old family ties there."

She was quiet for some time before saying, "I didn't realize you had family."

"A brother is there, who is also my father, or so the legends say."

McKenna replayed the mythology of Galahad and the Round Table in her head. "You're kidding, right? Would that be Lancelot?"

The idea of another creature like Kellan existing on this earth had always been daunting, as was the possibility of meeting Lancelot du Lac in the flesh. Meeting another Blood Knight would prove that more of the legends were true in spite of the fact that no one had got anything straight. The Grail Knights seated at Arthur's Round Table had been supernaturally beautiful and undefeated in battle because they had actually been supernatural creatures. And a few of them still existed today. Somewhere on this earth there were six others like Kellan. Right here, right now, there was a new immortal addition to the gang—an ex-cop, ex-nurse potential vigilante named McKenna. That was the choice he had offered her, and the one she had taken.

But when thinking about meeting Lancelot, McKenna thought seriously about asking Kellan to turn the bike around.

"Not going to do that, either," he said, easily reading her mind.

"Brother and father, both? No wonder…" McKenna started to say teasingly, but found herself by the side of the road, in the grass, on her back before finishing the remark.

Seattle's lights were a dim glow in the distance. Overhead, stars shone like diamonds in a clear night sky. They hadn't gone forty miles from where they started and had to answer the call of their needy bodies. It had been like this since that first night. They couldn't seem to get enough of each other, and immortality had blown those needs way out of proportion.

Or hell, maybe this was still some kind of crazy soul business.

Kellan had stripped naked beside her, revealing his true feelings for his lover, his partner, his new immortal companion. McKenna heard his fangs drop. Inside her mouth, hers did the same. She had a hard time tearing her gaze from his impeccable body. When she did, she found him smiling.

And her soul—one that was her very own—sparked as she heard Kellan whisper, "I will love you...*forever*."

Because she was now strong enough to see that he did.

* * * * *

MILLS & BOON®

Helen Bianchin v Regency Collection!

316_MB520

MILLS & BOON®

nocturne™

AN EXHILARATING UNDERWORLD OF DARK DESIRES

A sneak peek at next month's titles...

In stores from 7th April 2016:

- **Dark Journey** – Susan Krinard
- **Otherworld Renegade** – Jane Godman

0416/89

"Hafiz, we're outside," Lacey reminded him, her voice hitching with scandalised excitement. **"You shouldn't be this close."**

He knew it, but it didn't stop him. She was his one and only vice, and he was willingly addicted. He had already risked everything to be with her. Each day he made the choice to risk everything for her. But now the choice had been taken away from him, and it was all coming to an end.

He bent his head and stopped abruptly. He should pull away. Hafiz remained still as he stared at Lacey's mouth. Their ragged breathing sounded loud to his ears. One kiss could bring him peace or could set him on fire. One kiss would lead to another.

ROYAL AND RUTHLESS

The power of the throne, the passion of a king!

Whether he is a playboy prince or a masterful king
he has always known his destiny:
Duty—first, last and always.

With millions at his fingertips
and the world at his command,
no one has dared to challenge this ruthless royal's desire…
Until now.

More **Royal and Ruthless** titles:

Kate Walker
A THRONE FOR THE TAKING

Caitlin Crews
A ROYAL WITHOUT RULES

Kim Lawrence
THE HEARTBREAKER PRINCE

PRINCE HAFIZ'S
ONLY VICE

BY
SUSANNA CARR

MILLS
BOON

Published in Great Britain 2014
by Mills & Boon, an imprint of Harlequin (UK) Limited,
Eton House, 18-24 Paradise Road, Richmond, Surrey, TW9 1SR

© 2014 Susanna Carr

ISBN: 978-0-263-90906-7

Harlequin (UK) Limited's policy is to use papers that are natural,
renewable and recyclable products and made from wood grown in
sustainable forests. The logging and manufacturing processes conform
to the legal environmental regulations of the country of origin.

Printed and bound in Spain
by Blackprint CPI, Barcelona

Susanna Carr has been an avid romance reader since she read her first Mills & Boon® Modern at the age of ten. Although romance novels were not allowed in her home, she always managed to sneak one in from the local library or from her twin sister's secret stash.

After attending college, and receiving a degree in English Literature, Susanna pursued a romance-writing career. She has written sexy contemporary romances for several publishers and her work has been honoured with awards for contemporary and sensual romance.

Susanna lives in the Pacific Northwest with her family. When she isn't writing she enjoys reading romance and connecting with readers online. Visit her website at: www.susannacarr.com

Recent titles by the same author:

SECRETS OF A BOLLYWOOD MARRIAGE
A DEAL WITH BENEFITS
 (One Night with Consequences)
HER SHAMEFUL SECRET
THE TARNISHED JEWEL OF JAZAAR

**Did you know these are also available as eBooks?
Visit www.millsandboon.co.uk**

To Sarah Stubbs,
with thanks for her guidance and encouragement.

CHAPTER ONE

HER LOVER'S PICTURE was on the front page of every paper in the small newsstand.

Lacey adjusted the dark sunglasses that concealed her bright blue eyes and squinted at the newspaper on display. Although the headline was in Arabic, the print was big and bold. She could tell that something important had happened. Something that could explain the jubilant attitude that shimmered in the marketplace. No doubt Prince Hafiz had made his countrymen proud again.

She wondered what he had done this time as she requested the daily English paper in halting Arabic. Did he add a fortune to the royal coffers? Convince another industry to make the Sultanate of Rudaynah their headquarters? Win an award?

She decided it would be best to wait until she got home before she read the paper. Lacey took another glance at the pictures of Hafiz that covered the stall. His expression was solemn, but it didn't stop the secret thrill sweeping across her heated skin. It was unnerving that Hafiz could elicit that kind of response through a photograph.

The photo was an official head shot the palace systematically offered to the press, but while the image was familiar, it always grabbed the reader's notice. No one could look away from Prince Hafiz's mysterious dark eyes and harsh mouth. He was devastatingly handsome from his luxuriant black hair to his sharp bone structure. Women watched him from afar, too awed of his masculine beauty.

Or perhaps they sensed his raw power beneath his sophisticated manners. Lacey had instantly recognized the sexual hunger lurking below his ruthless restraint. His primitive aura was a silent warning that most women heeded. But for Lacey, it drew her closer.

She had found Hafiz's relentless self-discipline fascinating. It had also been a challenge. From the moment they had met, she had been tempted to strip him from his exquisitely tailored pinstripe suit and discover his most sensual secrets.

Just the thought of him made her impatient to get back home. She needed to return before Hafiz got there. His workload would crush a lesser man, but he still managed to visit Lacey at nightfall.

The blazing sun began to dip in the desert sky, and she didn't want to contemplate how Hafiz would respond if she weren't home.

He never asked what she did during the day, Lacey thought with a frown. At first his lack of interest had bothered her. Did he think time stood still for her until he appeared?

There were moments when she wanted to share her plans and ideas, even discuss her day, but she had always held back. She wasn't ready to reveal the work she had done. Not yet. Lacey wanted to show Hafiz what she was capable of. How she could contribute.

She wanted to show that she was ready to make his sultanate her permanent home.

It hadn't been easy. There were days, weeks, when she had been homesick. Lonely and bored. She had missed her wide circle of friends and colorful nightlife, and she craved the basic comforts.

It was aggravating that the newspaper hadn't been delivered today at her penthouse, but that wasn't surprising. After living in the small Arabian country for almost six months, Lacey still hadn't gotten used to sporadic service, frequent power outages and laborers arriving at work anywhere from three hours to three days late.

Her connection to the outside world was just as erratic. The communication services were usually down, like today. When they were running, the content was heavily censored.

Definitely not the lifestyle she had enjoyed in St. Louis. Not that she was complaining, Lacey hurriedly assured herself. She was willing to forego many comforts and conveniences for the one thing she couldn't get back in the States: Hafiz.

Lacey shivered with anticipation and handed the coins to the newspaper boy. She practiced her Arabic and felt a sense of accomplishment when the young man understood her. Lacey shyly tugged at the bright orange scarf wrapped around her head and tucked in a wayward strand of hair.

Maybe she was ready to show Hafiz what she had learned over the past few months. She wasn't fluent and didn't know everything about the culture, but she was getting impatient. It was time to meet his family and friends.

Lacey bit her lip as she imagined making that demand. The idea made her uncomfortable. She had been stalling. Not because his family was royal but because she was worried she would push too soon.

Lacey didn't want to give an ultimatum. The last time she'd taken a stand she had lost everything. She wasn't ready to lose Hafiz. Unlike her parents, who had no problems walking away from her in pursuit of their dreams, Hafiz hadn't been able to bear leaving her and had brought her to his home. Well, not his home, but his home country.

As much as she wanted to be part of Hafiz's life and share her life with him, she needed to be patient. She had to trust that Hafiz knew what he was doing. Lacey sighed deeply. She wasn't used to allowing another to take charge.

But she was in a country that followed different codes of conduct. She was also in love with a prince, and she didn't know much about royal life. Her presence in Hafiz's world required delicacy.

Lacey was amazed that Hafiz could even breathe among all the rules and regulations. But not once did he complain. His strong shoulders never sagged from the burden. The man was driven to attack every challenge and reach a goal he never discussed, but Lacey guessed that world domination was just the beginning. His obligations were never far from his mind. That is, until he was in bed with her. Then the world stopped as they fulfilled every fantasy their bodies craved and every wish their hearts desired.

Pleasure nestled low in her stomach, beneath the stifling black gabardine caftan. Lacey stuffed the English newspaper into her plastic shopping bag that contained the crimson desert flowers. She hoped the article offered good news, although she couldn't imagine the press saying anything less than flattering.

She hurried off the curb, and the blowing horn of a filthy truck had her jumping back to the sidewalk. Reddish clouds billowed from the dirt road and settled into a fine layer on her soft black boots.

She waved her hand in front of her face, blinking away the grit. Lacey wrinkled her nose at the tart smell of animals, car fumes and rotting sewage. She knew the small country just recently came into wealth, but if this was a decade of progress, she was grateful she hadn't seen the unenlightened country.

A memory flickered of Hafiz talking about his country when they had first met. He'd spoken with love and pride about the rich heritage and romance of the desert. Hafiz had described the tribal music and the exotic spices lingering in the starry nights. When he'd told the story of how the sultanate had been named after the first sultana, Lacey had thought Rudaynah had to be a romantic paradise.

Never trust a man's idea of romance, Lacey decided as she determinedly stepped into traffic. The high-pitched ring of bicycle bells shrieked in her ears as she zigzagged her way across the street. She dodged a bored donkey pulling a cart of pungent waste matter. A bus whipped past, her plastic bag swatting against one of the male passengers hanging outside the overcrowded and rusted vehicle.

Lacey hurried to her apartment in earnest. Shadows grew longer and darker as the sun dipped precariously closer to the horizon. She nodded a greeting to the armed guards at the gates of the condominium complex. The men, all in olive green uniforms and sporting bushy mustaches, waved her in without a pause in their conversation.

She scurried across the bare courtyard, pausing only as a big insect with a vicious-sounding buzz flew in front of her. Gritting her teeth as she shuddered with revulsion, Lacey turned the corner to access the private elevator that would lead her straight to the penthouse apartment.

She halted when she saw a man waiting for the elevator. Lacey barely had time to gasp as her mind snatched a flurry of disjointed images. A white flowing robe. A golden chord over the white *kaffiyeh* that covered his hair. She didn't need to see the man's face to sense the impenetrable wall of arrogant masculinity. Of power and privilege. There was only one man who enjoyed a life with no limitations or impossibilities.

"Hafiz?" she whispered.

Prince Hafiz ibn Yusuf Qadi whirled around. "Lacey?" He moved forward and stared at her. He slowly blinked and frowned. His sexy and glamorous mistress was wearing a shapeless caftan and a hideous scarf. There wasn't a hint of makeup on her pale face, but she was still a stunning beauty.

"What are you doing down here?" Prince Hafiz plucked off her sunglasses. He needed to see her eyes. He could always tell what she was thinking and feeling when he met her bright blue gaze.

After he snatched the glasses, Hafiz pushed down the head scarf and was rewarded with a cascade of copper-red curls. His fingers flexed. He wanted to touch her hair. Fan it out and allow the last rays of the sun to catch the fiery color. Sink his fingers into the soft weight as he kissed her hard.

Instead, he slowly, reluctantly, let his hand fall to his side. He gripped her sunglasses until the tips of his fingers whitened. He could not touch her. Not here, not in public. One graze, one brush of skin, and he wouldn't stop.

It didn't help that Lacey wanted to greet him with a kiss. The sight of her closed eyes and parted lips whirled him back to the first time he'd seen her. That fateful night he had entered the luxury hotel near the St. Louis waterfront.

The lobby had bustled with activity and there was a piano bar to the side. The deceptively languorous music had caught his attention, but it was her singing that had made him turn around. Soft and clear like the voice of a well-bred lady, but so rich and velvety that it sparked his wicked imagination.

And when he had seen her, his heart had slammed against his ribs. Lacey was an intriguing mix of contrasts. She had looked like an innocent girl, but her voice held a wealth of experience. Her red hair had flowed past her shoulders like a veil, touching the simple blue evening gown. It should have been a modest dress that covered her from her slender neck to her delicate ankles, yet it had lovingly clung to every curve.

Hafiz had known she was trouble, but that hadn't stopped him from walking toward the piano as she'd coaxed a longing note from the ivory keys.

She hadn't seen his approach as she closed her eyes and raised her flushed face to the sky, swept away from the music. And he had allowed her to take him with her.

Hafiz forced himself to the present and away from the untroubled past. His gaze drifted to the voluminous black gown veiling her body from his eyes. For some reason, that irked him. "What are you wearing?"

She opened her eyes and frowned before she placed her hands on her hips. The movement gave him some indication of where the soft swells and curves were underneath her outfit. "I could ask the same about you," she said as her wide eyes roamed over his appearance. "I have never seen you like this. It's straight out of *Lawrence of Arabia.*"

Lacey's voice was deep and husky as the desire shone in her eyes. When she looked at him like that… His skin flushed and pulled tight. How did this woman make him this hot, this fast, without even touching him?

His body hardened, and he gulped in the hot desert air. He could take Lacey against this hidden corner and capture her cries of ecstasy with his mouth within minutes. All he needed was… Hafiz shook his head slightly. What was he thinking? The last thing he needed was for the sultan to discover he had a mistress living in the shadow of the palace.

"This is a *dishdasha,*" he explained gruffly as he tried to contain the lust that heated his blood. "I wear it for royal functions. Now explain what you are doing outside alone."

She held up her plastic bag and lightly jostled the contents. "I went shopping."

"Shopping," he repeated dully.

"Yes, I wear this whenever I leave the apartment." She glided her hand down the black gabardine with the flair of a game show model demonstrating a prize.

"I know Rudaynah only asks tourists to dress modestly, but I don't know if I fall in that category. I'm not quite a tourist, but I'm not quite a resident, am I? I didn't want to take any chances."

Hafiz barely heard the question. *Whenever she left?* She had done this more than once? Routinely? What did she do? Where did she go? And with whom?

It wouldn't be with a man. He knew he could trust Lacey. She had fallen in love with him that first night and saw no reason to deny it.

But he didn't like the possibility that she had a life apart from him. He was the center of her world, and he didn't want that to end. "Whenever you leave?" he asked as his eyebrows dipped into a ferocious frown. "How often do you go out?"

"You don't need to worry about me." Lacey's smile dropped. "Or are you worried that one of your friends or relatives will meet me?"

Hafiz heard the edge in her tone and felt her impatience. He surrendered to the need to touch her and delve his hands into her hair. He needed to feel the connection that sizzled between them.

Hafiz spanned his fingers along the base of her head and tilted her face up. "I thought you spend your days playing your music," he murmured distractedly.

"And dreaming about you?"

"Of course," he said with a slanted smile.

Her smooth brow wrinkled as she considered what he said. "I can think of you while I'm shopping. I'm talented that way."

"No." His sharp tone stanched any argument. "No more excursions. You don't know the language or the country."

"How else am I going to learn if I don't get out and—"

"You have servants who can shop for you. Yes, yes." He held his hand up as she tried to interrupt. "You've already told me. You're not comfortable with the idea of someone waiting on you. But they are here to take care of you."

"You can't hide me inside all the time," she insisted as she pressed her hand against his chest. His heart thudded from her touch. "I'm not Rapunzel."

"I know," he said resignedly. She often mentioned that European fairy tale. She once told him the basic story line, but someday he needed to read it in case there was more he should know.

Lacey leaned against the wall and sighed. Hafiz flattened his hands next to her head, her sunglasses dangling from his loose grasp. He stared at her mouth, his lips stinging with the need to kiss her.

But this was as close as he would allow himself. If he leaned into her softness, he wouldn't leave.

The tip of her tongue swept along her bottom lip. "Hafiz, we're outside," she reminded him, her voice hitching with scandalized excitement. "You shouldn't be this close."

He knew it, but it didn't stop him. She was his one and only vice, and he was willingly addicted. He had already risked everything to be with her. Each day he made the choice to risk everything for her. But now the choice was taken away from him, and it was all coming to an end.

He bent his head and stopped abruptly. He should pull away. Hafiz remained still as he stared at Lacey's mouth. Their ragged breathing sounded loud to his ears. One kiss could bring him peace or could set him on fire. One kiss would lead to another.

As if he were in a trance, Hafiz grazed his fingertips against her brow. He caressed her cheek, wishing it were his mouth on her. Hafiz swallowed hard as he remembered how her skin tasted.

He shouldn't be with her. No, it was more than that. He shouldn't *want* to be with her. Lacey Maxwell was forbidden.

Wanting Lacey went against everything he had been taught. He should only find honorable and chaste women from his sultanate attractive. Yet the only woman he noticed was Lacey.

She was bold and beautiful. Instead of hiding her curves, she flaunted her body. She showed no shame in her desire for him. And instead of trying to tame him, Lacey encouraged the wild streak inside him that he had tried so hard to suffocate.

The sound of his heartbeat pounded in his ears as he stroked Lacey's jaw. She tilted her head, exposing her slender throat. He wanted to sweep his fingers along the elegant column and dip his hand beneath the caftan. He wanted to hear her shallow breaths turn into groans and whispers.

But that would be reckless. Hafiz dragged his thumb against her lips. He traced the shape of her mouth over and over until her lips clung to his skin.

Lacey turned her face away. Hafiz gripped her chin and held her still. With a growl of surrender, he bent down to claim her mouth with his.

"Hafiz," she whispered fiercely. "We will be seen."

That warning could form ice in his sizzling veins

like no other. His chest rose and fell as he reined in runaway needs. With great reluctance, he drew away.

"We should leave before one of the neighbors spots me," Lacey said shakily as she pulled the scarf over her head.

Disappointment scored his chest as she tucked her glorious hair away. "I don't like seeing you covered up like this." He never thought about how he would feel seeing his woman veiled, but it felt intrinsically wrong to conceal Lacey's captivating beauty and character.

"Believe me, I don't like wearing it." She reached for her sunglasses. "It's like an oven, but it makes me invisible and that's all that matters."

He flashed a disbelieving look. "Lacey, you could never be invisible."

Her smile was dazzling as she blushed with pleasure. It was as if he had given her the ultimate compliment.

"Take off your scarf," he insisted in a rough whisper. "No one will see. Everyone will be at prayer." Hafiz wondered why he resented the scarf and sunglasses so much that he was willing to risk the chance of discovery. He reached for her arm and pulled her close.

"Don't be too sure. Most people acted like they were ready to celebrate tonight. I don't know why—" The plastic bag fell from her wrist. She bent down to retrieve the contents, and he followed her descent. Her sharp cry startled him.

"Lacey?" He looked down at the cracked cement floor and didn't understand what was wrong when he saw the dark red flowers resting unblemished on the floor. He almost missed the English newspaper

with his picture on the front page. The bold headline grabbed him by the throat and hurtled him into
despair.

Prince Hafiz to Marry

CHAPTER TWO

LACEY STARED AT the engagement announcement. Her mind refused to comprehend the words. "Marry?" she whispered. Her wild gaze flew to Hafiz's harsh face. "You're getting married?"

She waited in agony as he rose to his full height. He looked very tall and intimidating. Almost like a stranger.

Lacey didn't realize she was holding her breath until he answered. "Yes."

The single word sent her universe into a spiral. "I don't...I don't..." She stared at the headline again, but the pain was too raw, too intense. She hurriedly stuffed the newspaper and flowers back into the bag.

Her hands shook as the rage and something close to fear swirled inside her. Fear of losing everything. Pure anger at the thought of Hafiz with another woman. The fury threatened to overpower her. She wanted to scream at the injustice and claw at something. Stake her claim. Hafiz belonged to her.

"You have been with another woman." She couldn't believe it. "All this time, you were with someone else."

Hafiz's eyes narrowed at the accusation. "No. You

have been the only woman in my life since I met you in St. Louis a year ago."

She was the only woman, and yet he was going to marry another? Lacey fumbled with her sunglasses and tossed them in the bag. "Then how are you...I don't understand."

He braced his feet a shoulders' width apart and clasped his hands behind his back, preparing for battle. "I met the bride today and she agreed."

Lacey's mouth gaped open. "You just met her?" She snatched the flicker of hope and held on tight. "So, it's an arranged marriage."

Hafiz let out a bark of humorless laughter. "Of course."

"Then, what's the problem?" She moved slowly as she stood. Her arms and legs felt limp and shaky. She lurched as she stepped on the hem of her insufferable caftan. "Say that you won't get married."

He looked away. "I can't." Regret tinged his voice.

Lacey wanted to stamp her foot and demand a better answer, but she knew she wouldn't get it. Not with his shuttered expression and the regal tilt of his stubborn chin. "It's not like you're the crown prince," she argued, "although I don't understand that since you're the oldest son. But this means you have more freedom."

Hafiz's eyes closed wearily for a brief moment. "For the last time, the sultan chooses the next in line for the throne. My father chose my brother. And, no, I don't have any freedom in this matter, even though I will never rule. In my case, I have less."

She didn't want to hear that. Thick emotions already clogged her aching throat. "You should never have agreed to marry this woman," she said as her voice wobbled.

He turned his attention back to her. "I gave my consent," he said gently. "I can't take it back."

What about the promises he made to her? The ones he made first. The ones about how they would be together. Didn't those promises matter? Didn't *she* matter?

"Why did you agree in the first place?" She held the plastic bag to her chest. She would rather hold on to something solid and strong like Hafiz until the emotional storm passed, which would still leave her feeling battered and stinging with pain, but he would prevent her from breaking. "You should have refused."

"I couldn't this time." Hafiz winced the moment he revealed too much. He pressed his lips into a straight line.

Lacey stared at him with open suspicion. "This time?" she echoed. "How long have you been looking for a wife?"

"Could we not discuss this here?" he bit out tersely. "Let's go back to the apartment." He guided her to the elevator, keeping a firm hand on her arm as she still weaved from the unpleasant shock. He pressed the call button, and she watched as if her life depended on it, but her brain couldn't register the simple, everyday action.

"Marry," she repeated and shook her head. "I don't believe this. Why didn't you tell me?"

"I am telling you." He kept his eyes on the descending lighted floor numbers.

"Now. After everything is settled." She couldn't be bothered to hide the accusation in her voice.

He spared a glance at her. "Not quite, but it is official as of this morning. I wanted to tell you before you found out from another source."

That explained the missing newspapers. "How considerate." She felt his start of surprise from her bitter sarcasm, but she didn't care. Hafiz was getting married. To someone else. The knowledge stabbed at her heart. It was a wonder she didn't break from the piercing force. "When is the wedding taking place?"

"After Eid." His answer was almost swallowed by the clank and thump of the arriving elevator.

Eid. That holiday came after the month of Ramadan, if she recalled correctly. She remembered something being mentioned in the paper about that coming soon. "Three months?" she made a guess.

He held the sliding metal doors open for her. "More or less."

Lacey walked into the elevator compartment, her head spinning. Three months. She only had three months with Hafiz.

What was she thinking? She had no more time left. Oh, God. She wasn't strong enough to handle this. She was going to shatter from the pain. Hafiz was an engaged man. Off-limits. And she never had any warning.

Her mouth suddenly felt dry as she instinctively pressed the burgeoning wails and sobs into silence until they were ready to burst from her skin. "You should have told me you were looking for a wife."

"I wasn't. I have no interest in getting married. I held it off for as long as possible."

Lacey reeled back in shock. Hafiz had no interest in marriage? *At all?* Not even to her? If that was the case, then what had the past six months been about?

"My parents were looking for a wife for me," he clarified sternly.

"But you knew they were," she argued. "You knew this was going to happen."

Hafiz said nothing and pressed the top floor button several times as the elevator doors slowly shut.

Winning that point of the argument was a hollow victory. "How long have they been looking?" A part of her wanted to know, the other part wanted to deny that any of this was happening.

He stood silently, his jaw tightly clenched. A muscle twitched in his cheek. Lacey thought for a moment he didn't hear her and was about to repeat the question when he finally answered. "A couple of years."

"A…couple of *years*?" She couldn't possibly have heard that correctly. Lacey folded her arms across her chest. "From the time that you knew me, from the very first time you *propositioned* me, you were also on the marriage market? And not once did you find the chance to tell me?"

Why would he? Lacey thought bitterly. He hadn't considered her to be in the running. She was just a bit of fun on the side. A temporary distraction. Oh, she was a fool.

"Marriage negotiations are delicate and complex," he explained as impatience roughened his words. "It could have taken even longer to find a suitable match."

Suitable. She sneered at the term. It was a code word for the right bloodline and the right upbringing from the right family. Not a blue-eyed American who was also an unemployed nightclub musician.

Oh, and suitable meant someone who was pure and virginal. She mustn't forget that.

The injustice of it all flared to new heights. "Not once did you tell me, and yet I dropped my entire life to be with you." Her voice raised another octave. "I moved to the far-off corners of the earth, to this hell—"

"The Sultanate of Rudaynah is not hell." His low growl was similar to that of a wild cat ready to pounce.

"—And exist solely for you and your pleasure! And you don't have the decency to tell me that you're getting married?" Her eyes narrowed into a withering glare.

He gestured with his hands. "Calm down."

"Calm down?" She thought now was as good a time as any to rant. She was ready to punctuate her tantrum by throwing her shopping bag at his sinfully gorgeous face. "Calm down! No, I will not calm down. The man I love, the man I sacrificed everything for is throwing it all away right back into my face," she hissed, her cheeks hot with fury. "Believe me, this is not a time to calm down."

Hafiz was suddenly in front of her. He made a grab for her, but she raised her hands, warding him off. Lacey fought the urge to burrow her head into his shoulder and weep.

"I am not throwing you away, damn it. How could I?" he asked as his bronze eyes silently pleaded for understanding. "You are the best thing that has ever happened to me."

Lacey looked away and tilted her head against the corner. She needed something to lean against anyway

as her knees were incapable of supporting her. A buzzing filled her head. She took short, even breaths of the
stifling air and blinked back the dark spots.

As the elevator made its slow, rocky ascent, Lacey
realized that Hafiz must be equally unnerved by the
turn of the events. He had cursed. Another first for
the day. Hafiz never, ever cursed. But then, he always
controlled the situation and his environment with the
same iron will he used over his temper.

Over himself, really. The man never drank alcohol
or gambled. He did not live in excess. His sculpted
muscles were that of an athlete in training. He barely
slept, too busy working to improve the living condi-
tions of Rudaynah. When he wasn't fulfilling his royal
and patriotic duties, he met every family obligation.
Even marry his parent's choice.

The only time he went wild, the only time he allowed his control to slip, was when they were in bed.
Lacey winced, and the first scalding teardrop fell.

Tears streamed out of her eyes and burned jagged
lines down her hot cheeks. Why had she thought Hafiz
was considering a future with her? Not once did he
mention the possibility of happily-ever-after. Never
did the word "marriage" ever cross his lips.

But the dream had been harbored deep in her heart,
secretly growing. It had been incredibly naïve and
wrong to think all she had to do was be patient. She
thought that if she came here and slowly entered the
culture, she would eventually stand publicly by Hafiz's
side as his wife.

Only that dream died the moment Hafiz pledged
himself to another. She gasped as the words plunged

into her heart. The surrounding blackness she had been fighting back swiftly invaded her mind.

Pledged to another...

The buzzing grew louder and almost masked Hafiz's shout of alarm.

"Lacey!" Hafiz caught her as she slid down the wall. He plucked off her scarf, and her head lolled to one side. He supported her head with his shoulder and noted that her unnaturally pale face was sticky with sweat. He patted her clammy cheek with his hand. "Lacey," he repeated, trying to rouse her.

Her eyelashes fluttered. "So hot."

He gathered her in his arms. The ill-fitting black gown bunched around her slender figure. "I'll take care of you," he promised, holding her tighter. And he would, he vowed to himself, until his last breath. No matter what she thought, he would never cast her aside.

The elevator finally stopped on the penthouse floor. He searched her features, vaguely aware how her curly long hair hung defiantly like a copper flag and her bare legs dangled from the crook of his elbow, exposing her ivory skin for the world to see. If they were caught in this compromising embrace, so be it. Lacey's safety and comfort were always top priority, but now it was more essential than his next heartbeat, Hafiz decided as he stepped out of the elevator and onto the open-air hallway to the apartment.

The sun was setting. Dark reds and rich purples washed the sky as evening prayers were sung from a nearby loudspeaker. Hafiz kept his eyes out for any potential trouble, but he saw no one strolling the grounds or outside the condominiums across the courtyard. But from the domestic sounds emitting from the neighbors' homes on the other floors, the situation could change in an instant.

Carrying Lacey to her front door at a brisk pace, Hafiz noted he wasn't even breathing hard from lifting her. She weighed barely anything. He glanced down at her face and the fragility struck him like a fist.

Not for the first time did he wonder if moving Lacey to Rudaynah had been the best decision for her. Life in hiding had taken its toll. Why hadn't he seen that before? Or did he not want to see it?

Lacey stirred as if she was acutely aware of his perusal. "I'm fine," she murmured and tentatively ran her tongue over her parched lips.

"No, you're not." He leaned heavily against the doorbell and waited at the iron grille door until the American servant wearing a loose T-shirt and cargo pants came to the door.

"Your Highness! What happened?" Glenn asked as he unlocked the door bolts with economical movements. His craggy face showed no alarm, but his watchful eyes were alert. His body, lean from many years of military training, vibrated with readiness to act on the first command from his employer.

"It's all right. She fainted from the heat." Hafiz kicked off his sandals at the door and moved past the older man. "I'll get her into the shower. Have your wife prepare something very cold and sweet for her to drink."

"I'm sorry, Your Highness." Glenn raked his hand over his bristly gray hair. "She said—"

"It's all right," he repeated, calling over his shoulder as he made way to the master bedroom. "Lacey has always had a problem following directions."

"I'm not dead, you know," Lacey said with her eyes closed. "I can hear every word."

"Good, because I do not want you venturing outside again without Glenn," Hafiz said as he stepped into the large room where he spent many hours exploring Lacey's body and revealing the darkest recesses of his heart. This time the sumptuous silks and oversized pillows didn't stir his hot blood. He wanted to tuck Lacey between the colorful sheets and not let her out of bed until she regained her vibrancy. "He is your bodyguard and—"

"He is to play the role of my next of kin if any questions are asked because single women are not allowed to travel alone in this country," Lacey ended in a monotone. She let out a slow, stuttering sigh that seemed to originate from somewhere deep inside her. "I know."

"Then, don't let it happen again." He pushed the bathroom door open with his bare foot. Slapping the light switch outside the door with the palm of his hand, he entered the windowless room now flooding with light.

"It won't."

The determination in her voice made him hesitate. He cautiously watched her face as he set her down gently, sliding her feminine curves along his length. For once her expression showed nothing. Her eyes veiled her feelings. Usually her eyes would darken with righteous indignation, glow with rapturous delight and twinkle with every emotion in between. The sudden change in her behavior troubled him.

He wanted to hold her close until he could read her thoughts, but Lacey had other ideas as she moved away from him. "Can you stand on your own?" he asked.

"Yes." She took another step back and shucked off her cloth boots. The movements lacked her usual energy.

He kept one hand outstretched in case he had to catch her as he started the shower full blast. Hafiz turned his attention on Lacey and quickly divested her of her black caftan.

"Lacey!" His startled hoarse cry echoed in the small room. The sight of her barely-there peach lingerie was a shocking contrast against the conservative cloth. Hafiz's body reacted immediately. The heavy black material dropped from his fists and flopped on the wet floor.

"What?" She inspected her arms and legs. "What's wrong?"

He cleared his throat, wishing he could also clear the sharp arousal tightening his body. "You're supposed to wear several layers of clothes under the caftan." He unhooked the front closure of her bra, his knuckles grazing her breast. He saw the tremor in his hands. He was acting like a callow youth.

"Are you kidding?" She skimmed the high-cut panties down her legs and kicked them aside. "I would boil alive."

His gaze traveled as the peach satin landed on the black fabric. The searing image branded in his mind. The way he would look at women in the shapeless caftan was forever changed. He swallowed roughly as he controlled his baser instinct. "What if you had gotten caught?"

"No one would have found out. You are the only person who has shown enough nerve to get that close." She arched her eyebrow in disapproval.

And he was going to keep it that way. "Here, get under the water." He pulled her to the showerhead.

"Oh! Ow!" Lacey squealed in dismay as the icy cold spray hit her body. She jumped back and rubbed her hands over her arms. "This is so cold."

"You'll get used to it in just a minute," he replied as he always did to her comments on the lack of heated water. The familiarity calmed him while her beaded nipples made his brain sluggish.

"You can leave now," she said through chattering teeth. She looked away from him and tested the temperature by dipping her foot in the cold water.

He leaned against the door and folded his arms across his chest. "I don't want you passing out in the shower."

"I won't. Now go before your royal gown gets soaked." She shooed him away with her hands.

She had a point. The bathroom, already hot as a sauna, was in the traditional Rudaynahi design, with the exception of a European commode. The concrete floor had a drain and was also to be used as the shower floor. Since there was no plastic curtain or glass shower door, the water was already spraying every inch of the bathroom.

"If you're sure," Hafiz said and flashed a wicked smile. "But I can just as easily take it off."

She glared back at him. "I'm sure."

His smile turned wry at her ungracious rejection.

He shouldn't have made the offer. He knew that but went for it anyway. "I'll be outside," Hafiz said. Lacey didn't respond as she stuck her head fully under the spray.

He stepped out of the bathroom and almost collided with the housekeeper who carried a small tray into the bedroom. The tall frosty glass of juice rattled against a plate of figs and dates.

"How is she doing?" Annette asked as she set the tray on the bedside table. "Do we need to call a doctor?"

"No, she's not sick." The uncertain look of the older woman irritated him. If he truly felt Lacey needed medical care, he would call the American doctor who'd already discovered that cashing in favors from a prince was worth more than any currency in a country that relied heavily on the bartering system.

The physician was brilliant and up to date on medicine. Hafiz had seen that firsthand when Lacey arrived in the country and had drunk water that had not been purified. That week had been torture, and Hafiz was insistent that she was given the best care, no matter what. Hafiz would never place secrecy above Lacey's well-being, and it stung to have someone silently questioning his priorities.

"She's overheated," he explained, keeping the defensiveness out of his voice. "The shower is already doing wonders."

"We threw away the newspapers like you requested, but we never thought Lacey would leave to get one." The woman twisted the pleat of her yellow sundress with nervous hands and slid a worried glance at the closed bathroom door.

"It's no one's fault," he said. No one's but his own. He should have prepared Lacey for the possibility of his wedding, but he'd held on to the hope that his intended bride would have declined the offer. "Please, find something light for her to wear."

"Of course." The housekeeper gratefully accepted the task and opened the doors to the armoire, revealing gossamer-thin cotton in every color of the rainbow.

Hafiz walked into the simply appointed drawing room and tried to recapture the peace he always felt whenever he stepped into this home. Decorated with an eclectic mix of wood tables carved in the severe Rudaynahi style and chunky upholstered sofas from the Western world, Lacey had managed to add her upbeat personality with tribal throw rugs and colorful paintings from local artisans.

The apartment was more than a home. It was a haven. It was the only place he felt both passion and peace. The only place in the world he experienced unconditional love.

Hafiz walked slowly to the grand piano that sat in the middle of the room and under the carefully positioned spotlight. It had been incredibly difficult shipping the instrument into the country. Flying in a piano tuner every couple of months was no easy feat, but seeing Lacey's joy and listening to her soulful music made it all worthwhile.

He fingered the sheet music scattered on the polished black wood. The woman had the talent to become a successful recording artist. Hafiz had told her enough times, but she always shook her head in disagreement. Music was a big part of her, but she didn't want to be consumed with the ladder of success like her parents, who were still striving for their big break. She didn't have the desire.

But she stored up all her passion for him. Did that make him feel less guilty in whisking her to his country? The edges of the sheet music crinkled under his fingertips. Because she had no interest in pursuing a career? Because she didn't have family ties?

Hafiz pondered the question as he walked to the doors leading to the balcony that overlooked the Persian Gulf. He admitted that it made it easier to ask her to drop everything and follow him. To stay in the apartment and wait for him. Not once had she complained or shown resentment until today.

And she had every right. He had risked everything for more time with Lacey. The relationship they had was forbidden. And now, as of today, it was impossible.

Only Hafiz didn't allow that word in his vocabulary, and he wasn't willing to let the idea invade his life with Lacey.

"What are you still doing here?" Lacey asked at the doorway on the other side of the long room.

Hafiz turned around. Lacey's wet hair was slicked back into a copper waterfall. She had changed into a pink cotton caftan that clung to her damp skin. Gold threads were woven into the fabric and sparkled like stars.

"Are you feeling better?" he asked, silently watching the housekeeper duck into the kitchen.

"Much. You're free to go." She walked toward the front door.

"Lacey, we need to talk."

"No kidding, but I don't want to right now." She

gripped the thick door handle. "You have had years to think about this. I have had less than an hour."

"Lacey—" He crossed the room and stood in front of her, prepared to take the brunt of her anger and soak up her tears.

"I want you to go." She flung open the door.

Hafiz's shoulders flexed with tension. Every instinct told him to stay, but he knew what she said made sense. It was strange to have her as the calm one and he filled with impetuous emotions. He didn't like the role reversal.

Hafiz agreed with a sharp nod. "I will be here tomorrow after work." He leaned down to brush her cheek with a gentle kiss.

She turned her head abruptly. "Don't." Her eyes focused on the hallway outside the iron grille.

His heart stopped. Lacey had never rejected his touch. "What are you saying?" he asked in a low voice as his lungs shriveled, unable to take in the next breath.

The muscles in her throat jerked. "You shouldn't touch me." The words were a mere whisper. "The moment you became engaged, the moment you chose another woman, we no longer exist."

Hafiz grasped her chin between his thumb and forefinger. "You don't mean that," he said, staring at her intensely. As if he could change her mind through his sheer willpower.

"Yes, I do."

He swallowed down the rising fear. "Obviously, you are still suffering from your collapse." The tip of his thumb caressed the angry line of her bottom lip.

Lacey yanked away from his touch. "I'm thinking quite clearly. You made your choice." She took a step back behind the door, shielding herself from him. "And this is mine."

"You are going to regret those words. You can't send me away." He stepped toward her, ready to prove it.

Lacey's glare was so cold it could have frozen the desert air seeping into the apartment. "Do you want me to cause a scene in front of this complex to get you to leave?"

Her threat surprised Hafiz. That wasn't like her. She knew his weak spots but had always protected him. Now she was so angry, she was becoming a dangerous woman.

Would she try to hurt him because he was getting married? No, not Lacey. She was loyal to him...but when she thought she didn't have any competition. How could he convince her that this marriage was in name only?

He decided to change his strategy. "I will return," he said, shoving his feet into his sandals. The expensive leather threatened to snap under his angry motions. "And you will be here waiting for me."

Defiance flared in her blue eyes. "Don't tell me what to do. You have no right."

"You still belong to me, Lacey," he announced as he left. "Nothing and no one will change that."

CHAPTER THREE

THE WHITE ROBES slapped angrily against Hafiz's legs as he stormed into his office. He would rather be anywhere else but here. Although the palace's murky shadows descending on the spartan rooms were good companions to his dark mood this evening.

"Your Highness." His private secretary clumsily hung up the phone. The withered old man bowed low, his fragile bones creaking. "His Majesty wishes to speak to you."

Hafiz set his jaw as dread seeped inside him. The day couldn't get any worse. The sultan didn't command appointments from his eldest offspring unless there was or would be an unpleasant event.

"When did he make this request?"

"Ten minutes ago, Your Highness," the elderly man answered, his focus on the threadbare Persian rug. "I called your cell phone and left several messages."

Of course. He had turned off his phone so he wouldn't bend to the overwhelming need to call Lacey. His show of confidence that she would follow his orders was going to cost him in more ways than one. Hafiz wanted to roar with frustration, but he needed to stay calm and focused for the sultan.

Hafiz turned and checked his appearance in the gilt-edged mirror. He didn't see anything Sultan Yusuf would find offensive, but the ruler didn't need to hunt long for something to disapprove about his son. Unable to delay the inevitable, Hafiz set his shoulders back and strode to the palace offices.

When he entered the sultan's suite, Hafiz stood respectfully at the double doors and waited to be announced. As one of the secretaries hurried to the massive wooden desk to convey the message to the sultan, Hafiz grew aware of the sideway glances and growing tension. He coldly met the employees' stares one by one until the gazes skittered down in belated respect.

Sultan Yusuf dismissed his secretaries with the flick of his hand. The men hurried past Hafiz and through the doors. Their expressions of grateful relief concerned him.

The sultan continued to sit behind his desk and read a note on thick white paper. He took his time to deign to acknowledge his son's presence. "Hafiz," Sultan Yusuf finally said.

Hafiz approached the sultan. "Your Majesty." Hafiz gave the briefest deferential nod as defiance flowed through his veins.

The sultan tossed the paper on to his desk. "Be seated."

The lack of mind games made Hafiz suspicious, which it was probably supposed to achieve. Hafiz sat down on the chair across from the desk. Tradition dictated that he should keep his head down and his gaze averted. He was never good at tradition.

The sultan leaned back in his chair, steepled his fingers, and studied Hafiz. Not even a whisper of affection crossed his lined face. "You are very fortunate that the Abdullah daughter agreed to the marriage."

Fortune had nothing to do with it. It didn't matter who his bride was. He was marrying this woman for two reasons. It was his royal duty and it was another step toward redemption.

"This girl knows about your—" the king's fingers splayed apart "—misspent youth, as does her family."

Hafiz clenched his teeth and willed his hands to stay straight on his knees. He would not respond. He would not allow his father to spike his temper.

"They will use that knowledge to their advantage as the wedding preparations draw closer. The dowry is not nearly worthy enough for a prince. We're fortunate they didn't demand a bridal price."

Hafiz still said nothing. His teeth felt as if they would splinter. His fingers itched to curl and dig into his knees.

"Have you anything to say, Hafiz?"

He did, but most of it wasn't wise to say aloud. "I regret that my past mistakes still cost our family." And his regret was as honest as it was strong. Nothing could erase the suffering he'd caused Rudaynah. The simple truth destroyed him, and his life's mission was to prevent any future suffering from his hand.

"As do I." Sultan Yusuf sighed heavily. "The reason I'm telling you this is that I expect many maneuvers from the Abdullah family." He smacked his lips with distaste as he mentioned his future in-laws. "Any male relative could trick you. Talk you down the dowry. Say you made a promise or agreement when there was none."

Annoyance welled up inside Hafiz's chest. From

years of practice, his expression didn't show his feelings. Hafiz negotiated multi-million-dollar deals, brokered delicate international agreements and increased the wealth of this country ten times over. But his family didn't respect his accomplishments. They only remembered his mistakes.

"You will have no interaction with the Abdullah family," the sultan commanded. "All inquiries must be directed to my office. Do you understand, Hafiz?"

"Yes, Your Majesty." He didn't have a problem following that order. If that was the purpose of the meeting, Hafiz wondered why the sultan didn't dictate a memo so he didn't have to speak to his son.

"After all," the ruler continued, "your mother and I cannot afford another scandal from you."

Hafiz closed his eyes as the pain washed over him. He should have seen that coming.

"This marriage must happen." The sultan tapped an authoritative finger on the desk. The thud echoed loudly in Hafiz's head. "If the engagement is broken, it will shame this family."

Shaming the family was his sole specialty. The statement was left unspoken, but Hafiz could hear it plainly in his father's manner. It wasn't anything his conscience hadn't shouted for more years than he cared to remember.

"You've already lost your right to the throne because of your poor choices," Sultan Yusuf said with brutal frankness. "If you harm this agreement, I will make certain you lose everything you hold dear."

Did his father think he would try to sabotage the wedding agreement? Hafiz was stunned at the possibility. Hadn't his actions proven he would sacrifice his personal wants for the good of the country?

"But, if you do not cause any delay or scandal—" he paused and sliced a knowing look "—I will give you the one thing you desire."

Hafiz flinched. His mind immediately went to Lacey. A white-hot panic blinded him. Did the sultan know about her?

"Marry the bride I choose, and you will resume your rightful place. You will become the heir to the throne once again."

Lacey's fingers dragged against the ivory keys of her piano, but she didn't play a note. She couldn't. The music inside her had been silenced.

Glenn and Annette had retired hours ago, but she couldn't sleep no matter how hard she tried. Her body felt limp and wrung out, and her mind craved for oblivion.

What was it about her? Why was she so easy to discard? First her parents and now Hafiz. She didn't understand it.

Lacey always held on to the belief that she would have bonded with her parents if they had taken her on the road with them. They would have remembered her birthdays and special occasions. They wouldn't have forgotten her all those times or accidentally left her to fend for herself on school vacations. If they hadn't sent her off to live with distant relatives or family friends, she would have some sort of relationship today with her mother and father.

But now she knew her parents didn't get the full blame. There was something wrong with her. It didn't matter how freely and completely she gave her love; she would not get it in return. She was unlovable.

Lacey stood and walked to the balcony doors and peered outside. No lights glowed against the darkness. Outside appeared silent and empty.

If only her mind would quiet down like the town below her. She leaned her head against the glass pane that was now cool from the desert night. The moment Hafiz had left, fragmented thoughts and fears had bombarded her mind. She'd paced her room as unspoken questions whirled through her head. She'd stared numbly at the walls for hours.

No matter how much the housekeeper had tried to tempt her with food, Lacey refused to eat. Her throat, swollen and achy from crying, would surely choke on the smallest morsel. Sustenance meant nothing and she had curled up on Hafiz's side of the bed. There she had muffled her cries in his pillow when one more minute of living without him became unbearable.

Her mind felt as chaotic as the clothes jumbled inside her suitcase. She packed her belongings, which were pathetically few. It was a mocking symbol of the emptiness of her life before she'd met Hafiz and her barren future without him. Only now she had even less, because she was leaving everything behind along with her heart.

Lacey frowned, trying to hold her emotions together. There were too many things she had to do, like finding a new home.

Lacey pressed the heels of her hands against her puffy eyes. The business of breaking up was beyond her. She needed a fresh start. Somewhere that held no memories. A place where Hafiz couldn't find her.

Not that he would follow her across the world. He'd made his choice. And it wasn't her. It was never going to be her.

She didn't want to know anything about the woman who got to share Hafiz's life. The one who would wear his ring, bear his name and carry his children in her womb. Lacey blinked as her eyes stung, but she'd already used up her tears.

Lacey twisted around when she heard the key in the lock. Hope stuttered through her exhausted body as Hafiz entered. He halted when he saw her across the room.

"Hafiz." She instinctively moved toward him like a moth to a flame. "What are you doing here?"

She stared at him, memorizing every detail. He was dressed like a laborer. While the outfit was an unusual choice for a member of the royal family, Hafiz lent a sophisticated elegance to the rough work clothes.

The simple tunic was as black as his short hair. The cotton sluiced down his muscular chest and skimmed past his knees. His jeans strained against his powerful legs as he slid his feet out of scuffed sandals. His high-tech watch was nowhere to be found, but the royal ring gleamed proudly on his hand.

"I wasn't sure you would be here." His hands clenched and unclenched the keys.

Lacey guiltily flashed a look in the direction of the bedroom where her bags were packed and stowed away under the bed. "And you're checking up on me?" she asked as her eyebrows arched with disbelief. "You could have called."

"No. I came here to say goodbye." He set down the key with hypnotic slowness. "Tonight."

She froze as the words pummeled her bruised heart. Tonight? Her chest heaved, and she struggled for her next breath. "Now?"

Hafiz nodded. "I had a meeting with the sultan earlier this evening." He stared at the keys as though he wanted to snatch them back. "If any of my actions prevent the forthcoming marriage, I will lose everything."

"Your father threatened you?" she whispered in horror.

"The sultan warned me," he corrected. "And I can't help but wonder if he knows about you. Maybe not your name or where you live, but that I have someone like you in my life."

Someone like you... The phrase scratched at her. What did that mean? More importantly, what did it mean to Hafiz?

She stood in front of him, and placed her hand on his arm, offering him comfort. Not that he needed it. Hafiz had the strength to stand alone. "You shouldn't be forced to marry someone you don't love."

Her words seemed to startle him. "Lacey," Hafiz said in a groan as he cupped her cheek with his hand. "A royal marriage never has anything to do with love. It has always been that way."

She closed her eyes as she leaned into his hand, knowing it would be the last time he would caress her. She gathered the last of her self-discipline and withdrew from his touch. Energy arced and flared between them.

"I will miss you, Hafiz," she said brokenly as her throat closed up. The tears she thought couldn't happen beaded on her eyelashes.

Hafiz let out a shuddering breath. He swept his fingertip against the corner of her eye, taking her tears with him. The moisture clung to his knuckle, and he rubbed it into his skin with his thumb, silently sharing her agony.

The image took a chink out of her hard-earned resolve. Lacey wrapped her arms around her stomach before she crumbled altogether. "I had so many questions to ask you, and now I can't remember what they were." All except for one that danced on her tongue. "Did you ever love me?"

Silence throbbed in the air.

Lacey blinked at the question that had tumbled from her mouth. *Of all the things to ask,* her mind screamed.

Hafiz went unnaturally still.

"I don't know why I asked." She shrugged as her pain intensified. "Please, don't answer that."

The words were ripped from deep within her. She desperately wanted to know the answer. She never questioned it before, but she had been living in a fantasy.

Lacey had always felt Hafiz loved her. It was in his touch, in his eyes, and in his smile. But he never said the words, even when she chanted her declaration of love in the height of ecstasy.

It was too late to find out. If he didn't love her, she would never recover. If he did love her, then she would never let go. Even if he was married, even if he kept her hidden. And she couldn't let that happen.

Hafiz frowned. "Lacey…"

"Ssh." She silenced him by pressing her fingers against his parted lips. *"Please."*

He covered her hand with his and placed soft kisses

in the heart of her palm. "I don't want you to leave," he said against her skin.

"Then, come away with me!" She impulsively tangled her fingers with his and pulled him away from the door. His torn expression shamed her. She drew back and let go of his hand. "I'm sorry. That was wrong."

He moved swiftly and crushed her against him. "I can't leave Rudaynah," he whispered, his breath ruffling her hair. "And you can't stay. I don't know what I'm going to do without you. I'm only half alive when you are not around."

He didn't want to give her up, but he had the strength to do it when she wanted to ignore the inevitable. Hafiz would flourish without her while she wilted into a slow death. "In time, you'll forget all about me."

He tightened their embrace. "How can you say that?"

"You will," she predicted with a sigh. It happened to her before, and nothing she did would stop it from happening again. "You need to leave." Now, before it became impossible. Before she threw herself at his feet and begged him to stay.

"Yes." He gradually relaxed his hold but didn't let go. "This was already a risk."

She looked up into his face. The scent of the desert night clung to his warm skin. The steady and strong beat of his heart pounded under her hand. The passion he felt for her shone in his eyes. This was how she wanted to remember him. "Goodbye, Hafiz."

He lowered his face and gently brushed his mouth against hers. Like Lacey, he kept his eyes open, needing to commit this last kiss to memory. The unshed tears in her eyes blurred his image. Lacey's lips clung to his. The craving to deepen the kiss radiated between them. She felt his need to carry her away and the struggle to leave her behind.

"I have to go," he murmured against her mouth.

"I know." The world tilted as he withdrew, and his arms dropped away from her. She felt exposed and weak. A single tear spilled down her cheek. "I wish…" She stopped and bit her lip.

"You wish what?" When she didn't answer, he grabbed her upper arms with his large hands. "Tell me," he pleaded, his fingers biting into her flesh.

"No." She shook her head. She had to be strong and ignore her wants. For both of them. "I wish you… happiness."

Hafiz shook her slightly until tendrils of her hair fell in front of her face. "That was not what you were going to say. Don't end this on a lie," he ordered, agony threading his voice. "Don't leave me with a half-spoken wish, so that I will go mad trying to figure out what you wanted to say."

Lacey looked away. She'd ruined the moment, all because she couldn't let him go. "I can't."

"Tell me what you wish," he said against her ear, teasing her willpower with his husky voice full of promise. "I will make it come true if it's in my power."

"I wish we…" She swallowed. Damn her weakness! "I wish we had at least one more night."

She saw the gleam in Hafiz's bronze eyes. Her request unleashed something dark and primitive inside him. He wanted to claim her, possess her so completely that she would never forget him. As if she could.

"I can grant you that wish," he promised as his features sharpened with lust. "Tonight."

"No." Lacey shook her head. They had to stop now. If she went to bed with him tonight, she would do everything in her power to keep him there. "We can't. You are an engaged man. The sultan has warned you—"

"This is my wish, too." He gathered her close and lifted her in his arms before he strode to the bedroom. "Don't deny me one more night."

CHAPTER FOUR

LACEY CLUNG TO Hafiz as they entered her bedroom. The bedside lamp offered a faint glow in the large room, casting shadows on the unmade bed. Hafiz barely broke his stride when he kicked the door shut.

She wasn't sure why he wasn't rushing to the bed. Lacey felt the urgency pulsating between them. This was the last time they would be together. They had to get a lifetime into one night.

The unfairness of it all hit Lacey, and she tried to push it away. She didn't want to focus on that. She wasn't going to waste her last moments with Hafiz on something she couldn't control.

The only thing she could do was make one beautiful and lasting memory. Have something that could ease the pain when she thought about the love she lost.

Hafiz stood by the edge of the bed, and Lacey knelt on the mattress before him. She pressed her hands against his cheeks and looked deep into his eyes.

She bit the inside of her lip to prevent from speaking when she saw Hafiz's sadness. It wasn't like him to show it, but the emotion was too strong; he couldn't contain it. Lacey closed her eyes and rested her head against his chest. She wanted to ease his pain. Take it away from him.

She was hurting, too. It hurt knowing that after tonight she wouldn't see him, and she couldn't touch him. She wouldn't be allowed anywhere near him.

Her shaky breath echoed in the room.

"Lacey?" Hafiz's voice was tender as he smoothed his hand against the crown of her head.

She tilted her face up and sought his mouth. She poured everything she felt into the kiss. She held nothing back. The pain and the anger. The love and the unfulfilled dreams.

The heat between them wasn't a slow burn. It flared hot and wild. Lacey sensed the dangerous power behind it, but this time she didn't care. In the past they danced around it, knowing it could rage out of control. This time she welcomed it. Encouraged it.

Hafiz bunched her caftan in his fists. She knew it was a silent warning. He needed to leash his sexual hunger, or it could become destructive.

She didn't think that was possible. There was nothing left to destroy. She wanted to climb the heights with Hafiz and disregard the possibility of plunging into the depths.

Lacey wrenched her mouth away from Hafiz. Her breath was uneven as her chest rose and fell. She watched him as she tore off her caftan, revealing that she wore nothing underneath.

As she tossed her clothes on to the floor, a part of her warned her to slow down. This was not what she wanted their last night to be like. She wanted it soft and romantic. This was primal and elemental. And she couldn't stop. She didn't *want* to slow down.

Hafiz shucked off his tunic, exposing his muscular chest. She reached out with the intention to trail her hand down his warm, golden skin. Instead she hooked her hand over the low-slung waistband of his jeans and pulled him close. She gasped as the tips of her breasts rubbed against his coarse chest hair.

Hafiz stretched his arms and wrapped his hands around the bedposts. His move surprised her. He didn't gather her close or take over. He was giving the control to her.

It was a rare gift. Hafiz was always in control. She watched him as she boldly cupped his arousal. A muscle bunched in his jaw, but he said nothing. He didn't move as she teased him with her hands. She lowered the zipper and pushed his clothes down his legs.

She wasn't gentle as she stroked him. She felt the tension rise inside him and felt the bedposts rattle under his grip. But even a man like Hafiz had his limits. He suddenly growled and grabbed Lacey's arms.

His kiss was hard and possessive. Her heart raced as the anticipation built deep inside her.

Hafiz tore his mouth away, and she tumbled down on to her back. She was sprawled naked before him. The ferocious hunger in his eyes made her shiver as the excitement clawed at her. She needed Hafiz, and she would go mad if she had to wait.

"Now," she demanded. She almost couldn't say the word, her chest aching as her heart pounded against her ribs. She rocked her hips as the desire coiled low in her pelvis.

Hafiz didn't argue. He grabbed the back of her legs and dragged her closer. Her stomach gave a nervous flip when she saw his harsh and intense expression.

After he wrapped her legs around his waist, Hafiz ruthlessly tilted her hips. She felt exposed. Wild and beautiful. Vulnerable and yet powerful.

Her heart stopped as he drove into her. Lacey moaned as she yielded, arching her body to accept him. There was no finesse or sophistication. Her hips bucked to an ancient rhythm as she met his thrusts.

She wanted to hold on to this moment and make it last, but she couldn't tame the white heat that threatened to overpower her. Lacey closed her eyes and allowed the sensations to claim her as she cried out Hafiz's name.

Hours later, they lay together. Lacey's back was tucked against Hafiz's chest. Her long hair, tangled and damp with sweat, was pushed to the side as he placed a soft kiss on her neck. The blanket and sheets were in disarray on the floor, but Lacey didn't feel the need to warm their naked bodies. Hafiz's body heat was all she needed.

Lacey deliberately took an even breath and slowly exhaled. She wasn't going to cry. Not yet. She didn't want Hafiz's last memory of her to include that.

She focused her attention on their joined hands, barely visible in the darkened room. She idly played with his hand, rubbing his palm and stroking the length of his fingers. Hafiz did the same, as if silently memorizing every inch of her hand.

They were so different, Lacey decided. Hafiz's hand was large and strong. Hers was more delicate. Her job as a pianist relied on her hands while Hafiz never used his for physical labor. His skin was golden and hers was ivory.

Her fingers clenched his. She stared at their clasped hands, noticing the soft shine of Hafiz's royal ring. She glanced at the window, her heart aching with knowing, when she saw the light filtering through the gap in the curtains.

The night had ended. Their time was over.

Lacey was reluctant to point it out. If Hafiz wasn't going to comment on it, why should she? After all, they didn't define when night ended. The people of Rudaynah didn't start the day until close to noon.

She knew she was grasping for more time. Lacey bit her lip as she watched Hafiz twist his fingers around hers. She wanted to grab his hands and hold them tight.

She was in danger of never letting him go.

Lacey glanced at the window again. They had not squeezed out every minute of their night together. How long had they spent gazing in each other's eyes, holding each other, not saying a word? But she wouldn't regret those quiet moments. They meant something to her. It made her feel connected to Hafiz.

Lacey swept the tip of her tongue along her bottom lip before she spoke. "It's morning."

Her voice shattered the peaceful silence. She felt the tension in Hafiz's muscles before his fingers gripped hers.

"No, it's not," Hafiz replied in his deep, rumbling voice as his warm breath wafted against her ear.

She frowned and motioned at the window. "It's sunrise."

"I disagree." Hafiz gently turned her so she lay on her back. "The sun is still rising. It isn't morning yet. We still have time."

He wasn't ready to end this, either. Lacey gazed lovingly at his face above hers. She brushed her fingertips along his jaw, the dark stubble rough against her skin.

"I love you, Hafiz."

A dark and bittersweet emotion she couldn't define flashed in his eyes. Hafiz slowly lowered his head and bestowed a gentle kiss on her lips.

She didn't move as he placed another soft kiss on her cheek and yet another on her brow. It was more than saying goodbye. He touched her with reverence.

She closed her eyes, desperate to hide her tears, as Hafiz cupped her face with care. He tipped her head back against the pillows and kissed her again. His mouth barely grazed hers.

Lacey wanted to capture his lips and deepen the kiss. But Hafiz slid his mouth to her chin before leaving a trail of kisses along her throat.

She swallowed hard as Hafiz darted his tongue at the dip of her collarbone before pressing his mouth against the pulse point at the base of her throat. She gasped as he suckled her skin between his sharp teeth and left his mark on her.

He didn't need to brand her. She was already his, and nothing—not time, not distance—would change that.

"Hafiz…" she said in a moan as she reached for him. He stopped her and wrapped his hands around her wrists before lowering her arms on the mattress.

"Shh," he whispered as he settled between her legs. He continued his path and kissed the slope of her breast. Lacey arched her spine as he teased her with his mouth.

Hafiz knew how to touch her, how to draw out the pleasure until it became torment. She hissed between her teeth as he laved his tongue against her tight nipple before drawing it into his hot mouth.

She fought against his hold, wanting to grab the back of his head, needing to hold him against her chest, but Hafiz didn't let go.

As sweat formed on her skin while she trembled with need, Hafiz silently continued his descent down her abdomen. Lust, hot and thick, flooded her pelvis. She rocked her hips insistently as Hafiz licked and nibbled and kissed her.

His path was slow, lazy and thorough. She glanced at the window. The sunlight was getting brighter and stronger.

Hafiz bent his head and pressed his mouth on her sex. Lacey moaned as she bucked against his tongue. He released her wrists to spread her legs wider. Lacey grabbed his head, bunching his short hair in her fists as he pleasured her.

She tried to hold back, wanting to make this last, but her climax was swift and sharp. She cried out as it consumed her. Her hips bucked wildly as she rode the sensations.

Her stomach clenched with anticipation as Hafiz slid his hands under her hips. His touch was urgent. She opened her eyes to see him tower over her. There was a primitive look in his eyes as he knelt between her legs.

She felt the rounded tip of his erection pressing against her. Hafiz entered her fully, and she groaned with deep satisfaction. She watched as he closed his eyes and tipped his head back as he struggled for the last of his control.

Lacey's flesh gripped him hard as she felt her body climbing fast toward another climax. She bucked against Hafiz, and he braced his arms next to her. He recaptured her hands and curled his fingers around hers.

"Hafiz…" she whimpered as he rested his forehead against hers. She went silent as he met her gaze. She allowed him to watch her every emotion and response flicker in her eyes. She hid nothing as she climaxed again, harder and longer.

And when her release triggered his, she didn't look away. Lacey let Hafiz know how much pleasure she received from watching him. She heard his hoarse cry before she closed her eyes, allowing exhaustion to claim her.

Lacey's eyes bolted open. The first thing she heard was the drone of the high-speed ceiling fan. Then she noticed the sheets tucked neatly around her body.

Panic crumbled on top of her. She jackknifed into a sitting position and looked at Hafiz's side of the bed. It was empty.

"No," she whispered. "Noooo." She pushed the sheets away as if he would suddenly appear.

She wildly looked around the room. She knew she'd asked for this night only, but she wished she had asked for more. Much more. Even if she knew it wasn't possible, she would have thrown her pride to the wind and begged for more time.

Lacey stumbled out of bed and grabbed for her

robe. Hafiz's side of the bed was warm. There was a chance that he was still there.

"Hafiz?" she called out with a nervous tremble as she tied the sash of her robe. The silence taunted her. Biting down on her bottom lip, she opened the bedroom door. Hope leached from her bones as she stared into the empty drawing room.

Lacey slammed the door shut and ran to the window, her bare feet slapping against the floor. She ripped the curtains to the side and searched the quiet streets.

Her heart lodged in her throat as she saw the familiar figure walking across the street.

For a brief moment, Lacey thought she was mistaken. The man didn't stride through the streets with regal arrogance. Hafiz walked slowly. Hesitantly. His head was bowed, his shoulder hunched.

She raised her fists, ready to beat at the glass and call for him to turn around.

Instinct stopped her. She knew it was hard for him to walk away. Probably just as difficult as it was to let him leave. She had to be strong. For him, if not for herself.

She pressed her forehead against the window, letting her fingers streak against the glass. "Hafiz..." she cried weakly.

Her eyes widened as she watched him slow to a halt. It was impossible for him to have heard her whimper. Hafiz turned slightly to the side and caught himself before glancing at her window.

Her heart pounded until she thought her ears would burst from the sound. She needed one more look. Just one more so she could carry it with her to ease her loneliness. She needed another look to remember that she was loved once.

But she also didn't want him to turn around. She needed him to be strong. She needed to see his strength and know that he was going to be okay. That he was going to stand alone as he had before he met her.

Lacey pressed her lips together, her breath suspended as Hafiz paused. Tears cascaded down her cheeks as she felt her future clinging to this moment.

Hafiz straightened his shoulders and resolutely turned away. Lacey felt shell-shocked. Her future took a free fall into the dark and desolate abyss.

It was a bittersweet sight for her to see Hafiz stride away. She stared at him, sobbing noisily until he turned the corner. Her gaze didn't move from the empty spot just in case he changed his mind. Her vision blurred and her eyes stung as she kept watch for the possibility that he needed to steal one more glance.

But it wasn't going to happen. He was strong enough for the both of them. The knowledge chipped away at her as she sank against the wall into an untidy heap.

It was over. They were no longer together.

Lacey felt as if she was going to splinter and die. And she had no idea how she was going to prevent falling apart without Hafiz holding her tight and giving a piece of his strength to her.

CHAPTER FIVE

HAFIZ REALIZED HE must have looked quite fierce by the way the office workers cowered when he strode in. *Too bad,* he thought as he cast a cold look at a young businessman who had the misfortune of being in his eyesight. Hafiz didn't feel like altering his expression.

Usually he looked forward to coming into his downtown office in the afternoon once he had met all of his royal duties for the day. It felt good to get out of the palace that was as quiet as a mausoleum. Although it had been built by his ancestors, the historical site—or the people inside it—didn't reflect who he was. The royal viziers were too concerned with protocol and tradition. They didn't like any new idea. Or any idea *he* had.

The royal court seemed to have forgotten that he was brought up to serve and look after the sultanate. His education and experience had been focused on international relations and business. He had so many plans and initiatives to improve the lives of his countrymen, but no one wanted to listen to the prince who had fallen out of favor. That would change once he married the sultan's choice.

He strode to his desk and noted that, unlike his

troubled mind, everything in his office was in order. The modern building, complete with state-of-the-art equipment, usually crackled with energy from dawn to dusk. The sultan and the palace had no say in what went on in these offices. Here Hafiz had the freedom to explore and take risks.

The young men he employed outside of the palace were unquestionably loyal, efficient and brilliant. They were men who were educated outside of Rudaynah, but returned home so they could make a difference. They spoke Arabic and English fluently, usually within the same sentence. They were comfortable in business suits and traditional Rudaynahi robes. Men very much like him, except for a few drops of royal blood and a few years in the world that had stripped away any idealism.

From the corner of his eye, Hafiz saw his executive secretary hurry toward him. One of the office assistants was already at his desk, trying to look invisible while carefully setting down a mug of coffee. The bitter scent was welcoming since he hadn't slept for days. Hafiz walked around his desk, determined to lose himself in his work.

"Good afternoon, Your Highness," the secretary said cautiously as he tugged at his silk tie. The man eyed him like he would a cobra ready to strike. "The changes in your schedule have been entered—"

Hafiz's attention immediately began to fade, which was unlike him. He was known for his focus and attention to detail, but he had been distracted for the past few days. Perhaps he was coming down with something. It had nothing to do with Lacey. He did not wallow in the past. He didn't focus on the things he couldn't change. He had moved on from Lacey.

Lacey. He refused to look at the window, but the pull was too great. Hafiz reluctantly looked outside, his gaze automatically seeking Lacey's penthouse apartment. A few months ago, he had picked the office building specifically for the view. He had found himself staring out of the window throughout the workdays, even though he knew he wouldn't catch a glimpse of Lacey. The knowledge that she was there always brought him peace. Until now.

The buzzing of his cell phone shattered his reverie. His gut twisted with anticipation and dread. Only a few people had this number. He grabbed the phone and looked at the caller ID. Disappointment crashed when he saw it wasn't Lacey. Hafiz dismissed his secretary with the wave of his hand and took the call.

"Your Highness? This is Glenn," Lacey's body-guard quickly said to identify himself. "I'm sorry to call you, but we've hit a setback. Our exit visas have been delayed."

"Nothing works on time in Rudaynah." Hafiz rubbed his hand over his forehead and gave a short sigh of frustration. A sense of unease trickled down his spine. Was the palace behind this? Did they know about Lacey?

Hafiz discarded that thought. The palace wouldn't be concerned about an American nightclub singer. "Did they say why?"

"No. I bribed the right government officials, sat down and had tea at the chief of police's office, but I'm not getting any information."

Hafiz glanced out the window again. He had to

get Lacey out before her presence could ruin everything he had worked toward. "Ordinarily I would have
someone from the palace make a special request with
the right official, but that would bring unwanted attention. We will have to wait it out. They should be
ready in another day or two."

"Yes, sir."

"Would you please put Lacey on the phone, and I'll
explain it to her." He shouldn't talk to Lacey. After
all, they had said their goodbyes. He wanted that night
to be their last memory, but he also didn't want her
to think he had abandoned her when she needed assistance.

There was a beat of silence, and Glenn cleared his
throat. "Miss Maxwell is not here, sir."

"What?" Hafiz stared at Lacey's apartment. She
had promised that she wouldn't venture out again.
"Where is she?"

"She is at the Scimitar having tea with friends."

Hafiz's muscles jerked with surprise. *Friends?*
What friends?

His gaze darted across the skyline to the luxurious
hotel. The tall building was like a glass and metal spiral reaching out to the sun, reflecting the rays against
the dark windows. "I don't understand."

"I apologize, sir. I would have accompanied her,
but I was dealing with the exit visas. She had left before I got back."

Lacey had friends? Hafiz felt his frown deepen.
Lacey had a world outside of the apartment. A world
that didn't include him. He wasn't sure why he was
so surprised. Lacey had a large group of friends in
St. Louis.

But she never talked about these friends. That was strange. Lacey told him everything. Or he thought she did. Why had she been hiding this information?

"Who are these friends?" Hafiz asked tersely, interrupting Glenn's excuse. If one of them had a male name… Hafiz gritted his teeth and clenched his hand into a fist.

"No need to be concerned, sir," Glenn replied. "These women are above reproach. They are the wives of ambassadors and government ministers."

Hafiz went cold as he remained perfectly still. His ex-mistress was socializing with the most influential and powerful women of Rudaynah? The very mistress he broke up with so he could marry another? Hafiz slowly closed his eyes as the tension wrapped around his chest and squeezed. Glenn was incorrect. He had every reason to worry.

Lacey always thought the tearoom at the Scimitar was an unlikely mix of cultures. She stared at the plate that offered scones and slices of cinnamon date cake. A copper *cezve* for Turkish coffee sat next to an ornate silver teapot. A golden table runner with an intricate geometric design lay on top of the white linen tablecloth.

"You look so different in Western clothes," Inas told Lacey as she nibbled on a fried pastry ball that was dipped in a thick syrup. "I hardly recognized you."

"I feel different," Lacey admitted as she self-consciously tucked her hair behind her ear. She felt undressed wearing a simple green dress with long sleeves and a high neckline. Her makeup was minimal, and her shoes had a low heel. She was covered, but it didn't feel as if it was enough. "It's strange not wearing a caftan."

"Why the sudden change?" Janet, an ambassador's wife, asked as she patted a linen napkin to her bright red lips. Tall, blond and willowy, Janet had lived in the sultanate for years but chose not to wear the native clothes, no matter how warm the weather turned. "We're still in Rudaynah."

"I'm trying to get used to my old clothes," Lacey explained, but it wasn't the whole truth. When she'd first moved here, Lacey had originally chosen to wear the scarves and caftans, believing it was the first step to enter this world. Now she realized it had been a waste of time. "Although I really didn't fit in here."

"Nonsense." Inas flipped her long black braid over her shoulder. "You were one of my hardest-working students. So determined. If you had stayed here a little longer, I'm sure you would have become proficient in Arabic."

"Thank you." She had wanted to surprise Hafiz with her grasp of the language. One of her goals had been to watch his face soften when she declared her love in his native tongue.

"I don't know what our charity is going to do without you," Janet said with a sigh. "We made great strides once you joined. Are you sure you have to leave right away?"

"Yes, we need to move. It's urgent for my…uncle to get to his next work project." Part of her wished she could have left on the first flight out, but she was finding the idea of permanently leaving Hafiz very difficult. "We're just waiting for the exit visas."

"Those are just a formality," Inas insisted. "But if

you're still going to be here this weekend, you must attend my daughter's wedding reception. The marriage contract ceremony is for family only, but the reception is going to be here for all of our friends. Oh, and you should see the dancers we hired for the *zaffa* procession!"

"I would like that." She had heard every detail about the upcoming wedding and wanted to be there to share her friend's special moment. But her moments with Hafiz had come first, and she had reluctantly declined because it would have interfered with her time with him.

What had Hafiz given up to spend time with her? Lacey frowned as the thought whispered into her mind. She shouldn't compare. Hafiz was a busy and important man.

"Most of the royal court will be there because my husband and the groom's father are government ministers. I know you couldn't attend before because your aunt and uncle had a previous engagement, but this will be the last time we see each other. Extend the invitation to them and…" Inas frowned when the quiet buzz of conversation suddenly died. She set down her teacup, her gold bracelets tinkling, as she looked over her shoulder. "What's happening?"

"I'm not sure," Janet murmured as she craned her neck. "Everyone is looking at the door to the lobby."

"Oh, my goodness," Inas whispered and turned to face her friends. Her eyes were wide with delight. "It's the prince."

Lacey flinched at her friend's announcement. Her heartbeat stuttered over the possibility of seeing Hafiz again. "Which one? Which prince?"

"The oldest. Hafiz."

Lacey struggled for her next breath when she saw Hafiz being escorted through the tearoom. He effortlessly commanded attention. It wasn't because the aggressive lines of his dark business suit emphasized his muscular body, or the haughty jut of his chin. It wasn't because he walked like a conqueror or because of his royal status. It was because he exuded a power that indicated that he was a valuable ally or a dangerous opponent. This was someone who could ruin a man's life with the snap of his fingers or steal a woman's heart with a smile.

Hafiz strode past her, never meeting her startled gaze. His face was rigid, as if it had been hewn from stone.

He didn't see her. Lacey's lips parted as she stared after him. How was that possible? She would always capture his gaze the moment she walked into the room.

A thousand petty emotions burst and crawled under her skin. She wouldn't give in to them. She shouldn't care that she was invisible three days after he left her. She expected it. That would have always been her status in public had she stayed with Hafiz.

And she didn't want a life like that, Lacey reminded herself, closing her eyes and drawing the last of her composure. She didn't want to come in second, even if it meant a life without Hafiz. She refused to be on the side. She wouldn't be an afterthought again.

"He's gorgeous," Janet said in a low voice as they watched Hafiz stride out of the tearoom to what she suspected was the private dining areas.

"So is his fiancée," Inas informed them. "I know the Abdullah family."

Lacey winced. She wished she hadn't heard that. She didn't want to know anything about the woman who got to marry Hafiz. It was easier for her that way.

Janet leaned forward. "What is she like?"

"Nabeela is the perfect Rudaynahi woman."

Lacey's muscles locked. Now she had a name to go with the woman. Somehow that made it worse. She didn't want to put a name or a face to the person who got the man she loved.

"She has been groomed for life at the palace. Her parents were hoping she would marry a royal adviser or minister. They never thought the sultan and his wife would choose her to become a princess. She'll make a good wife for Hafiz."

No, she won't. He's mine. The thought savagely swiped at her like a claw. It tore at the thin façade she'd carefully constructed after finding out about Hafiz's wedding, exposing the truth that bled underneath. It punctured the festering pain she tried to ignore.

She knew Hafiz was going to be married, but she didn't allow herself to think past the wedding. She thought of Nabeela as the bride. She'd never thought of them as a couple. As partners. As husband and wife.

Lacey looked down hurriedly, the table weaving and buckling before her eyes. The knowledge made her physically ill. She knew it wasn't a love match, but it didn't stop the bilious green ribbons of jealousy snaking around her heart.

Her poisonous emotions ate away at her until she felt like a brittle, hollowed-out shell. A series of primal responses, each sharper than the previous one, battered her mind, her heart and her pride.

"Well, I heard it's not Nabeela's beauty that made Prince Hafiz accept," Janet said in a sly tone.

Lacey wanted to change the topic immediately. But she was scared to open her mouth, not sure if her secrets or a scream of howling pain would spill out. She stared at her teacup and forced herself to reach for it. She didn't like how her hands trembled.

"Rumor has it that the sultan and the prince made an agreement," Janet whispered fiercely. "If he marries this Nabeela without incident, Hafiz will become the crown prince."

Lacey's breath hitched in her throat. She set the cup down before it snapped in her hands. So that was the reason. It made sense, and she didn't question it.

Lacey sank back in her plush chair and tilted her head up. She stared at the mosaic ceiling made of lapis lazuli as the low murmur of different languages faded into a hum. The clink of fine china blurred into nothing as her thoughts spun wildly.

She always knew Hafiz was ambitious. Driven and determined. A man like Hafiz couldn't give up the chance of the throne. Even if it meant discarding his mistress. Although now she wondered if it had been a difficult decision for him. She couldn't compete with a crown.

She should have seen the signs. After all, she had been in this position before. Her parents had been just as driven, just as single-minded with their dreams to become rich and famous. Once they decided having a child was holding them back, they had abandoned her with a swiftness that still took her breath away.

But this time she hadn't looked for signs because she thought they were in love. She had wanted to believe that this time she wasn't the burden. That she was not only welcomed into Hafiz's life, but that he would move heaven and earth to be with her.

When was she going to learn? She did not inspire that kind of devotion. No one would ever love her like that.

"What about his brother?" Lacey's voice sounded rough to her ears. She pushed her plate away with tense fingers. "I thought he was the crown prince."

"Ashraf?" Janet asked. "Yes, I wonder how he feels about this new development. He's been the heir to the throne for a decade."

"A decade?" Lacey repeated slowly. "How old is he?"

"Just a few years younger than Prince Hafiz," Janet said, glancing at Inas for confirmation. "He became the heir to the throne when Hafiz lost his birthright."

Lacey blinked slowly as a buzzing sound grew in her ears. "Hafiz lost—?" She gripped the edge of the table as her heart fluttered against her rib cage. "I mean...*Prince* Hafiz? What do you mean by birthright?"

"He was in line to be the next sultan," Janet explained.

Lacey tilted her head sharply. Her arms went lax as she slumped in her chair. She felt as if she was missing a vital piece of information. "He was *supposed* to inherit the throne? When did this happen?"

"How do you not know this?" Inas's eyes widened as she leaned over the table. "I thought we covered this during your history lessons."

Lacey slowly shook her head. "How can a prince be displaced in the line of succession?" She was hesitant to even ask. Did he renounce his right? Did he commit a heinous crime? Neither sounded like something Hafiz would do. "You have to do something really bad, right?"

"I don't have all the details on that, but I can tell you this." Inas gave a cautious glance at the tables surrounding them before she went on. "It had something to do with a woman."

Lacey felt her lungs shrivel up as the bitter taste of despair filled her mouth. Hafiz lost everything over a woman? Numbness invaded her bones, protecting her before she doubled over from the intense pain.

"What woman?" Lacey asked dully. She must have been extraordinary for Hafiz to take such a risk. It didn't make sense. The man would do anything to protect and serve his country. He did not put anyone before his duty. Hafiz did not put *himself* before Rudaynah.

"I heard it was a mistress," Janet said quietly. "A series of mistresses."

Inas shrugged. "One woman is all that it would take to lose the throne."

A mistress. No, *mistresses*. She shouldn't be surprised. Hafiz was incredibly sophisticated and knowledgeable in the bedroom. Yet for some reason she felt as if her role in his life was different from all the other women. That she was somehow special.

Maybe she was special. Maybe… Lacey clenched her hands together under the table. She should stop trying to make her relationship with Hafiz into a fairy tale.

But why had he risked everything again by bringing her to his sultanate? By starting the relationship in the first place? What provoked him to flaunt authority and break the rules again?

Again? There was no indication that he went without a mistress after he lost his right to the throne. Lacey went cold. Was bringing his mistress to the sultanate something he did often? Did he get a new model every year? Lacey slowly closed her eyes. Her jaw trembled as the hot tears stung her eyes.

She needed to figure out what was going on. She wanted to go home, lock herself in her room and curl up in a ball to ward off the anguish that was crashing against her in waves. But first she had to leave the tearoom before she embarrassed herself.

Lacey opened her eyes and kept her head down before anyone saw her distress. "Oh, look at the time!" she said as she barely glanced at her wristwatch. "I didn't realize it was so late."

Her movements felt awkward as she rose from the table and said goodbye to her friends. The flurry of hugs and promises did nothing to calm her. Her heart pumped fast as she struggled with the information about Hafiz's past.

She turned and saw one of the hotel bellmen standing in front of her. His blue uniform was the same color as the mosaic ceiling. "Miss Maxwell? Are you leaving?" the young man asked. "A Mr. Glenn called for you. He says it's urgent."

"Oh!" She clumsily patted her purse and realized she didn't bring her cell phone because it hadn't been charged due to another power outage. "Is there a phone I can use?"

"Please follow me to one of the conference rooms, and you may contact him in private."

"Thank you." She hurried after the bellman, her legs unsteady after the surprise she had received. She felt dizzy, as if her world had been knocked off its axis. Lacey was out of breath by the time she reached the conference room. She managed to give the man a simple nod as he opened the door with a flourish.

She stepped inside the long room and felt the door close behind her. The conference room was intimidating with its heavy furniture and arched ceilings. The thick blue curtains were pulled shut, and the silence was oppressive.

Lacey frowned when she noticed there was no phone on the oversized conference table. She inhaled the familiar scent of sandalwood that never failed to stir a deep craving inside her.

Hafiz.

It was her only warning before her spine was pressed up against the wall.

Strong arms bracketed her head. Hafiz's broad shoulders were encased in an expensive suit jacket. She wanted to cling on to them. She looked up and saw that Hafiz's face loomed above hers.

He was just a kiss away. After convincing herself that she would never be able to touch him, having him so close was overwhelming. She leaned forward as her eyelashes drifted shut.

"What the hell are you up to, Lacey?" Hafiz asked through clenched teeth.

CHAPTER SIX

SHE STIFFENED AND her lashes fluttered. Hafiz's brown eyes shone with cold anger. Lacey's stomach quavered at his ferocious look. It was not the kind of greeting one lover gave to another.

But then, they weren't lovers anymore. Any momentary fantasy she harbored broke like crackling ice. They might have been alone in the room, but they were not together. They were acquaintances. Their past was erased as if it never existed. She needed to remember that.

She rested heavily against the wall as if it was the only thing in the room that seemed to be able to support her. She tilted her chin and looked directly at Hafiz. "Good afternoon to you, too, Your Highness," she replied as tears pushed against the backs of her eyes.

"Lacey," he bit out. "I want an answer."

She pressed her lips together and dug her fingers against her purse. Lacey wished she could turn off her emotions with the same effortlessness as Hafiz. She wished his cool treatment didn't feel like a slap in the face.

She looked away and wrapped her arms around her middle. She couldn't handle the lack of intimacy in his dark eyes. She already missed the aura of shared secrets that cocooned them for a year.

She felt as if she was being tugged into a sandstorm and had nothing to hold on to. She could only rely on herself. It had always been that way. When she first met Hafiz, she thought she wouldn't be so alone in the world. Now she understood that it had been an illusion.

"I was having tea with a couple of my friends," she said, hating how her voice cracked.

"Why is this the first I've heard about these so-called friends?"

"You never asked." Lacey felt the flare of anger. "You never asked about my day or how I was coping living in this country." The anger burned hotter, and she ducked under his arm and walked away. "You just assumed I spent every waking moment in my apartment. Did you think I powered down until you returned?"

"If you wanted to share something, there was nothing and no one holding you back." Hafiz's eyes narrowed as he watched her move to one end of the table. "Why am I hearing about this now?"

She shrugged. Some of it was her fault. She was reacting in the same way as when she had felt her parents' interest slipping. She'd known if she wanted to retain Hafiz's attention, have him keep coming back, she needed to be positive. She had to be entertaining, and put all of the focus on him. If she had been too needy, he would start to distance himself.

"How is someone like you friends with an ambassador's wife? Or the wife of a deputy minister?"

Lacey raised her eyebrow and met his gaze. She

would not show how much those words hurt. "Someone like me?"

"You know what I mean." Hafiz rubbed the back of his neck with impatience. "You don't share the same status or have the same interests."

"So, what you're really asking is how a mistress became friends with respectable women?" she asked in a cool tone.

"Yes." Hafiz crossed his arms. "That's exactly what I'm saying."

The room tilted sickeningly for a moment. Did he know what he was saying? Did he care? She closed her eyes and swallowed. "You do realize that you're the one who made me a mistress."

"And you accepted the offer."

His indifference cut like a knife. A sarcastic rejoinder danced on her tongue like a hot pepper.

"Why are you friends with these women," he asked, "and why did you meet with them today?"

"Do you know why I play the piano?" Lacey asked as she pulled out a chair and sat down at the head of the table.

Hafiz gave her an incredulous look and spread his arms out wide. "What does this have to do with the women you were with?"

"A lot of people think I play piano because I grew up in a musical environment," Lacey continued as if he hadn't spoken. "My parents are musicians, so, therefore, I must have their interests rub off on me."

Hafiz leaned his shoulder against the wall. "Get to the point, Lacey."

"My parents didn't care if I took up a musical instrument or not. I thought that if I learned how to play the piano, and played exceptionally well, I could be part of their lives. They would take me on the road with them and I wouldn't be left behind all the time."

"And?"

The corner of her mouth twitched as she remembered her parents' harsh and immediate rejection to that plan. How her father had declared that one of the benefits of the road trips was taking a break from being parents. "It didn't work. But for some reason, I thought it would work this time."

Hafiz frowned. "This time?"

"When you invited me to live here, I thought we were building toward a future. A life together." She hastily looked away. She was embarrassed by her ignorance, her belief that they would live happily ever after. "And I worked to make this my new home. Inas is very proud of her heritage and she used to be a teacher. She's been my Arabic and history tutor."

"You've been learning Arabic? I've never heard you speak it."

She saw the deep suspicion in his eyes and a dull ache of disappointment spread through her chest. "I wasn't ready to show off my language skills just yet. I'm nowhere near fluent."

His mouth twisted, and she knew he didn't believe her. "And the ambassador's wife?"

"I met Janet at her charity against hunger. We've been working together for the past six months." Her voice trailed off when she noticed that she was following the same pattern and getting the same results.

Both times she had placed all of her energy into another person's interest. Both times she had thought the commitment would pay off. That they would see how she fit seamlessly into their world and welcome her with open arms. At the very least, appreciate her efforts.

It shouldn't be this hard to keep her loved ones in her life. She had to stop giving her all to people who didn't want it. Didn't want her.

"And you just happen to become friends." Hafiz's voice broke through her thoughts. "With the two women who could destroy everything I've worked for if they mention a rumor to one of their powerful friends or husbands."

"Is that what you're worried about?" Lacey began to tap her fingers on the table. "In all our time together, I've never done anything to hurt you. Why would you think I'd do that now?"

"Because you thought I would marry you one day, and instead I'm marrying someone else. You want revenge."

"Wait a minute! Are you saying—" She sat up straight and pressed her hands against her chest. "Do you think I'm trying to—"

He speared her with an icy cold glare. "Hell hath no fury like a woman scorned."

"Scorned woman? You've scorned me? No, you've sacrificed me, but—"

"And you needed to hit me back." He widened his arms as if offering her another shot.

"You think I have the power to hurt you?" she asked through barely parted lips. She realized that she did have that power, temporarily. "That's why you didn't tell me. I never thought you were a coward. And you aren't. You just don't give information unless it's in your interest."

She bit the inside of her lip as he walked to her, his stride reminding her of a stalking panther.

"Explain yourself, Lacey," he said softly with just a bite of warning.

"The agreement between you and the sultan," she said hurriedly. "The one about you becoming the crown prince if you marry his choice of bride."

Surprise flashed in his dark eyes before he placed his fists on his lean hips. "How do you know about that?"

Lacey dipped her head as the last glimmer of hope faded. So it was true. He gave her up for a chance to become the next sultan. "Everyone knows."

"The agreement came after I was engaged," he said stiffly before he turned around. "I don't know why I'm explaining this to you."

You mean, to someone like you, Lacey silently added. "Do you want to be the sultan?"

Hafiz's shoulders grew rigid as he turned around. "Of course. I know I can do the job. For the past ten years, I've worked hard to prove it to others."

"Don't you want to do something different?" she asked.

"Why would I give up this opportunity?"

Why would he, other than to have a life that would include her? It wasn't worth the sacrifice. And he supposedly made the decision to end their relationship *before* the sultan's offer.

"Look at the impact you've made on your own," she pointed out. "Think of what else you could do without the interference of the palace."

"You don't understand, Lacey," he said wearily as

he thrust his fingers in his dark hair. "I was born for this. It's my destiny."

"I know. It's why you push yourself." Her toe tapped a nervous staccato beat before she dove into uncharted territory. "It's not out of ambition, is it? You're looking for redemption."

He tilted his head as if he was scenting danger. As if she was getting too close to his secret. Too close to the truth.

"You lost your birthright ten years ago. That's why your brother was chosen over you. And you've been trying to get it back."

She knew the truth. Shame swept through Hafiz. It burned through his veins, and he instinctively hunched his shoulders to ward it off.

He looked at the floor, unable to meet her eyes, even though she had the right to judge him. "How do you know about that?" he asked hoarsely.

The tapping of her toe halted. The silence vibrated around him. "I wish I had heard it from you."

Hafiz said nothing. He wished he could have denied it, but he'd withstood the disgrace for nearly a decade. It should be no different now.

But it was. He didn't want Lacey to know about his mistakes. About the person he used to be.

Lacey was the first to break the silence. "Why didn't you tell me?"

Because he was a better person when he was with Lacey. He could be the man he wanted to be, the prince he strived to become for his country. She believed he could do the impossible, and he knew he could with her by his side. Had she known about his past, would she still have believed? He knew she wouldn't.

But Lacey knew now. And her opinion meant the most to him. He didn't know how he would stand up against her disillusionment. "It's not something I'm proud of."

"So you hid it from me?" she asked. He heard the anger wobbling in her voice. "You only showed me one side of you? I thought we had been closer than that."

Hafiz pulled open a curtain and let the bright sunlight stream in the dark room. The image of his beloved country didn't soothe the twinge inside him. He was drowning in regret and there was no hope of escape.

He bunched his hands into tight fist, imagining the relief if he punched through the glass. He could hear the shattering window in his mind, but he wouldn't act on the impulse. But, oh, what he wouldn't do to get out of this room…away from Lacey's steady gaze.

"You were just a teenager when you lost your title as crown prince?"

"No, I was an adult. I was twenty-one." Hafiz had a feeling that was the easiest question he would be facing from Lacey.

"Really?" She made a sympathetic cluck with her tongue. "That's harsh. Being twenty-one is all about pushing the limits. Pushing boundaries."

He shook his head. It should have warmed his heart that Lacey automatically defended him, but he knew it wasn't going to last. "It's different for me."

"Because you're a prince? The heir to the throne?"

"Because my country came into a great deal of

wealth when I was eighteen. I was sent to the States to get an education. To learn how to protect and grow the wealth." He took a deep breath and turned to face her. "Instead I spent it."

Her eyes widened as her mouth open and shut. "All of it?" she croaked out.

"No. It doesn't matter how many millions I spent." The amount was branded into his soul for eternity, but the numbers could never convey the suffering of others. "I spent it. I stole it." He still flinched at the stripped-down version of his action. "I stole the money from the people of Rudaynah for my own pleasure. I was the playboy prince the tabloids love to hate."

Lacey stared at him as if he was a stranger to her. It was better than looking at him with the disgust he felt for himself. "That doesn't sound like you at all."

"It was me," he said brutally. "Look it up. The sultan tried to hide the story, but you can find it if you look hard enough. My spending habits had been legendary," he said, humility threading his voice.

"What stopped it?"

"The sultan received reports and called me home. The moment I returned I saw how Rudaynah had yet to see any progress. It humbled me. Shamed me more than any lecture or punishment."

Lacey frowned. "And your punishment for spending the money was losing your right to the throne?"

"No. I was stripped of any responsibility or authority. Of any rights or privileges. I was spared getting lashes because of my royal status. I didn't leave Rudaynah until I could regain my father's trust. And

I still didn't leave the borders until I felt it was necessary."

"But that doesn't explain to me how you lost your birthright."

The punishment he'd received was paltry considering his crime, but the sultan didn't want people to know the whole story. "One of the reports the sultan received had to do with my mistress at the time."

"I see," she said stiffly.

"You don't see." He looked directly in her blue eyes and braced himself. "My mistress became pregnant."

Lacey turned pale, but she regained her composure. "Is it yours?" she asked brusquely.

"I found out too late that she had an abortion," Hafiz said, the bitterness corroding inside him. "I've often wondered if the sultan campaigned for and funded it. Not directly, of course," he added cynically.

"I still don't understand—"

"Don't you get it, Lacey?" he barked out. "I couldn't uphold the expectations placed on me. I proved I wasn't leadership material." The list of his sins bore down on him. "I used the money for my own pleasure. I couldn't make my country proud. I couldn't provide the security of giving a rightful heir to the throne. But most of all, I couldn't protect my unborn child."

"Hafiz," Lacey said grimly as she walked toward him. He braced himself for her to launch into a tirade. For a stinging slap. It wouldn't hurt nearly as much as her disappointment.

She surprised him by placing a gentle hand on his arm. He looked down at her, bemused by the sincerity gleaming in her eyes. "Don't let your mistakes define you. You are a good man."

He drew back. She still believed in him. How could she? Wasn't she listening? "You're biased, but thanks."

"Give me some credit. I wouldn't give up everything familiar for a playboy prince. I certainly wouldn't follow any man to the ends of the earth."

"I believe the term you're looking for is 'this hell'," he reminded her.

Lacey looked chagrined but wouldn't be deterred. "And Rudaynah needs you. The mistake you made will serve you well." She paused, obviously searching for the right words. "You have risen from your past like…a phoenix from the ashes. You're stronger and smarter. You have worked hard all these years to take care of your countrymen."

But he would never regain the trust of the people. His brother kept his distance, as if poor judgment was contagious. His own parents couldn't stand the sight of him.

"I am not the kind of man you're trying to make me out to be." But he wanted to be. He wanted to deserve her admiration.

"You're good for Rudaynah. This sultanate needs you," Lacey insisted and cupped his face with her hand. "If I thought otherwise, I would take you away with me."

Hafiz leaned into her touch just as his cell phone rang. They both jumped as the harsh sound echoed in the cavernous room.

"Don't answer it," Lacey whispered.

"It would be Glenn. He would only call if it was important." He reached for the phone and answered it. "Yes?"

"Our exit visas have been denied," Glenn said.

A coldness settled inside Hafiz as he considered what that could mean. "Did they give a reason?"

"No, but they were acting strange. As if it hasn't happened before. What do you want me to do next, Your Highness?"

"Let me get back to you." Hafiz ended the call and pressed the phone against his chin as he stared out the window. He quickly analyzed the sultan's latest move and what it represented. He didn't like any of the answers.

"Is something wrong?" Lacey asked.

"Your exit visas have been denied," he murmured as he considered his next move.

"I thought the process was just a formality." Lacey gasped, and she clapped her hand over her mouth. "Your father knows about me. He knows I'm your mistress."

"Let's not jump to conclusions. It could be a clerical error." Hafiz wanted to calm Lacey, but he knew his answer wouldn't soothe her.

"This doesn't make sense. Why can't I leave the country? Wouldn't your father give me the red carpet treatment to the first car out of here?"

"Not necessarily," Hafiz replied grimly.

Lacey pressed her lips together. "What's going on?"

"There's a possibility," he said, emphasizing the word, "that the sultan sees your presence as an advantage to him. It would make me the most agreeable groom."

"I don't like the sounds of that," Lacey said. "Am I in trouble? Is he going to use me to get to you?"

"I should have predicted it," Hafiz muttered. "The sultan had done this before."

"When? Ten years ago?" Lacey took a deep breath. "Hafiz, I need to know. What happened to your last mistress? The one who got pregnant?"

CHAPTER SEVEN

HAFIZ LEANED AGAINST the windowpane and closed his eyes as the guilt swamped him. He never forgot that time in his life, and he refused to forgive himself. The actions he took, the mistakes he made were part of him and had influenced his decisions to this day. And yet, he tried not to look too closely and inspect his flaws.

"Her name was Elizabeth," he said quietly. "I had already earned my reputation as the playboy prince when I met her in Monte Carlo."

"What was she like?" Lacey asked.

"Beautiful. Professional. Ambitious."

Lacey frowned. "You make her sound cold and unfeeling."

What he had shared with Elizabeth had nothing to do with warmth and affection. "She made her way through life as a mistress. Our relationship had been purely physical, and we both wanted it that way."

Because he hadn't been interested in romance or commitment. He had been too busy partying, gambling and exploring the world outside of Rudaynah and royal life.

Hafiz forced himself to continue. He knew Lacey needed to hear this. "We had only been together for a few months when I found out she was pregnant." Hafiz looked away. "I didn't handle the news well. I wish I could take back that moment and react differently."

"What did you do?" Lacey asked.

He didn't want to give a voice to the memories that haunted him. The moments that had demonstrated what kind of man he had been. Only he hadn't acted like a man.

"I was furious. Scared," he admitted with a sigh. "I knew that a baby was going to change everything. I swore the baby couldn't possibly be mine. I didn't *want* it to be mine."

Lacey rested her hand against his shoulder. "I can't imagine you acting like that, Hafiz."

"It was me. A spoiled and selfish prince who knew his freedom was about to be taken away from him. I accused Elizabeth of being unfaithful. I wasn't going to let her trap me or extort money from me." Hafiz raked his hand through his hair. "I hate the way I treated her."

"That may have been your first reaction, but I'm sure you saw reason once you calmed down."

Hafiz shook his head. Lacey thought too highly of him. He slowly turned around and faced her. "I left Elizabeth," he said, watching the surprise in Lacey's eyes. He hunched his shoulders as the remorse weighed heavily on him. "My father had demanded that I return home, and I used that as a way to hide from my responsibilities."

Lacey stared at him in disbelief. "You wouldn't do that."

"That was the lowest time of my life. I was trying to hide what I had done and conceal the person I was.

Hide everything from the sultan and my countrymen. At times, I tried to hide the truth from myself."

"Impossible."

"It wasn't that hard to do. I wanted to convince myself that Elizabeth was the villain. I believed she tried to trick me and that she got what she deserved for attempting to get her claws into a prince."

"When did you decide she was not the villain?"

"It wasn't just one event. I started seeing how I treated everyone during that time. I should have treated her better. I had cut off all contact. And somehow I had convinced myself that I did the right thing."

"Did you try to find her after that and make it right?"

He nodded. "I wasn't able to travel, but I wasn't going to let it stop me. I was done making excuses. I had one of my representatives track her down." Hafiz took a deep breath. "But I was too late. Elizabeth had gotten an abortion."

The silence permeated the room as Hafiz remembered getting that call. He had shattered from the grief. He had never been the same man after knowing he hadn't protected and provided for his unborn son.

"I was furious at myself," Hafiz said quietly. "If I had shown Elizabeth any concern or any sign that she could depend on me, she wouldn't have taken extreme measures."

"And you think your father was behind that?"

"I'm sure of it. Elizabeth had hinted it to my representative, but I think she was too afraid to speak plainly. She was afraid to cross the sultan, with good reason."

"Should I be afraid?"

"No," Hafiz said. "You can depend on me. I will not abandon you."

Lacey moved closer to him until her hip brushed against his. "I'm sorry. I'm sorry that my presence in your life is causing so many problems." The air around them pulsed with energy, but Hafiz didn't reach out for her. His fingers flexed, but his hands stayed by his side.

"You're not a burden," he said gruffly. Having Lacey in his life had been a gift.

Lacey leaned forward and pressed her forehead against his shoulder. Hafiz tensed and remained where he stood. It was still a risk. If someone walked into this room and saw him alone with Lacey...he didn't want to think about the consequences.

Hafiz cleared his throat and took a step away from her. "I have to go. I know how to fix this."

"What are you going to do?" she called after him as he strode to the door.

He set his mouth into a grim line. "Whatever it takes."

"This wedding reception is one of the most lavish I've seen. I don't know how Inas and her husband paid for it," Janet said a few days later as they slowly made their way through the crowded ballroom to the buffet. "I can't wait to eat."

"Where are the men?" Lacey asked. The ballroom was packed with women. Bright, garish colors swirled around Lacey and her friend Janet as the conversations swelled to an earsplitting decibel. Heavy perfumes of every imaginable flower clashed against one another.

"They are in the ballroom across the hall having

their party," Janet informed her. "The men and women in Rudaynah don't celebrate together. This way the women can literally let their hair down and dance."

Lacey glanced at the stage where the bride sat. It seemed strange to Lacey that the newlywed couple would spend their wedding reception apart. Did it signify what was yet to come? That the marriage meant separate paths, separate lives, for the couple? Was this what all marriages were like in this country?

She studied the group of relatives on the stage surrounding the bride. "I still don't see Inas."

"We'll find her. By the way, I love what you're wearing. I thought you had given up wearing the traditional caftan."

"Thank you." Lacey glanced down at her pale blue caftan. She hadn't been certain about the transparent sleeves or the modest neckline. The skirt flared out gently, and the intricate embroidery design that ran down the front of the caftan matched her slippers. "I wanted one chance to wear it before I leave."

"Did you get your exit visas sorted out?"

"Uh…yes," she lied. "I'll be leaving very soon." As in tonight. But she couldn't let anyone know that.

She glanced at her jeweled watch and winced. The wedding reception had started late, and she should have returned home by now and gathered her things.

"Janet, why don't you go on ahead to the buffet? I have to leave."

"Already?" She shook her head. "You're going to miss the professional dancers and the wedding march. Not to mention the food!"

"I know, but I'm glad I had a chance to be here. I just hope leaving early doesn't offend Inas."

"She'll understand," Janet said as she hugged Lacey goodbye. "You'll probably find her near the door greeting all the guests."

Lacey fought her way through the cluster of women. She couldn't help but wonder if Hafiz's wedding reception would be like this. She pushed the thought aside. She wasn't going to torture herself imagining what Hafiz's wedding to another woman was going to be like.

Lacey saw her friend near the entrance. "Inas!" She waved and hurried to greet the mother of the bride. "Inas, this wedding is beautiful. And your daughter!" She glanced at the woman on stage in the back of the ballroom. The young woman wore an embroidered red gown and veil. Heavy gold jewelry hung from her wrists and throat. "She looks like a princess."

"Lacey, I'm so happy to see you." Inas gave her a kiss on each cheek. "And you wouldn't believe who is here!"

The woman almost squealed. Lacey couldn't imagine who would cause this level of excitement. "Who?"

"Inas?" An older woman's voice wafted over them. Inas's demeanor changed rapidly. Her smile widened, and she trembled with exhilaration. Inas struggled to lower her eyes as she gave a curtsey to the woman. She folded her hands neatly in front of her as she spoke respectfully in Arabic.

Lacey took a step back. Her instincts told her to melt into the crowd and disappear.

"Allow me to introduce you," Inas said as she grasped Lacey's elbow and brought her forward. Lacey stared at the older woman who wore a white scarf over her gray hair and a brocade caftan that concealed her body.

"Your Majesty, this is Lacey Maxwell. I tutored her in Arabic while she was visiting our sultanate. Lacey, this is the Sultana Zafirah of Rudaynah."

And Hafiz's mother. Lacey's knees buckled, and she quickly covered it up with a shaky curtsey.

She glanced at the sultana through her lashes and found the older woman inspecting her like a mangled insect carcass. It took every ounce of willpower for Lacey not to meet the woman's gaze. *This was probably why Hafiz didn't want you to meet his family.*

Lacey covertly looked at the exit and wondered how she was going to extract herself from this situation. Her mind went blank as panic congealed in her throat. "I understand one of your sons will be married soon," Lacey said in what she hoped was a respectful tone. "Congratulations."

The sultana stiffened, and Lacey wondered if she had broken some protocol. "Thank you," Sultana Zafirah said with a sniff.

Lacey hesitated, uncertain how to proceed. "I'm sure Miss Abdullah will be a worthy addition to your family."

The sultana gave a careless shrug. "More worthy than my son."

A startled gasp quickly evaporated in Lacey's throat as indignation mushroomed inside her chest. How dare the sultana say that about Hafiz? Lacey was stunned that the woman would say it to a stranger. There was no telling what was said in private.

Lacey looked away and fought back her words. Didn't Sultana Zafirah see how much her son worked and sacrificed to correct his mistakes? Didn't she care that he strove to become worthy, all the while knowing he would never reach his goal? Or was the sultana unwilling to recognize what her son has already achieved?

Tears smarted Lacey's eyes as hope shriveled up inside her. Why did Hafiz want to be with his family instead of her? The idea alone was like a knife sliding between her ribs before it gave a vicious twist. Was this what he really wanted?

How could she leave Hafiz here to face this alone? But deep down, she knew she wasn't an ally. She was a liability. She was going to leave so Hafiz could become the man he wanted to be. She wanted Rudaynah to benefit from his ideas and leadership, and she wanted the people to recognize his worth and abilities.

On a purely selfish level, she wanted her sacrifice to mean something. She wanted it be worth the pain, if that was possible.

The ballroom suddenly plunged into darkness. The initial squeals from the crowd turned into groans of people who were used to power outages. Lacey blinked wildly as the darkness shrouded her. She could already feel the difference in temperature as the air conditioner silenced.

"Nothing to worry about, Miss Maxwell." Sultana Zafirah said. The royal entourage bumped Lacey as they quickly surrounded the sultana. "The generator will turn on soon."

"Yes, Your Majesty."

The emergency lights gradually came on, casting an eerie green over the wedding guests. Just as every-

one cheered, the lights blinked and flared before shut-
ting off.

"No, no, no." Inas said. "This cannot happen at my
daughter's wedding."

"I'll go see if there are any lights on in the hotel,"
Lacey offered. Sensing she only had a few minutes
before the lights and power returned, she slowly retreated.

Using the flurry of activity to her advantage, Lacey
turned around and made her way to the exit. Her hands
brushed against the heavy metal door. She wrenched
the handle, opening the door a crack, and found the
hallway was just as dark as the ballroom. The moment
she passed the threshold, she breathed a sigh of relief.

As much as she wanted to celebrate her friend's
special moment, she found the business of marriage
in Rudaynah too depressing. It wasn't a union of two
hearts as much as it was a business alliance. The com-
bining of two families and two properties.

The lights came back on, and she heard the mur-
murs of delight from the ballroom. Lacey hurried
down the steps to the main lobby when she saw a familiar figure in a gray pinstripe suit waiting at the
bottom of the stairs.

"Where have you been?" Hafiz asked, glancing at
his wristwatch. "We were supposed to meet at your
apartment."

"Hafiz?" She remembered that the sultana and the
most influential people in the country were in the next
room. He was placing himself at risk. "You can't be
here. It's too dangerous. Your—"

"I'm fully aware of it," Hafiz said as he fell into

step with her. "If you want to get to Abu Dhabi to-night, we must leave now."

"I'm sorry I'm late. I'm never late."

Hafiz set his mouth in a grim line. "My limousine is waiting right outside the entrance. Once we leave, then we will discuss what you were doing with my mother."

Lacey stiffened as she heard the accusation in his tone. How did he find out about that? She didn't have to see Hafiz's face to know he was angry. But why was he blaming her?

"I didn't know the sultana was going to make an appearance. How would I?"

Hafiz muttered something succinct as he ushered her out the hotel. Guilt slammed through her. She didn't want to be a hindrance. She hated being the cause of his troubles.

Lacey paused. She wasn't a hindrance. She wasn't a liability. The only thing she was guilty of was loving a man who didn't think she was good enough to marry.

CHAPTER EIGHT

HAFIZ KEPT HIS anger in check as he got into the waiting limousine. Tonight he had to send away the one person who mattered the most to him. He wanted to rage against the world, destroy everything around him and allow the fury to consume him. Instead he closed the car door with deliberate care.

The car jerked into full speed. He barely glanced at Lacey sitting regally on the other side of the back seat. He didn't trust himself to speak or look at her.

What was it about this woman? Did she trigger a self-destructive tendency in him? Why had he been willing to risk everything for Lacey? What made him lower his guard when they had been in danger of discovery? Why couldn't he have fallen for someone who would make his life easier?

"I have nothing to say." Lacey stared straight ahead. "I did nothing wrong."

He sliced his hand in the air. "Yes, you did," he replied in a low growl. In the past Lacey's hurt would have destroyed him until he did everything in his power to make her happy, but at the moment he wished she would see the world through his eyes.

"I don't have to explain myself," Lacey continued.

"My friend introduced me to your mother. She thought I was worthy enough to meet the sultana. Why don't you?"

"Does your friend know everything about you?" The words were dragged from his mouth. "Is she aware that you are the prince's mistress?"

"Of course not." Lacey said and rolled her eyes.

He speared a hard look at Lacey. She had spent half a year in his country but still didn't have a basic understanding how the Sultanate of Rudaynah worked. He risked everything to help her tonight. It would be scandalous if he were found alone with a woman. If it were discovered that she was his mistress, the results would be cataclysmic.

"I'm sorry if my meeting the sultana made you uncomfortable," she said angrily.

Was she? Had she not suggested a few days ago how he was better off without that title? Lacey had to be furious that her dream life ended abruptly while he was offered the one thing he had relentlessly worked toward. It wouldn't take much to crush his chances, but Hafiz didn't want to believe Lacey could be that diabolical.

"No, you're not. You want me to be uncomfortable and worry. You're enjoying it." Hafiz grabbed a hold of the door as the limousine took a sharp, fast turn. "I want to know the whole truth. How long have you known my mother?"

"I just met her," Lacey insisted. "It's not like we had an in-depth conversation."

Hafiz shook his head. Her eyes shone with innocence, and yet he didn't trust that the meeting was happenstance. She could have arranged to meet the sultana and dropped a few bombshells. He didn't want to think of how many times those blue eyes possibly duped him in the past.

"I swear, I didn't tell her anything."

And yet, despite careful planning of keeping his family and private life separate, his mother managed to meet his mistress. "This is not happening," he muttered. Being introduced to a mistress or concubine was considered a deep offense to the sultana. If the truth came out, he would pay the penalty for it. "You planned this, didn't you?"

"Planned what? An introduction with your mother?" Lacey asked listlessly, as if the fight had evaporated from her. She looked out the window at the dusty city streets whizzing past them.

"You hinted at it when you first arrived here. How you wanted to meet my family. Then it turned into a bold request and finally a demand."

Lacey rubbed her hands over her face and gave a deep sigh. "That was before I understood our relationship was completely forbidden. That I was somehow beneath you and not good enough to meet your family."

Beneath him? Where did she get that idea? "I told you that it was complicated."

"But you didn't tell me that it was impossible." She returned her attention to the window as if she couldn't bear to look at him. "I should have known something was up when you didn't introduce me to your friends. I was so naïve."

"I have nothing to apologize for."

She shook her head. "You brought me over here

under false pretenses. I thought we were going to live together."

Hafiz's mouth dropped open in surprise. "I never made that offer. Us, together in the palace?" He shuddered at the thought. "We would have been cast out in seconds."

"Obviously you and I had different ideas about being together. I didn't think you would hide my existence from your family."

"And when you realized that meeting them wasn't going to happen, you decided to take matters into your own hands."

"Like my introduction to your mother? What would be the point?" She turned to face him. "What do you think I did? Just walk up to her and say, 'Hi, I'm Lacey. I'm Hafiz's mistress and I hope to continue even after he's married?' Do you really think I'm capable of that?"

He stared at her with disbelieving horror as something close to panic clenched his stomach. "You would if you thought it would help."

"Help?" She watched him with growing suspicion. "Help what?"

"To stop me from getting married." She would eventually realize that he wasn't going to stop it. He accepted that his future wasn't going to be happy or loving. He had known that for the past decade.

"For the last time," she said, her voice rising, "I was not trying to wreck your wedding. I am going against every instinct I have by not fighting for you." She tilted her head back and rested it against the seat. "Is that what makes you so suspicious? You gave me up and thought I would fight for you. For us. Because I immediately backed off, I must be up to something?"

"You think I gave you up easily? That there was no thought involved, no hesitation? I had put off my marriage for as long as possible so I could be with you."

"You put off your marriage so you could get a better deal," Lacey said through clenched teeth. "Like getting another shot at becoming the crown prince. Then you couldn't get rid of me fast enough."

"Lacey, I am not your parents. Try not to compare me with them. I didn't discard you to pursue my life's ambition."

Lacey's eyes narrowed into slits. "Don't bring my parents into this."

"You think I'm abandoning you out of ambition just like your parents. You act as if my life is going to overflow with happiness and abundance once you're out of my life. Do you think your parents had a better life without you?"

"Yes!" she bit out.

Hafiz drew his head back and stared at her. "You're wrong, Lacey. They missed out on so much."

"No, you are wrong. I held them back from what they really wanted in life. Once I was gone, they pursued their passion. They are happier than they've ever been."

Did she think he wouldn't look back at their time together? That he wouldn't feel the regret of letting her go? "Why do you act like I'm giving you up for something better? I am entering a marriage with a stranger," he reminded her.

"You made a choice, Hafiz. And it wasn't me. It was never going to be me."

A thought suddenly occurred to him. *She had been waiting for this to happen.* "You're not fighting for me because deep down you knew I was going to have to make a choice one day. And you knew it wasn't going to be in your favor."

"I'm not fighting for you because I know we have run our course." She gave a sharp intake of breath and tossed her hands in the air. "I should have just kept our relationship to a one-night stand and be done with you."

"Excuse me?" Anger flashed hot and swift inside him. What he and Lacey shared could not have been contained in one night.

"I knew you were trouble, but that didn't stop me. No, quite the opposite." She shook her head in self-disgust. "And, let's face it, you weren't thinking about forever after one night with me."

Hafiz wearily rubbed his hands over his eyes. "All I knew is that I couldn't stay away."

"And you kept coming back. I would count the days until we could see each other again. I thought you felt the same way, too."

"I did." The anticipation that burned in his veins, the excitement pressing against his chest had never waned.

"No, it's only been recently when I realized we had approached this affair very differently. I was so happy in love that I wanted to share it with the whole world. You wanted to keep this relationship secret because you were ashamed."

"For the last time, Lacey, I am not ashamed—"

"No, not of me." Her jaw trembled as she tried to hold her emotions in check. "You were ashamed that you couldn't stay away. After all those years of resisting temptation, of demonstrating your willpower, your strength, you couldn't stay away. An ordinary woman, a nobody, was your weakness."

He closed his eyes, momentarily overwhelmed. She was right. He didn't like how Lacey saw right through him. Understood him better than he understood himself.

"I am Prince Hafiz ibn Yusuf Qadi," he said quietly. "I have spent the last ten years proving that I am worthy of that name. I had purged every wild impulse, and nothing could tempt me off the straight and narrow path. And then I met you."

"You make me sound like I'm a vice. Something you need to give up to be a better person."

Hafiz was too deep into the memory to reply. "And then I see you at the piano in a hotel lobby. I didn't even stop to think. I was drawn to your singing as if I was a sailor listening to the sirens."

"Being attracted to me does not show weakness of character. Falling for me is not a sin."

"It is if you are a prince from the Sultanate of Rudaynah."

She crossed her arms and stared at him. "And yet, you asked me to live here. I thought it was because you loved me. No, it's because you see me as some kind of bad habit that you couldn't give up."

Fury flashed through him, and he held it in check. "You don't have that kind of power over me. No one does."

"Especially a young woman who doesn't understand the royal court politics or influential people. That's why you felt safe to bring me over here."

He scoffed at her statement. "Having you here was never safe."

"I thought you trusted me. I thought that made me different from everyone you knew. It made me special to you. But that's not it at all, is it? It's that you contained the situation. You made sure I wasn't in a position to break your trust."

"Not a lot of good it did me," he muttered.

Lacey's fingers fluttered against her cheeks as if she was brushing something away. "I wish I didn't know any of this. I wish I could have left Rudaynah the night I found out about your engagement."

Hafiz remained silent. He knew he should feel the same way. She was his weakness, his vulnerability, but he didn't want her to go.

"That night had been magical," she said softly. There was a faraway look in her eyes. "It was the right way to say goodbye. I would have left here believing that…what we had was special. That I had been special."

Hafiz clenched his hands. He wanted to tell Lacey how special she was to him. But what purpose would it serve? What they had was over. It could not continue.

"You think I'm bad for you," Lacey said. "That I'm proof of your bad judgment, or that I symbolize all of those wild impulses you couldn't get rid of. One of these days you're going to realize that I was the best thing that had ever happened to you." She pointed her finger at him. "Someday you'll realize that everything I've done was to protect you."

"I don't need your protection, Lacey." He shook his head. "It was my job to protect you."

Lacey blinked rapidly as if she was preventing

more tears from falling. "I wanted to be your confidante. Your partner. My goal was to help you be the best prince you could be."

"And in return, you would become a princess." Hafiz grimaced. Even as he said it, he knew that wasn't her true motivation.

"If you believe that, you don't know me at all." Her shoulders drooped as if she didn't have the energy to fight anymore. "I thought you knew everything about me," Lacey announced dully as she pulled her hair away from her face.

"And you know everything about me," Hafiz said. "I confided in you when I shouldn't have."

Lacey jerked at his harsh tone and slowly turned to meet his gaze. "Why do you continue to believe that I would betray you?"

Her question was carried out with a wispy puff of air. The wounded look in her eyes threatened to shatter him inside. He drew from the dark edges that hovered around him, knowing he had to be callous, and knowing he was going to regret it.

"Because you are a mistress. A fallen woman. Betrayal is your only power against me." Hafiz knew what he said hurt her where she was most vulnerable, but it was his only guarantee. That cold response would prevent Lacey from trying to hold on to him and what might have been. He had to protect her even if it meant tearing down the love she felt for him.

The darkness surged through Hafiz, and he struggled against the cold bitterness invading his body. He'd battled it before, only this time he had to do it alone. In the past, Lacey was the only person he knew who could stem the flow.

"If I'm a fallen women, you shouldn't be seen with me. So, why are you still here?" Lacey asked in a withering tone. She folded her arms more tightly and crossed her legs. Hafiz wondered if it was an attempt to get as far away from him as possible. "Stop the car and I'll get out."

"That's enough." Hafiz's tone held a steely edge. "I'm making sure you get on that helicopter."

She gave a haughty tilt of her chin. "I'm perfectly capable of finding my way."

"I'm sure you could, but you don't have access to the palace."

"Palace?" Hafiz saw her tense as a sound of panic rumbled in the back of her throat; she turned abruptly to her window. When she didn't see anything on her side of the limousine, she frantically searched out his window.

He knew the minute she saw the towering mud brick walls that surrounded the palace. The historical site was constructed as more of a fortress than the home of a sultan. It wasn't opulent or majestic. The curved buildings, domed roofs and large archways were made out of clay. The buildings were functional and cool against the desert heat.

It was also designed to intimidate the enemy. Lacey had a look of unease as they passed through the guarded gates, and she got the first good look of the palace. Hafiz held back his assurances. He needed her to focus on leaving without looking back.

"I can't see you again," he began.

Her eyes dulled with pain. "I don't want you to."

Hafiz scowled at her statement. "I mean it, Lacey."

"I do, too. I'm not really big on sharing." Her chin

wobbled, and she blinked back the moisture from her eyes. "Don't contact me unless you've changed your mind and only want me."

That wasn't going to happen, Hafiz thought. It couldn't.

The limousine lurched to a stop next to the helicopter pad. Hafiz immediately stepped out of the car and reached for Lacey's hand. When she hesitated, he grasped her wrist. Fierce sensations scorched his skin from the touch. He grimly ignored the way his pulse tripped and assisted her outside.

Her long hair blew in the desert wind, and he escorted her to the pilot who was waiting by the helicopter. After Hafiz yelled instructions over the noise, Lacey climbed in. He tried to assist her, but she batted him away. He flashed a warning look at her.

The warning dissipated as he looked into her eyes. Even after what had happened, after everything they'd said, he wished for one more kiss. He was desperate for it and felt the pull. His mouth craved her taste and her softness. The yearning pierced at him like swift jabs of a knife, because he knew after this moment, circumstances would snatch Lacey away from him.

He looked away. The darkness inside him eclipsed the pain of knowing this was the last time he would see her. Their paths would never cross, and he could never contact her again. He wouldn't know where she lived or if she was safe. She would disappear but linger in his mind as he worried and wondered.

"Your Highness," the pilot shouted, breaking through Hafiz's thoughts. "We need to leave now."

Hafiz hesitated. He couldn't make a clean break

from Lacey, no matter how much he wanted to. How much he needed to, for both their sakes.

He glanced at her and met her gaze. No tears escaped her eyes. She didn't speak. Didn't move, but he knew she struggled for composure. He knew her poise was for his benefit. It was her way to prove that she would be fine.

She looked so beautiful and elegant. Regal. Hafiz thought his heart was going to blast through the wall of his chest. Lacey was more beautiful than when he first saw her. He was fortunate to have known and loved her, and she would never know. His throat closed shut as his strength seeped out of his bones.

He had to tell her. He had thought it would be kinder not to say anything. Not to give her the answer because it would have given her hope. Something to fight for. But he could not let her go with the belief that she didn't matter.

"I love you, Lacey."

Her lips parted, and she stared at his mouth. She frowned as if she had heard incorrectly. As if she had heard what she wanted to hear.

"You may think I hate you or I'm ashamed of you," he said over the whine of the helicopter, "but it isn't true. I took all of these risks because I love you. I will always love you."

She began to reach out as the helicopter started to lift off. Hafiz wanted to grab her hand, but he forced himself to back away.

He watched her, unblinking, as the helicopter rose into the sky and turned, taking his love, his last chance of happiness, away from him.

But he didn't deserve happiness. He didn't deserve a life with Lacey.

Hafiz remained where he stood when every instinct screamed for him to run after Lacey. A ragged gasp escaped his raw throat as he watched the helicopter fly off until it was no longer a speck in the air. The silence sliced deep into his dreams and wishes until they lay tattered at his feet and darkness descended in his heart.

CHAPTER NINE

"LACEY, MY WORK shift is about to start," Priya shouted over the music. "Are you going to be okay? I feel weird leaving you alone."

"That's sweet of you, but you don't have to worry." Lacey smiled at her roommate. She felt bad that Priya felt the need to mother her. And drag her to this party so she would get out of the apartment. "I'm going to be fine. It's been a while since I've been to a party, but it's all coming back to me."

"Good," Priya said with a nod. "I know you've been mending a broken heart, but you are too young to spend all your time working at the hotel and staying in bed."

"You're right," she said as her roommate walked away. Taking a small sip from the beer bottle she had been nursing for an hour, Lacey stood at the sidelines and watched her coworkers mill around the pool room located in their housing complex. It was an eclectic mix of young people in swimwear and colorful sundresses. While some splashed around in the pool and others danced to the blaring music, most of the guests nibbled on the spicy snacks and drank the boldly colored concoctions.

Once Priya left the party, Lacey closed her eyes and exhaled. She would stay another five minutes and then leave.

She still wasn't sure why she'd chosen to stay in Abu Dhabi, but it had proven to be a good decision. The rich nightlife had allowed her to find a job performing at the hotel lounge. She'd also managed to make a few friends within the month she arrived. She was determined to get out and meet more people. Forget the past and make up for lost time.

Sometimes determination wasn't enough. Her time in Rudaynah had changed her. Marked her in ways she hadn't considered. Lacey glanced down at the purple bikini she wore and the wispy sarong around her hips. These days she wasn't comfortable showing too much skin. She preferred the modest dress code she had to follow once she was outside the housing complex.

"Lacey!" Cody, another American who worked in the hotel, was at her side. His wide smile, unbuttoned shirt and bright red swim trunks conveyed his casual attitude toward life. He liked to flirt with her, and while she knew it didn't mean anything, she tried to discourage it.

"You haven't danced once the whole time you've been here." He held out his hand. "We need to fix that."

She hesitated for a second. She knew the invitation wasn't going to jump-start her love life, but the idea of dancing with another man—touching another man—felt wrong.

It's just a dance. It's no big deal. But she knew Cody would try for more. How could she explain to him that she didn't feel whole or intact? That she was definitely not strong enough to even expose herself to a lighthearted fling or a one-night stand?

Looking into Cody's face lined by the sun rather than by hardship, Lacey realized falling in love again was impossible. She felt the corners of her mouth quirk as she considered her foolishness. What was she worried about? She was safe with Cody and every other man. No one could measure up to Hafiz.

"Okay, sure. Why not?" She set down her beer and took his hand. Lacey didn't feel any thrill of anticipation when he placed his other hand on the curve of her hip or when her fingers grazed his bare skin. She felt no excitement, no awareness. Nothing.

But, quite honestly, she hadn't felt a thing since the helicopter touched down in Abu Dhabi a month ago. She went through the motions of living, but she felt dead inside. She had a feeling it was going to be like that forever. And still she didn't worry over the possibility.

As Lacey danced in Cody's arms, she wondered how long the song would last. She knew that if Hafiz had been her dance partner, she would have wanted the music to go on forever.

Hafiz. She had to stop thinking about him. Lacey abruptly pulled away just as the song changed into something harsh and angry.

Cody motioned for her to keep dancing, but she wanted to go home. No, that wasn't true. She wanted to find Hafiz.

But that was not going to happen, Lacey reminded herself. He didn't want her near him. She was a vice. A sin. Hafiz's words ricocheted through her head.

Nothing had changed. Nothing ever would. She had to move on.

"Don't hold back, Lacey!" Cody yelled as he jumped up and down to the drumbeat.

Move on. Start now. Fake it until you make it. Lacey swayed to the music. She wished it had the power to make her forget everything. But the music didn't reach her heart or fill her soul like it used to.

She needed to feel it again. Music was part of who she was. It was more than her livelihood; it was how she expressed herself and how she found solace. She couldn't let Hafiz take that away from her, too.

Lacey pushed harder as she danced. She moved her shoulders and swished her hips to the beat of the drums. The music still didn't reach her.

She pulled and pushed her body to move as far as it would go, wishing that the numbness that held everything back would break. That the music would grow louder until it seeped inside her. If that didn't work, then she hoped the dancing would exhaust her so she could sleep without dreaming.

From the corner of her eyes, Lacey saw that someone wore all black. A jacket...no, a suit. The formality was at odds with the party. The darkness was out of place among the bright rainbow colors. But there was something familiar about the person's movement. What was it that... Her heart lurched, and she went still.

Hafiz. She froze as the wild hope and surprise ripped through her. Hafiz was here? No, that was impossible. She blinked, and he was suddenly gone. Lacey rubbed her eyes. Was she now having hallucinations about him along with her dreams?

Her pulse skipped hard as she quickly scanned the crowd. Why did he seem so real? Shouldn't her memory become hazier as time went on?

She frowned as she resumed her dancing. Her memory was definitely playing tricks. Lacey didn't understand why she envisioned him in a black linen jacket, collarless shirt and black trousers. Usually she remembered him in a pinstripe suit, in traditional robes, or in nothing at all.

Lacey squeezed her eyes shut as she tried to discard the images of Hafiz in various stages of undress flickering through her mind. *Forget about him,* she decided as she forced herself to dance. *It's time to start living again.*

Hafiz watched Lacey dance, her body moving with the same earthiness as when they shared a bed. It had been four weeks since he'd seen Lacey. Since he had declared his love. It felt like an eternity. He shouldn't be here, and yet he couldn't stay away.

Now he wished he hadn't given in to the impulse. Anger and indignation swirled inside him, ready to explode. From what he could see, Lacey was the center of the party. She wasn't laughing or smiling, but her intense expression suggested that nothing mattered more than exploring the music.

He glared at the bikini and sarong she wore. It flaunted her curves instead of hiding them. The bikini top lovingly clung to her breasts. Her nipples pressed against the fragile fabric. The sarong hung low, emphasizing her tiny waist and the gentle swell of her hips.

His gaze traveled down her taut stomach. The ivory

skin was sun-kissed, but she had lost weight. Pining for him? Hafiz glanced around the party and scoffed at the idea as he crossed his arms. He wished. More like too much partying.

The brightly colored sarong teased his senses, and he couldn't drag his gaze away from her bare legs. He remembered how they felt wrapped around his waist as he drove into her.

When Lacey rolled her hips, Hafiz's restraint threatened to shatter. Where was a voluminous caftan when you needed one? He was beginning to see the advantages.

Lacey was surrounded by cheering men, and she unknowingly taunted them with the thrust of her hips. Hafiz swore she was more sensual than any belly dancer without even trying. Did she know that these men would do anything to get her into bed? They couldn't hide the desperation to take his place in her life.

Had they already?

The possibility fueled his bitter jealousy. He could not hold back any longer. He stepped through the circle of the men posturing for Lacey's attention and reached for her. Hafiz grasped her wrist and was painfully aware of the heat coursing through him from the simple touch.

Lacey opened her eyes just as he slid her against him. Blood sang through his veins as her soft breasts pressed against his hard chest. He shuddered as his control slipped. After a month without her, every primal instinct told him to pounce and never let her go.

"Miss me, Lacey?" he murmured in her ear.

He watched as she blinked at him. His chest ached

as he waited, wondering how she would greet him. Would she push him away? Would she welcome him with the same cool friendliness she'd welcome an old acquaintance? Or would she treat him with indifference?

"Hafiz?"

He drew her closer as the people and the noise faded around them. He had eyes only for Lacey. She pressed her hands to his face. "I can't believe you're here," she whispered.

He held her hand and pressed his mouth against her palm. "You did miss me," he said, purring with satisfaction.

"Of course I did." She wrapped her arms around his neck and held him fiercely. "How can you ask?" she asked against his chest.

"Let's get out of here," he insisted as he drew her away. He was too impatient to taste Lacey's mouth on his. He needed her more than his next breath. "I want you all to myself."

Hafiz held her hand tightly as he guided her out of the party as if he couldn't risk losing her. As if she might break away. He was striding to the elevators that would whisk them to her apartment when he abruptly turned and pulled her into a shadowy corner.

It had been too long. He wasn't going to wait anymore. He pressed her back against the corner and braced his arms against the walls, trapping her. "Show me how much you missed me."

Lacey didn't hesitate and claimed Hafiz's mouth with hers. The one touch, one kiss, was all it took for the numbness to disappear. Her skin tingled, her heart pounded against her chest, and blood roared in her ears as she violently came back to life.

She still couldn't believe it. Hafiz had come for her. He chose her over his fiancée and his duty. Over his country. He chose *her*.

Lacey pulled away and stared at Hafiz. She searched his face, noticing how much he had changed in a month. His features were harsher, the lines and angles more pronounced. The sexual hunger in his eyes was ferocious.

She trembled with anticipation and grabbed his jacket lapels. Hafiz wrapped his hands around her waist and ripped off her sarong. He tossed it on the ground with an impatience she'd never seen in him.

She knew Hafiz was almost out of his mind with lust. He was desperate to touch her. To taste her. She understood this driving need, but the intensity was almost painful. She felt as if she could explode from it.

Hafiz pushed the bikini top away and exposed her breasts. They felt heavy under his hot gaze. Lacey almost wept as Hafiz captured one tight nipple in his mouth. She raked her fingers through his hair, encouraging him closer.

Lacey gasped at the primal, almost savage way he stripped her bikini bottoms from her hips. She could tell that his control was slipping. He couldn't hold back. This reunion was going to be hard, fast and furious.

She couldn't believe she had this power over him. That they had this power over each other. Lacey liked how his fingers shook as he tore the flimsy piece of fabric from her trembling legs. She bit her lip when he roughly cupped her sex.

"Now," she muttered. "I need you in me now."

Hafiz didn't follow her demands. Instead he dipped his fingers into her wet heat. Lacey panted hard as her flesh gripped him tight and drew him in deeper.

As Hafiz stroked her with his fingers, Lacey pressed her mouth shut to prevent a throaty moan from escaping. They were hidden as the party continued around them. No one could hear them, no one could see, but old habits died hard. She couldn't risk being discovered, but she couldn't bear the idea of stopping.

Lacey dove her hands under his shirt and slid her fingers along his hot, flushed skin. She wanted to rip his clothes off his perfect body, but that would take too much time. She smiled when his breath hitched in his throat as his muscles bunched under her touch. He countered with the flick of his finger inside her. She shuddered as the fiery sensations swept through her body.

"Now, Hafiz. I can't wait any longer." She heard the metallic sound of his zipper and rocked her hips with impatience. She gulped for air and inhaled the musky scent of his arousal. Her chest ached with excitement as he lifted her up and hooked her legs over his hips.

He entered her with one smooth thrust. Hafiz's long groan rumbled from his chest, and he didn't move as if he was savoring this moment. His penis stretched and filled her, but Lacey couldn't stay still. She wanted more—needed everything Hafiz had to give her. She rolled her pelvis slowly and was rewarded with a warning growl before he clenched his fingers into her hips. Hafiz withdrew and plunged into her again and again.

She eagerly accepted each wild thrust. Lacey held on to Hafiz tightly and closed her eyes as her climax forked through her. Her heart faltered as the fury rushed through, taking the last of her strength. Her mind grasped on the only thing that mattered—he had chosen her above all else.

"This bed is too small," Hafiz complained in a murmur as he held Lacey in his arms. She lay on top of him, naked and warm. She rested her head against his chest, and he threaded his fingers through her long hair.

He was right where he wanted to be.

"It's fine," she said sleepily.

Fine? He shook his head at the thought. His feet dangled off the edge, and his shoulders were almost too wide for the bed. The mattress was as thin and cheap as the sheets.

It was too dark to see all of Lacey's bedroom, but he could tell that it was tiny with just a few furnishings. It was nothing like the apartment she had in Rudaynah.

"We should go to my hotel suite," Hafiz suggested. "It's more comfortable. Bigger." *Better.* He felt Lacey deserved more. How did she wind up here?

"Mmm-hmm." Lacey made no move to get up.

He slid his hand down and caressed her spine. He felt her shiver of pleasure under his palm. "Do you like Abu Dhabi?" he asked.

"Mmm-hmm."

"Why did you choose to live here?" He had been astounded when he discovered she was still in the UAE. He thought she had gone home. Back to St. Louis. "Did you know someone? Had business contacts?"

"I didn't know anyone," she said with a yawn. "But I applied for some jobs, did the necessary paperwork, and I got this one at the hotel."

"Adventurous of you," Hafiz said as he cupped the base of her head and held her close. He didn't like the idea that she was all alone in the world. That there was no one looking out for her. Protecting her.

"You sound surprised," Lacey said. "May I remind you, I moved to Rudaynah sight unseen? Some people consider that adventurous. My friends thought it was crazy."

"That was different. You had me to take care of you."

"I've been looking after myself for as long as I can remember."

"You let me take care of you," Hafiz said. The words echoed in his mind. She *let* him. She had given her trust in so many ways, and he took it for granted.

"It wasn't easy for me," Lacey admitted as she pressed her mouth against his chest and gave him a kiss. "I didn't want to be dependent on you."

Lacey Maxwell wasn't cut out to be a mistress, Hafiz decided. Most women took the role because they wanted to be taken care of.

"What's wrong with depending on me?" he asked. "On anyone?"

"I remember what it was like when I had to rely on my parents. They really didn't want to deal with me."

His fingers tightened against her. Anger flared inside him as he imagined a young Lacey, ignored and neglected. "You don't know that."

"I do." There was no sadness in her voice. She spoke as if she was giving the facts. "They have not reached out to me once I've been on my own. It's better this way. I know I made the right decision to cut them out of my life."

A cold chill swept through Hafiz. *"You're* the one that walked away?"

"I tried for years to be the daughter they wanted and needed. But I couldn't earn their love or attention. I walked away and didn't look back."

His heart started to race. He had always thought Lacey was tenacious. It was one of her most admirable traits. He had seen her practice a piece of music until she got it right or talk him through a work problem even if it took all night. But even she had limits. "But…they're your parents."

"And that's why it took me so long to walk away. I kept thinking circumstances would change. But they didn't see any need to change. They weren't being malicious. They were extremely selfish. It took me years to forgive them, but I'm not trying to make them love me anymore."

Hafiz couldn't shake the fear that gripped his chest. He had always felt that Lacey's love was unconditional. It was the one thing he could count on. Yet Lacey had walked away from the strongest bond a person could have. He thought that once Lacey loved someone, it was forever.

This changed everything.

"Lacey." She felt a large hand cupping her shoulder, rousing her out of the best sleep she'd had in a long, long time. "Lacey, wake up."

She peered through bleary eyes. A whisper of a smile formed on her lips when she saw Hafiz looking down at her. Last night hadn't been a dream. "Come back to bed," she mumbled drowsily and patted the mattress next to her.

"It's time to get up, Sleeping Beauty," he said with a smile.

She looked at him and noticed for the first time that he was already dressed in his black T-shirt and trousers. His hair gleamed with dampness from a recent shower.

Lacey sighed and stretched, murmuring in protest at the twinges in her muscles. "Sleeping Beauty isn't my favorite fairytale princess," she said as she rubbed the sleep from her eyes.

"You prefer Rapunzel?" he asked. "I finally read that fairy tale you kept talking about."

"Really?" She slowly sat up in bed and pushed her hair away from her face. "What did you think of it?"

Hafiz's mouth set in a grim line. She suspected he was going to ask something but wasn't sure if he would like the answer. "Did you see me as the prince who saved the day, or did you see me as the witch who trapped Rapunzel in the tower?"

Lacey blinked, startled by the question. The corners of her lips tilted into a sad smile as she wrapped the bed sheet around her nude body. "It took me a while before I realized that you were the Rapunzel in the story."

Hafiz jerked his head back. "That's not funny."

"I'm serious. Think about it," she said. She knew she should have kept her opinion to herself. What man would want to be compared to Rapunzel? But it was too late, and she needed to explain her way of thinking. "Rudaynah was your tower and you were trapped."

"I am not trapped," he said stiffly. "I have duties and obligations, but that is not the same thing."

"Those expectations were holding you back. The sultan was more interested in how you acted than what you accomplished."

"I don't want to talk about that right now." The flash of annoyance in Hafiz's eyes indicated that the topic would be discussed at length later.

"It doesn't matter. It's the past. You're free now," she said with a wide smile. "You escaped the tower. Although I'm sure you would want to visit the sultanate every once in a while. It is your homeland."

Hafiz tilted his head and stared at her with incomprehension. "Lacey, what are you talking about?"

"You left Rudaynah. Didn't you?" she asked slowly. "We agreed that we wouldn't see each other unless you chose me and only me."

"I never agreed to that."

She tried to remember what had been said that night. Hafiz had said he loved her. It was the one thing that held her together when she wondered what it all had been for.

"You love me. You found me," she said softly. "But you're not staying?"

Hafiz sighed. "No."

She flinched as his answer clawed at her. It tore her to shreds before she had a chance to ward off the pain. "And you're still…"

"Getting married. Yes."

Those three words ripped away the last fragment of hope. She closed her eyes and hunched her shoulders. Hafiz hadn't chosen her. He hadn't chased her across the world to get her back.

CHAPTER TEN

HE WAS STILL getting married to Nabeela. The stark truth sliced through her. He'd failed to mention that important piece of information before he possessed her body and soul throughout the night. The rat. The snake.

She couldn't believe he would do this to her. Again. How many times would she fall for this routine? "Get out," she ordered hoarsely, clutching the sheet against her.

"What?" Arrogant disbelief tinged his voice.

"I thought you chose me. I'm such a fool," she whispered, gently rocking back and forth. It felt as if she was bleeding inside. She was going to drown in it.

Hafiz exhaled sharply. "I am choosing to be with you."

"Temporarily," she said. "You came here for sex." She stiffened and looked at the bed before scrambling off of the mattress. She gave a fierce yank to the bed sheets that covered her body. Her body, which she'd freely given to him with her love hours before.

He splayed his hands in the air. "I didn't plan it."

"Right." This from a man who was in control of everything and everyone around him. "You didn't plan to travel to Abu Dhabi. You didn't plan to search for me. You didn't plan to take me against a wall minutes after you found me."

He rolled his shoulders back as if he was bracing himself for a direct hit. "I traveled here for a meeting. I'm staying at this hotel, and I didn't know you were still in Abu Dhabi until I saw the poster at the hotel lounge about your performance."

Just when she thought she couldn't feel any worse. He hadn't come here just to find her. He didn't go out of his way to seek her. She stared at Hafiz, not sure if she was going to burst into tears or start laughing maniacally at the unfairness of it all.

She needed to cover herself. Protect herself. Lacey grabbed her robe that had fallen on the floor. "You needed to scratch an itch. Why? Your fiancée won't sleep with you until the wedding night?"

His eyes darkened. "I have no contact with my future bride because it is an arranged marriage. It is not a love match."

As if that was supposed to make her feel better. The muscle in her cheek twitched with fury. "It's probably best that way. You don't want her to find out how rotten to the core you are until after the vows are exchanged."

"Lacey, I apologize for the misunderstanding."

"Misunderstanding? There was no misunderstanding. You withheld that information because if I knew you were still engaged, I wouldn't have welcomed you with open arms."

"Don't be too sure. We have a connection that is too—"

"Connection?" She gave a harsh laugh. "No, we have

a past. That is it. You severed that connection when you got me out of your life as quickly as possible."

"We still have something," he argued. "That's why I came to check up on you and—"

"You came to have sex because you're not used to going without." Lacey thrust her arms through the sleeves of her robe. The fiery orange silk felt like needles across her sensitive skin. "And you knew I wouldn't deny you. Especially since you had lied to me and said you loved me."

Hafiz drew back. "That wasn't a lie."

She glared at him, fighting the urge to strike out with her nails unsheathed. "Your timing was suspicious."

He placed his hands on his hips. "Suspicious?"

"You tell me that you love me the moment before I was out of your life forever. Was it a way to keep me dangling on your hook? That way, when you looked me up, you didn't have to work too hard to get back into my bed."

"I told you in a moment of weakness," he said in a low growl. "I didn't want you to look back and think the year we spent together meant nothing."

Their time had meant everything to her. It had been the one time when she felt safe and wanted. She had honestly believed during the months in Rudaynah that they had been growing closer and that their relationship could weather anything.

"You could have told me you loved me at any time, but you didn't. Why?" She took a step closer and pointed her finger accusingly at him. "Because saying those words at the last minute meant you didn't have to do anything about it."

He raked his fingers through his hair. Lacey had the feeling he wanted to grab her by the shoulders and shake her. She took a prudent step back.

"If you don't believe me," Hafiz said in a clipped tone, "that is your problem."

Lacey glared at him. Wouldn't a man in love want to express his emotions? Wouldn't he show it with grand gestures and small, intimate moments?

But not this man. No, not Prince Hafiz. He wasn't going to lower himself and try to convince her. He wasn't going to waste his energy on proving something that didn't exist.

"You want to forget everything I did for you? For us? Go right ahead," Hafiz said. "I love you and nothing is going to change that."

"What am I supposed to think? You say you love me when you are engaged to another woman." She tied the sash of her robe with enough force that it could have ripped.

Hafiz ground the heels of his palms against his eyes. "I'm not replacing you."

"Of course not," Lacey said as she walked out of the bedroom. "I would have had to be part of your life for Nabeela to replace my role."

Hafiz followed her into the main room with long, brisk strides. His presence made the apartment feel smaller, as if it couldn't contain him. Lacey wished Priya had not had the night shift. She wanted him to leave and could have used some backup right now. Knowing what kind of man he was, Hafiz wouldn't leave until he got what he was after.

"You made sure I wasn't part of your world," Lacey continued. "I thought I needed to earn that privilege because I was a foreigner and a nobody. Now I realize that nothing I did would have made a difference. It just wasn't going to happen."

She was done trying to earn love. It didn't work. She had twisted and bent herself into knots, determined to give her all and make her relationships work. She had made Hafiz the most important part of her life, and he could not do the same. He had accepted her love as if it was his due, but he did not see her as a priority in life.

No more. Hafiz did not value her role in his life, and he wasn't going to. From now on, she would put herself first because no one else would. She would not settle or compromise.

She heard Hafiz's cell phone ring. Lacey whirled around and saw him retrieve it from his pocket. "Don't you dare."

He frowned as he glanced up from the touch screen. "I'm just—"

"No, you are not answering that phone. I don't care if Rudaynah suddenly disappeared from the face of the earth. It can't be as important as what's going on here."

"Lacey, don't be—"

"I'm serious, Hafiz. For once, I am your top priority. The most important person in your life is right in front of you, so put the phone away."

Hafiz's austere face tightened, clearly holding his anger in check.

"If you'd rather take the call," she said coldly, "then leave and don't come back."

Her heart was pounding as the phone continued to

ring. Hafiz silently turned off the ringer and returned the phone to his pocket as he held her gaze.

Lacey tried to hide her surprise. She had never given him an ultimatum like that. She had always been reluctant, always knowing that he held the power in the relationship. She'd believed that if she made any demands, placed any expectations on him, he would exchange her for another woman.

It turned out that he'd done it anyway.

"I am marrying Nabeela, but the marriage is in name only," Hafiz assured her.

"What exactly does that mean?"

"It means that we will not live in the same suite of rooms in the palace. It means that we will see each other on official occasions, and, even then, we won't stand next to each other."

Lacey's eyes narrowed as she listened to his explanation. "And this is what you want?"

"It's not about what I want to do. It's about meeting my obligations. Meeting the expectations of my country and my family."

"Will you consummate the marriage?"

His nostrils flared as he reined in his patience. "It is required by law."

The idea of him in bed with another woman made her sick to her stomach. How would he feel if she chose to sleep with another man? Claimed it was required? Hafiz would do everything in his power to prevent that from happening. Why did he think she wouldn't respond in the same way? Because she was a woman? Because as a mistress she had no claim on him?

"Will you have children?" she asked.

The muscle in his jaw twitched. "As the second in line to the throne, I am not required to have an heir."

She noticed he didn't answer her question. "But you won't be second in line," she reminded him. "You will be the crown prince if you marry Nabeela."

"That is the sultan's promise, but I don't know if or when it will happen. I need to be the crown prince," Hafiz admitted. "I didn't expect to get a second chance, and I have to take it."

"It's what you want most," she said in a matter-of-fact tone. He wanted it more than he wanted her. "It's what you strove for all these years."

"I had abused that power ten years ago. If I get the title back, I can make amends. I can show that I'm different. That I am the leader that they need."

Power. It was all about the power. "But the sultan has the ultimate power. And he can strip your title whenever he sees fit."

"That is true, but I won't let that happen. I know how to protect what is mine. This time no one will intimidate or harm those who are important to me. This time I have the power to fight back."

Lacey shook her head with resignation. That sounded like the Hafiz she knew and loved. "You already have that power," she pointed out. "You don't need to be a prince to use it."

He reared his head back as if she had said something blasphemous. "I disagree. Taking care of Rudaynah is my purpose in life. I can't do that if I'm not their prince."

Lacey tried to imagine what Hafiz would be like without a royal title. He would still be arrogant and influential. People would continue to clamor for his attention and advice. But would his countrymen allow him to represent the sultanate if he wasn't a prince, or would they treat him as a celebrity? She didn't know.

"I may not agree with you every time, Lacey, but I always listened. You made me look at the world differently. I missed the way we used to talk," Hafiz said.

Lacey looked away. "We didn't talk. I was your mistress, not your girlfriend. We had sex. Lots and lots of sex."

"Don't," Hafiz said harshly. "Stop rewriting our history."

Was she guilty of that? Lacey sank her teeth into her bottom lip. She had felt loved and adored when she was with Hafiz. He had been generous and caring. Maybe it wasn't just about sex.

"Think about the times you listened to the troubles I had on a project or my concerns for the sultanate," Hafiz said quietly. "You gave me advice and ideas. I knew I could count on you to give me honest feedback. Your opinion always mattered to me."

"And now you have Nabeela for that."

"Nabeela won't look after my best interest. She can't drive me wild. She can't love me the way you do."

"Then break the engagement," she whispered.

He froze and turned his head away. "No, Lacey," Hafiz said as he took a step back.

"You don't have to do this to redeem yourself. You have made up for your mistakes years ago."

"I don't deserve forgiveness."

"You don't deserve a loveless marriage," she insisted. "I know what it's like to be unloved. To be surrounded by indifference. It chips away at you until you become a shadow of yourself."

"I can't break the engagement. It's too late."

Lacey closed her eyes as the pain flashed through her. "And you can't walk away from me. So, what do you plan to do?" She slowly opened her eyes as it occurred to her. "You plan to have both of us?" she asked in a scandalized whisper.

Hafiz remained silent as he watched her closely.

She felt the blood drain from her face. "You need to leave right now. I can't believe you would insult me this way."

"I told you, my marriage would be in name only. It's not a real marriage. It's not even a relationship."

She thrust her finger at the door. "Get out," she said, her voice trembling with outrage.

Hafiz sighed and went to collect his jacket. "Give me one good reason why this won't work."

"I don't want to be your mistress." At one time in her life, she gladly accepted the role. It had been the only way she could be in his life. She'd gratefully accepted the crumbs he offered, but now she knew she deserved more.

"But you can't be my wife," he murmured.

"You made sure that couldn't happen. Even if you didn't accept Nabeela as your bride, I still wouldn't be your wife. Because I was a mistress. *Your* mistress."

"That's not the only reason."

"Because you don't think I'm worthy of the title."

"That's not true," he said, grabbing her wrists with his large hands, forcing her to stand still as he towered over her. "I love you and I want to spend the rest of my life with you. This is the best compromise I can make."

"Compromise." Her lips curled with disgust as she said the word. "I'm done compromising."

"There are rules," he said in an impatient growl.

"Break them," she suggested wildly. "You've done it before."

"And I regret it every day. This is different."

"Here's a thought. Stop hiding me from the world and present me to your family with pride. Show them that it's not a sin to love me. Tell them that I am everything you need and that I'm the one you will marry."

"That isn't going to happen. Ever."

Lacey looked down at her bare feet. She had gone too far. She had made an ultimatum that showed the limit of his love for her. She should have known, should have been happy with what he offered, but she couldn't. She wasn't going to take a smaller and demeaning role just to stay in his life. That wasn't love. That was the first step on the path to her destruction.

She had to protect herself. She suddenly felt weak, so much so she couldn't raise her head to meet his gaze. Lacey took a deep breath, the air hurting her raw throat and tight chest.

"And this, what we had together, isn't going to happen again," she said in a low rush. It took all of her strength to raise her head and meet his gaze. "I need you to leave now."

She saw the calculating gleam in his eye just as she heard a key fumbling in the lock of the front door. Lacey turned just as her roommate rushed in.

"Lacey! Why haven't you been answering your texts?" Priya asked as she slammed the door closed.

Priya looked flustered. Her topknot threatened to collapse, and her name tag was crookedly pinned on her black blazer. She appeared out of breath, and her face gleamed with sweat.

"Are you all right?" Lacey asked as her roommate openly studied Hafiz. "Priya, this is—"

Priya raised her hand. "Prince Hafiz, the guy who broke her heart."

Lacey straightened her spine and clutched the lapels of her robe. "How do you know that? I never told you his name."

"No need." Priya swiped her finger against the screen of her phone. "It's all right here in full color."

"What are you talking about?" The lethal tone in Hafiz's low voice made Priya hesitate.

"This." She turned the phone around to show a picture of Hafiz and Lacey in a hot embrace at the party. It was a good quality picture from someone's phone. There was no denying that Prince Hafiz was the man in the picture. Lacey's face was partially hidden, but her identity didn't matter. The fact that her bikini-clad body was plastered against Hafiz was damning enough.

The sharp twist of dread in Lacey's stomach almost made her sick. She clapped a shaky hand against her mouth.

"How many pictures are there?" Hafiz asked.

Lacey's gaze clashed with his. Her eyes widened as she remembered those stolen moments in the corridor outside the party. They hadn't been aware of their surroundings as they made love. What if their recklessness had been caught on camera?

Oh, God. What had they done? It had been madness. Lacey watched Hafiz's gaze harden, no doubt considering the repercussions.

"I've only seen this one so far."

So far. Lacey wanted to sit down before she tumbled to the floor. Hafiz was right. She was his vice. No, she was his poison. She was going to ruin everything for him.

"Who sent it to you?" Lacey asked. "Maybe we can get them to delete it from their camera." Maybe they would luck out. Maybe one of their friends had no idea who Hafiz was and sent it to Priya because she was in the picture.

"I don't know," Priya said as she pressed the screen. "One of our friends was sharing pictures of the party. But it's only a matter of time before someone finds out Hafiz is the playboy prince. Once that happens, there's no containing this."

CHAPTER ELEVEN

HAFIZ STARED AT the image on the small screen. The picture revealed everything. He had greeted Lacey with an intensity that indicated they were more than acquaintances. The passion, the love, the desperate yearning was evident in his expression.

Why? Why hadn't he been more careful? He knew the risks. Did he think the rules only applied when he was home?

He hadn't been thinking. The moment he had seen Lacey's picture in the hotel lounge he had been on the hunt for her. He should have resisted the urge. He had not contacted Lacey for a month and managed to get through each day. But that didn't mean he hadn't thought of her constantly.

"Hafiz?"

He jerked at the sound of Lacey's voice. His gaze slammed into hers. He saw the concern and the tears. But it was the defeat in her eyes that slayed him. Lacey always looked at him as if he was invincible. That he could achieve the impossible.

Now she wasn't so sure. Not when it looked as if he would lose everything over a damning photo.

Priya cleared her throat and only then did Hafiz remember she was in the room. He was always like this when he was around Lacey. Nothing else mattered. It was becoming a major problem.

"I'm going to give you guys some privacy," the roommate said as she started to back away. "Lacey, text me when the prince is ready to return to his hotel suite."

"Why?" Lacey asked.

"If this picture gets out, other photographers will try to find me. A picture of me is worth a lot of money, especially if it includes you," Hafiz explained.

He remembered how this worked. It was humbling that he was in the same predicament that he'd found himself in ten years ago. It didn't matter how much he had tried to control his wilder impulses, he had not changed at all.

Priya nodded. "I can get you to your room unseen."

"Thank you." He returned his attention to Lacey. She crossed her arms tightly against her body and began to pace.

The moment Priya closed the door, Lacey whirled around to face him. "I had nothing to do with this."

Hafiz narrowed his eyes. He wasn't sure what Lacey was talking about, but he often found being silent was the best way to get information.

"I did not set you up," Lacey said. "I know you think that I'm out to sabotage your wedding, but I wouldn't do that."

"You wouldn't?" he asked softly. The thought hadn't crossed his mind. He knew his appearance had been unexpected, and Lacey's attention had been focused on him from the moment they had reconnected. He knew he could trust Lacey about this.

The fact that she immediately leaped to the conclusion that he would suspect her bothered him. He didn't trust easily, and yet he trusted Lacey more than anyone. But since his trust wasn't blind or absolute, Lacey thought he didn't trust her at all.

"Of course, I wouldn't. Do you think all mistresses are manipulative schemers who would do anything to maintain their lifestyles?"

"You aren't like any other mistress." Lacey hadn't been motivated by money, status or power.

"I wouldn't know. I have nothing to compare," Lacey said as she continued to pace. "But, believe me, I am not interested in returning to Rudaynah and maintaining the lifestyle of secrets and hiding."

"Hate Rudaynah that much?"

"I don't *hate* it," she corrected him. "There were parts of it that I found intolerable, but I also saw the beauty and wonder."

Hafiz doubted she could list what she found beautiful. "No, you hated it."

"I hated that I was separated from you," she said. "I hated that we had to hide our relationship."

"Our relationship is about to be brought out into the open," he murmured. He would have to deny it, but no one would believe him. It was clear in the photo that he was intimate with Lacey. And if they had photos of what happened immediately after that embrace… He would protect Lacey from the embarrassment, no matter the cost or the consequences.

"Do you think I forced your hand?" Lacey stopped pacing and stood directly in front of him. "I didn't. I don't know how to convince you that I have nothing to do with this picture. I don't have any proof. But once I find the person who is responsible…"

Hafiz was momentarily fascinated as he watched her shake her fist in the air. He hadn't seen her like this. She was in full protective mode. Of *him*. He took care of Lacey, not the other way around.

"I know you don't have anything to do with it," Hafiz said.

She lowered her fist and gave him a sidelong glance. "You do?" She said the words in a slow drawl.

Hafiz nodded. "It's not your nature." He knew that, but it hadn't stopped him from accusing her in the past. He had let his past experiences with women cloud his judgment.

"Just like that?" She snapped her fingers. "A month ago I couldn't have lunch with a few friends without you accusing me of betrayal."

"I had jumped to conclusions," he admitted. "I thought…"

"That I would retaliate because I was kicked out of your life with little ceremony?"

He felt his mouth twitch with displeasure at her description. Their relationship ended abruptly, but he did not kick her out.

"Something like that," he admitted. "I'm sorry I considered that was a possibility. I know you're not that kind of person. You are loyal and sweet. Innocent about the world, really."

"That's an unusual choice of words for a mistress."

He raked his fingers through his hair and exhaled. "Stop calling yourself a mistress."

She looked at him with surprise. "Why? That was my role in your life. We weren't a couple. We weren't partners. We led separate lives during the day and spent the nights together. Only you didn't stay all night."

"No, I didn't." It had been a test of willpower every night to get out of Lacey's bed and return to the palace.

"Where is this coming from?" Lacey asked as she planted her hands on her hips. "You don't have to pretty up the past, Hafiz."

"I don't want people to think the worst about you." He should have considered that before he brought her over to Rudaynah, but all he had cared about was having her near.

"You don't want them to know that I was a mistress?" She tilted her head as she studied his expression. "Or is it that you don't want people to know about your role?"

Those words were like a punch in the stomach. Was that the real reason he didn't want Lacey to wear that label? He was a prince, was held to a higher standard, but he had brought Lacey to his world by any means necessary.

"Because deep down that goes against what you believe in, doesn't it, Hafiz? You don't want to be the playboy prince, but you had a kept woman. Instead of making a commitment or having a relationship based on mutual feelings, you made arrangements with a woman so you could have exclusive access to her body."

"Our relationship was more than just sex," Hafiz said in a growl. Not that anyone would see it that way.

"The palace may have some questions about that if they see that picture." Lacey dragged her hands down her face. "What are we going to do about it?"

Hafiz went still. "*We?* No, you aren't getting involved with this."

Lacey rolled her eyes. "We're in this together, and we're going to get out of it together."

He was conflicted. Hafiz had always appreciated it when Lacey was ready to fight alongside him, but he didn't want to drag her into this battle.

"No one can see your face in the picture," Hafiz insisted. "You can't be identified. Let's keep it that way."

"It's only a matter of time," Lacey said. "Someone at the party is going to remember what I wore and how you dragged me out of the party."

"It was late, and people had been drinking. No one can be too sure what happened."

"Anyway," she continued, "I don't care if people know it's me."

Why didn't Lacey care about her reputation? A public scandal never died. He hadn't thought much about his until he destroyed his reputation and took the slow, hard road to repair it. He knew it would be much worse for a woman.

"I care." Hafiz knew his voice sounded harsh, but he had to get Lacey to understand. "If you get caught up in a scandal with me, it will cling to you for the rest of your life. You will always be known as the woman who slept with the playboy prince."

Lacey lifted her chin. "I've done nothing to be ashamed about."

"Nothing?" he asked with a tinge of incredulity. "We lost control. We made compromises and excuses even when it went against everything we've been taught. Everything we believe in." He turned away from Lacey. "And even though we swear that we won't meet again, that we won't think about what might have been, we break our promises. The moment we see each other, we destroy everything we tried to create."

The silence pulsed between them.

She made him dream about a life he had no right to pursue. Hafiz winced as resentment shot through his chest. He took in a deep sigh, and he realized nothing had changed. No, that wasn't true. When he was with Lacey, everything he felt was sharper and stronger. Life after Lacey was going to be excruciating.

He needed to be strong and not give in to his wants. He had done that for years until he met Lacey. After disappointing a nation, he had sacrificed his happiness to make amends. He could do it again, but he had to stop teasing himself with the fantasy of life with Lacey.

"Hafiz," Lacey said in a husky voice, "there are many reasons why I love you. You have worked hard to make up for your mistakes. You try to be a good man, a good son and a good prince. I have always admired your willpower and your strength. But your one weakness is me."

Hafiz wanted to deny it.

She slowly shook her head. "All this time I've hated the idea that I'm your one and only vice. Your weakness. But it's true. I am making you into the man you don't want to be."

"That's not true. I like who I am when I'm with you."

"You like sneaking around?" she asked. "Breaking

promises? Feeling guilty because you shouldn't love a woman like me?"

"No," he admitted gruffly.

"Would you have acted this way with another woman? Would you make love to her in public?"

Hafiz wanted to lie and say yes. But even when he was known as the playboy prince, he had always been aware of his surroundings. But when he was with Lacey, nothing else mattered. It wasn't just a weakness. It was a sickness.

"You know what kind of woman I want to be?" she asked.

He knew. She never said it out loud, but he knew of her plans and dreams. Lacey wanted to be a woman surrounded by love and family.

"I can tell you that I didn't grow up thinking I wanted to be a femme fatale. I didn't want to be the kind of woman who ruined lives."

"You're not ruining my life. My—" He stopped. He wasn't going to think it. Voice it. His royal status was part of his identity and the one true constant in his life. It was not an obstacle that kept him from being with Lacey.

"I'm a problem for you, Hafiz. What do you think is going to happen if this photo gets out? What will the sultan do?"

Hafiz gritted his teeth. He wasn't going to tell Lacey. She would try to protect him and keep him in Abu Dhabi. "I can take care of myself."

"No, that's the wrong way to go around it," Lacey said. "That's expected. You'll probably use the words that every powerful man has used when denying an affair. I will take care of this."

Hafiz's shoulders went rigid. "No, you will not."

"Why not?" Lacey's eyes lit up, and she held up her hands. Hafiz knew that look. Lacey had a plan. "This is what we're going to do. If the picture gets published, I'll take the blame."

"Not a chance."

"Listen to me, Hafiz." She placed her hand on his arm as she pleaded. "It's so simple. I'll tell people that I saw you at this party, and I came onto you. You rejected my advances."

He wasn't going to let anyone think that his woman was an indiscriminate seductress. "The picture says otherwise."

"Pictures lie." She dismissed his words with the wave of her hand. "No one knows what happened before or after. It's very possible that I propositioned you. It's just as possible that you declined my offer."

Hafiz gave her a disbelieving look. He couldn't remember a time when he refused Lacey. "No."

She squeezed his arm. "It will work."

He placed his hand over hers. "No, it won't. I am not hiding behind a woman."

She jerked her hand away. "Excuse me?"

He leaned closer. "And no one is going to believe you."

"Yes, they will."

"Not when every gossip site is going to drag up my playboy past and follows up with my former lovers."

He felt the weight of his past on his shoulders. Why had he thought he could erase those moments? And why did it all have to be dug up now?

"Lacey, there is a very real chance that someone

took a picture of us after the party." He was furious at himself that he'd put her in this position.

She blushed a bright red. "If they had a picture, they would have already used it, right?"

"No, they would hint that something even more scandalizing is coming out," Hafiz said. "Stir up interest and sell it to the highest bidder."

"Hafiz, I'm sure there aren't any more pictures," she said in a shaky voice. "We would have seen someone."

He wasn't so sure. They had been lost in their own world. "I need to call a few people and find out if someone is shopping the pictures," he said as he turned on his cell phone and walked to the door.

"Good. And I—"

He halted and turned around, stopping her with one warning look. "You will stay here."

She glared at him. "You have no say in the matter. Anyway, I have to go to work in a couple of hours."

"Promise me that you won't try to fix this," Hafiz said in a low tone. "I need you to trust me on this. Let me handle it."

"But—"

"I won't let you down."

She hesitated, and Hafiz knew what she was thinking. He had let his former mistress down. Back then, he had abandoned his woman when she was vulnerable and in need. At that time, he didn't have the power to protect what was his from the sultan. Now he did, and he wasn't going to let anything happen to Lacey.

"Fine," she said through clenched teeth. "I will hang back…for now. But if I see that you are in trouble, I am—"

"No, you won't." He didn't care what she was planning to do. He wasn't going to let it happen. Hafiz grabbed the door handle and was about to cross the threshold when he turned around. "And, Lacey, one of these days you will realize that I don't need saving."

CHAPTER TWELVE

LACEY LOOKED OUT on the audience and gave a warm smile as she played the last note on the piano.

Why am I wasting my life doing this? she wondered. *Why do I still feel as if my life is on hold?*

Her smile tightened. The spotlight above her felt extraordinarily hot as sweat trickled down her spine. There were only a few people in the hotel lounge on the weekday afternoon.

That was not unusual, Lacey decided as she rose from the bench and bowed to the smattering of applause. It was common to see a few businessmen sitting in the audience at this time of day. They all had a dazed look from back-to-back meetings or constant travel.

She knew they weren't really listening to the music. If asked, they wouldn't remember her or describe her hair in a tight bun or her black lace dress. They were here because they didn't want to return to their quiet hotel rooms. They didn't want to be alone.

Lacey knew how they felt. She had struggled with loneliness before she had met Hafiz. It permeated her life and had been the theme in all the songs she had performed.

And when she met Hafiz, she had felt a connection between them. It had excited and frightened her. She didn't want to lose it. She didn't want it to end.

She glanced around the lounge and noticed Hafiz was not there. He knew when she was going to perform but he didn't stop by. Hafiz had always claimed that he enjoyed listening to her music, but now she wondered if that was just an empty compliment. Or perhaps he enjoyed it when she performed only for him.

She knew he wouldn't be there, but yet she still couldn't stop the disappointment dragging her down. Did he not show up because he was too busy or because he didn't want to be seen in the same room with her?

It shouldn't hurt. She was used to Hafiz not being part of her life. If he had shown up, she would have been unreasonably happy. Thrilled that he graced her with his presence.

And even with the decision that she wasn't going to let him treat her this way anymore, Lacey knew she would weaken her stance. She wanted him in her life no matter how little time she got with him.

Her dreams were not as grand as Hafiz's goals. Her plans for her life wouldn't lead her on the road to glory. At times what she wanted in life seemed impossible. But that didn't mean her dreams were less important than Hafiz's dreams. She needed to remember that.

What she wanted in life was to be with Hafiz. Build a life together and have a family. Create a home that was filled with love, laughter and music.

Lacey quickly got off the stage and glided between the empty tables. There was no use yearning for that

kind of life. She wasn't going to get it. Not while she
was on this path, waiting, hoping for Hafiz to change
his mind.

Maybe she was Rapunzel. Lacey's footsteps slowed
as the thought crashed through her. Oh, hell. She *was*
the one who was stuck. She kept following the same
pattern, waiting for a different outcome.

This was why she felt like her life was on hold. She
was waiting for Prince Hafiz to reach out, take her
away from her tower, and carry her away with him.

Not anymore. As much as she loved Hafiz and would
greedily accept whatever he could spare, she didn't want
a part-time love. She couldn't agree to sharing him.

She wanted a love that was exclusive and one that
would last. She was willing to work for it, willing to
give up a lot to make it happen. But she would not be
his mistress or long-distance lover. She deserved more
than that.

Lacey hurried through the hotel and headed for the
staff housing. An enclosed garden separated the em-
ployee residences from the hotel. She usually found
it peaceful walking past the fountains and ponds, inhaling the fragrance of the brightly colored flowers.
Today the formal garden seemed too big.

"Lacey?"

Her pulse gave a hard kick when she heard the familiar masculine voice. She whirled around and saw
Hafiz. Her heart started to pound as she stared at him.
He was devastatingly handsome in his black suit. The
severe lines of his jacket emphasized his broad shoulders and lean torso. He looked powerful and sophisticated. She was very aware of her cheap lace dress and
secondhand shoes.

"Hafiz?" she whispered and frantically looked around the garden. "What are you doing here?"

"What do you mean?" he asked as he approached her. "I'm staying at this hotel."

"I mean you shouldn't be seen speaking to me. The last thing you need are more pictures of us together."

"The picture has been deleted," he said.

"Oh." Lacey knew that it was the wisest course of action, but getting rid of the picture bothered her. She realized it was because she had no pictures of them together. It was as if all evidence of them together had been erased.

"Why do you look upset?" Hafiz asked. "I took care of it just like I said I would."

"I had no doubt that you would be successful." Hafiz always got what he wanted. Except her. It made her wonder just how much he really wanted her in his life.

"You don't have to worry about it being released."

"I wasn't worried," she said, crossing her arms as a gentle breeze brushed against her skin. "I don't care if people know I'm with you."

Hafiz frowned. "You don't care if people know that you were a mistress?"

Did she care that people knew she didn't hold out for a wedding ring? That she accepted whatever Hafiz offered so she could be with him? No, she didn't regret those choices, but she knew she couldn't make them again.

In the past she'd thought accepting his offer to live in Rudaynah was one step toward a future together. Now she understood the rules. She either got to be his mistress, or she didn't get to be with him at all.

If he asked her to be his mistress now, she would decline. Even if he was unattached, even if he moved out of Rudaynah. It would be hard to say no, but these days she placed more value on herself and her dreams.

"I just finished working," Lacey said as she took a few steps away.

"I know," he said as he moved closer.

"I didn't see you in the lounge." Lacey bit down on her lip, preventing herself from saying anything more.

He frowned at her sharp tone as if he sensed an emotional minefield. "I wanted to be there."

"Something more important came along?" she asked with false brightness. "Something better?"

"You know why I couldn't be there."

"No, I really don't." She had automatically accepted the belief that they couldn't be seen together, and yet, here they were alone in a garden, deep in conversation. It felt as if he chose when he could and could not see her. "Explain it to me. Why were you not there to support me?"

"Did you need my support?" he asked.

"Yes." She never asked because she didn't want to set herself up for rejection. Her parents had not taken the time to see her perform while she was in school or early in her career. Hafiz had only seen her a few times early in their relationship.

"You have performed on stage countless times," he pointed out.

"Doesn't matter. I was always there for you, behind the scenes and in the shadows. I didn't stand next to you during ceremonies and events, but I supported your work. Why don't you support mine?"

His eyes narrowed. "Where is this coming from?"

"You wouldn't understand," she said as she closed her eyes. She realized she surprised him with her demand. It was rare to demand anything from him. She had spent so much energy trying to be part of his life that she didn't expect him to take part in hers.

"Lacey, the next time I'm here, I will sit in the front row and watch your entire performance," he promised.

She went still. "The next time you're here?"

"I'm leaving Abu Dhabi in a few hours," he said. "It's time for me to home."

He was going back. Lacey shouldn't be surprised, but she was struggling not to show it. "You are returning to Rudaynah?"

"I have to go back." His tone suggested that there had never been a question. "I'm still the prince. I have obligations."

"And a wedding?" she bit out.

Hafiz tilted his head back and sighed. "Yes, I am getting married."

"Why?" Lacey asked as the hopelessness squeezed her chest. "I've seen what kind of marriage you're entering. It's bleak and lonely. There is no happiness, no partnership and no love. Why are you doing this?"

"Because this is what I deserve!" he said in a harsh tone.

She gulped in air as she stared at Hafiz. "You're still punishing yourself for something you did over ten years ago," she said in a daze. "Hafiz, your countrymen have forgiven you. In fact, they adore you."

"It's not about my country. Yes, I accepted an arranged marriage because it is my duty. But I don't deserve a love marriage. Not because I'm a prince. It's because of what I did to Elizabeth."

"Your mistress who had become pregnant?" she asked. "I don't understand."

"I discarded her and I denied my son. I had a chance to take care of them, but instead I abandoned them. I treated them worse than how your parents treated you."

"Don't say that," Lacey whispered. "You are nothing like my parents. You value family. Your children will be your highest priority."

"I don't deserve to become a father after what I did. I neglected my responsibilities because I had been selfish. One day my brother will have a son, and he will become the heir to the throne."

She was stunned by his words. Lacey had always known that Hafiz would make a good father. He would be attentive but allow his children to forge their own paths and make their own mistakes.

"All this time," Lacey said, "you've been avoiding a love marriage and creating a family because of the way you treated Elizabeth?"

"Yes," he said. "It's only right."

"No, it's not. I'm sure Elizabeth has moved on."

"That doesn't matter," Hafiz replied. "My suffering doesn't end because she can accept what happened in the past. What I did was unforgivable."

"You have suffered enough," Lacey declared. "You have sacrificed your happiness for years while you've taken care of Rudaynah. You did everything you could to be the dutiful son and the perfect prince. When is it going to stop?"

"I don't know. What if the selfish and spoiled prince

is the real me? What if the playboy prince is underneath the surface, ready to break free?"

"It's not," Lacey insisted. "What I see before me is the real you. Caring and loving. Strong and protective. This is the man you're supposed to be."

"I want that to be true, but I can't take that risk. I am going back to Rudaynah and marry Nabeela, who understands that this marriage is nothing more than a business arrangement."

"This is crazy!"

"But I promise, Lacey, I will be back one day."

"How? When?" She frowned. "Why?"

"Why? Because I'm not giving up on us."

Her eyes widened. "Are you saying that you want a long-distance relationship?"

"Yes," he said as he reached for her. "We did it before when you lived in St. Louis."

She snatched her hands back. "That wasn't what it was. You kept visiting me because you couldn't stay away."

"It started out that way."

"And then you visited more frequently. Your trips were longer. But you never made the commitment."

"I was faithful to you." His eyes flashed with anger. "I haven't been interested in another woman since I met you."

"We weren't living together. Your main residence was somewhere else. And it was the same in Rudaynah. We were in the same country, the same city, but we lived separately."

"So what?"

Lacey crossed her arms and hesitated. She wasn't asking for marriage, and she wasn't asking for forever, but she knew she might be asking for too much. "If you want to be with me, then you have to make the commitment. You have to live with me."

"We can't." His answer was automatic.

"You mean, *you* can't."

"I just explained why I can't," Hafiz said. "If you expect a commitment from me, you are setting yourself up for disappointment."

"And I don't mean living in the same town or in the same hemisphere," she continued. "We will share a home and live as a couple."

"You can't return to Rudaynah."

"I know." She rolled her shoulders back and met his gaze. "You will live elsewhere."

"You mean leave the sultanate?" He angrily barked out the word, but she could see the fear in his eyes. The fear of losing her again. "Do you understand what you are asking of me?" He splayed his hands in the air.

"Yes, I'm asking to you to make a choice." And she had a feeling that she was setting herself up for rejection. "You asked me to make the same choice when I moved to Rudaynah."

"That is different. You didn't have obligations that tied you down to one place."

"It's not different. I made a choice of staying home or being with you. I chose you."

Hafiz took a deep breath. "Lacey," he said quietly, "I wish I could live with you. You are the only woman I've ever loved."

"But you don't want anyone to know it." She felt the first tear drip from her eyelashes, and she dashed it away with the side of her hand. "You love me as long as nothing is expected of you."

"That is not true." Hafiz's voice was gruff. "I want to take care of you. I want to be with you. Share a life together."

"You mean share *part* of your life," Lacey said. "You want to give me the occasional day or weekend. That's not good enough. I want it all."

He splayed his hands in the air. "You are asking me to do the impossible."

"Then there is nothing you can do but—" her breath hitched in her throat "—walk away."

Hafiz stared at her with incredulity. "I tried to do that, but I can't. I won't!"

"You have to," she pleaded, her tears falling unchecked. "If you really love me, if you really want the best for me, you will."

"What's best?" He flinched as if she slapped him. "Suddenly I'm not good for you?"

"You have to set me free." She didn't realize how hard it would be to say those words. Hafiz's devastated look made her want to snatch them back. It took all of her courage to continue. "Let me find a life where my needs are equal to everyone else's."

"What do you—" Hafiz's eyes lit with brutal understanding, and he recoiled from her. "You mean you want to find another man," he spat out.

"If it comes to that." Lacey knew it wasn't possible, but she couldn't let Hafiz know that, or he would continue to pursue her. "I need someone in my life who will put me first, just like I place him first. I can't have that kind of life with you."

"I have always put you first," he said in an angry hiss. "I took care of you the best way I knew how.

I—" He covered his face with his hands. "I would die for you."

Lacey believed him, and it bruised her heart. She didn't want him to die for her. She wanted to share her life with him. The thought speared her chaotic mind. Everything became clear.

She swept her tongue across her lips as her jittery heart pounded against her chest. "If it was between living with me or dying for the good of Rudaynah, which would you choose? The ultimate shame of loving me or the highest honor of serving your country?"

Hafiz was frozen in silence. She held her breath in anticipation as Hafiz dragged his hands from his face. She saw all of the emotions flickering in his ashen face. Shock. Pain. Hesitation.

"That's what I thought." She dragged the words out of her aching throat as hope shriveled up and died inside her. Hafiz might have loved her and he might have trusted her, but he couldn't be proud of her. He couldn't respect himself for loving her.

Nothing she could do would change that. She wasn't going to make the mistake of trying to earn her way. She wasn't going to think that being patient and uncomplaining would be rewarded.

"You need to leave and never come back," she said as she marched away. "Right now."

He shook his head. "I am not leaving. Not until you listen."

"I've listened, and I know nothing is going to change. I need to leave to protect myself. Goodbye, Hafiz," she said, her voice breaking as she fled.

CHAPTER THIRTEEN

SHE HAD TO protect herself. Hafiz silently leaned back in his chair and listened to the business presentation given in his conference room, but he turned Lacey's words over and over in his head. *I need to leave to protect myself.*

From him. Hafiz clenched his jaw as the hurt stung through his chest. It was that thought that had kept him up at night for the past week. Why did she think he was harmful to her? He would never touch her in anger or deny her anything. Everything he did for Lacey was to support her. Protect her.

Hadn't he proved it in Abu Dhabi when he'd kept the pictures from being released? Hadn't he spent lavishly on her throughout their affair? How did her life get worse because of him?

He was the one who needed to protect himself. He could have lost everything if their relationship had been revealed. He was addicted to Lacey Maxwell and risked everything for her. Why didn't she see that?

But instead she cut off all contact. She gave up on them. She abandoned *him*.

Hafiz wanted to believe it was for the best. She was a distraction he couldn't afford. He had almost everything he worked for just within his grasp. His work to improve the lives in the sultanate was making progress. He had made Rudaynah a wealthy country. He would regain the title of crown prince that had been stripped from him.

So why did he feel as if he had failed Lacey?

I need someone who will place me first.

Lacey's words echoed in his head. He was a prince. He could not make a person more of a priority than his country.

Because he was a prince, he was not the man she needed. The knowledge devastated him. Most women would have accepted that. Most women would have been thrilled with the arrangement he offered Lacey.

But not Lacey. She wanted the one thing he couldn't give her. No, *wouldn't* give her. His duty to the sultanate may have sounded noble, but she understood him too well. All this time he thought he was trying to make up for his past sins, but he was just as driven hiding the fact that he was a man who couldn't meet the high standards placed on him.

All he managed to prove was that he was not worthy of Lacey Maxell.

He had worked hard to make up for his mistakes, and he was a prince who was respected and admired. But was he the man he wanted to be? No. He was making the same mistakes.

Despite the punishment he had received for having a kept woman in the past, Hafiz had made Lacey his mistress. Not his girlfriend or wife. He hadn't thought she needed that status. He had treated her as a sexual convenience instead of the woman he loved.

Hafiz had known about Lacey's upbringing, but he

had done nothing to make her feel safe in the relationship. She had been neglected and abandoned. Marginalized in her family. Instead of showing how grateful he was that she was in his life, he had kept her on the sidelines of his life.

Hafiz frowned as he gave a good look at his affair with Lacey. He thought their relationship had been perfect. A dream. A fantasy. He thought he had been generous and good to Lacey, but he had failed her.

He had to fix this. Somehow he would show Lacey that she was the most important person in his life. She thought it could only be demonstrated by marriage, but that was wrong. Marriage was about alliances and property. It was about lineage and power.

He would prove to Lacey that marriage had nothing to do with love.

Lacey sighed as she tiredly unlocked the door to her apartment. The stupor that had encased her almost a week ago when she left Hafiz now felt cracked and brittle. Exhaustion had seeped in. She couldn't wait to tumble into bed, regardless of the fact that it would be cold and lonely.

She pushed the door open and stumbled to a halt as she was greeted by Damask roses everywhere. Lacey inhaled the heavy fragrance with her gasp of surprise. The front room looked like a garden with red and pink flowers.

An image splintered through her mind. St. Louis, in the hotel's penthouse suite. Hafiz dragging a rose bud along her naked body. Longing swept through her as a flush of red crept under her pale skin.

"Lacey, I have to know," her roommate Priya said

as she strolled into the room, wearing wrinkled pajamas. "What have you done to deserve all these flowers?"

"They're for me?" Her stomach clenched. She'd sensed they were. Only one person would send her flowers. Only one man would make such a grand gesture. Trust Hafiz to disregard her demands and to this extent. Suddenly she was a challenge that he had to overcome. "Uh…nothing."

Priya cast a disbelieving look. "No guy goes through all this trouble without a reason," she said as she walked over to one oversized bouquet and stroked the fragile petals. "And this one is very sure he has no competition. He didn't sign the cards."

Lacey felt her mouth twist into a bittersweet smile. Hafiz didn't need to say anything because the flowers said it all. He wanted to remind her of the passion between them, the love they shared and of what she was turning her back on.

As if she was in a trance, Lacey walked from one bouquet to the next. The shades of pink and red thawed the coldness inside her. She felt the vibrant flowers questioning her choice to exist without Hafiz. Lacey sighed, knowing she should have ignored the bouquets and gone straight to bed.

"Prince Hafiz doesn't want you to forget him," Priya said with a sigh and placed her hands on her hips. "As if you could."

"I'm not getting back together with him."

"If you say so," her roommate said softly.

She bent her head and brushed her cheek against the soft petals. "I've learned that being with him wasn't worth the tears," she lied.

"No guy is," Priya muttered.

Lacey pressed her lips together. Hafiz was worth it. What she had really learned was that he didn't think *she* was worth the sacrifice or the struggle. Hafiz desired her, he may even believe that he loved her, but he didn't love her enough.

"I should call...and tell him to stop," Lacey said. She needed to let him know that she couldn't be wooed like the first time. She understood the rules now. Another affair with him would destroy her.

"Uh-huh." Priya rolled her eyes. "Right."

Was she kidding herself? Lacey wondered as she grabbed her cell phone from her purse and headed for her bedroom. Maybe those flowers stirred up a longing she didn't feel strong enough to deny. Maybe she was desperate to hear from Hafiz, and she was jumping on to this weak excuse. Lacey knew she should talk herself out of it, but instead she paced the floor as she called, wondering why she hadn't deleted his number. She held the phone to her ear with shaky fingers.

"Hello, Lacey."

She halted in the middle of her room. "Hafiz." She closed her eyes, tears instantly welling. Her heartbeats stuttered as a shiver swept through her. He sounded so close to her, as if his mouth was pressed against her ear, ready to whisper sweet nothings. Lacey curled her head into her shoulders, wanting to hold on to the feeling, wanting it to be real. "Thank you for the flowers, but I don't think you should be sending me presents," she said huskily. She gritted her teeth. She needed to be firm.

"Why?" His voice was silky and smooth, heating her body from the inside out.

Lacey frowned. Why? Was he kidding? Wasn't it obvious? "Because it's not—" she resumed pacing as she searched for the word "—appropriate."

"When have we ever been appropriate?" Hafiz's sexy chuckle weakened her knees.

She had to follow through and tell him to stop. She had to be strong. "I mean it," she said sternly, hoping he didn't catch the slight waver. "I don't want anything from you."

"That's not true."

She closed her eyes as his low voice made her skin tingle. It wasn't true. She wanted everything from him. But why would he give it to her? After a year of eagerly accepting whatever he offered, she knew Hafiz thought he could wear her down. That this was some sort of negotiation.

She couldn't live that way anymore. She deserved more. She deserved everything. She refused to settle.

"I've already told you that I'm not interested in married men."

Hafiz was quiet for a moment. "What if I broke the engagement?" he asked.

Her breath hitched in her throat. "Would you?" Her knees started to wobble. Was it because of her? Was he going to give the palace an ultimatum? "Could you?"

"I'm not interested in marriage."

"Oh." She sank on the bed. So many emotions fought inside her, struggling to surface, that they felt as if they would burst through her skin. Hope soared through her, and realization pulled her down. He may no longer be the playboy prince, but he also had no interest in marriage. With her, with anyone.

As much as she didn't want him to get married, she

also wanted to weep because she couldn't be with him and never would. "But it's only a matter of time before the palace can prove why marriage is necessary."

"I don't need a wife to be a good prince."

"Now, there you are wrong," Lacey said as she lay down on the bed and drew her knees to her stomach. "You need a woman at your side. A family of your own."

"I had that with you," he reminded her, his voice filled with such tenderness that she ached. "But Rudaynah wouldn't recognize it like that. The palace would never accept it."

And the ties that bound him to Rudaynah were too powerful for her to cut. Hafiz might withstand the burdens placed on him, but not if he held on to her. Lacey winced with pain as she had to make a decision, her face already wet with tears. She had to be the strong one, or they both were headed for destruction.

She took a deep breath. She could do this. She had to do this and take the brunt of the fall. Even if it meant she would wither and die, she would do it, as long as Hafiz thrived and flourished. "What we had was good." She choked out the words. "But we can never recapture it."

"Lacey?" Hafiz asked in an urgent tone.

"No more presents." She thought she was going to gag on her tears. "No more trying to… No more…." She disconnected the call and turned off the phone.

Lacey curled up into a ball as her spirit howled with agony. She clutched the phone, the last tangible connection she had with Hafiz, to her chest. Her weary body convulsed as she cried.

She wished she could disintegrate. But she knew

the ramifications of her decision were just beginning. She had to live without Hafiz, and she had to
be ruthless about it. Starting now. It meant leaving
Abu Dhabi. Tonight. Without a trace. Without hope.

Hafiz stood at the arched window and watched the
laborers set up the decorations along the route to the
palace. The colorful flags and banners celebrated his
upcoming nuptials while street vendors displayed wedding souvenirs.

He wished he could be as excited about the week-
long ceremony. Maybe, if it had been a different bride.
A woman with copper hair and a smile that warmed
his heart. A woman he loved and who fiercely loved
him in return.

"Having second thoughts?"

He turned to the sound of his brother's voice. From
the concern lining the crown prince's face, Hafiz knew
he must look like hell.

Ashraf strode down the open hallway, the desert
morning wind tugging his white robe. His younger
brother looked how a crown prince should. Hafiz felt
scruffy and tarnished in comparison in his tunic and
jeans.

That was no surprise. Ashraf was the perfect son.
The perfect prince. And did it all effortlessly when
Hafiz failed spectacularly.

While Ashraf embraced tradition, Hafiz always
questioned it. Hafiz was tempted by the world outside of Rudaynah, and Ashraf preferred to stay home.
Hafiz couldn't resist the charms of an inappropriate
woman. From all accounts, his brother lived like a
monk, nothing distracting him as he fulfilled the role

of the heir apparent. One day he would be the benevolent sultan this country needed. Rudaynah would be in good hands with Ashraf on the throne.

"I was thinking about something else," Hafiz said.

"*Someone* else. A woman," Ashraf guessed. "And from the look in your eyes, not the woman you are about to marry."

Hafiz nodded. "Her name is Lacey Maxwell."

No recognition flickered in his brother's eyes. "Who is she?"

"She's my…" Mistress? The term bothered Hafiz. It had been Lacey's status, but the word minimized her place in his life. She was not a sexual plaything. The label of mistress didn't describe her generous spirit or inquisitive mind. It didn't explain how important she had been in his life.

"She's yours," Ashraf said simply.

"She should be my bride." It hurt to say it. He hadn't said it to Lacey, and now it was too late. He gave voice to the idea, even though he knew it couldn't happen. And yet…Hafiz pushed away from the window.

"I know that look," Ashraf said. "Whatever you're thinking, just forget about it."

"You don't know what's going through my mind," Hafiz said with a scowl.

Ashraf grabbed Hafiz's arm. "Back out of this wedding and you could lose everything."

Okay, so his brother was a mind reader. "I've already lost everything," Hafiz replied.

"Not quite. This is just wedding nerves," Ashraf said, his fingers biting into Hafiz's arm. "Marry the sultan's choice and keep this Lacey Maxwell on the side."

"No, she deserves better. She should be the one who should have my family name. I don't want to hide how I feel about her anymore."

"Listen to me, Hafiz. I'm giving you advice even though it's against my best interest," Ashraf said. "I understand you will be made crown prince once you marry."

The pause between them sat uncomfortably on Hafiz. "Does everyone know about that agreement?" he finally asked. "Don't worry, Ashraf. Knowing the sultan, he will find a loophole to prevent that from happening."

"Typical Hafiz," Ashraf muttered. "You always think someone is going to betray you. That they are destined to fail you."

"I'm cautious," Hafiz corrected. "The more I know of this world and the more I understand people, I become more cautious."

"That shouldn't include your family." The shadows darkened on his face. "Despite what you may think, I didn't betray you when I became crown prince. I had to preserve the line of succession."

Hafiz drew back, astounded by the guilt stamped on his brother's face. "I don't blame you. I blame myself. I'm sorry you were dragged into this. In fact—" Hafiz tilted his head as a thought occurred to him "—you were affected most of all by what happened."

"You have the chance to redeem yourself and reclaim the title of crown prince."

"Maybe I don't want it anymore," Hafiz said. "Maybe I found something better."

"Like the title of Lacey's husband?" Ashraf asked in disbelief.

He wasn't worthy of that title. He had disappointed Lacey too many times. But he was willing to spend the rest of his life earning the right to be with her.

"You are very close to regaining your birthright," his brother said. "Don't ruin it now."

He was very aware of completing his ten-year quest, and yet he didn't think it was going to happen. He didn't believe it should happen. "Sometimes I think ruling Rudaynah was never my destiny."

"What has gotten into you?" Ashraf asked. "This isn't you talking. This is Lacey."

Lacey made him look at his life differently. She showed him what really mattered. "Perhaps I was only supposed to hold on to the crown prince title temporarily."

Ashraf gave him a suspicious look. "Do you really believe this, or are you trying to talk yourself into giving it up again?"

"I was holding on to the title until you were ready."

"You were born a crown prince," Ashraf said, his voice rising with anger. "You were destined to take care of this country, just like you were destined to marry for duty."

"I marry tomorrow," Hafiz said, grimacing.

His brother studied him carefully. "If you don't marry, you will be exiled. For life."

Hafiz flinched. He lifted his head and allowed the cool breeze to glide across his skin. Inhaling the scent of palm trees and sand warmed from the sun, he felt the land beckon his Bedouin blood. He opened his eyes and stared at the dunes in the distance, feeling the depth of his connection to his ancestors.

"Marry their choice of bride." Ashraf gave him a

firm shake. "You were going to before. What could possibly have changed?"

"I found out what life was like without Lacey." Life without any contact with his woman was slowly destroying him. Hafiz returned his attention to the horizon, wondering where she could be. She'd vanished, sending her message loud and clear. *Don't follow me. Don't find me. Get on with your life.*

"Do you have any idea what life will be like without Rudaynah?" Ashraf asked.

Living away from the land he loved was a misery all of its own. No matter where he had been and how much he enjoyed his travels, his heart always heard the call from the land of his people. Sometimes the ancient call brushed against him like a haunting song. Other times, it crashed against him with the beat of tribal drums. "I've lived elsewhere," Hafiz finally said.

"But always knowing that you could return in an instant," Ashraf pointed out.

Hafiz closed his eyes, and his shoulders sagged. Was he wrong to consider life with Lacey when she'd made it clear she'd moved on without him? Was it foolish to hope for the impossible or was his faith in his love being tested?

"No matter what happens, you are my brother, and that will never change."

Hafiz inhaled sharply as the emotion welled in his chest. Ashraf would never know how important it was to hear those words. He stepped forward and embraced his brother.

Ashraf returned the embrace. "And when I reign," he promised fiercely, "you will be invited back to Rudaynah with open arms."

"Thank you." His words were muffled into his brother's shoulders.

Ashraf stepped away and met his brother's gaze. "But our father could reign for years. Decades. Are you willing to risk exile for that long?"

Hafiz realized he couldn't answer that. What did that say about him and the strength of his love for Lacey? "I don't know."

"Rudaynah is a part of you," his brother reminded him. "You can't deny that."

"But Lacey is a part of me, as well." To deny that was to refuse the man he was. The man he could potentially be.

"Then for the next twenty-four hours you need to decide which one you can live without." Ashraf pressed his lips together as his stark face tightened with apprehension. "Because this time, my brother, there's no second chance."

CHAPTER FOURTEEN

THE ELEGANT SURROUNDINGS in the lounge seemed a world away from the trendy nightclubs and blues bars of her past. She *was* a world away, Lacey decided as her fingers flew over the piano keys. Istanbul was a culturally diverse city, but it wasn't home.

Home. Lacey gave a slight shake of her head. A simple word but a complicated idea. Home wasn't St. Louis. She had no family or connection there. Nor was it Abu Dhabi. While she had friends in the beautiful city, she didn't feel as if she had belonged.

She chose to move to Istanbul because it felt like a bridge between Hafiz's world and hers. She tried to take the changes in stride, but she felt the loss of everything familiar. Of everything she'd left behind.

The only time she had felt at peace was in the penthouse apartment in Rudaynah. Lacey didn't know why she missed that place so much. She had been hidden and isolated. She couldn't count on the basic necessities. She'd had difficulty living in the sultanate, but that apartment had been the one place where she and Hafiz could be together.

She wondered what had happened to the apartment. Hafiz undoubtedly got rid of it. He no longer needed a hideaway, since he would live in the palace with his wife.

Lacey's fingers paused on the piano keys for a moment as the pain ripped through her. She continued to play, her touch a little harder, as she imagined Hafiz as a newlywed.

The last news she read about Rudaynah was about the preparations for his wedding. After that, she stopped searching for information about the sultanate. It didn't matter if his marriage was arranged or if his bride was incompatible. Hafiz would do whatever it took to make the marriage work. Even give up the woman he loved.

When the audience applauded while the last mournful note clung to the air, a uniformed waiter approached the piano. "A request." He presented his silver serving tray with a flourish.

The Damask rose lying on the cream card caught her attention. The sight of the pale pink flower was like a punch in the stomach. They were just like the roses Hafiz used to send her.

Lacey swallowed and hesitated before she took it from the waiter. Her hands trembled as she nestled the fragrant flower between her fingers before picking up the card.

She stared at bold slashes in black ink. Lacey blinked, scrunching her eyes closed before opening them wide. She stared incomprehensively at Hafiz's handwriting.

It couldn't be. It looked like Hafiz's scrawl only because she was thinking of him. She was always thinking of him. But the request was for the song Hafiz always wanted her play. It had been their song.

The clink of stemware clashed in her ears. The murmur of different languages boomed in her head. She wet her suddenly dry lips with the tip of her tongue. "Where did you get this?" she asked huskily. She felt as if she was paralyzed with shock.

"That man." Lacey's heart leaped into her throat as the blood roared in her ears. From the corner of her eyes, she saw the waiter pointed in the direction of a window that offered a breathtaking view of the Bosphorus strait. "Well, the man who had been over there," he said with a shrug and left.

Lacey's shoulders tightened, and her pulse continued to pound a staccato beat. Had it been Hafiz? If so, then why did he leave once he found her? Had he given into temptation to see her one more time and thought better of it? She couldn't stop the pang of betrayal even when she wanted him to stay away.

Lacey cast a furtive glance around the lounge, ignoring the disappointment that flooded her bones. She didn't understand how Hafiz had found her. She thought she had made it impossible for him to follow, but then the prince never gave up on a challenge. The more difficult the test, the more determined he was to conquer.

She returned her attention to the rose in her hands. She thought she would never hear from Hafiz again. She had been his vice and the one thing in the way of his goals. No matter what she did, she could never give him what he needed.

This time he had stayed away longer. She knew it was because of his upcoming wedding. It had been ridiculously easy to avoid all news sources after that tidbit of information. She wouldn't have been able to look at his wedding pictures or cope with comparing herself and his chosen bride. But why did he seek her out? Was the pull just too strong to deny?

Rubbing the rose petals with short, agitated strokes, Lacey gave into temptation and brought the exquisite flower to her nose. Inhaling the delicate fragrance, she relived everything from the instant Hafiz invaded her life to the moment she'd retreated from his.

Regret seized her heart until the last of her strength oozed out. With clumsy fingers, Lacey set the pink flower aside on the grand piano. She couldn't cope with the sweet ache of remembering.

Her gaze fell upon the card again, wincing at the song title. The lyrics had captured how she felt about Hafiz. About them. She'd had so much faith in their love. She had believed anything was possible.

Now she knew better. Lacey wanted to crumple the card in her fists and toss it away. She knew the song by heart, had sung it to Hafiz countless times, but she no longer had the resilience to play the song. It held a glimpse of her innocent, carefree days. It was a testament of her naïve love.

And she still loved Hafiz. That was how naïve she truly was. Even though he was forbidden, married and out of reach, she still loved him.

Her love was actually stronger than when she first played the song. It might be as battered and bruised as her heart, but her feelings reached a depth she couldn't have even imagined a year ago.

Lacey paused at the thought, her fingers curved over the ivory keys. She couldn't play it. Not now, not here. This was a song just for him, not for a roomful of strangers. She would only bare her soul for Hafiz.

She *wouldn't* play it, Lacey decided, despite his request. Even if he were here, she wouldn't cave. If he were watching over her, she would play him a different song, one that offered another message but still held a poignant memory. The song she played when they first met.

Her determination wavered as the first few chords twanged deep in her heart. She would have stopped altogether, but an inner need overrode her misery, guiding her through the song. Her smoky voice was coaxed out of her raw throat, occasionally hitching and breaking with emotion. She closed her eyes, fighting back the tears as the last note was wrung out of her, depleting her remaining strength.

The enthusiastic applause sounded far away when she felt a shadow fall over her. Lacey froze, instinctively ducking her chin. She knew who was standing next to her before she inhaled a trace of the familiar scent of sandalwood.

Lacey was reluctant to look up. She wasn't strong enough to see Hafiz and let go of him again. But she also wasn't strong enough to deny herself one more glance.

Cautiously opening her eyes, Lacey saw the expensive leather shoe on the traditional Persian rug. Her chest tightened as her gaze traveled along the black pinstripe trousers. She remembered every inch of Hafiz. The crimson red tie lay flat against his muscular chest, and the suit jacket stretched against his powerful shoulders.

Her pulse skipped hard as she looked at Hafiz's face. Her skin flushed as she stared at his harsh, lean features. When she looked into his eyes, Lacey felt the full force of his magnetic power crash over her.

Hope and devastation escaped her fractured heart. *Hafiz*.

She couldn't turn away. "What are you doing here?" Her voice croaked.

"Why didn't you play my request?" he asked softly. His voice skittered across her skin, blanketing it with goose bumps.

Lacey gnawed her bottom lip. She didn't expect the gentleness. His reticence was surprising. In fact, it bothered her. Where was the primal man who made a fierce claim on her?

She cringed as she remembered how she'd misunderstood his motives the last time he sought her out. She wasn't going to repeat that mistake. "That's not an answer," she said as she reached for the flower.

Hafiz's watchful eyes made her feel awkward. Her simple black dress suddenly felt tight against her chest and hips. The silky fabric grazed against her sensitive skin.

"When are you taking your break?" he asked.

"Now." She covered the keys and stood up abruptly. How could she work when he was nearby? At the moment, she didn't care if she received a reprimand for her boss or got docked in pay. "What are you doing here?" she repeated as she stepped away from the piano.

He arched his eyebrow in warning. "I'm here for you."

Lacey's brisk stride faltered when she heard the words she craved. But she knew better. There had to be a catch, a dark side to her deepest wish. She kept walking and sensed him following her.

"Hafiz, we've been through this," she said, grateful for her firm tone that came out of nowhere. "I am not available every time you're in town. I'm not a one-night stand. And I don't sleep with married men."

"I'm not married."

Lacey whirled around and stared at Hafiz. "What? How is the possible?"

"Is that why you didn't play my request?" his voice rumbled.

The rose threatened to snap, and she relaxed her grip. "No. Why are you not married? You were supposed to have your wedding after Eid."

"I refused." A shadow flickered in his dark eyes. Lacey had a feeling his refusal wasn't as easy as he made it sound.

"When? Why? I don't understand. You had to. There was no way out of it."

"I found a way." Hafiz dipped his head next to hers. "Why didn't you play my request?" He was so close, sending a burst of sensations spraying through her veins. "Because you thought I was married?"

Lacey stopped in front of the lounge's entrance and folded her arms across her chest. He wasn't married. The relief swirled inside her, only to be pulled down by a heavy sadness. One day Hafiz would have to marry, and she wouldn't be the bride.

"Did you forget the words to the song?" he asked softly. "Like you tried to forget us?"

She didn't know if it would be wise to explain anything. To encourage a love that was impossible. "You wouldn't understand," she finally said.

"You don't know that," he said as he placed his large hand against the gentle swell of her hip. The contact nearly undid her. Lacey stiffened, fighting the urge to sway into his body and melt against his heat.

She needed to calm down before her heart splintered. Lacey cleared her throat. "I don't play that song anymore. It reminds me of our time together."

His fingers flexed against her spine. "And you regret what we had?" Hafiz's penetrating eyes made her feel vulnerable and exposed. "Do you regret loving me?"

Lacey exhaled wearily. Nothing could be further from the truth. In a way, her life would be so much easier if she regretted her love. "I told you that you wouldn't understand," she said as she strode away.

She didn't get very far. Before she knew it, her back was pressed against one of the alabaster columns. The Damask rose fluttered to the champagne-colored carpet as Hafiz barricaded her with his strong arms. Her eyes widened anxiously as he leaned into her. "Make me understand," he growled.

The anguish deepened the lines of his stark face, and she struggled with the wrenching need to erase it from him altogether. Lacey tilted her head in the direction of the piano. "I don't play that song because it's about you. How you changed my life, how you changed me. How much you mean to me and what I would do to keep you." She pressed her clammy palms against the column, but they streaked against the cool, slick surface. "And that is why it belongs *only* to you."

Comprehension flashed through his bronze eyes. "Ah." Hafiz straightened and removed his hands from the alabaster.

Lacey frowned at his sudden retreat. She'd revealed more than she was comfortable with, and this was how he responded. "Ah, what?" she asked defensively, doing her best not to feel slighted. Why was he pulling away? "I knew you wouldn't understand."

"No, I do." The corner of mouth slowly slanted up. "It's how I feel when I give you this."

She watched with growing alarm as he removed his royal ring from his finger. The gold caught the light. Lacey stared at it, transfixed, unable to move until Hafiz grasped her wrist.

Lacey bunched her hand up into a fist. "What are you doing?" she asked in a scandalized whisper. She struggled to keep her arm flat against the column.

"I'm giving you my ring." He easily plucked her hand and moved it closer to him.

Her knuckles whitened as her tension grew. There was no way she was going to let him. She knew the rules, but she could only imagine the consequences of breaking them. "But, but—it's a royal ring." She gestured wildly at it. "Only someone born into royalty is allowed to wear it."

"And," Hafiz added as he leisurely caressed her fingers, enticing them to unfurl, "I'm allowed to give it to the woman I want to marry."

Lacey's hand tightened, her short fingernails digging into her palm. Her mouth gaped open as the remainder of her argument dissolved on her tongue. "Marry?"

"Yes." His gaze ensnared her. The depths challenged. Tempted. Pleaded. "Marry me, Lacey."

"I—I—" she spluttered, unable to connect two words together. Her heartbeat drummed painfully against her breastbone. "I...can't."

"Why not?" Hafiz didn't sound crestfallen. His

taunting tone indicated that he was primed and ready to argue. And win.

Her gaze clung on to the ring. It looked big and heavy. It belonged on Hafiz's hand, not hers.

"I'm not from the right family," she blurted out. She knew her shortcomings.

"I disagree," Hafiz said confidently. "You are the only family I need. Together we will create the home we always wanted."

And he would give it to her. He would be loving and protective. Hafiz would do everything in his power to make her feel safe and secure.

She felt herself weakening, but she couldn't let that happen. She had to be strong. Strong enough for the both of them. Lacey struggled to voice another reason. "I'm your mistress."

"You are my heart," he corrected in a husky voice. "Marry me."

"I can't marry you." Her firm statement trailed off in a whimper. She frowned ferociously and tried again. "I can't return to Rudaynah."

His hand stilled against hers. "Neither can I," he confessed.

His words froze her racing thoughts. Hafiz couldn't return to Rudaynah? What was he saying? "What?" The startled question tore past her lips as she stared at him with horror.

"I've been exiled." He broke eye contact, the frown lines burrowing into his forehead. "Banished for life."

Her hand fell from his. "Why?" she cried out, but instinctively she knew. "Because of me?" She sagged against the column as tears burned her throat and eyes.

Her body threatened to collapse into a broken heap on to the floor.

"Because I refuse to give you up again," Hafiz said, his voice rough with emotion. "I was given the choice to remain in my homeland or be with you. I chose you."

Hafiz chose her. He gave up everything he wanted for her. It didn't make her feel triumphant. The news destroyed her. Lacey struggled to contain the sob rising in her throat. "You shouldn't have done that."

"I don't want to stay in Rudaynah if I can't have you at my side."

She wanted to be at his side, but not if it cost him his world. "You say that now, but one day you're…"

"I refuse to hide how I feel about you, Lacey," Hafiz said in a low voice as his eyes flashed with determination. "I have nothing to be ashamed about."

"How can you say that? After all you did, you didn't get the respect you deserve. Your father exiled you." Lacey cringed as she said those words. She knew how important his status was to Hafiz.

She'd sacrificed everything, but she wasn't able to give Hafiz the one thing he needed. He hadn't redeemed himself in the eyes of his family. He would never gain the recognition that belonged to him.

Lacey covered her face with her hands. She didn't want this to happen. She had done everything in her power to prevent Hafiz from losing the world he fought so hard to keep.

"Hafiz, you can't give up being a prince," she begged. "Not for me. Not for anyone. It's who you are."

"No, it's not." His voice was clear and steady. "I am myself, I am who I want to be, when I am with you."

"No… No…"

"I'm not fully alive unless I'm with you," he said as he wrapped his fingers around her wrists and lowered her hands. "I'm not myself when you are not around. I love you, Lacey."

Tears dampened her eyelashes. "That can't be," she whispered. "It's impossible."

He cupped his hand against her cheek. The gentle touch contrasted with the demand in his eyes. "All I know is that this ring belongs only to you. *I* belong only to you." He held the glittering royal ring in front of her.

She slowly shook her head. "Hafiz…" Her eyes widened when he bent down on one knee in front of her.

"Lacey Maxwell, will you do me the honor of marrying me?"

EPILOGUE

"LACEY, WHERE ARE you?" Hafiz looked over the assembly of dignitaries that crowded the throne room and spotted his wife lurking in the shadows. As she turned, the diamonds in her hair shimmered under the chandelier lights.

Pride swelled in his chest as she made her way through the sea of evening gowns and military uniforms. Hafiz watched statesmen and socialites respectfully lower their heads when she passed, but his attention was focused on his woman.

It amazed him how Lacey's regal image concealed her passionate nature. Just thinking about it, he was tempted to sink his fingers in her copper red hair and pull down the sophisticated chignon. The rose taffeta caftan encrusted with iridescent pearls teased his senses as it skimmed her curves with each step she took.

When Lacey drew close, he captured her hand. "The coronation is about to start," Hafiz informed her and entwined his fingers with hers.

Lacey's uncertain smile tugged at his heart. He swore it gleamed more brightly than any jewel or medal in the room. "I'm sure the vizier said I'm not supposed to be here."

"You are right where you belong." He made a mental note to give the adviser a more explicit explanation of the new protocol. No one was going to hide his woman. No one was going to separate him from his wife.

The first few notes of the procession march filtered through the throne room. Exhilaration pressed against his chest. Soon Ashraf would be crowned sultan, and then he and his brother would bring Rudaynah to its full glory. The revitalizing plans that Hafiz dreamt for years could now be realized.

Lacey cast a troubled glance at the empty throne. "Do you regret—"

He shook his head. "No, I have everything I want," he replied truthfully. Most importantly, he had Lacey. He shared a life with the woman he loved and trusted.

She also helped him realize that he didn't need a royal title to take care of his countrymen. In fact, he was more successful without the restraint of royal protocols and rituals. For the past few years they'd traveled worldwide while promoting the Sultanate of Rudaynah's resources to other countries and international businesses.

And now with the passing of his father, Hafiz could return to Rudaynah any time he wanted.

It had been a bittersweet homecoming. Hafiz had felt like a stranger in his own country until Lacey lured him to the dunes. She knew that once he visited the desert, he would reconnect with the land.

The corner of his mouth kicked up in a wicked smile as he remembered how he and Lacey had spent those cold desert nights. His mind buzzed with anticipation as he rested his hand on her stomach. It was fate to have his first child conceived in Rudaynah.

Lacey's eyes widened from his possessive touch. "Stop that!" she whispered fiercely as she tried to dislodge his hand with a subtle push. "The formal announcement isn't until the end of the month. People will speculate."

Hafiz lowered his head and brushed his mouth against hers. "Let them talk."

* * * * *

MILLS & BOON®

Why shop at millsandboon.co.uk?

Each year, thousands of romance readers find their perfect read at millsandboon.co.uk. That's because we're passionate about bringing you the very best romantic fiction. Here are some of the advantages of shopping at www.millsandboon.co.uk:

* **Get new books first**—you'll be able to buy your favourite books one month before they hit the shops

* **Get exclusive discounts**—you'll also be able to buy our specially created monthly collections, with up to 50% off the RRP

* **Find your favourite authors**—latest news, interviews and new releases for all your favourite authors and series on our website, plus ideas for what to try next

* **Join in**—once you've bought your favourite books, don't forget to register with us to rate, review and join in the discussions

Visit **www.millsandboon.co.uk**
for all this and more today!